FOR MOTHERS ONLY

Some may be shocked. Others will believe this is just a wildly imaginative novel. But, Mothers, whatever you think, hold on to your long-haired, wide-eyed daughters until you've read this book! Mr. Glemser has obviously known a 'stew' or two, and—shocking, kooky, wild or wicked—he tells it exactly like it is!

THE FLY GIRLS

BY BERNARD GLEMSER

Originally published under the title

GIRL ON A WING

THE FLY GIRLS
Originally published under the title
GIRL ON A WING

*A Bantam Book / published by arrangement with
Random House, Inc.*

PRINTING HISTORY

*Random House edition published August 1960
2nd printing.......October 1960
Bantam edition published March 1963
2nd printing.........April 1963
3rd printing...........July 1969*

4th printing

5th printing

6th printing

7th printing

8th printing

9th printing

10th printing

11th printing

*Bantam Books are published by Bantam Books, Inc., a subsidiary
of Grosset & Dunlap, Inc. Its trade-mark, consisting of the words
"Bantam Books" and the portrayal of a bantam, is registered in the
United States Patent Office and in other countries. Marca Registrada.
Bantam Books, Inc., 271 Madison Avenue, New York, N.Y. 10016.*

PRINTED IN THE UNITED STATES OF AMERICA

For Phyllis Jackson

The author wishes to express his gratitude to
the many hostesses, pilots, and other airline personnel
who generously gave their time and expert knowledge
to help with the technical matters in these pages.

1

I guess I am just a plain dumbkopf, as my former friend N.B. would say. For example, when I had finally finished packing I found that I still had plenty of time on my hands, and I went down to the drugstore on the corner of Mac-Dougal and called Mother to say good-by. Why? To what purpose? What's Hecuba to me, or I to Hecuba?

Mother lives in the old house in Greenwich. It has a big garden, full of trees and moss, and a little stream flows through it. Very picturesque.

I said, "Well, good-by, Mother. I'm just leaving."

"Leaving?" she said in that fat sleepy voice of hers. "So soon? Oh, my poor baby. Promise me you'll take care of yourself."

"Yes, Mother."

"Promise you won't do anything dangerous."

How stupid can a woman get? "Yes, Mother."

Then she said with a sweet laugh, "By the way, dear, now that you have a job again I told the bank they can stop paying your allowance. Is that all right?"

"Certainly," I said.

So there, like the breeze, went $250 paid promptly on the first of every month. She stopped it when I went to work in the toy department at Macy's, and when I worked for Lever Brothers, and when I worked in the art gallery on Fifty-seventh Street. Not that it mattered so much, money isn't so important in my life, but it's the principle of the thing that gets under my skin. Mr. Cooper, our lawyer, explained it all to me once. There was a definite clause in Father's will by which Mother was supposed to pay me that $250 each and every month come hell or high water. You can't argue with her, though. She's a lost cause.

While I was near a telephone I decided to call Tom Ritchie at his advertising agency: another gesture by dumbkopf. What a blessed word that is. It explains everything.

"Ritchie," he said in his on-the-ball voice, and I could practically see him, sitting upright at his desk, casual but sharp, cool but hot. Maybe he was expecting a call from the vice-president in charge of the canned-tuna-fish account.

"Hi, Tom," I said.

"Oh. It's you."

"Yes. It's me."

"How damned nice of you to call."

"I'm just leaving, Tom. I just wanted to say good-by."

"You mean," he said, "you're going through with this crazy idea?"

"Yes," I said.

"You stupid half-witted bitch," he said, and he began to argue with me; and after listening to him for half a minute I hung up. All I wanted to do was say good-by nicely, like old friends, but all he wanted to do was make me feel bad. You can't have a relationship like that, where one part of the relationship acts like Hitler.

I shouldn't have called him, I shouldn't have called Mother, I should have walked out cold on everybody and everything, exactly as I planned it in the first place; and as I went back to my room I thought about being such a soft brain. To hell with Tom Ritchie, I thought: he took my virginity and now he wants to take my soul. And to hell with Mother, too, for being what she is.

Angel was waiting in my room, and Eena, my Lesbian friend who helped me to do my packing. Eena is five by five by five, even in her corsets, and she has a voice that always gives me a shock—pure deep-down Chaliapin. She put up some bookshelves for me when I moved into the room, and maybe she hoped something beautiful would blossom as a result. But never. It couldn't. Still, I'm very fond of her.

I said, "Hi, Angel."

"Man," he said. "Endsville."

"Yep," I said.

He was small and skinny and he had a beard that wouldn't grow and he wore a greenish-brown suit that was eight sizes too large for him and, God, he looked dirty. Poor little old Angel. He'd come from Cuba or somewhere, and he was a poet, and every so often they would let him read his poems in the Overnite Café. He had a trick, while he was reading, of showing the audience all the punctuation by making signs in the air, and I remember one night he read a poem which was dedicated to me. It was called *The Girl with the Level Eyes*, and he nearly broke his arm as he read it. The last stanza went something like this:

2

Love!!!
What??? Love again!!!
A running nose in the darkness,,,
A scream in the night!!!!!!!
But, beware! O! Girl! With! The! Level! Eyes!
I am dynamite!!!!!!
I am an earthquake!!!!!
Me!!!!
You????

It caused a sensation, particularly with those last four question marks. Everybody knew it was meant for me, and
when Angel sat down, absolutely exhausted by this effort,
some of the beat characters in the café made hissing noises,
as if I'd deliberately infected the little man with typhoid.
So Angel, exhausted as he was, jumped up again and made an
impassioned speech in defense of women and the hydrogen
bomb, and then gave me his dark glasses, and I was accepted back in the fold. I do not, incidentally, dig that level
eyes bit. All my life I have been told I have level eyes,
and it doesn't make any sense because as far as I can see
nearly everybody has level eyes, and why make such a
production out of it in my case? Level-Eyed Thompson,
that's me.

"I brought a bottle," Eena said, growling like an old bulldog. "I couldn't let you go away dry."

"Oh, no," I said. "You shouldn't have, Eena." She was
generous and outgoing, even if she did have a personality
problem. I always felt sorry for her. God knows, it's hard
enough to find someone of the right sex to love; it must be
a hundred times harder to find somebody of the wrong sex.

She'd brought a bottle in a brown-paper bag so that I
wouldn't guess what it was. I'd guessed, of course. It was her
usual brand, Old Paralysis. I didn't want a drink, I didn't
want to go away with the smell of liquor on my breath,
but I figured that my plane wouldn't be leaving for two
hours and the smell would wear off by then. So we all sat
down on my three-legged sofa, and we had a drink, while
Eena boomed into my right ear and Angel slobbered into
my left ear. They were my friends, they were being friendly,
but I scarcely heard a thing. I sat looking around the room,
thinking, Mon Dieu, I lived here for six months, here, in
this squalor, twelve feet by eight, the ceiling dripping plaster,
the rug chewed by silverfish, no air, no light coming through

3

the dirty yellow window, no heat coming out of the peeling radiator. And for what? To discover the real Thompson, to experience beatitude? I had parties here, Angel read me his punctuation here, Eena tried to love me here, all kinds of people laughed and shouted and screamed here, they slept on the floor here and they vomited on the floor and once they poured lighter fluid on my *Oxford Book of English Verse* and tried to set it alight (they tried to burn Shelley, and Keats!); and it all should have had some deep-down effect on me, all this squalor and all this noise and all this reaching out: but what?

It wasn't too bad on the whole. I had only used up one forty-fourth of my life searching for fulfillment in Greenwich Village; and as I thought this profound thought, Big Top Charlie walked into the room without knocking, grinning from ear to ear and flexing his biceps.

"Hey," Big Top said. "You ain't gone yet."

"No," I said. "I ain't gone yet."

Eena said, "Hi, Big Top, have a drink."

"Poison," he said.

He walked over to the sofa and ruffled my hair. It was like having your hair ruffled by one of those machines that dig excavations for skyscrapers. I can't describe Big Top Charlie. The first time I saw him I practically swooned onto the sidewalk. He was just leaning against a wall on MacDougal, his hands in the front pockets of his chino pants, his ankles crossed, and I had the feeling that the wall would surely collapse—he was so fantastically massive. He was about six feet tall, and about six and a half feet across the shoulders, and about fifteen inches around the waist, and his muscles bulged as I have never in all my life seen muscles bulge. You couldn't miss them: he wore a white polo shirt a couple of sizes too small for him and the sleeves were turned up to the very top of his arms. His skin was deep deep gold, his hair was blonder than mine, his eyes were bluer than mine, he was so damned Nordic all over that it made my heart stop beating. Those muscles! That godlike smile! Those blue blue blue blue eyes! Let me add quickly, I'm not the first female to become hysterical over Big Top. It happens all the time. I daresay he could pick himself a different female every hour on the hour if he wished; but he doesn't wish. He explained it to me the first evening we were together. We'd been having a cappuccino in some espresso joint, and after a while he said

we couldn't sit there all night, why didn't we go somewhere else to talk, like my room. Sure, I said, why not;
and I walked out into the smelly darkness of West Fourth
Street with him as if I were walking right into Paradise.
I didn't know much about men, except for those miserable
few minutes with Tom Ritchie at the bottom of the garden
in Greenwich, and I was a full twenty-one-and-a-half years
old, and I couldn't turn away from so sublime an experience
as Big Top Charlie and his fifteen-inch waist—no girl could.
I was almost in a coma as we climbed the four flights of
stairs to my room, I couldn't open the door because the key
kept disappearing between my fingers, but finally I over-
came every obstacle and we were sitting side by side on my
three-legged sofa, and I waited for the sky to come crashing
down on my head. And then Big Top gave me his celebrated lecture on the effects of lovemaking on the male
organism. Boy! Big Top certainly opened *my* eyes! Love
was great for women: they thrived on it. But for a man
it was worse than suicide. It was just a long slow lingering
death. It robbed a guy of all his essential juices, not to mention his calcium, his sodium, and his phosphorus. It turned
his bones to dry twigs and it turned his muscles to little
rags that flapped in the wind. It sapped the will, it de-
composed the brain cells, it turned a man's insides to mush.
And he told me these gruesome facts with such authority
that I began to hate myself, I began to feel like the Harlot
of Babylon. Vile, horrible creature! To think of turning Big
Top Charlie's beautiful muscles to rags! To think of robbing
him of his phosphorus!

That was my Village romance. Eena hung around for
weeks hoping to get me on the rebound.

When I finished my drink I said, "I'm sorry, kids, I have to
leave now if I'm going to catch my plane."

"Listen," Eena said. "You don't have to go to Albuquerque.
Why the hell do you want to go to Albuquerque anyway?"

"It's my big chance," I said. This was the story I'd told
everybody except my mother and Tom Ritchie: I was going
to Albuquerque to work as a model. I couldn't explain that
I was through with living here, that I had to get away. I
said, "Big Top, help me carry my suitcases to a taxi."

He looked at me with his innocent blue blue eyes. "Gee. I
can't. I have this strained back, see? I can't lift noth'n."

I should have known. He was always scared out of his wits that he might strain one of his precious muscles.

Eena said, "I'll help you, honey." She tucked a suitcase under her left arm and then picked up the other two as if they were just filled with helium. I carried my hatbox and my purse. Big Top followed us, whistling, and Angel followed Big Top, moaning, and somehow I felt as if I were walking out to my own funeral. We found a taxi on Sixth Avenue, and when all the luggage had been thrown in, Eena grabbed me and kissed me on the side of the mouth, and I felt the wetness of her tears. I just said, "So long," to Big Top Charlie, but I couldn't say anything to Angel—he was running back to MacDougal Street like a rabbit.

I told the driver to take me to the East Side airlines terminal, and I sat back and began to breathe again. It was amazing: all of a sudden, within a minute of leaving Eena and Big Top and Angel and the Village generally, I had this absolutely marvelous feeling of relief and excitement, exactly as if my sinuses had been clogged up and now they'd unclogged. I wanted to sing at the top of my voice because I'd left that squalor and meanness behind me, I would never any more have to pretend that I was crazy about dirt, and Zen, and Being and non-Being, and poetry that stank as if it had come out of a MacDougal Street garbage pail. Maybe it's biological, but in the long run this way of life isn't meant for a female. At least that's what I found: the whole thing got to be a bore.

The taxi driver turned to me at a traffic light and said, "Are you flying, miss?"

It was a funny question. I wondered what he was after. I said, "Yes, I'm flying. South." Like a duck.

"From Idlewild, or La Guardia?"

"Idlewild."

He said, "Look, miss. You'll have to take the bus from the airlines terminal, right? Plus you'll have to pay the redcaps to carry your bags, right? So for a few pennies more I'll take you all the way and you can sit back in comfort. Isn't it worth it?"

"What do you mean, a few pennies more?"

"I'll tell you what I'll do," he said. "The whole trip, five bucks."

"Okay."

"Okay?" He sounded surprised that I'd accepted his proposition without any argument.

"Sure."

"It's a pleasure to meet someone sensible," he said. "Some folks will break their backs to save a few lousy pennies."

Sensible, I thought: oh, brother, if you only knew. But it was a fair deal and it fitted in with my mood. Whenever you're starting a new life, give the flag a wave. Bust a gusset or two. Celebrate. Even if it's only riding all the way to Idlewild in a taxi when you could just as easily have gone by bus. As it happened, I could well afford the luxury. I was loaded. I had fifty dollars in my purse, plus a hundred and fifty in traveler's checks, which still left a balance of two hundred and eighteen in my bank against a rainy day, together with a few E Bonds. And all this wealth was left after, literally, an orgy of buying new clothes, mostly at Lord and Taylor, because, for this new life, I absolutely had to have a new wardrobe practically from the feet up. All my old clothes were worn-out or moth-eaten, except my beaver coat, and I wouldn't have any use for that where I was going: South. When I totted up what I'd spent on all those dresses and things I was slightly chilled—$433.87. It was worthwhile, though; I had a marvelous feeling of serenity knowing that practically every single thing in my three suitcases and hatbox was spanking new, except for my hairbrush and a few other trifling items.

The taxi driver was a nice friendly man: he just let me sit quietly in the back of his cab to think my own thoughts, while he concentrated on his job of driving. But taxi drivers are taxi drivers, and I suppose I couldn't really expect this one to remain alone and apart for ever; and eventually he said in a gentle sort of way, "What's your destination, miss?"

I thought I'd told him earlier. "Idlewild."

"I mean, where you flying to *from* Idlewild?"

"Oh, California." It was the first place that came to my tongue.

He hesitated. "That's funny," he said. "I had an idea you told me you was flying South."

He must have been worried about his ears letting him down, and I did my best to reassure him. "That's right," I said. "I'm going South for a quick visit with my aunt, and *then* I'm going to California. California is where I'm *really* going."

7

Immediately, it struck me as very very strange. Normally I don't lie. I don't invent stories. Yet here I was telling this innocent taxi driver that I was going somewhere I wasn't going, and I'd done the same to everybody I knew in the Village. New Orleans, California, Albuquerque—why? I felt like a murderess escaping from the scene of her crime. Or, more precisely, like an animal covering up its spoor so that it couldn't be tracked. That's what it was; and once I had the explanation I felt better. I wasn't turning into a pathological liar, after all. I was merely starting a brand-new life in another part of the forest, and I didn't want my old life to follow and catch up with me. I wished now that I hadn't broken down and told Mother and Tom Ritchie where I was going and what I would be doing; I wished I'd kept my big mouth shut. If you're planning to be a jungle cat creeping off into the undergrowth, be a jungle cat.

The taxi driver had a fine monologue with me about California, and by the time we reached Idlewild he'd almost convinced me that I was actually going there. The climate! The sunshine! The people, so relaxed! He had me all agog at the golden prospect, and in a burst of gratitude I gave him a dollar tip. At once, bingo!—something wonderful happened. No sooner had he deposited my three suitcases and hatbox on the sidewalk than two Marines marched out of the crowd and said, "Can we be of service, ma'am?" They looked like twins, straight and tall and lean and cropped, as Marines are, and deadly serious.

It did my heart good. I hadn't been a girl, in a sense, for six months—just a young hag, a figment of Jean Paul Sartre's imagination; and here, like a flash, I was a girl again, capable of raising the hopes of the United States Marine Corps. I said, fluttering a little, "Why, it's awfully nice of you, but I was only looking for a redcap—"

"George," said one.

"Roger," said the other.

There wasn't any harm in it. Nothing was going to come of it. I walked between them; people smiled at us; my ego was uplifted, and so was theirs. Young men seem to like carrying suitcases for girls the same way a dog likes to carry a bone.

But there was something else as we marched into the airport, far more important. I'd been to Idlewild many times, and each time was exciting because it's so vast and active and vital, with thousands of exotic people bustling hither and thither, and scores of voices booming over the public-address system, and dozens of planes taking off every minute, and lights flashing, and arrows pointing—it just leaves me utterly breathless. In the past, though, I'd come here merely as a passenger, or as a visitor seeing somebody off: one of the crowd. This time was different. There was a new and wilder excitement because I was entering deep, deep into all this tremendous activity, although practically nobody was aware of it yet: this was my own new world. I'd chosen it deliberately, and I trembled as I stepped into it.

One of my Marines said politely, "Which airline did you want, ma'am?"

"Magna International Airlines, please."

The other Marine said, "You wouldn't by any chance, ma'am, be going to Portland, Maine?"

"Oh, I wish I were," I said. "I'm terribly sorry. I'm going to Spartanburg, South Carolina."

"Too bad," they said. But they didn't falter. They marched me right over to the Magna International Airlines counter, and deposited my three suitcases and my hatbox in front of the weighing machine. I shook hands with them and said, "I do hope we'll meet again," and they said, "Have a pleasant trip, ma'am," and went off quite contentedly.

The clerk behind the counter was almost the same type: cropped and scrubbed, good-looking, broad-shouldered. "Can I help you?" he asked.

I opened my purse and handed him my white-and-red envelope with the green form inside.

"Well, well, well," he said. "Another one."

I didn't understand. "I am?" I said.

"Yes, indeed." He picked up a telephone, spoke mysteriously into it, waited, put the receiver down, scribbled something on my envelope, and said, "Flight 21A. Gate 12."

"Thank you," I said.

He looked me up and down very critically, as if he were an expert at a certain kind of statistics. Five feet seven. 36-24-34. Then he winked. "You'll do fine," he said. "Welcome aboard."

2

Flight 21A was due to leave at two twenty-five. I was half an hour ahead of time when I arrived at Gate 12 and only a few people were standing there, but as I waited in line more and more people appeared, until I began to wonder. Could such a huge crowd get onto one airplane? It seemed impossible, unless it were a rubber expandable airplane. Magna International Airlines, I thought, I trust you are aware of what you are doing.

At a few minutes past two the loading started. I might have known. When I reached the gate the harassed little man on duty took one look at my green form and said curtly, "Wait at the rear, please, with the other girls."

Everything happens to me that can possibly happen. I'm used to it. I said, "Which other girls?"

"Just wait at the rear," he snapped. "We'll call you when we're ready for you."

I pushed my way to the rear of the crowd and saw three of the girls the snappy little man had referred to. They were unmistakable: tall, good-looking, nicely dressed. They stared at me sadly, and I stared at them sadly.

"Hi," the tallest of them said. "Are you another of the rejects?"

"I guess so."

She said, to make sure, "You're going to the training school in Miami Beach?"

"That's what I thought until the little man turned me away."

"We're all in the same boat," she said. "Come and join the gang. I'm Donna Stewart and these two are—what are your names again, girls?"

"Annette Morris," one of them said. She was a brunette. The other said, "Mary Ruth Jurgens." She was a pale, expressionless blonde with cold gray eyes. They were both attractive, but Donna Stewart outshone them by a million miles. She had reddish hair and eyes that were the most fabulous emerald green, and a warm, gay personality.

10

I told them my name. Then I said, "Does anybody know what's happening around here?"

Donna said, "It's just the usual stuff with airlines. They're all fouled up. I guess they're loading the regular passengers first, and they'll squeeze us in if they have space." She laughed cheerily. "And if they don't have the space, well, it's just too bad. I'll be delighted to spend the night in New York City."

"Why?" I asked.

"Because I've never been in New York City, that's why," she said. "I'm just a simple country girl from New Hampshire."

I said, "I've been living in New York City, and you can have it."

"If we're stranded here tonight," Donna said with the sweetest smile, "you can show me the town. Do you know all the hot spots?"

"Sure."

She touched my arm with the tips of her fingers, and we were friends from that moment.

"Hey, girls," Annette whispered. "Look what's coming."

We looked, and then we stared. The thing that was coming was a girl, and she was unbelievable. She was simply the loveliest girl I've ever seen. I hate to say anything like that, it's too easy, but in this case it happened to be true. Her face was perfectly oval, her skin was porcelain, her eyes were like a cat's, hazel-gold, and she had the blackest, glossiest hair swept up from her forehead and curling down her back. She was dressed like a movie star, in a rather extravagant fashion—a tight black suit with ruffles on the hips, and a hat festooned with gold leaves—but the most impressive thing about her was the signal she gave off. It was pure female voluptuousness.

When she reached us she threw out one hand dramatically and said, "Ha. You are for Miami Beach the training school which waits the airplane, yes?"

I made a stab in the dark—although it wasn't completely in the dark; my instinct is usually right about this particular thing—and answered in Italian, "Yes, we're all waiting to go aboard this airplane. Please join us. And permit me to introduce myself. My name is Carol Thompson."

She looked me up and down with cold interest, as if I might be edible if cooked for twelve hours and then left

11

to simmer. I was a little suprised that she didn't open my mouth and examine my teeth. She said, "Ah-hah. You speak Italian?"

I thought so. I mean, I'd just spoken four sentences to her in Italian. I said, "Yes."

She cocked her head to one side. "Where you pick up these cheap Italian accent?"

I said, still in the language I thought I spoke so fluently, "In Florence. My uncle has there a bordello, small, but of good repute. It is possible you have heard of him. His name is Signor Atkinson." I've always felt, if you're going to trade insults, *trade* them. Don't beat about the bush.

Apparently I was too subtle. She said, "These is not accent of Florence, these is just cheap accent. I am of Rome. I am Alma di Lucca."

Out of the blue, Donna asked in a cool, bitchy voice, "Not the *Countess* Alma di Lucca, by any chance?"

Alma stiffened. *That* little arrow hit its mark. She did not look at Donna, she did not reply. I thought, Well! What do you know! We have a war on our hands. Already. In one minute. This might be highly interesting.

Donna yawned. "We have to pass the time somehow, fellers. Who plays bridge?"

The snappy little man came over to us after a while and said, "I'm sorry to keep you back like this, girls, but it couldn't be helped." He worried over a few scraps of paper attached to a clipboard which seemed to be his badge of office. "Let's see, now. How many of you are there?"

"We are five," Alma said. "Any person can count us. Five."

"Are you expecting any more?"

"We do not expect," Alma said. "It is your job to expect. We shall now climb on the airplane to fly where we are flying?"

I approved of the way she put things, but the man evidently didn't hear her. He made some ticks with a pencil on one of his pieces of paper, and frowned. Then he looked us over, made some more ticks, and frowned again. Poor little chap. He seemed to have so much on his mind. Here we were, three perfectly charming girls, plus a ravishing dreamboat from Italy, plus me; and he treated us as if we were so many bales of cotton filled with boll weevils. For the first time, then, I realized the demands that the airline business makes on its minions.

Finally he said, "Okay. You can go aboard. The hostesses will take care of you. Go to the aft loading ramp." He sounded as if he'd given everything up in despair.

Annette asked, "Where's aft?"

"At the *rear*," he said hopelessly. "My God, don't you know where *aft* is?"

Alma said, "If she know, she did not ask. You please be polite, sir, or I report you to Mr. Benjamin."

That seemed to stun him; and as we walked through Gate 12 I asked, "Gee! Who's Mr. Benjamin?"

She said, "Very useful person. Big executive. Very important." Then she smiled. "But just a ghost. I invent him, in the imagination. Scare everybody, very much. I say Mr. Benjamin to them, they jump."

I'd never thought of that. Boy! She certainly had something there. She ought to patent it. Everybody needs a Mr. Benjamin in the background to help smooth life's rougher spots.

I began to go to pieces as we came close to the big Boeing. It looked so majestic, so patient, standing there waiting for us, its wings swept back, its engines thrust forward, its tail tall and sharp against the cool sky. It was like, I thought, some gigantic wild orchid; or a huge white fish pierced by a huge white boomerang; or, even more ridiculously, the Arab's steed (*my beautiful, my beautiful*) on a colossal scale; and I wanted to reach up and pat its nose out of sheer love for it. I love airplanes, and I shall always love them, and when I'm near one it turns my bones to jelly.

Mary Ruth Jurgens and Annette went up the ramp first; then Alma; then Donna and myself. At the top of the ramp another harassed little man in a raincoat checked our tickets and silently allowed us to pass. A hostess was waiting at the cabin door, and all at once, at the mere sight of her, I felt as if I'd arrived here straight from the Casbah. It was a maddening and humiliating moment. I'd been feeling pretty well satisfied until then, unconsciously glowing as a result of being picked up by those two Marines. Here, though, was the living proof that I was still, relatively speaking, a Greenwich Village bum. Her russet uniform was immaculate, her hair under its cute hat was immaculate, her com-

13

plexion was immaculate, her hands were immaculate, she was as crisp and bright as a brand-new silver dollar.

"Hi, girls," she said to Donna and me. "Welcome aboard."

"Hi," we said.

It was her turn to check our ticket envelopes. "Okay," she said, and handed them back to us. Then she whispered, "You two have seats in the first-class section, forward."

"We do?" I said. "What about the others?"

"They're in the coach section. We have to fit you in wherever we can."

She motioned us into the cabin. Another hostess beckoned to us to come down the aisle. She said, "Keep going, girls," and we walked on and on and on, and it felt like the longest walk I had ever taken in my life. I heard Alma say hoarsely, "Carola!" but I couldn't respond. I am such an idiot about airplanes: I guess I was in a sort of a trance. My eyes only saw the vista before me, and it seemed endless, endless, swathed in azure blue and soft white. A third hostess took us in charge after we'd walked the first mile, and then a fourth hostess showed us to our seats, and I found myself sitting beside a man in a light gray suit. His tie was light blue, and in general he matched the color scheme of the plane. I was content. Heaven.

Before we began to move there was a great deal of palaver, which I listened to with interest. One of the hostesses made a charming speech over the public-address system, welcoming us to Magna International Airlines' jet 707 flight 21A. She introduced the other hostesses, and then herself; she gave us a delightful talk about the many new and interesting features of our airplane; and then she went on at great length about oxygen. I'd never given this subject much thought before.

"Ha! Oxygen!" the man beside me said.

"I beg your pardon, sir?"

"It's for operations," he said.

He had a rather scratchy gruff voice, and I wondered if I had heard him correctly. I looked at him; and he looked at me, caught my eye, and turned away again. But I thought I had a clue. His face was thin and drawn and ascetic, very sensitive. I glanced down at his hands. The fingers were long and tapered. A surgeon, I decided, just like that. Who but a surgeon would comment about oxygen being used for operations?

14

One of the hostesses walked down the aisle with an oxygen mask in her hand, showing everybody how to use it. In the ceiling of the plane, over each row of seats, beside the individual reading lights and the gadgets that blow air on you, there were cunningly concealed trap doors; and when these trap doors popped open, oxygen masks dropped down and dangled in front of you, so that you had your own personal supply. All you had to do was breathe normally, holding the mask over your nose and mouth. Nothing could be simpler.

This procedure was completely new to me, and perhaps I was too wide-eyed with wonderment. The man beside me said, "Don't let them scare you with this oxygen stuff. It's nothing. Just a lot of rigamarole."

"I'm not scared, really."

"Good. Just relax. You'll be okay."

He gave me a friendly, reassuring smile. He's nice, I thought: he means well. But I changed my mind about him. In spite of his fine features and his delicate hands, he didn't sound exactly like a surgeon. A dentist, more likely. Dentists are always reassuring people, telling them to relax. *Don't clench your teeth, now. Just relax. You'll be okay.*

Then, in a few minutes, we were moving slowly past the hangers, out to the runway. We waited; and suddenly the plane came alive. The man beside me folded his arms, closed his eyes, and went to sleep, following his own advice. We began to go forward in an amble, we began to run, we were sprinting, galloping along at a tremendous pace; and then, without any sensation, we were up, going through patches of thin white mist and scraps of yellow cloud. There was blue water below us, and spits of land, and groups of tiny white houses; and I thought, it's really the most astonishing thing in the whole world—it works every time. You take a de luxe railroad train, and stick wings on it, and stick engines into the wings, and it *flies,* it actually *flies* and stays in the air. I've had it explained to me a thousand times, why a plane stays in the air, but the scientific facts simply won't do. It's purely a miracle.

I can sit back now and without any effort recall every second of that take-off, but it wouldn't be of great interest to anybody except a person who cares about flying the same way I do. The basic question really is, Thompson, what is there about airplanes and flying in them that stirs you up to such an extent? And the answer is, I'm darned if

I know the answer. I am enough of a Bryn Mawr girl (and one year was enough, and plenty) to recognize that an airplane is an absolutely unmentionable symbol which I am subconsciously always seeking; and the act of flying is fraught with sexual significance to such a degree that one can only write about it in a document that's going to be buried in a time capsule for the next thousand years. But what nobody has ever succeeded in explaining to me is, why should I forever be craving symbols when I can have, without the least bit of effort, the real thing? I mean, it would have been only too easy, ever since I was about sixteen years old, to have had an utterly scintillating sex life with all the trimmings—instead of which, here I was at twenty-two practically as pure as the driven snow, except for that one time when I had the hiccups in the garden at Greenwich and Tom Ritchie took advantage of my weakened state. I don't blame him, damn him. It's been a natural activity of young males from the day when life started in a swamp somewhere in Asia; and he did tell me afterwards, over and over again, that he wanted to marry me as soon as he had the canned-tuna-fish account sewed up. Still, this isn't an explanation of my obsession with airplanes, my alleged seeking after symbols of rampant masculinity. Incidentally, that is the most extraordinary experience, being seduced while you have the hiccups. I was fond of Tom Ritchie, and I always had a normal girlish interest in the whole subject of what goes on between males and females at those moments which are usually described in novels (so explicitly) by four dots; but nothing registered too clearly on this occasion because I was too preoccupied with the upper half of me going *hic* every second. Trust Thompson to foul it up when she's losing her virginity. The greatest moment of my life, according to all the books I've read: and I swear, all it *was* was four dots. I daresay I might have put up a ladylike fight if I'd been my usual self, but with those hiccups I was simply helpless. When it was all over I just lay there on the grass going "Hic, hic," like a run-down alarm clock, and Tom Ritchie looked at me in disgust, as if he'd done everything in his power to cure me but I was just too doggone stupid to respond to his medicine. A girl could get the idea from this that sex is somewhat overrated, particularly if a character like Big Top Charlie is the next big thrill to turn up in her life. But, no. I didn't lose all hope. I didn't abandon all my ideals and illusions. I have to admit, though, that these two experiences, Tom and Big Top, left me mildly disenchanted, and if it came to a choice I'd just as soon sit down to a good steak or a broiled Maine lobster.

We were climbing (just as the advertisements proclaim) without a whisper of sound, without a trace of vibration, when something went *Snap!* in my ear and a deep, virile voice said, "Hello, everybody. This is the Captain. H'm. You might like to know that we'll be flying at five-eighty miles an hour, altitude of 'proximately twenty-eight thousand feet, estimated time of this trip—h'm—two and a half hours. We don't anticipate any adverse flying conditions. That's all. Thanks." *Snap!* A peppy little speech, with hardly a wasted word. I could see him at the controls in the cockpit, surrounded by dials and levers and switches, lean and tanned and dangerous, secretly despising all these passengers who were fouling up his beautiful machine: a dedicated man, with strong wrists covered with fine silky black hair, and black eyebrows, and keen eyes peering into the distance. And I thought, perhaps that's where my fate lies. Perhaps. It wasn't too likely, on the facts I'd read. Eighty-four percent of all airline pilots are married, which leaves a mere sixteen percent available for the joys of romance with girls like me. The odds are kind of stacked, because there are an awful lot of girls like me. Zillions, that's all.

Then, as the Captain finished his announcement, the man beside me gave a little sigh, unfastened his seat belt, and took out a pack of cigarettes and a gold-plated Zippo lighter. He looked at me out of the corner of his eye, hesitated, and then said, "Would you like a cigarette, miss?"

I hesitated too, for a fraction of a second. And the peculiar thing was, in that fraction of a second my whole nature changed. I said, "Why, thank you, sir, I would love one," and gave him a big bright smile.

Now I had learned a long long time ago that I shouldn't accept a cigarette from a strange man. No matter how innocent the offer is, it's a trap. One miserable little cigarette and you're under an obligation to the man, you have to talk to him and listen to him tell you all about his family and his work and what he did in Philadelphia last Tuesday, and you never know how or where it's going to end. Particularly when you're a girl traveling alone, one simple word can lead to the most embarrassing complications. So, in the past,

17

I've tried to act in a ladylike way and avoid getting involved with stray men.

But in the fraction of a second that I hesitated in this case, a great many thoughts came into my mind, including a sort of complete visual recording of my interview with the man from Magna International Airlines at the main offices on Park Avenue a couple of weeks ago. How an interview that lasted nearly two hours can flash through your mind in a fraction of a second is something I can't explain. Maybe it goes to prove that the human brain can still occasionally hold its own with an IBM machine.

The name of the man at Magna was A. B. Garrison—the A. stood for Arnold. The room he interviewed me in was enormous, acres and acres of bare office, and as I entered the room he called in a cheery voice, "Hello, Miss Thompson, good to meet you, come and sit down," smiling welcomingly as I walked the long mile to the chair beside him. I knew what he was doing, of course: he was sizing me up for first impressions—how I looked, how I walked, how I reacted to his "Hello," how I returned his smile, and so on. He was fortyish, plumpish, easygoing, and I guess he realized that I knew he was sizing me up because as I sat down he chuckled and said, "Don't be nervous, Miss Thompson, this is going to be quite painless." What he convinced me of, from the first moment, was that he wanted to help. He was shrewd as the dickens, and I knew that I couldn't possibly put anything over on him even if I tried; but I also had this good encouraging feeling that he was on my side. While we were talking a very dignified lady named Mrs. Montgomery joined us. She sat down beside Mr. Garrison after he introduced us, but most of the time she merely listened to our conversation and made no comment.

On Mr. G.'s desk lay an enormous application form which I had filled in a few days earlier, consisting of at least ten thousand questions ranging from my measurements (bust, waist, hips, shoes, hat, height, weight) to my present marital status, location of missing teeth, visible scars, schools attended, degrees if any, employment record, have you discussed this application with your parents, and so on and so on. Questionnaires as long as your arm seem to be de rigueur these days; even if you apply for a job as a street cleaner you have to tell the story of your life and have psychiatric tests and say what you think an ink blot reminds you of; and if this doesn't smack of *Izvestia* I don't know what does. But there was one priceless item in the Magna questionnaire that stopped me dead in my tracks: State briefly how you use your spare time. This, I thought when I came to it, is the living end, this is straight out of *Das Kapital,* and I toyed with the idea of giving a really snappy answer to that one like, *How I use my spare time cannot possibly be stated briefly.* Or, *This matter is between me and my Maker.* Or, *Am always open to interesting suggestions.* Finally I thought, Oh, the hell with it; and wrote, "Reading and swimming." Dull but safe. No bureaucrat could object to that.

Mr. G. began to go through my application form more or less at random, and I couldn't guess where he was leading, if anywhere. He wasn't in a hurry, just friendly, and even jolly at times.

"You haven't had any serious illnesses, Miss Thompson?"

"No, sir."

"You're an only child? No sisters, no brothers?"

"That's correct, sir."

"I see you were at Bryn Mawr for one year. Why only one year? Was the work too difficult for you?"

"Oh, no. I just quit."

"Why?"

"I got awfully bored. I wanted to go out into the world."

"To travel?"

"To do anything. Just to get out and do things."

"But you managed to travel quite a bit. I see you've been to Canada, Mexico, England, France, Italy, et cetera. Did you get to visit all these places after you left college?"

"No, sir. Before. During vacations."

"Did you go alone? Or with your family? Or friends?"

"I went to Mexico by myself. My father took me to all the other places. He used to travel a lot."

Mr. Garrison looked at the form for a few seconds. "I notice you haven't entered your father's occupation. Of course, you don't have to, if you'd rather not. It isn't too important—merely for our records."

"My father's dead, sir. That's why I didn't answer the question."

"Oh, I'm sorry."

"His occupation was writing travel books. That's how I

came to do so much traveling. He used to take me along with him sometimes."

"Travel books?" Mr. Garrison said. "H'm. Was his name Gregg Thompson, by any chance?"

"Yes."

Mr. Garrison looked pleased. He turned to Mrs. Montgomery. "Did you ever read any of those Gregg Thompson travel books?"

She had a quiet, cultured voice. "Indeed. Many of them. I found them quite delightful."

"Same here," Mr. Garrison said. "Absolutely topnotch. He had a real gift."

I wanted to cry.

Mr. G. changed the subject. "You speak French, Italian and Spanish. Fluently?"

"Fairly fluently."

"Enough to keep up a conversation?"

"Oh, yes. As long as it isn't too technical."

"How did you come to learn so many languages, when you only completed one year of college?"

I said, "I can't help myself. I'm kind of a fool about languages. I just seem to pick them up. I guess by osmosis, or something."

"You picked them up when you were traveling with your father?"

"Yes, sir. For the most part, anyway."

"I see. Incidentally, do you do much reading?"

"Yes, sir. I read a lot. I used to read all the time."

"A bookworm, eh?"

The way he said it made me laugh.

He went on, "I see that you put down reading as one of the ways you use your spare time. The other thing is swimming. You swim a lot, too?"

"As much as I can. I love it."

"You mean, splashing around in a pool, having a good time with your friends?"

I said, "Oh, no. That's awful. What I meant was real swimming."

"I don't follow you," he said. "*Real* swimming?"

"Long-distance stuff," I said.

"Don't tell me you're one of these girls who swim the English Channel."

I laughed again. "Not quite. But up in Canada we had a cabin on a lake, when my father was alive, and I used to swim across the lake and back every morning. It was about three and a half miles, altogether."

"Did you do this alone?"

"Mostly. That's the fun of swimming. You can be alone." For the first time, his voice became gloomy. "Miss Thompson, you aren't alone very often on a big airliner."

Oh, God, I thought: I've trapped myself. I've said all the wrong things. That item in the questionnaire which I despised so much, which I answered so casually, has backfired and caught me out. Because, what kind of girl is Mr. G. looking for, to fly on Magna International Airlines planes? Obviously, girls who are healthy, happy, smiling, outgoing. And what kind of girl had I just proven myself to be? A morbid introvert. The kind of girl who's always slinking into a dark corner to read some utterly miserable book. The kind of girl who sloshes across a lake for hours, to avoid her fellow human beings. I'd told the man so, out of my own mouth.

He didn't appear to notice that I was in a panic. He went on to chat about other things. Pay, for example. He explained that girls were only accepted conditionally, which meant for a period of four weeks of training—and even this could be terminated at any time—and only after this training was completed were they given a contract. During training, they got forty-five dollars a week, out of which there was a deduction of fifteen dollars for rent, plus further deductions for uniforms, social security, etc. Was I prepared to accept this?

"Yes," I said.

"I also have to tell you," he said, "that we have extremely high standards during training. It's rather tougher than Bryn Mawr. Any girl who gets less than a ninety percent average is sent home."

"Oh," I said. *Ninety percent average!*

He leaned back in his chair and said, "Miss Thompson, there are just a couple of things I'd like to say. First: I'm impressed by your qualifications, specially your facility with languages. If you join the company it might be some time before you could fly on our international routes—we have a general rule that the girls don't fly international until they've completed two years of domestic flying. At the same time, we have something of a shortage of girls with the right qualifications. You understand that?"

"Yes, sir."

"Now," he continued: "When we hire a girl we don't lay down any hard-and-fast conditions about how long she has to stay with us. We realize that any girl is liable to find another career that's more attractive—such as getting married and raising a family." He folded his arms and paused for a moment. "Just the same, Miss Thompson, we'd naturally like to have *some* assurance that we wouldn't lose you a week or two after you finished your training. What's your feeling about this? Do you think of flying as a sort of interlude between other things? Or do you see yourself making a career of it?"

I said, "Mr. Garrison, I love flying. If the company takes me on, I would want to go on flying for years and years and years, until you have to carry me out to the plane in a wheelchair."

"Okay," he said. "Mrs. Montgomery?"

She said slowly, "I, too, find your qualifications impressive, Miss Thompson. Your languages, your personality, your background, are unusual. You have a very pretty smile, which will undoubtedly please a lot of our passengers. But I must impress on you: anybody can smile. This job is far more than that. It is much more than walking up and down an airliner looking glamorous."

I was half scared out of my wits by the solemn way she spoke.

She went on, "My dear, I admire your passion for books. I can also sympathize, very fully, with your desire to get far away from the crowd. Of course. We must all be alone sometimes. But—"

I quaked.

"But, Miss Thompson, we must all learn new disciplines. That is how we grow. That is how we develop and fulfill ourselves. If you join us, you will be alone rarely. You will be working in airplanes, with passengers who in some cases will depend on you completely. And that is the hardest of the disciplines you will have to learn—to give, give, give, freely and endlessly. Not to think of yourself. To forget yourself, and to exist only for these others."

I didn't know what to say.

She smiled. She looked lovely, suddenly, when she smiled. "Have I frightened you?"

"No, ma'am." But I was lying.

She stood up and walked across to me, and held out her hand. "I shall watch your progress with interest," she said.

22

Mr. G. said, "So will I."

Well: they would have been fascinated by my progress when the man beside me offered me a cigarette and I accepted it. My mind flashed over that entire interview, everything Mr. Garrison had said, and those sonorous words of Mrs. Montgomery; and in that crowded fraction of a second I thought, Okay, Thompson, here's your big chance. Forget yourself, forget you're an inhibited female from Greenwich, Connecticut, go into you new geisha-girl act, try it on for size.

Gad! It worked like a charm. I was such a perfect geisha, I almost began to lisp.

"Thank you," I said as I took the cigarette.

"Welcome," he said.

"Thank you," I said when he lit my cigarette with his gold-plated Zippo lighter.

"Welcome," he said.

I waited a moment to see whether he would take it from there. But no. The cat had his tongue. So I gave him an encouraging smile and said, "Are you going to Miami?"

It was one hell of a subtle question. The plane was only going to Miami, with no in-between stops. But that's the way we geishas start the ball rolling. A nice easy pitch that the guy can't miss even if he's blindfolded.

"Yeah," he said. He looked delighted. "That's right. Miami Beach."

"Gee, I'm going to Miami Beach, too."

"Yeah?"

He seemed stumped at this point. He didn't quite know what to say next. I tried to give him a little assistance. "I've never been to Miami Beach before."

"You haven't?"

Boy, it was hard sledding. I said, "I hear it's fabulous. Those wonderful hotels, and the palm trees, and the sunshine."

"Yeah."

"Is it really as fabulous as they say?"

"Well, yeah. Kind of." The cat returned with his tongue. "Where you staying?"

"Let me see." I opened my purse and searched through the debris for the letter Mr. Garrison had sent me confirming my acceptance and telling me where I was to go and when. "Here it is," I said. "The Charleroi."

"The Charleroi," he said (except that he pronounced it in a sort of Americanized way: Charleyroy). "Well, that's a pretty nice all-around hotel. Not new, mind you. They built it two-three years ago. Don't let that worry you, though. It's real cozy. Matter of fact, Maxwell Courtenay is an old pal of mine. Quite a guy, Maxwell."

"Is he the manager of the hotel?"

"That's right." He leaned over confidentially. "Tell you what. My name's Nat Brangwyn. When you check in to the Charleroi, you tell Maxwell you know me. He'll do his best to see you're comfortable."

"Why, thank you."

He became slightly pink. "I'm in and out of the Charleroi every day. I might bump into you, eh?"

"Well, I hope so, Mr. Brangwyn."

"They have a nice bar there, the Souvenir Bar. Very quiet. We could have a drink, maybe."

"Well, thank you." But it went to prove my point—if you don't have a professional reason for doing so, *never* accept an innocent cigarette from a stranger. I'd only known Mr. Brangwyn for two minutes, and here he was making far-ranging plans for the future.

He became slightly pinker. "How about tonight?"

"I'm sorry," I said. "Tonight is out," and I went on to explain that I was going to Miami Beach to be trained as a Magna International Airlines flight hostess, and tonight was checking-in night, and I'd be busy getting settled. Why not? If he was in and out of the Charleroi every day he'd soon discover it for himself.

"Is that right?" he said in wonderment. "You're going to train to be a hostess?"

"Yes."

"And you're going to stay at the Charleroi?"

"Yes."

He blinked his nice blue eyes. "Well, gosh. Why the Charleroi?"

"That's where I was told to go," I said. "As far as I'm concerned it's just a roof over my head."

"Some roof."

"Why do you say that? I expect there will be other girls there who are taking this training course."

"No kidding."

I couldn't understand his attitude. I said, "At the very

least, there are four other girls who are flying on this plane."

He smiled broadly. "I get it."

"You get what?"

"Maxwell. I know what he's up to. He rented the fourteenth floor to the airline."

"Oh. Is that funny?"

"Look," he said gently: "The fourteenth floor, it's actually the thirteenth floor. Counted from the bottom up, that's what it actually is. The *thirteenth* floor. But no one wants to sleep on the thirteenth floor because it's an unlucky number. See?"

"Yes." It was coming through as a faint glimmer.

"So instead of labeling it the thirteenth floor, they label it the fourteenth floor. But the whole world still knows it's actually the thirteenth, and they won't sleep on that floor for all the tea in China. You see now?"

"Yes."

"So Maxwell solved his problem. The floor is taken off his hands by an airline for a bunch of airline hostesses, and he's sitting pretty. It's a stroke of genius. He'll be fighting them off."

"Fighting us off?"

"No. The guys."

"Which guys?"

"Miss," he said reproachfully, as if I were acting just too damned coy.

"My name is Carol Thompson," I said. "Which guys?"

"You know. All the single guys on the Beach. Not to mention all the married guys who think they'd like a little relaxation away from home."

"Mr. Brangwyn: you don't make that sound one little bit attractive."

He shrank down in his seat. "Believe me, I didn't mean to sound like that."

One of the hostesses interrupted in a soft voice. "Excuse me: we are now serving complimentary drinks. Would you care for anything, Mr. Brangwyn?"

"I sure would. Bourbon; with a little water on the side. How about you, Miss Thompson?"

"No, thank you," I said.

"Come on. How about a martini?"

"No, really—"

He said, "Bring the young lady a martini."

The hostess said very quietly, "I'm sorry, sir, Miss Thompson is traveling as a special passenger and I am not permitted to serve her a complimentary drink."

He bridled. "Why not? She's a human being like everyone else."

I said, "*Really*, I don't want a drink. *Honestly*, I don't."

The hostess slipped away. It was an awkward moment for her, and I felt sorry it had happened. People can cause such trouble by being well meaning. They argue and argue, defending your rights to life, liberty, and the pursuit of happiness, and all they do is start a riot.

"I don't get it," Mr. Brangwyn said. "What's the harm in bringing you a simple little martini? You think the airline would go broke?"

I said, "It's a rule, that's all. A rule is a rule."

"Yeah. But if a rule is a rule then it ought to be sensible."

I liked him. I didn't really want to like him, but he had something attractive. A sort of skinniness, a sort of sharpness, edgy and alive. He wasn't a surgeon, of course, he probably wasn't even a dentist—God knows what he was—and he didn't exactly elocute like Sir Laurence Olivier; but he was definitely likable.

I didn't want to be there when the hostess returned with his bourbon and water, so I excused myself and began to walk toward the rear of the plane. Donna Stewart was three seats behind me, and she beckoned me to lean down. Sitting beside her was one of the tiniest men I have ever seen, dressed in a cream-colored silk suit, with a white-on-white tie which was tacked down by an enormous old-fashioned pearl tie pin.

She whispered in my ear, "Guess what? He made me a proposition. Can you imagine!"

"You mean, this little guy?"

"He's a jockey. He told me he likes big horses and big women."

"Keep going, honey," I said. "You're doing great."

I walked on, back to the coach section. Annette Morris and Mary Ruth Jurgens were sitting side by side. Annette said, "Hi! Isn't it fun, flying on a real jet airliner?" I said, "It sure is." Then I said to the other girl, "Are you having fun, too?"

Her expression was definitely frigid. Her voice was harsh. She said, "Yeah."

That put an end to that conversation. I walked on until I

came to our fine Italian beauty, Alma di Lucca. "Hi," I said. This time I wasn't taking any chances: I spoke in my own language.

She did not answer. She was on an outside seat, and beside her sat a large elderly woman who was snoring heavily.

I repeated my salutation. "Hi."

She sniffed disdainfully, as if she almost wouldn't be caught dead speaking to anybody like me. Lord, what a pain in the neck she was.

I said, "What's eating you?"

She said, "I have been insulted."

"Is that so? Who insulted you now?"

"Why should you care a damn?"

"Give, baby, give. What's the trouble?"

She said, "See for yourself. Where do you sit? In the first-class seats. Where do I sit? With the pigs."

I wouldn't even stop to argue with her. I said, "Honey, just consider yourself lucky you have any place to park your can," and walked away.

I didn't return to my seat. I carried right on to the galley in the front part of the plane. I wanted to apologize to the hostess for the trouble with Mr. Brangwyn over that stupid drink, and I also thought the girls might let me peek at all the equipment they had there. If they weren't too busy, they might even give me a little advance information about what to expect at Miami Beach. I was really going there cold—nobody (except Mr. Brangwyn) had told me anything.

The two hostesses were in the galley, talking in low voices. They turned as I approached, and stopped talking. The girl who'd been involved with Mr. Brangwyn said, "Oh. It's you."

"Yes. I only wanted to tell you I'm sorry about—"

"Forget it," she said.

They were both rather pale and tense, I thought. I said, "Is something wrong?"

"You really want to know?" she asked.

The other girl said, "Leave her alone, Lucille."

There was a strange tension suddenly between the three of us. I couldn't understand why.

"She wants to know, she might as well know," Lucille said. "It'll be all over the front pages of the Miami newspapers, anyway." She looked at me with a thin smile. "The

27

Captain just picked up a radio flash. One of our planes crashed at the Tokyo airport."

"Oh, no!" I said. "One of *our* planes?"

"Yes."

"Oh, God, how awful."

"That's right. *How awful.* There were three of our girls aboard, plus the crew—"

The other hostess said again, "Lucille, leave the kid alone."

"Why shouldn't she know? Why shouldn't she know it isn't all glamour?"

The other hostess said to me, "Go back and sit down, honey. Don't mention this to any of the passengers, will you?"

"Of course not," I said, and went back to my seat. Great. Just great. A beautiful way to start.

3

We came into Miami International Airport like a huge white dove, flopped down softly, rumbled a little, and rolled along to the unloading ramp. "Here we are," Mr. Nat Brangwyn said. "Sure was a pleasure talking to you, Miss Thompson. And if I bump into you at the Charleyroy—" He was suddenly shy. His voice fell.

"Yes?"

"Maybe we might have that drink together, eh?"

"I hope so."

"Really?"

"Yes, really."

I'd made a conquest. And it was okay, because I liked him. He had something very unusual; I don't know what it was, but it made me feel comfortable sitting next to him.

We freed ourselves of our seat belts, stood up, and prepared to leave. Mr. Brangwyn looked at the trap door in the ceiling overhead and said with a smile, "I told you not to worry about the oxygen, didn't I?"

"You certainly did."

"It's for the birds."

I waited for Donna at the foot of the ramp, enjoying the delicious hot smell of an airplane that's just finished a long trip. Mr. Brangwyn said, "I have a car here. Could I give you a ride to the Charleyroy?"

"Thank you, but I have to wait for the other girls."

He didn't argue. "Well," he said. "Good-by, now." He walked away with a quick, light, bobbing walk, his eyes on the ground.

Then Donna joined me with her conquest, the jockey. He was really a miniature. She didn't introduce him, she simply said, "Well, Mr. Muirhead, here's my friend, so I'll say by-by. Thank you for making the trip perfectly delightful."

Quite a speech. He seemed bowled over. He gazed up at her with yearning—she literally towered over him—and said in a pathetically squeaky voice, "Thank *you*. Thank *you*. By-by. By-by. See you soon. Eh?"

"I hope so, Mr. Muirhead."

He said significantly, "Remember, now. *Remember*."

She laughed. "You bet I'll remember."

He trotted away, and when he was out of earshot I said, "Remember what?"

"The proposition he made me."

"What's the proposition?"

"Well, he has a suite at a hotel called the DeVinne. And he said any time I felt I'd like a little privacy, I could just come over and stay in his suite. *Any* time."

"Day or night, I suppose."

"That's the idea."

We walked toward the airport building, and suddenly I was conscious of the deep clear sky and the freshness of the air and a delicate sweet fragrance, the fragrance of tangerines. I said, "Donna! You're in Florida."

"So I am," she said, and brightened. "Oh, boy! Florida!" She sniffed. "God, smell that air!"

"Isn't it wonderful!"

"Oranges," she said. "I smell oranges."

"So do I." Or tangerines, in my case. I could smell the sunlight and palm trees and coconuts, and when a large butterfly floated over my head I could smell that, too—very faintly, like the new kind of glue they have on the back of postage stamps. Whimsical but pleasant.

Donna said, "Incidentally, you made quite a hit with Mr. Nat Brangwyn, didn't you?"

"How do you know his name?"

"Mr. Muirhead told me. He knows Mr. Brangwyn. I gather everyone in Miami knows Mr. Brangwyn."

"Oh? How come? Is he the mayor, or something?"

"He's a gambler," Donna said.

"A *what?*"

"A gambler. He gambles on the horses, and card games, and things like that."

"Are you on the level?"

"That's what Mr. Muirhead told me. He said Mr. Brangwyn does okay for himself. The income tax people are trying to collect a hundred and fifty thousand dollars from him, but he's a smart cookie and keeps slipping out of their clutches."

"Seriously?"

Donna said, "Honey, that's what the little man *told* me. I haven't been able to check it. But the little man sounded as if he *knew*. That's all."

"Gee," I said, without any enthusiasm. I was right, though. He wasn't a surgeon, or even a dentist. A gambler. I'd never met a gambler before, and here I'd been sitting beside one for two and a half hours without knowing it. I might have asked him to show me how to play pinochle, a game I can't even pronounce.

Inside the airline building we went right to the Magna International Airlines counter, as Mr. Garrison had instructed in his letter. The clerk showed no enthusiasm over our arrival. He said, "There'll be a bus to pick you up and drive you to the Charleroi. Just wait out front."

"Carola!" Alma screamed from a hundred yards away.

Everybody turned to stare, first at her and then at me. She strode over to us, her bosom bouncing with indignation. "They put me in the third-class tourist coach like an animal in the farmyard," she said. "Then you run away from me like I stink. Why?"

I said to her in Italian, "Hold your tongue. I am here, am I not? Do you expect me to wait for you like your servant?"

Unexpectedly, tears came to her beautiful hazel-gold eyes. She said, "Carola."

I returned to the language of my birth. "Okay. We're going to collect our luggage. Stay close."

The bus was a riot. I don't often laugh at buses, but when I saw this one I just stood and almost laughed my head off. It was half the size of a normal bus, and somehow you had the impression it was fresh from a beauty parlor where it had had its eyebrows plucked, and a facial, and a manicure. The outside had been painted the prettiest shades of baby blue and baby pink, and along the side, in neat gold letters, were the words,

MAGNA INTERNATIONAL AIRLINES
HOSTESS TRAINING SCHOOL

to make sure everybody understood why it was such a pretty, feminine-type bus. The windows were very large and sparkling bright, but it was surprising that the airline had forgotten to hang some flowered curtains. And where were the ribbons?

"It looks," Donna said, "like a traveling brothel."

"Ssssh," I said.

31

"Don't shush me," she said. "Am I right or am I wrong?"

"You're right."

"Brother! If we're going to ride around in this we ought to have some interesting experiences. I never saw a bus before that was a clear incitement to rape."

The driver was a short, chunky man named Harry. He wasn't feminine in the slightest way, thank God, even though he wore a short-sleeved flowered shirt that made your eyes water. He had a neck like a wrinkled bull, and massive brown arms, and he didn't turn a hair when he saw all our luggage piled on the sidewalk. Donna had seven suitcases, no less; Alma had six; Annette and I had three each; Mary Ruth Jurgens had two. In addition there were hatboxes and cartons and radios and record players. But Harry didn't mind. He loaded everything in the luggage compartment chuckling as if he'd never enjoyed himself so much. He seemed to understand the elementary truth that girls can't travel anywhere without taking with them practically every single thing they own.

Then we were off, and I saw Miami Beach for the first time.

It gives you a shock. I have to admit it. I'm fairly blasé about show places, after the traveling I did with my father. I managed to see most of the resorts on the Mediterranean, St. Tropez and Cannes and Nice and Monte Carlo and Portofino and so on, and they all gave me a thrill, although my father despised them, and now and then I'd have to pretend to despise them too. Miami Beach gave me a quite different kind of thrill, much more like the thrill I always get from seeing Rockefeller Center at Christmas. Except, of course, that this was semitropical. We came to it over the Venetian Causeway in the early-evening light, and it was just unbelievable. The patterns were all so exciting, hard white against the crystal blue of the water and the deepening blue of the sky; below us, the lush little islands, and the fancy cruisers, and the huge slow-wheeling pelicans, all adding light and shadow and movement to the patterns.

"Carola, it is like Naples, it is exactly like Naples," Alma said in rapture.

"Are you crazy? It's nothing like Naples."

"I mean, the colors. And everything look so rich."

"What do you mean, rich?"

"So much money."

32

"Just get it into your head," Donna said to her: "Everybody in America is a millionaire. Even the taxi drivers."

Alma said happily, "Yes, I know."

We began to drive along Collins Avenue, past one huge hotel after another; and we were bug-eyed as we stared out of the window. Those hotels are just fantastic—shining, immaculate, each one challenging its neighbor. The sidewalks were crowded. The roadway teemed with Cadillacs and Lincoln Continentals and Jaguars.

"Frankly," Donna said, "I don't believe it."

"Ah," Alma sighed.

Harry suddenly swung the bus onto a broad driveway lined with palm trees—the utterly upright kind, Royal palms. We curved around an immaculate lawn which was set with three fountains spraying high in the air, and then we pulled up outside an enormous portico filled with pillars and glass doors and satin-chrome fittings and doormen in magnificent blue uniforms.

"Here you are, girls," Harry said cheerfully. "All change."

Alma panted, "These is Hotel Charleroi?"

"Yes, ma'am. This is it."

"Oh, boy," Donna said.

"Gee," Annette said. Mary Ruth Jurgens was silent.

Men like Harry are the salt of the earth. They really are the kindliest and friendliest and most helpful people in the whole world. He said, "Listen, girls. There's a heap of fellers with nothing better to do hanging around in the lobby, but don't you take the least bit of notice of 'em. Just you go right to the elevators, and go right up to the fourteenth floor, and you'll find Miss Pierce and Miss Webley there, sitting at a little table, and they'll take care of you. Me and the boys will be up with your luggage soon as we unload it."

So, shaking like leaves on an aspen tree, we descended from the bus. Two grinning blue-uniformed doormen assisted us down. Two grinning doormen held two glass doors open for us to pass through. Inside, scores of men were standing around a great sumptuous lobby, grinning at us like idiots. We marched to the elevators. The starter, dressed up like a French admiral, grinned at us; one of the elevators was waiting with its doors open, and the elevator boy had his head hanging out, grinning at us. I wish to God somebody would explain to me in words of one syllable what is so hilariously funny about five girls walking into a hotel.

Grin, grin, grin—you'd think we were tattooed all over with dirty stories.

"Fourteenth floor?" the elevator boy said, grinning like a mule. I wanted to slap his big ears back.

"Yes," I said.

The doors of the elevator slid together as if they were made of silk. The elevator went up, I suppose, but there wasn't the slightest vibration and it was quiet as the grave. Then the doors slid open silkily again, and *bam!* After those few seconds of living in a noiseless vacuum I had the feeling I was stepping out into a madhouse. Girls. Thousands of girls, running around in all directions, all gabbling at once; girls and girls and girls and girls, like the sultan's harem. They were all young, and they were all good-looking, and they all had perfect figures, and I developed an inferiority complex on the spot. Gad, the competition here was going to be something fierce.

Donna said, "Pandemonium, by George."

"Stay with me, Carola," Alma said. "Do not lose me."

I knew exactly what she meant. Annette and Mary Ruth Jurgens didn't speak; they simply stared.

I said, "Let's find Miss Pierce and Miss Webley. That's the first order of business."

They were sitting at a small table in the corridor, sweating a little but otherwise unruffled. One of them, a handsome brunette about twenty-six years old, looked up at us and said, "Hello, girls. Have you just arrived? Good. I'm Janet Pierce, and this is Peg Webley."

Miss Webley was as blond as a blonde could be, and as pretty as a picture. She had soft, wavy golden hair—not heavy and straight, like mine—and melting blue eyes, and a real peaches-and-cream complexion, and cute dimples. She was gentler than Miss Pierce, but just as efficient in her own way. "Hi, girls," she said. "It's bedlam, I know, but don't worry. It'll simmer down soon. Tell me your names, and where you're from, so I can check you in."

We were checked in. Alma di Lucca, of Rome, Italy (they gave her a big welcome); Annette Morris, Albany, New York; Mary Ruth Jurgens, Buffalo, New York; Donna Stewart, Handsbury Notch, New Hampshire; me, Greenwich, Connecticut (because that was my home address).

"Now," Miss Webley said, "let's see where we can locate you." She and Miss Pierce put their heads together, frowning over a large floppy piece of paper marked off in squares. A floor plan, I assumed.

Alma said, "Please. I wish to be with Carola, Miss Thompson."

"Why?" Miss Pierce asked immediately.

"Because I am stranger in these country. Carola, Miss Thompson understand me, I understand her. We already have great love for each other."

Miss Pierce gave me a suspicious look. I couldn't blame her. I explained, "What Alma means is, I speak a little Italian. That's all. I guess I can help her out with the language problem."

"Do you wish to room with her?" Miss Pierce asked.

"Whatever you say, Miss Pierce." I tried to sound casual, but I couldn't help feeling bitter. It's always the same. I always fall flat on my face in the mud. I mean, I'd scarcely opened by mouth, and here I was already suspected of Lesbian tendencies. My old friend Eena would have been tickled to death.

Miss Webley said in her clear, sweet voice, "I think we can arrange for Alma and Carol to be together. Let me see: we have only one girl in 1412, so far, which means we can get four of you in there—we're set up for five girls in each apartment. Alma, Carol, Annette, Mary Ruth, you'll be in 1412. Donna, you'll be in 1401."

Donna said, "Thank you."

"Okay, girls," Miss Pierce said, "go and find your rooms. Your luggage will be coming up the freight elevator, at the far end of the corridor." She frowned at me, as if she'd already tabbed me as the world's number one troublemaker. "There's just one thing I want to stress: you may not leave the hotel this evening. We don't want you to go sauntering out to do some sightseeing—you'll have plenty of time for that. Miami Beach will be here for the next month. What we want you to do tonight is get unpacked and settled in because, believe me, you have a hard week ahead of you. Furthermore, we want you all to assemble here at seven-thirty this evening. Do you think you'll remember the time? Seven-thirty sharp."

"Seven-thirty," we said.

We trudged off. I was melancholy about losing Donna. We'd hit it off pretty smoothly, and I had a feeling I was going to need a friend.

The door of 1412 was closed. I tapped on it, and a voice said, "Who's there?"

"Us," I said, and walked in. A strapping girl with long red hair was standing by a bed unpacking a suitcase. She looked at us in surprise and we looked at her in surprise. She wasn't wearing anything except a black garter belt.

I said, "Hi," and explained that the Misses Webley and Pierce had sent us. She wasn't especially enthusiastic. Maybe she'd expected to have the apartment entirely to herself. She said, "Oh, well. Make yourselves at home. I'm Marcia Matthews."

I didn't like her. I couldn't help myself. It was just a feeling I had in my bones. She went on unpacking, a rather surly expression on her face, and she didn't make a move to slip into a robe. This didn't bother me too much, although, frankly, I don't feel the female form divine will stand too much exposure. For my money, it's altogether too blobby. I'm delighted that poets and painters and sculptors and males generally make a habit of going into ecstasies over girlish flesh (what the hell *else* can they go into ecstasies over, as far as females are concerned? Their cooking?), but female nudity leaves me absolutely cold.

Not Alma. She was livid. Italian girls are brought up pretty strictly on the whole, usually by nuns; and they're madly Victorian about certain things although they're surprisingly earthy about other things. She went snorting around the room, and finally she marched over to Matthews and said, "Hey! You! Meess! You think these is Turkish bath?"

"Huh?" Matthews said, stepping back in alarm.

"You go round with everythings hanging out all the time?"

"What's that?" Matthews said.

Alma leaned forward and sniffed at her. Then she leaned back holding her nose. "Ugh," she said loudly. "Feesh."

"Don't you dare!" Matthews cried.

It's a well-known fact that any Italian girl can out-insult any other ten girls in the world. I dragged Alma away before she could say anything else; Matthews hurriedly put on a robe; and then I led Alma to the freight elevator in search of our luggage. I said to her, "Listen, you mustn't pick a fight with that girl, we have to live with her for a month." She said scornfully, "Pooh. In Italy we throw her in the river."

We'd just brought the last of our suitcases to the apartment when Donna strode in looking grim. She didn't so much as glance at me. She said in the voice of authority, "Is there a party by the name of Matthews in here?"

Matthews piped up, "Yes. That's me."

Donna glared at her. "*You're* Matthews?"

"Yes. Marcia Matthews."

"Matthews," Donna said, "you certainly fouled everything up. You're supposed to be in Apartment 1401. What the hell are you doing in here?"

"But—" Matthews said.

"Miss Webley is busting a gut out there," Donna said. "Not to mention Miss Pierce. Boy, are you starting off on the wrong foot. Come on, baby, pick up your things and get the hell where you belong."

"But I'm practically *unpacked*," Matthews wept.

"Out," Donna said.

I began to feel sorry for the poor kid now. We weren't making life easy for her. Donna stood over her cracking a whip, and at last she went, bag and baggage. But I couldn't help breathing a sigh of relief at the thought that I wouldn't be seeing that garter belt again, and I think even Alma breathed a sigh of relief. At least Alma and Donna knew where they were with each other—enemies to the death. This Matthews character was an unknown quantity.

Donna said, "Okay if I move in?"

"Sure it's okay," I said. "But how did you do it?"

"I just went and asked Miss Webley. She said, certainly, she had no objections to a switch if I could arrange it with the other girl."

"Gad," I said, "you switched, all right. You practically gave Matthews nervous convulsions for life."

Donna said, "That's something my father taught me: when you're making a trade, never show any signs of weakness. It's fatal."

I was glad, anyway. It was good to have Donna back in the fold. There we were, the five of us together, just as we'd started from Idlewild on Flight 21A.

The apartment consisted of a large living room, plus a slightly smaller bedroom, plus a positively lavish kitchenette, and the usual bathroom facilities which amounted to one bathroom; but the most marvelous thing of all was that the windows overlooked the ocean. Directly below, you could see the grounds of the hotel, palm trees (strung with Chinese lanterns), a big kidney-shaped swimming pool, a long row of cabañas, and the broad golden beach; then, beyond, the ocean spreading for miles and miles and miles, changing from emerald green inshore to silvery green where the Gulf Stream flowed through it; and over this endless ocean hung a whole infinity of sky, more sky than I could remember seeing at any time in my life. It was breathtaking.

Annette and Mary Ruth chose to share the bedroom. Alma, Donna and I took the living room. Most of the regular living-room furniture had been moved out, of course, and the management had moved in three beds and three chests of drawers, which really left little room for anything more than a smallish table and two very small armchairs. Donna took the bed under the window, since she came from New Hampshire and was accustomed to oodles of fresh air before breakfast; I was in the middle; and Alma was nearest the door because this was the furthest she could get from Donna and, also, she was terrified of air because it might give her TB. A third reason was that she'd be nearer the bathroom, and she had an absolute passion for bathrooms. We discovered this too late. She'd lock herself in, and come out after several hours with an innocent look, carrying her huge make-up kit under her arm but without a trace of make-up on her face; and God knows what she did in there. Maybe she took time out to read Dante's *Inferno*.

We unpacked until seven-thirty, bumping into each other and screaming bloody murder over closet space, and then we went out into the corridor as we'd been instructed by Miss Pierce. We assembled around the little desk with everybody else, and very soon the place looked like Grand Central Station on Christmas Eve, except that instead of people, there were just girls. Girls. Girls everywhere. Most of them had dressed up a little for the occasion; and, honestly, they threw me. I mean as a *bunch*; as a swarm of females gathered in one spot. They were fantastically attractive. And more than being attractive, they had such a clean, healthy, fresh aura. I guess in Hollywood you could gather together a bunch of starlets and they'd be a sort of collective knockout; but they'd never have the special quality these girls had, the freshness, the eagerness, that clean, untouched-by-human-hands look.

Miss Pierce and Miss Webley were standing behind the desk, and standing with them were three men, all wearing the queer defensive expressions that men always put on when they're in a situation like this, hopelessly outnumbered by the female of the species. One of them I recognized —Mr. Garrison, who'd interviewed me in New York. The other two I hadn't seen before.

Miss Pierce tapped on the desk with a pencil and called out, "Quiet, girls." She waited until the buzz had died down, and gave Mr. Garrison a little nod; and he stepped up onto a chair and began to speak to us. He wore a light-tan suit and as he spoke he kept his hands behind him, under his coat tails. His plump face was pink.

He said, "Girls, I'm not going to make a long speech," and that immediately prepared me for the worst. He looked us over before he went on. "Up to now, our hostess training was carried on in Pennsylvania, and we housed the girls wherever we could, in private homes and motels and so on. It was a little uncomfortable, but I want to make this point: it worked. Some of our finest girls came out of that training setup."

He looked us over again. "Today, for the first time, thanks to the generous co-operation of Mr. Maxwell Courtenay, we have a setup that surpasses our fondest dreams. You girls are being housed on one entire floor of one of the finest hotels in Miami Beach." He looked down. "Or should I say *the* finest, Mr. Courtenay?"

Mr. Courtenay said modestly, " 'One of the finest' will do, sir."

"Right," Mr. Garrison said. "Now then. You girls will have at your disposal not all but practically all of the facilities of this magnificent hotel. You will be permitted to use the swimming pool at any time, and swim from the beach when the lifeguard is on duty. You may use the solarium. Et cetera, et cetera. But there are certain facilities which you may not use. Repeat, *not*. For example, you will not be permitted in any of the bars. We've prepared an instruction sheet which Miss Pierce and Miss Webley will pass out in a few minutes, giving the rules in detail."

He put his hands in his jacket pockets. "*I* don't have to go into those rules in detail. When you read them you'll see for yourselves that they make simple common sense. And furthermore, I think I know you. There are forty of you here: forty. And in my considered judgment, every one of you is a person of innate good manners, of innate good breeding. No matter what walk of life you're from, that's one thing I looked for in you, and—I trust—found. So I feel sure of this: you will observe not only the *printed* rules, but the unprinted ones too."

He put his hands behind his back again. "Now, finally. Why are you here? What are you doing here? Why did you come here?" He smiled happily. "I'll tell you. It's bad news. You didn't come here to spend a glamorous month at the Hotel Charleroi, with all expenses paid by Magna International Airlines. No, indeed. You came here to work. And without wishing to scare you, let me tell you you will be working hard, very very *very* hard, for most of the time you stay here. The reason is easy to state: you have a tremendous lot to learn. Let me emphasize that. You're here to *learn*, and this kind of learning is hard hard *work*. That's all I have to say, and I wish each and every one of you the best of luck."

We gave him a big hand. I didn't really dig what he was trying to tell us; I mean, it was all kind of wrapped up in a thick layer of words. Nevertheless, it sounded good, so, clap-clap and bravo.

Before he stepped down he invited Mr. Courtenay to say a few words, and Mr. Courtenay clambered up on the chair. He was a short man with a rugged, handsome face like Julius Caesar, beautiful gray wavy hair that was brushed back behind his ears, and small, white delicate hands. He wore a black jacket, a black vest, and striped trousers: as distinguished as all get-out.

He said, "Ladies. It is my privilege to welcome you to the Hotel Charleroi. We are *happy*, we are *delighted*, that you are here with us. Believe me. We are *honored*. We are also very proud, for we are aware that you represent the cream of young American womanhood, the very cream. Therefore, whatever we can do for you will be done humbly and happily. Call on us whenever you wish, for we are here to serve. Bless you, ladies, each and every one of you. I thank you."

That, too, got a big hand. I mean, what else can you do when you're called the cream of young American womanhood? So, clap-clap, and hip-hip-hurrah.

The third man wasn't called on to speak. I was sorry. He looked fairly interesting, even though he wore horn-rimmed glasses. He wasn't even introduced to us. He just stood, with one of those blank intelligent expressions of his face, and I didn't have a clue. I said to Donna in a low voice, "Who's the horn-rimmed glasses?" and she said, "Sweetie, I'm a stranger here myself. He's probably from the FBI." Some help.

The men beat a hasty retreat after all the fine phrases, and we were left with Miss Pierce and Miss Webley.

No nonsense with them. No stuff about ladies, and cream of young American womanhood. No, *sir*. Trust a woman any time to state the facts as she sees the facts. Leave romance to the boys.

Miss Pierce took the chair. She was as good-looking as anybody present, with blue-black hair and very alive brown eyes and a beautiful mouth; but you only had to meet those brown eyes for a fraction of a second to realize that she saw right through you to your backbone.

"Girls," she said, and when she spoke not a sound was heard, not a funeral bell. "There are a couple of points I want to clear up. First: *you* are responsible for your apartments, not the hotel staff. You will make your own beds, maintain absolute cleanliness, and so on. There will be daily inspections."

Right on the line. Not a wasted syllable.

"Second: your actual training will be held not here, but at the airport offices. You have been divided into two groups, or classes. The first will leave the hotel in the school bus *promptly* at a quarter of eight. The second will leave *promptly* at a quarter past eight. The driver has instructions not to wait for anybody not seated at those times. Okay?"

It was okay if she said so.

"Finally," she said, "as Mr. Garrison told you, we're going to distribute mimeographed sheets stating all the rules that apply to your stay here. However, it's getting rather late, and some of you may not be able to read too clearly at this time of night; so I'm going to read the rules to you here and now. In this way, none of you can claim that any particular rule got mislaid before you saw it. Here goes."

She read the rules for half an hour. Then we tottered back to our apartments to lick our wounds.

4

Donna expressed it for all of us. She said, speaking to me, "Listen, cream of young American womanhood, isn't there something in the Constitution about all persons being entitled to life, liberty, and the pursuit of happiness, and all that stuff?"

I said, "Not the Constitution. The Declaration of Independence."

"Okay, okay, let's not get too technical. What I want to know is, what the hell are they trying to do to us?"

I said, "My guess is, they think they're trying to protect us from ourselves."

"Is that so?" She growled, "People talk about what's going on in Siberia. Ha. They ought to see what's going on right here, under their very own noses."

That, I think, was stretching it a bit. I mean, there wasn't any need to exaggerate. What had happened, as far as I could see, was that Magna International Airlines had merely copied its rules from the rules of the Women's House of Detention. Nothing more. There had been a few changes, of course. For example, instead of referring to *prisoners* they always referred to *student hostesses;* but actually these two terms were completely interchangeable. Someone in the Magna organization was just being tactful.

The mimeographed sheets started off with a kind of general preamble. Nothing definite. Just vague threats:

Welcome to Miami Beach. We are glad to have you aboard and hope you will enjoy your four weeks of incarceration at the Hotel Charleroi. May we first impress on you that the highest standard of conduct is expected from all prisoners, or student hostesses. Prisoners, or student hostesses, must at all times behave like ladies. Violation of this basic rule is a serious offense.

"That means," Donna said, "three days' solitary."

Then, after the preamble, it went on to be specific. Prisoners staying at the Hotel Charleroi were expected to respect all hotel property and would be held personally responsible for any damage. We were to treat all guests at the hotel with courtesy. We were not allowed into any bars in this hotel, or in any other hotel on Miami Beach. We were not permitted to imbibe any alcoholic liquor in the hotel, and any prisoner who was found intoxicated during training was subject to immediate dismissal.

Then it went on about personal appearance. Prisoners were expected at all times to be perfectly groomed. Prisoners were never to appear anywhere in the hotel unless attired in good taste. Prisoners were to maintain the highest standards of personal appearance, including care of complexion and proper use of cosmetics; care of hands and fingernails; hair care and styling; weight and figure control. Furthermore, except in bathing areas, prisoners must be fully attired when appearing in public; and full attire was spelled out. It meant stockings and girdles.

"Great," Donna said bitterly. "Stockings and girdles. My cup of happiness runneth over."

"Oh, boy," Annette said. "That means we wear stockings and girdles to class, and when we go out for a walk—"

I said, "Even if you go down to the lobby to mail a letter."

Donna said, "What beats me is why the hell they don't make us *sleep* in stockings and girdles."

I said, "Don't be flippant, now."

Then the rules went on to Social Life. It was explained, in an apparently reasonable way, that because of the pressure of training our social life had to be limited to a slight extent, so that we had ample time for study and rest. Then the facts were stated in capital letters:

WEEK NIGHTS (SUNDAY THROUGH THURSDAY)
    (1) NO DATING
    (2) MUST BE IN ROOMS BY 10:30 P.M.

It couldn't be any clearer. No dating, must be in rooms by ten-thirty. Sunday through Thursday.

"Sunday!" Donna screamed. "Sunday night I have to be in by ten-thirty!"

"Yep," I said.

But we had a little more latitude on Friday and Saturday nights. We were permitted to have dates, and we didn't have to be in until 2:00 A.M. Furthermore, one could get permission in special cases to leave town over the weekend, to stay with friends or relatives. I couldn't see that this affected me, but Donna pounced on it. "Well, thank God," she said. "I have friends and relatives all over Florida that I haven't seen in years. At least I'll get to visit them in the weekends and take my girdle off for forty-eight hours."

Finally, the law of all laws was laid down. It was in cast-iron, lawyer-proof language. At no time were male friends or relatives to visit student hostesses on the fourteenth floor of the Hotel Charleroi. Equally, at no time were student hostesses to visit male friends or relatives, in any room or apartment in the same hotel. By kind permission of the management, male friends or relatives could be entertained in the hotel lobby, and there only.

"Ridiculous," Donna said.

Annette said, "Well, I suppose the whole idea is that they want us to work, whatever the work is. After all, it's costing them a terrible lot of money to bring us here, and to stay in this hotel for a month. So they have to lay down a whole lot of rules."

Donna said, turning to Mary Ruth Jurgens, "You feel like that, too?"

"Me?"

"Yes, you. Incidentally, what do we call you? Mary, or Ruth, or what?"

"Mary Ruth."

"A double-barreled name, eh?"

"Some people save their breath, call me Jurgy. Please yourself."

"Okay, Jurgy," Donna said. "What's your feeling about all these crazy rules?"

"It's their airline."

"Sure, it's their airline; but that doesn't give them the right to order us around like cattle."

Jurgy said, "They didn't hand me an invitation to come here. I asked them. They say I have to wear a girdle and stockings, okay, I'll wear a girdle and stockings. That's all."

Donna looked at her with interest. "Jurgy: what did you do before you came to this place?"

"Why?"

"I'm just asking, honey. You don't have to get your Irish up. If you don't want to tell me, don't tell me."

"I was a waitress in a hotel, the Thripp Hotel, in Buffalo. Before that I was a waitress in a diner."

44

Donna turned away from her. "Annette, what did you do?"

"Gee, I was just a secretary in a bank."

"That's a nice quiet job."

"Yes, very quiet. That was the whole trouble with it. It was just too quiet."

Donna called, "Hey, Alma, what do you think about all these rules?"

"Excuse?" Alma said. She was unpacking methodically, folding undergarments and stowing them away in her chest of drawers. The rest of us were sitting on my bed, except Jurgy, who stood stiffly with her back against the wall.

"I said, 'what do you think about all these rules?'" Donna repeated. "No men in your room, and things like that."

"Ah," Alma said. "I tell you what I think. I think American girls are so innocent, that is what I think."

"Is that so?" Donna said.

Alma shrugged her shoulders. "Rules. Rules are rules. They are there. If you can follow them, you follow them. If you cannot follow them, then be careful the policeman on the corner does not catch you."

"I'll remember that," Donna said, and laughed.

She ruffled Annette's pretty chestnut hair. "You know what, kids? I'm dying of thirst. Annette, honey, take a look in the icebox for me. See if there are any ice cubes."

"Okay," Annette said.

"Carol, open that gray suitcase for me, will you?"

I had a strange feeling. "What do you want out of the suitcase?"

"I have a bottle of gin stashed away. We can all have a drink and relax."

I said, "Nope," and Annette on her way to the icebox stopped dead in her tracks.

"Oh, come on," Donna said, laughing.

"No, sir," I said.

She stopped laughing. She said quietly, "You know, I thought you were different."

She was mistaken if she thought she was going to break my heart with that old gag. I said, "Let's get this straight. I'm no square. If you want a drink, you go right ahead and have one. It's your privilege."

"Is that so?"

"Look," I said. "You know the rules. My God, we've just this minute finished *reading* them. Any time you feel like breaking a rule it's okay with me, and I guess it's okay with everyone else in this apartment. We won't squeal. But don't get us involved. Okay?"

"That suits me," Donna said. "I don't mind drinking by myself. Anybody who'd like one is welcome."

I said, "Fine. Now I'll tell you what you do. You take your bottle, and you take your ice, and you go and lock yourself in the bathroom. We won't disturb you. Any of you girls want to use the john before Donna locks herself in?"

"Ha ha ha, very funny," Donna said.

I said, "I'm serious."

"Really?"

"Yes. Really."

She looked at me. She had the most amazing green eyes, full of the devil. She said, "Okay, little woman. You win."

"No, no," I said. "No, no. Don't let me stop you. There's the bathroom. It's all yours."

"You won your point, Carol. Don't rub it in."

She stood up and stretched herself. "No drink," she said wonderingly. "I never thought I'd live to see the day." She cocked her head sideways, as if she were listening to something that was happening inside herself. "You know what?" she said. "I'm *starving*." She looked at her watch. "Holy smoke! No *wonder* I'm starving! It's a quarter of nine. Do you realize I haven't eaten anything since six o'clock this morning?"

Annette said, "I have some crackers you're welcome to."

Jurgy said, "I have some candy bars. You're welcome to those."

"Kids, you don't understand. I'm *hungry*. I want a steak. And shall I tell you a secret? I'm going out this minute to get one."

There was dead silence.

She became aware of it.

"My God," she said. "What rule have I broken now? You mean, if I want a steak I have to eat *that* in the bathroom?"

I held my peace. Annette spoke up. "No. It's only that Miss Pierce said we mustn't leave the hotel this evening. Remember?"

And at this Donna flew right off the handle. It was absolutely the last straw. She stormed up and down the room screaming about Nazi Germany and Soviet Russia, she threw her shoes at the wall, she began to tear her hair, until I grabbed her by the arm and said, "Hey, take it easy, simmer down. You can't go *out*, but I bet there's a cafeteria right here in the hotel where you can get a hamburger."

She yelled, "I don't want a goddam hamburger, I'm a big girl, I need nourishment, I want a T-bone steak."

"Okay," I said. "I haven't eaten all day, either. I'll come with you."

Alma called, "Carola. You take me with?"

"You're hungry, too? Sure. Annette? Jurgy?"

Annette and Jurgy said they would stay. They had their crackers and candy bars.

I said, "Okay, Donna. Let's go."

A strange look came into her green eyes. She said, "This is a pretty fancy hotel, isn't it? I bet they have a pretty fancy restaurant." She glanced at me sharply. "Thompson, you can't go like that."

"Like what?"

"In those clothes."

"Why not?"

"Rule 325," she bawled. "You are not to appear anywhere in the hotel unless properly attired. Rule 699. You are to maintain the highest standards of personal appearance. Rules? By golly, I'll give you rules until they come out of your ears. All the dolls downstairs will be in evening dress. That's what you're going to wear."

"Are you crazy? Evening dress to go down to eat a hamburger?"

"Right." She called to Alma. "You have an evening gown?"

Alma drew herself up. "But certainly."

"Crawl into it."

"Listen, Donna," I began; and she turned on me murderously and said, "If you don't stop getting in my hair I'm going to clobber you, but good. There's no rule against *eating*, is there? And if we're going to *eat* we have to *dress* appropriately, don't we? So get cracking, baby, because I'm going to give you just fifteen minutes to put on all your war paint. Understand?"

If anybody had asked my opinion I would have said it was impossible. But proclaim it from the housetops: a girl can get superficially clean, changed, powdered, earringed, the whole works, in sixteen minutes flat, even with two other girls underfoot during that entire period. You need some kind of driving force to keep you going, and on this occasion the driving force was Donna Stewart, who screamed at us every second of the time because she thought she was going to drop dead of acute starvation before we reached the elevators. She missed her vocation, that babe. She should have been working for the Pharaohs when they were building the pyramids. Annette and Jurgy sat on my bed watching us. They didn't say a word. They just stared. I daresay it was the wildest thing they had seen in their lives.

We looked fairly presentable, I must admit. I was wearing a little gold number I'd picked up at Lord and Taylor, and gold slippers. Alma was wearing something utterly stupendous in black lace, with a huge red rose at her bosom; and she was so gorgeous that she just about knocked your eye out. And Donna was simply a dream walking, in a baffling gown—I couldn't figure out how it was put together, it was all so subtle—in a fantastic soft color that I can only describe as misty Spanish moss, or old cobweb. It did everything in the world for her figure, and her green eyes, and her swooping red hair.

I said to her, "Donna! Where did that gorgeous gown come from?"

"Schiaparelli," she said. Offhand. Just like that.

I said, "For a little old country girl from New Hampshire you sure know your way around. Didn't you tell me you'd never been to New York? How do you order gowns like this in the backwoods? Through the Sears, Roebuck catalog?"

"I got it at Filene's in Baaahston," she said. "You ever hear of Baaahston?—Who's seen my purse? What did I do with my purse?"

It was on her bed.

She sat down and opened it, and turned it upside down so that all the contents fell out, including about thirty pennies, some dimes, three quarters, two diamond rings, and a roll of bills the size of her fist.

I said, "Donna! That *money!*"

"That's what I was looking for," she said. "We'll need some to pay for our dinner. I don't have to take it all, do I?"

"For crying out loud, how much do you have in that roll?"

"Twelve hundred dollars," she said. "My old man gave it to me this morning as a going-away present." She pulled off a single hundred-dollar bill and stuffed it into a tiny silver lamé evening purse she was carrying. "That should be enough, shouldn't it?"

I said, "Boy, I hope so." I'd figured that it might be a big night and that I might be stuck with the check, and I'd thoughtfully put all of seven dollars and a fifty-cent piece in my purse. Alma, I suspected, had a one-dollar bill pinned securely with a big safety pin somewhere near her navel. And I don't think either of us was being skinflinty. I mean, we were all getting the same basic forty-five a week, less fifteen for rent, and less various other deductions; and how much can you budget for a hamburger in these circumstances? What was obvious at once, of course, was that Donna happened to be one of these people who didn't have the faintest idea what money means. A twenty-dollar bill, and a fifty-dollar bill, and a hundred-dollar bill all looked alike to her: just bills, just money, just something the government printed so that she wouldn't have to carry a trunk full of pennies when she went to Filene's in Boston.

Alma said, "We go? Or we not go?"

"We go," Donna said. "Annette, sweetie, do me a favor. Put these things back in my purse, will you?"

Annette scrambled off the bed. "But you can't keep all this money just lying around, Donna. And these rings."

"Oh, don't worry," Donna said.

"I'll hide your purse in the closet," Annette said.

Donna laughed. "Okay."

"A moment," Alma said. She selected one of the diamond rings, slipped it onto the third finger of her right hand, examined the effect critically, and said to Donna, "You mind? I wear this tonight?"

"Sure. Help yourself."

We went out to the elevators, and a few peasants with their hair in curlers and wearing raincoats to cover their nakedness looked at us with out-popping eyes. Poor slobs: student hostesses going about their menial tasks.

To be absolutely truthful, we didn't do the Hostess Training School any discredit. And, something I hadn't specially noticed before, we were all kind of high up in the air. I was wearing three-inch heels. Alma, who was about my height,

49

five-seven, was wearing four-inch stilettos, and so was Donna. Add four-inch heels to a girl who's nearly five-nine in her stocking feet and you have something très formidable.

The elevator boy went pale when he saw us. No grins this time, oh, no. Between us we were about fifteen feet taller than he was, and if he'd given us the slightest provocation we could have beaten his brains out on the spot. We were no longer comic characters who were being kept out of harm's way on the fourteenth floor. We were ladies. We had dignity. I had a few seconds to think about this as the elevator vacuumed down. It was almost incredible, but I'd come from the garbage cans of Greenwich Village —when? Only a few *hours* ago. Thompson, the tomato of Washington Square. And here I was, dressed like a girl, smelling like a girl, feeling like a girl, a dream, a dream, a dream, going for my first hamburger in the Hotel Charleroi on Miami Beach. It was glorious. I felt as if there were a rainbow around my soul.

The elevator stopped, the doors slid open, we stepped out, and hey presto!—that amazing thing happened that you read about in advertisements. It was a shared experience between the three of us: we felt the air become electric, eyes turned, we heard the buzz of whispered comment. All I could see in front of me were men. The word must have spread that there were forty selected females on the fourteenth floor, and here we were, three representative specimens. I wanted to turn and run.

Then immediately, from somewhere out of that palpitating air, Mr. Maxwell Courtenay materialized: black jacket, black vest, striped pants, the face of Caesar, tiny white hands. He wasn't a man you'd laugh at. He was tough enough, and you had to respect him. But he was shorter than I had thought, under five-six. He glanced at me and smiled. He glanced at Alma and smiled. Then he looked up at Donna as if she'd shot him through the heart.

I should have been prepared for it, no doubt.

"Ladies," he said, "what can I do for you?" But he said it to Donna, and I swear that as he said it he teetered up on his toes as if he were trying to gaze right into her eyes.

She said breathily, "Oh, Mr. Courtenay, we're from the fourteenth floor, the training school—"

"You do not have to tell me. I can see. Let me express to you how happy I am to have you here staying with us, how honored we feel to be permitted to participate—" He was so worked up, he wanted to recite his speech all over from the beginning.

Donna said, "Mr. Courtenay, what we were wondering was, do you have a restaurant, or snack bar maybe, where we could get a bite to eat. Do you? Just some little old cafeteria where we could have a little old steak, or something?"

I don't know why. She sounded like Scarlett O'Hara.

He was thunderstruck. "Do we have a restaurant?"

"Yes."

"Madame—" He paused. "Would you be kind enough to tell me your name?"

"Donna Stewart. And this is Miss di Lucca, and this is Miss Thompson."

"Delighted," he said. He gave each of us a stiff bow. Then he returned to Donna. "Please. Come with me. We have a little restaurant, yes, indeed. Permit me to escort you there."

He led the way with Donna. From behind, he was very broad-shouldered and a trifle bowlegged, and the top of his head was way below her chin. Not that I have the slightest feelings about people's height: it simply happened that the top of his head came below her chin, and he had obviously fallen for her like a ton of bricks, and history was repeating itself. You would think that smallish men would be inclined to chase after smallish women. Not so. At least not as far as Donna Stewart was concerned. First Mr. Muirhead, the jockey. Now Mr. Courtenay. I just dreaded to think what would happen if she ever happened to run into a midget.

"These is big hotel," Alma said to me. "Very nice furnish."

It sure was a big hotel, and it sure was nice furnish. We walked on and on, Mr. Courtenay ahead talking thirteen to the dozen to Donna, until at last we came to a vast open archway, with a thick red velvet rope across it and a uniformed flunky standing in front of the rope to open it and let you through if he thought you'd gone to the right school. Mr. Courtenay snapped a finger at him, and he cringed and opened that rope so fast he nearly broke an ankle.

Mr. Courtenay made a sweeping gesture. "Dear young ladies. This is our little restaurant. We call it the Sun King

Room, after—you recall?—Le Roi Soleil, the great and renowned Louis Quatorze. Kindly enter."

I couldn't say a word. We were at his mercy. He led the way, and we followed. I thought of the seven dollars and fifty cents in my purse, and the dollar bill pinned to Alma's navel, and I thought, Thank God Donna was farsighted enough to bring a hundred dollars. And even that might be a delusion. Because the Sun King Room was not merely vast; it was so tremendously decorated, and the tables were so big and so far apart and so covered with napery and glasses and silver, that any fool could see that a crust of dry bread would cost a fortune, particularly à la carte. The ceiling was covered with millions of yards of billowing gray satin, all gathered together at the center and fastened with a huge gold brooch in the form of a sunburst. There were gay murals on three of the walls depicting, I suppose, various amorous episodes in the life of Le Roi Soleil, but the fourth wall wasn't a wall at all. It was an enormous curved window, with an opening at one end which led to a terrace where a dance band was playing, and where a few couples were dancing.

"These is just like Rome," Alma said.

We were now a procession. Mr. Courtenay was preceded by a head waiter named Henri, and three regular waiters. The restaurant was full of people, and they all seemed highly impressed by our appearance in their midst. Donna in her Schiaparelli cobwebs, was undoubtedly the center of attraction, but Alma and I got our share of glances, and I felt myself blushing all the way down to my toes.

We reached a table at last. The waiters pulled out three chairs for us to sit on, they handed us menus that were approximately the size of the *New York Times* but constructed of sheepskin or something of that kind; and then Mr. Courtenay wound himself up and began to make another speech. He was obviously wild about oratory, and he couldn't open his mouth without a speech pouring out, and he delivered himself with such passionate unction that it was rather unnerving. "My dear young ladies," he said. "This is your first night with us at the Charleroi. Let me repeat what I said earlier. We are delighted, we are enchanted, to have you here. So, tonight, you must be our guests. The hotel is yours, I beg you, order whatever you please. Anything. It will be our pleasure."

He was staring at Donna as he spoke, and she opened her

eyes wide and beamed at him. "Why, Mr. Courtenay! Aren't you sweet! Girls, isn't Mr. Courtenay the sweetest man?"

He turned a deep red.

Alma was open-mouthed.

I was open-mouthed.

Mr. Courtenay said, "Henri will look after you. I shall return," and strode away.

Henri was a skinny man with a skinny neck, and he bent over us like a human hairpin, gurgling in an affable way. "Now. What would the young ladies prefer? Shrimp Botticelli, perhaps, to start?"

Just trying to *visualize* shrimp Botticelli made me sick to my stomach.

Donna said, "Henri, just bring me a double martini."

I said in a low voice, "Donna. Don't be an ass."

"What do you mean, honey?"

I said, "Look, we might be *surrounded* by people from the training school. If they see you with a double martini, baby, you're *out*. Remember the rules?"

She said, "You know something, Carol? For once you're right." She thought for a moment. "Listen, Henri. Bring me a double vodka, but put it in a water glass with lots of ice. Okay? We just have to camouflage it a bit."

"I understand, madame. You can trust me."

"Donna," I said.

She said earnestly, "Honey, I defy *anyone* to tell a glass of vodka from a glass of water at twenty paces. They're *identical*."

Henri said to her, "You wish to order dinner after the apéritif?"

I know exactly what I want, Henri. A T-bone steak, rare, and a small tossed green salad. Bring it just as soon as you can."

"Yes, madame." He turned to me. "Madame?"

"A hamburger and a cup of coffee."

He looked shocked beyond words.

I said, "Don't you serve hamburgers?"

"Not as such, madame. We have our own delicious *specialité*, filet mignon Barbarossa. It is very popular with our clientele."

"That's fine," I said. "But what is it?"

He sighed. "It is a hamburger."

"Okay. And coffee."

He turned to Alma. "Madame?"

There was a tiny wistful smile at the corner of her lips. There was a dreamy look in her honey-colored eyes. She said, "Groose."

Nobody spoke for a moment. Then Henri whispered politely, "You said groose, madame?"

"Yes. Groose. Groose. I am mad for groose."

Henri looked at me. He looked at Donna. He shrugged his shoulders.

I said, "Alma, you mean *goose*, don't you?"

She became very excited. "I do not mean goose. I mean *groose*. You hunt him with the guns. He hides. He is very cunning. You do not find him—"

Donna said, "Hell. She means a moose."

"I do not mean moose!" Alma cried. "Look! He is here in menu." She waved it wildly in front of Donna's face. "*Groose à la manière de la Château de Balmoral.* See for yourself! Scottish groose. From Scotland."

"Forgive me, madame," Henri said. "Of course: groose. You wish to partake of a bottle of wine with this?"

"But naturally," Alma said. "What you think with groose, Carola? A white wine, Orvieto, or Lacrima Christi? Or red? Nebbiolo? Santa Maddalena? Barolo?"

It was getting to be awfully wearing. I was surrounded by alcoholics. I said, "Alma. Remember the rules. You aren't allowed to drink in public. It's sudden death if they catch you. Can't you settle for a nice cold glass of water?"

She was white. "Me? I am of Rome. It is my duty to drink wine. Water! You know what water does? It makes rust! I do not want my pipes to be cover with rust." She said to Henri, "You have a good Orvieto, perhaps of 1954?"

"Yes, madame."

"We will partake."

Henri drifted away. The three waiters drifted away. Peace settled over our table. But gradually I became aware that half the people in that huge restaurant were staring at us. We were being sized up by hundreds of eyes, examined in minute detail; and the skin at the back of my neck began to tingle. And suddenly I realized that all these people knew who we were, three of those airline girls from the fourteenth floor, and that's why they were scanning us through high-powered telescopes. My God, we were really being sized up, and it made me so nervous that I began to twitch like a hamster. I took a pack of cigarettes from my purse and extracted one, and then remembered my manners and offered the pack to Alma and Donna.

"Thanks," Donna said, and took one.

"Thank you, Carola," Alma said, and she took one, too.

Donna gave us each a light with a small gold lighter she carried in her little evening purse; and suddenly I had another shattering thought. I said, "Oh, my God, are we allowed to smoke in public?"

Donna took a deep breath. "Why not?"

"There's a rule about smoking—"

"Listen," Donna said. "For Pete's sake, be your age. Are you going to have an orgasm every time we break some stupid, trivial, ridiculous little rule? What's the matter with you, Carol?"

I said weakly, "Donna, rules are rules."

Alma said, "Carola, calm yourself. The rule is, smoking is possible when you are sat."

"When you are *what?*" Donna asked.

"When you are sat. Sitted."

"There you are," Donna said to me icily. "And one more word from you about rules and I'll slug you."

One of the waiters cleared all the water glasses from our table, including the decanter; and another waiter arrived with three fresh glasses and a fresh water decanter; and so, with a little sleight of hand, Donna got her double vodka. Very neat. I didn't approve, because it all seemed just plain stupid, but I had to admire. Henri and his minions certainly knew their job.

We had to wait some time for the steak and the Barbarossa hamburger and the groose; and while we waited we began to talk. Within minutes we were prying into each other's private lives with the wildest enthusiasm.

Donna started it. She said to Alma, "Tell me something, cream. What brings *you* here?"

"Because I am hungry. I am starving. I could eat the ox."

I said, "No. Donna means *here*, to the training school."

"Ah-hah," Alma said. "Very good question." She answered it for about half an hour, and during that time our food arrived, including her bottle of Orvieto. She rhapsodized over the poor little groose, she sniffed disdainfully at the wine, and then she went right on with the story of her life and loves. I daresay she could have wrapped it all up in a few well-chosen words, but she had to tell everything in all its detail. Also, every now and then her English failed her and I had to step in and translate for Donna's benefit; and, frankly, my Italian wasn't good enough to cope with Alma's experiences. What had happened, by and large, was that she'd started work when she was sixteen in a little shop where they sold religious relics to tourists, and that's when she began learning English, so that she could sell the tourists all the religious relics they needed. Here she met a very nice gentleman friend (I could imagine) who found her a job in an automobile agency. Then she met a very nice gentleman friend who found her a job with an Italian airline, which led to her meeting another gentleman friend who found her a job with, no less, the representative of Magna International Airlines in Rome. There she met *such* a nice gentleman friend who (a) helped her to learn more English so that she now had this perfect accent, and (b) managed to get her a job flying as a hostess on some of the European flights. Then, when Magna began to look for girls to train for their international flights, she applied. Right here her tale became really complicated, because she didn't apply through her gentleman friend who was presumably working at Magna. That would have been too easy. By this time she had another gentleman friend who introduced her to a friend who had a friend, and *this* friend spoke to somebody at Magna in New York, and *they* said, Well, sure, this is just the kind of girl we're looking for, send her over. And so, here she was.

"Boy," Donna said. "You've certainly been around."

"A little," Alma admitted.

"You certainly made a lot of friends."

"A few," Alma said. She leaned forward confidentially. "Now I tell you something. You know what? I am frightened of airplanes. True. Every time, before I fly, I have the diarrhea of the stomach. Funny, eh?"

Donna said, "Why the hell do you want to fly, then? With your talent for picking up guys, I bet you could find some job that didn't give you diarrhea."

"A good question. I tell you." She nibbled for a moment on the leg of her groose. "Because," she said, "because, on the planes, you meet such a nice kind of peoples."

"Men peoples?" Donna asked.

Alma threw her head back, roaring with laughter. "Who else?"

Donna looked at her in a very odd way. She didn't say

anything, she just looked at her, at her hair and her eyes and her mouth and her throat and her breasts, and I think she was trying to add up in her mind what the effects of Alma's life amounted to. I mean, it was clear enough what Alma meant by a nice gentleman friend; she'd probably been sleeping around for years. And Donna, practically using a magnifying glass, went over her feature by feature, like somebody in a laboratory examining a guinea pig that had been put through a long series of tests. Well, there was no mistake about it: this particular guinea pig had come through in pretty good shape. True, Alma didn't exactly give the impression of an undefiled virgin who shrank away from the mere gaze of a man. At the same time, she didn't look used, as some girls do. She just looked like a normal, but very beautiful, Italian girl with lots of blood in her veins and a full supply of hormones.

I said, "Okay, Donna, you tell me something. What brought *you* here?"

"Hell," she said. "That's easy. I was just bored to death in New Hampshire. I lived there all my life. My old man is in the hotel business—" She looked around at the Sun King Room. "Nothing like this. We have a lodge near Mount Washington, with a ski tow and all that stuff, and cabins and stuff, and a shop where we sell sweaters and stuff, and rent out skis—you know."

I said, "It sounds wonderful."

"Oh, sure."

"Well?"

"*Well?*" she repeated. "Well, what? I got tired of looking at people on skis. I got tired of wearing those goddam Norwegian sweaters. I just suddenly decided last year I had to get clear away from it, or I'd go off my head." She smiled. "It struck me all of a heap—there must be other things going on in the world besides skiing. And you know what else? There must be other towns besides Boston. I was so damned restless and bored all last year, I wasn't good for anything. So I had this bright idea, and I wrote away to every airline I could think of, and finally I had an interview with Mr. Garrison in Boston; and here I am."

"How did your father feel about your leaving home?"

"Dad? Oh, Dad is the greatest guy in the whole world. He was swell about it. As a matter of fact, I think he was kind of relieved, because he could see I was getting restless. And another thing: my mother died seven years ago, and

Dad wants to get married again; but he's worried because he has an idea I won't get along with wife number two. He's dead right. I hate the bitch. She and I couldn't last a week under the same roof."

Alma said, "You have been affianced twice to be married?"

"I have?" Donna asked.

Alma stretched out her right hand. "You have these ring, and you have other ring upstairs."

Donna said indifferently. "Cream, that's nothing. I've been engaged a dozen times. Come spring, and the sap rises, this baby is ready to be led to the altar by anything in pants. A nice moonlight night has the same effect."

There we had to stop. A girl wearing a silver wig and an off-the-shoulder blouse and a sort of froufrou skirt skipped up to our table. Over her arm she carried a wicker basket filled with flowers. "Pardon me, ladies," she said. "I have a gift for you all, from a gentleman admirer." And she handed each of us a corsage of the most exquisite tiny orchids.

Donna asked, "From Mr. Courtenay?"

"Oh, no," the girl said. She smiled sweetly. "These are from Mr. Nat Brangwyn."

It was the biggest surprise in my life, or one of the biggest. I looked around for him, and there he was, about four tables away, alone, sipping a highball, wearing a white jacket and a dark red bow tie. He smiled and waved his hand, and I smiled back at him but I didn't wave.

He waited until we'd finished eating and then, rather hesitantly, he came over, looking more like an eminent surgeon than ever—thin and nervous and terribly sensitive. It was only when he began to speak that you realized he had a rather different background. But by the same token, when you *knew* his background you realized he had quite an aura of his own. You don't meet a real professional gambler every day. And any gambler who owes the federal government a hundred and fifty thousand dollars, and can hold the federal government at bay, is certainly worth a few minutes of any girl's time.

"Well," he said. "Miss Thompson. Hi."

I said, "Mr. Brangwyn, you shouldn't have sent over these lovely orchids."

"Why not? It's nothing."

I introduced him to Alma and Donna.

Donna said, "Mr. Brangwyn, these are the most beautiful baby orchids—I never saw anything like them. They're darling."

"Yeah," he said, hopping from one foot to the other. "They grow right here in Florida. It's a fact."

Alma held the corsage against her bosom, where it clashed hideously with her red rose. She didn't say anything. She just sighed, and ogled Mr. Brangwyn. I've never seen anybody use the ogle in real life like that: it turns up now and then in old television movies, and it gives you the queerest ideas of what prehistoric sex must have been like.

Donna said, "Mr. Brangwyn, won't you join us?"

He looked at me as if he were asking my permission. I said, "Oh, do. Please."

He sat down between Alma and Donna, so that he was facing me. He said, "Well, how's everything going? Is Maxwell Courtenay treating you right?"

Donna said, "Mr. Courtenay has been just angelic to us. He's so generous."

"Yeah, Maxwell isn't such a bad fellow when he sets himself out to try.—Hey! What am I thinking about? Let me order some drinks. What will you girls have?"

I said, before Donna could open her mouth, "Mr. Brangwyn, it's very kind of you, but we aren't drinking anything."

He seemed astonished. "No?"

"Really," I said. "Absolutely *nothing*."

"Oh, come along, now. How about some cognac?"

"Oh, boy," Donna said, "I'd love a cognac."

Alma said, "Ah! Cognac."

"Absolutely not," I said. And I couldn't quite understand it: how had I managed to get myself into this position? How had I come to be the calm, steady voice of Alcoholics Anonymous?

Mr. Brangwyn said, "A cognac can't do you any harm. Let me get a waiter—"

I said, "Look, Mr. Brangwyn: it's a rule, that's all. We aren't allowed to drink in public. Period."

Donna said, "We aren't even allowed to drink in secret, period."

Mr. Brangwyn said with genuine indignation, "What's the idea? You're in America, aren't you? You had this same identical trouble on the plane coming down, Miss Thompson. Listen, if this is the way Magna International Airlines treats its girls, I'm going to stop flying with them. There's plenty of other companies. Holy smoke—you're over eighteen, aren't you?"

"Yes," I said.

"Well, then. What's wrong with a simple drink?"

We went on discussing this burning question for some time, just going around in circles and getting nowhere, naturally; but one interesting fact emerged. There was Donna, absolutely ravishing, and there was Alma, absolutely luscious, and there was I, really nowhere in their class; and yet Mr. Brangwyn remained faithful to the friendship we'd started when we sat side by side on the plane. I could feel it, in the strange extrasensory way these things pass between people. He kept turning his eyes *to* me with a puzzled expression, he kept turning his eyes *away* from me with a puzzled expression, and I knew that I'd taken a definite place in his mind. It was flattering. His problem, with the other girls sitting at the same table, was how to express himself; and at last he said, "Well, if you can't have a drink I guess you can't have a drink. . . . Er, Miss Thompson."

"Yes?"

He couldn't quite look me in the eye. "Have you seen this terrace where they dance? Just out there. It's kind of nice."

"I've been admiring it."

He cleared his throat. "Would you care to take a turn?"

Oh, God! How complicated everything was! I tried to recall the rules from one to a thousand—was anything said about dancing under Chinese lanterns, were prisoners allowed to take a turn on the terrace?

"Go on, Carol!" Donna laughed. She knew why I was hesitating. "The band sounds just dreamy."

It did, too. It was playing South American music, very softly, and I'd been aware of it all through dinner. South American music, when it's sweet and low, just sends my blood sugar zooming.

I said, "I'd love one dance, Mr. Brangwyn. But just one. Then we really have to get back to our apartment."

He went ahead of me, and as we reached the entrance to the terrace I saw Mr. Garrison sitting at a table, with the man who wore the horn-rimmed glasses who hadn't made a speech when we assembled at seven-thirty. They were both staring at me coldly.

I wanted to die, then and there. I wanted, literally, to stop existing, and disappear into the ether and become merged with the great Nothingness. It sounds absurd now, but that's all I wanted to do, vanish in a little puff of blue smoke. I felt guilty as hell, even though I didn't know what I was guilty *of*.

I smiled at Mr. Garrison. I gave him the sweetest, friendliest smile that any girl, in the circumstances, could give any man.

He looked back at me as if I were one of the more hideous stone carvings on Easter Island. I was cooked, I knew it. I'd done everything possible to keep to the rules, and as usual I'd fallen flat on my face in the mud.

It's so damned unfair. Any time you feel you want to vanish in a cloud of blue smoke, your guardian angel just leaves you there to sweat the situation out on your own. I barely managed to crawl after Mr. Brangwyn, and the sweet low rumba they were playing on the terrace sounded like a funeral dirge.

I said, "Mr. Brangwyn, I'm sorry. You'll have to excuse me. I just don't feel like dancing."

He said, "Okay."

He couldn't have been any nicer.

I said, "I'd like to walk around for a minute; and then, if you don't mind, go back."

"Sure."

He didn't even try to hold my arm. We strolled under the illuminated palm trees, and I smelled the jasmine in the air and heard the faint wash of the ocean on the sands, and saw the stars in billions shining down on us. He said, "Was I right? Isn't it kind of pretty out here?"

"It's beautiful."

"But let me tell you something. Florida has a lot more to offer."

"It has?"

"Oh, sure. This is overcivilized. There's still a lot that's wild. Like the Everglades. You're liable to run into herds of wild pigs, alligators, almost anything."

"I've heard about the alligators."

"While you're here you ought to take the opportunity to see all these things. There's the Indian villages. Sponge divers. The Keys. A lot worth seeing."

I said, "We're only allowed to leave town in the weekends."

"That's okay. You can see them in the weekends."

"And one would need a car."

He said, "Well—"

"Mr. Brangwyn, I'm awfully sorry, but I really think I ought to go in."

"Sure. Sure."

We returned to the Sun King Room. Mr. Garrison and the man in the horn-rimmed glasses had mercifully left. I walked back to our table with Mr. Brangwyn and said, "Come on, kids. It's time to leave."

"It's only ten-fifteen," Donna said. "We can stay a few more minutes."

"On your feet," I said.

"You know who leave a minute ago?" Alma said. "These Mr. Garrison, with a friend, a man. I smile at him, but I don't think he notice. He leave in a hurry."

I put a five-dollar bill on the table for the waiters, I picked up my corsage, and I said to Mr. Brangwyn, "It was awfully nice seeing you again. And thank you for the orchids, they're lovely."

"My pleasure," he said. His eyes were sad, and puzzled.

We walked out. Donna said, "I want to find Mr. Courtenay. The least we can do is thank him for our dinner."

I said, "Donna, Mr. Garrison saw us. He was furious."

"Why on earth should he be furious?" Donna asked. "We haven't done anything wrong."

"I saw the expression on his face."

"Nuts," Donna said. "You're imagining things."

I guess I imagine things too easily. That night I dreamed about the plane crash at the Tokyo airport. It was just too damned vivid. I had a ghastly time.

5

We'd been divided into two groups in the simplest way—alphabetically. The break came at the letter N, which meant that Mary Ruth Jurgens and Annette Morris and Alma were in one group, the group which left the hotel at seven forty-five; and Donna and I were in the second group, which left at eight-fifteen.

Jurgy was apparently a natural early-morning riser. She was up promptly at six. She woke Annette, and then she woke Alma. The commotion that ensued woke me, because Alma began to scream at the top of her lungs that she wasn't going anywhere with Jurgy and Annette, she was only going with Carola because Carola was her only friend and the sister of her bosom, etc. It was getting to be pretty tiresome. I had to jump out of bed and console her, and in the end, very tearfully, she agreed to go with the seven forty-five group this once, and I swore that I would speak to Miss Pierce and Miss Webley and if necessary to the president of Magna International Airlines to arrange for our reunion. This first morning there was ghastly confusion in the vicinity of the bathroom, and Jurgy said to me, "Hey, Carol, we can't go through this every morning, we'll have to figure out some routine." I said, as an impartial observer, "Jurgy, I couldn't agree with you more." There was something about this girl that made me respect her. Not *like*, but *respect*. She was a cold fish, but she was awake from the minute she opened her eyes, she was quick, she was efficient, she knew just what she was doing. Annette, on the other hand, was a morning sleepwalker. When she fell out of bed she didn't have the faintest idea where she was, whether she was in Miami Beach, Florida, or Peking, China. She had to be led to the bathroom by the hand, and when the door closed there was the most shattering series of crashes and howls as she bounced off the various fixtures. What she really needed for a couple of hours was a Seeing Eye dog. Alma was worse. She was one of these people you abandon for lost as far as bathrooms are concerned. She couldn't be budged either by threats or honeyed promises, and after a while you gave up in despair because it was perfectly clear that she'd passed away in there, and the only thing to do was to send for Mr. Courtenay and his gang of merry plumbers, and *that* was going to be pretty embarrassing all round. Five girls who have to be perfectly groomed before they can go out and face the world, and one bathroom, provide a fascinating little problem in what might be called the science of social logistics. Add to this the fact that all the beds had to be made, and all clothes hung away, and everything in the apartment left spotless, and it turned into a problem in the science of confusion.

I said to Jurgy, "With all this going on, what are we supposed to do about breakfast?"

"We'll just have to grab a cup of coffee in the snack bar."

"There *is* a snack bar?"

"Or a cafeteria, or something. All hotels have them. But I reckon as soon as we get organized we can lay in some stuff and fix our own breakfast."

"Fix our own breakfast in all this pandemonium?"

"Why not?" She sounded utterly sure of herself. "I don't mind cooking. I had plenty of experience as a short-order cook."

I said, "Okay. We'll make a deal. You fix breakfast. I'll fix dinner. I don't mind cooking, either. Let's get together tonight and work out some menus."

She looked positively pleased. She positively smiled. There really was a human being under that cold expressionless mug.

The noise of the girls leaving didn't disturb Donna at all. She slept on placidly under the open window, one long bare arm outside the sheet, one hand cradling her cheek, breathing as gently as a baby. Finally I shook her shoulder; and she opened her eyes at once and said in the most natural way, "Hi, Carol." It took her exactly half a second to wake up completely, which impressed me to death. I'm not as bad as Annette, but I'm inclined to grope around for a while.

She reached under her pillow for a pack of cigarettes and her lighter, and then as soon as she had her cigarette lit she threw off her sheet, sat up, and looked out of the window. She was the only one of us who slept raw. I couldn't care less one way or the other, although Alma had muttered in her beard about it last night. I suppose Alma considered the nude male figure a perfectly natural thing to have around, whereas the nude female figure was reserved purely for feelthy postcards.

Actually, Donna had an almost neutral body. I mean, she was without any question a girl, but nothing had filled out to any considerable extent. She had small breasts and long narrow flanks, and practically no behind. By comparison, Alma was a mass of overlapping curves, like one of Rubens' alleged nymphs. Annette was curvy, too, a feminine little thing; but Jurgy and I were built in much the same way, with fairly standard adornments. When Donna was *dressed*, as she had been dressed last night in the Spanish moss, she outshone the whole world. She was a born clotheshorse, whereas healthy types like Jurgy and me receive only Paris' scorn.

"Boy!" Donna said. "Look at that ocean!"

"Isn't it something!"

She frowned. "You know, it's crazy lying in bed like this. We ought to take a swim every morning as soon as we wake up."

"We certainly ought."

"Okay. Tomorrow morning. We'll get up half an hour earlier and take a swim." She jumped out of bed energetically. "Gee! I *like* Florida. I do. As soon as I get myself settled in, I'm going to like Florida a lot."

"What do you mean, settled in?"

"Why," she said, surprised by my question: "As soon as I find myself a boy friend. You have a boy friend. Don't you think I deserve one, too?"

I said, "Well: there's always Mr. Muirhead, the jockey. Not to mention Mr. Courtenay."

She laughed. "You know what I admire about you, Carol? You can always cut me down to size."

"Get dressed, or we'll miss the bus."

I wanted to tell her to wear something fairly conservative this first day, but at the last moment I hesitated and decided it was none of my business, she could wear what she pleased. So I watched her put on a rather fluffy dark green blouse, with a rather flouncy black skirt, and a fine gold-chain necklace, and I didn't make any comment. I wore a black Lord and Taylor number which buttoned up the front with about thirty buttons, to discourage idle fingers, and the neckline came directly under my chin. I can't imagine what mad whim made me buy it originally, but I knew perfectly well why I chose to wear it today: I was merely scared of Mr. Garrison. I had an idea at the back of my head that Mr.

Garrison was displeased with me after our encounter in the Sun King Room last night; and I felt that if I ran into him again this morning I'd better look as demure as possible. No bosom. No hips. No neckline. Just a female shadow.

As Jurgy had predicted, there was a snack bar. It was off the main lobby, and it was called—as any idiot might have guessed—the Salon de Fragonard. Très chic. The walls were covered with paintings of buxom shepherdesses, all of them completely oblivious to the fact that their rosy bosoms were falling out every which way, and the waitresses were garbed as shepherdesses too, but with much stricter bodice control. Ye gods! Imagine being served your morning coffee by an unbosomed shepherdess! As Donna observed, any normal female would be sick to her stomach for the rest of the day.

Mr. Courtenay had shown a magnificent sense of reality by organizing a special seventy-cent breakfast for Magna student hostesses: papaya juice, scrambled eggs, and all the coffee we could drink at no extra charge. We wolfed everything in sight, and then we trooped out, with eighteen other girls, to our darling pink and blue bus. Harry was driving again, in a shirt covered with dolphins and sailfish, and we went buzzing through Miami Beach in the delicious early-morning sunshine. People stared, people waved (but we never waved back), a few gay blades wolf-whistled, and although we tried to be prim and proper we couldn't help breaking down into mildly hysterical giggles. It was partly sheer nerves, and partly the result of being a crowd, twenty girls with only poor old Harry to provide male companionship.

Magna International Airlines' offices were on a little side road near the airport. There were no hangars or airplanes here, although you couldn't miss the noise of the planes taking off just a few hundred yards away. These offices were purely for the administrative and training staff—an enormous concrete building two stories high. It was unglamorous outside and unglamorous inside, rather like a factory. I think I'd expected something wildly modern, stainless steel and dazzling glass and crazy observation towers with spiral staircases, reflecting the mad adventure of flying and the challenge of tomorrow, etc. But, no. It was just as utilitarian as it could possibly be.

Miss Webley was waiting for us in the reception room—the tall, sweet-faced blonde whom I'd liked so much. She smiled when she saw us and said, "Hi, girls! I thought I'd better be here to meet you and show you the way to the classroom, otherwise you're sure to get lost. Now stay close," and off she set briskly, leading us through miles and miles of narrow corridors. Then, at last, she led us into a big old-fashioned classroom complete with a blackboard and a battered old teacher's desk and rows of small desk-and-seat contraptions which looked as if they'd come directly from the original little red schoolhouse.

"Here we are," Miss Webley said. "It doesn't matter where you sit, just get settled for the time being. We aren't going to do very much serious work today because you'll be busy with a lot of red tape—having your physicals, and getting your records entered, and being measured for your uniforms, and—"

She was interrupted by Miss Pierce, who strode into the classroom with Alma. Dear Alma. What would I have done without Alma, how could I have lived all these years without Alma? She stood there with tears in her lovely eyes, while Miss Pierce and Miss Webley conferred in low tones.

Then Miss Webley called, "Carol Thompson."

I stood up.

She said, "Ah, yes. I remember now. You're the girl who's been helping Alma di Lucca. You speak Italian, is that right?"

"Yes, Miss Webley."

"Well, in that case, I think Miss di Lucca might transfer to this class so that you can continue helping her." She glanced at a paper on her desk. "Grace O'Malley, you will go into Miss Pierce's class to replace Miss di Lucca."

O'Malley went out dismally with Miss Pierce. Alma clambered into the seat at my left side. Donna was on my right.

Miss Webley continued as if nothing had happened. "Now, girls, as I was saying, we aren't going to be able to do very much formal work today because of your various appointments. But I want you to understand that this is your home base. Whenever you're through with your medical, or seeing the people in Records, I want you to return here, so that we can all keep track of each other. Is that clear?"

"Yes, Miss Webley." It was just like being back in kindergarten.

"Now there are one or two things I want to discuss—"

She stopped again. A girl wearing glasses walked to her

67

desk and handed her a folded slip of paper. Miss Webley read it, frowned at it, and then said, "Carol Thompson. Donna Stewart. Alma di Lucca."

"Yes, Miss Webley," we replied.

There was no expression in her voice. She said, "All three of you are to report to the Director of Training. Betty will show you to his office."

Betty was the girl wearing glasses. She waited at the door of the classroom as we clambered out of those strangulating desks. "This way, please," she said, leading the way down the corridor. "Up these stairs. We're on the second floor."

I said to her, "Who's the Director of Training?"

She looked at me as if I were crazy. "You've met him. Mr. Garrison."

"Oh," I said.

"What is these?" Alma said. "What is happening, Carola?"

"Nothing," I said. "Just relax." My mouth had become dry and my knees were buckling, but I felt strangely proud of myself for having had the foresight to put on my plain black dress.

We waited for about five minutes in a small anteroom, while Betty sat at a typewriter, crackling away like a machine gun. There was only one spare chair and I put Alma into it, mostly to keep her out of my range of vision. Donna was slightly pale, but she managed to keep the ghost of a smile on her lips, and when she glanced over at me I saw that her eyes were very bright. And another interesting thing, her eyes were a deeper green—they'd taken color from her blouse. I began to think of other people's eyes: for example, there was a boy whom I once knew named Oswald who had those trick eyes—they could change from blue to gray to green, almost to hazel, believe it or not, according to the tie he was wearing. Tom Ritchie's eyes were just button-brown. My father's eyes were a strange shade of blue, very deep, practically violet. My mother's eyes were cornflower blue—

The telephone on Betty's desk rang. She answered it with a flat, "Hello," put it down, and said, "Carol Thompson. Go in." She pointed at a door. "There."

Donna gave me a little flip of her hand. I didn't look at Alma. I went through the door and saw Mr. Garrison sitting at a big desk in a big room. Two other people were with him: Mrs. Montgomery, whom I'd met at the interiew in New York, and the man who'd been with Mr. Garison last night, the man with the horn-rimmed glasses who Donna guessed was from the FBI. I had a sort of glimmering now that she might have struck at the heart of the matter. He had gray eyes, I noticed, with black eyelashes.

Mrs. Montgomery said quietly, "Good morning, Miss Thompson."

"Good morning, Mrs. Montgomery."

Mr. Garrison held out a sheet of paper. "Miss Thompson." He meant that he wanted me to take the sheet of paper. I took it.

He said, "That's a voucher for your return trip to New York. Present it to the clerk at our counter at the airport. He'll see that you get onto the first available plane."

I looked at the paper. I suppose I looked at it with great care for several seconds. I couldn't read it because I couldn't focus, but it was clearly what he said it was. After I'd held it a sufficient length of time I handed it back to him; but he wasn't prepared to receive it and it fluttered onto the desk.

I said, "If you don't mind, Mr. Garrison, I'd rather not use this."

He snapped, "Why not?"

"I'd prefer to pay my own fare back to New York."

He said, "That's quite unnecessary—"

I said, "Also, I think I'd prefer to travel on a Pan American plane, or National, or Eastern. Not Magna International Airlines on this occasion. Good-by, Mrs. Montgomery, it was so nice meeting you." And I felt I ought to be polite to the man with the horn-rimmed glasses, even though we hadn't been introduced. I said to him, "Good-by, sir," and he looked at me in such an odd way that my skin suddenly crinkled all over, as if I'd touched an electric wire. It was terribly interesting, and I wished I could stay a little longer to investigate it in more detail; but I couldn't.

I began to walk out.

Mr. Garrison called, "Miss Thompson."

I stopped. I didn't turn to look at him.

He said, "Miss Thompson, don't you have any comment to make on your dismissal? Or on your behavior last night?"

I turned slowly. "Mr. Garrison, are you asking me to comment *now?*"

"Yes. If you have anything to say."

Boy, did I have anything to say. I said, "You've fired me.

You've ordered me to get out of Miami on the first available plane. And you want me to comment now? *Now?*"

He said, "You, and two of your roommates, left your apartment last night, went down to the main restaurant of the Hotel Charleroi dressed in what I can only call a provocative manner, ordered liquor with your meal, and then invited to your table a man who has the reputation of being a cheap gambler. You know our rules. Miss Pierce read them to you in detail. You know that above all we expect our hostesses and student hostesses to behave like ladies. Your conduct was utterly disgraceful, and there can only be one penalty for it: instant dismissal."

I don't know why it is, but whenever I'm hit by injustice I blow up, not with pure rage, but with words. Words build up in me, words, words, words, like clouds in a thunderstorm, and I begin to talk with an eloquence I don't normally possess. It's stupefying. I turn into a sort of girl William Jennings Bryan, pouring out my indignation in great rolling periods. It's so stupefying that I can't even believe it's me.

I said, "Mr. Garrison, I don't think you and I are living in the same country. We must be living in completely different countries. You've just punished me for breaking certain rules. Very good. Then, having inflicted your punishment, you ask me if I have any comment to make. I find this extraordinary. You see, in the country *I* live in—"

"Miss Thompson," he said.

"Do you mind if I finish, sir?"

"Just don't be cute," he said.

He'd asked for it, by God, and he was going to get it. There wasn't anything in the world he could do to stop me. "In the country *I* live in," I repeated, "there is an elementary principle of justice, inherited from our Anglo-Saxon forebears—"

"Miss *Thompson!*"

"—which provides that a person accused of a crime, whether big or small, shall be presumed innocent until he, or she, is proven, beyond any reasonable doubt, guilty—"

Mrs. Montgomery said gently, "Miss Thompson."

If she wanted to get into the act, too, she was more than welcome. I turned on her and said, "Mrs. Montgomery, at least let's be clear about this. Are we living in America, or aren't we? Is Magna International Airlines an American company, or isn't it?"

She looked at me sadly. "We did not presume you were

70

uilty, Miss Thompson. The evidence was only too con-
usive. You were in evening gowns when you entered the
staurant. A bottle of wine was brought to your table. You
ere joined by a man who, I understand, is a notorious
ambler, a certain Mr. Brangwyn. You and he subsequently
ent out onto the terrace together. Is this accurate?"

I said, "Yes."

She went on, "Whether you feel that our rules are op-
ressive, or juvenile, or unfair is beside the point. There
vere many people in the restaurant who must have observed
ou and your two roommates. Can you imagine their com-
nents? Here were three of our student hostesses, within a
ew hours of their arrival in Miami Beach carousing in an
xpensive restaurant and consorting with a known gambler.
Miss Thompson, do you think your behavior did anything
o enhance our reputation? Or do you think the evidence
ffers any alternative to instant dismissal?"

I'd met somebody who was a lot more eloquent than I
ould ever be, and I knew when I was licked. I said, "You're
bsolutely right, Mrs. Montgomery," and I turned to go
gain.

Mr. Garrison shouted, "Thompson! Come back here!"

So, a second time, I returned.

He glared at me. "Don't you have anything to say for
ourself? Apart from reciting the Bill of Rights? Don't you
ave any explanation of your behavior?"

I said, "What's the use? You've fired me."

He nearly jumped out of his skin. "You *are* fired. And
y George, I'll fire you again if you go on like this. What
vere you doing in that restaurant?"

"We were hungry, Mr. Garrison. We hadn't eaten all day.
We went down to get something to eat. That's all."

He looked baffled momentarily, but he made a fast re-
overy. "You had to change into evening gowns in order to
et something to eat, eh?"

"Mr. Garrison, we're staying in one of the most expensive
otels on Miami Beach. Any woman staying there, as a
natter of course, changes for dinner. Your rules absolutely
tate that we are at all times to be appropriately dressed. I
lon't know if you feel we ought to have changed into slacks
nd sweaters, but we felt, as *ladies*, that the only appropriate
lress was evening gowns."

He blinked. I went right on, before he could say anything,
"Furthermore, we had no intention of going into that res-

taurant—how could we possibly afford it on what Magr
pays us? But we met Mr. Courtenay in the lobby, and he
so sold on the idea that we're the cream of young America
womanhood, he took us into the Sun King Room as gues
of the hotel. We didn't have to pay a cent for our dinner, ex
cept that all I had was a miserable hamburger and a cup o
coffee, and for *that* I had to leave a five-dollar tip."

"You had wine, didn't you?"

I said, "Mr. Garrison, Miss di Lucca had wine. I didn'
Neither did Donna Stewart. And you may or may not realiz
this, but you aren't going to stop Miss di Lucca from drinl
ing wine. It's practically against her religion. She's an Italia
She wouldn't use water for anything except to take a bat
in."

He looked at Mrs. Montgomery. She looked back at hi
impassively. The other man lit a cigarette and stared up :
the ceiling. I was rather glad: I found those gray eyes o
his very disconcerting.

Mr. Garrison said, "You seem to have some pretty pat ex
planations, Miss Thompson. Let's see what you do with th
fellow Brangwyn. This cheap gambler."

I couldn't help taking one atom of sweet revenge. "M
Garrison, believe me, I'm not trying to be funny or any
thing. But you can't really call him a cheap gambler. H
owes the federal government a hundred and fifty thousan
dollars, and that's a lot of money in anybody's book."

Mr. Garrison was not amused. "You knew this?"

"Yes, sir."

"Then what were you doing in his company?"

And once again I blew up, like a balloon, with words. M
Garrison and Mrs. Montgomery had every right to defen
the honor and prestige of Magna International Airlines, bu
they had no right to act like the Spanish Inquisition. I sai
"Mr. Garrison, if you'd arrange for the FBI to investiga
every passenger before he or she is allowed to purchase
ticket, this wouldn't have happened. I sat next to Mr. Bran
wyn on the plane yesterday. I didn't *choose* to sit next t
him. I was *put* next to him. How was I to know he was
notorious gambler? He didn't offer to play cards with m
He didn't try to get me to bet on anything. He was actuall
just as nice and thoughtful as anybody could be. He ju
chatted about flying and oxygen and things like that. Whe
he came to our table last night he acted like a perfect gentle
man. Mrs. Montgomery, please tell me: what was the prop

72

procedure? Should I have caused a scene and ordered him to leave?"

She said, "But you *knew* he was a gambler?"

"I'd heard a rumor, that's all. You can't condemn a person on the strength of a rumor, or can you?"

"My dear, I can't tell you the answer to that question."

Mr. Garrison rubbed his cheeks up and down with the tips of his fingers. Then he sat back, like the man with the horn-rimmed glasses, and stared at the ceiling. Then he looked at me and said, "Do you intend to see this man again?"

"He's a friend of Mr. Courtenay, sir. He's in and out of the hotel all the time. It's going to be difficult to avoid seeing him, unless I take to dodging behind pillars every time he appears."

Mr. Garrison's manner changed suddenly. He became quiet and friendly and direct. He called me, unexpectedly, by my first name. He said, "Carol, it isn't our policy to tell our girls who they can see or who they can't see. Just the same, I'm sure you'll appreciate what we're up against here. No matter how harmless your relationship with this fellow is, it's going to cause gossip. It's going to give us a black eye. And if it comes to a choice between you and Brangwyn, and the reputation of the Hostess Training School, I won't hesitate for a second. You go. It's that simple. You understand?"

"Yes, sir."

"Good. Now, can I assume you won't see this man again?"

I wanted to cry. It was so cruel, so unfair. I wasn't in love with Mr. Nat Brangwyn, I didn't have any special feelings about him, he'd just been friendly and nice and shy, and I'd be prepared to swear he'd never do me the least harm. Why shouldn't I see him? And yet I could understand that what Mr. G. said was true. Gossip, scandal, a black eye—it was only too possible.

There was nobody I could consult. Mrs. Montgomery had her eyes averted from me, the man with the horn-rimmed glasses was in a sense not really there. I said, feeling as if I'd betrayed everything I believed in, "I'll try to keep out of Mr. Brangwyn's way."

Mr. Garrison said, "All right. You can return to your class." He added, "Take Miss di Lucca and Miss Stewart with you."

"Thank you, sir."

He said, "Incidentally, I'd like you to be the first to know. There's a new rule in effect as of today. Evening

73

gowns are not to be worn, repeat, *not to be worn* except on weekends and for special occasions. Will you tell your room mates that?"

"Yes, sir, I will.—What about Miss di Lucca's wine?"

He threw his pencil down. "Dammit. We'll consider that medicinal. Okay?" His eyes narrowed. "But if I ever see her reeling along a corridor or if I even smell it on her breath there's going to be hell to pay. Is that clear?"

I said, "Yes, sir," and withdrew.

I didn't mention any of this to Alma. I told Donna, though. At about ten-thirty, after visiting Records and signing various documents, we were led through a new maze of corridors to a cafeteria for a ten-minute break. Fortunately Alma was at another table. Miss Webley had gently diverted her all the way across the other side of the cafeteria to sit with two French girls who were in our class, Miss Webley being under the delusion that Alma and these French girls would immediately fall into each other's arms. As a result Donna and I were alone for a few minutes with our coffee and doughnuts, and I told her in brief outline about my appearance before the Inquisition, stressing the opening lines of Act One, Scene One, when Mr. G. handed me the voucher to return home instantly. I said, "Donna, let's not kid ourselves. They're in grim earnest, they mean every word they say. Either we toe the line, or we're out."

She said, "Carol, how old are you?"

"Twenty-two."

"I'm twenty-three," she said. She brushed her hair back. "I didn't go to college because I had to give my old man a hand running the lodge. I told you, didn't I, my mother died seven years ago, and until this prize bitch Marion turned up I was really the woman of the house. Dad just automatically left everything to me. A good weekend, we'd have eighty to a hundred guests staying, and I had to see they were properly looked after. I carried the full load; and what's more, Dad trusted me to carry it."

I said, "It sounds terrific."

"Hell's bells," she said: "We're grown women, aren't we? Why do they have to treat us like kids just starting high school? I'm not used to it any more. Honest, Carol, if they ever try to do to me what they did to you this morning there's going to be fireworks. I want this job, it means a lot to me, but I'll be goddamned if I'll let them treat me like

74

Little Orphan Annie. I like to drink, and I like having guys around, and there's no law that says I can't. Let's face it, Carol: what the hell does Garrison think he's running? A nunnery?"

I said, "Donna, I agree with you. But look at it from their point of view. They have forty of us at the Charleroi. They *have* to have some kind of law and order. Can you imagine forty girls going their own sweet way? It would be absolute hell, Dante's *Inferno* wouldn't be *in* it. You see that, don't you? It would be sheer chaos."

She thought about it for a moment and said reluctantly, "I guess so."

I said, "It's only for a month."

She laughed sourly. "I don't know if I can take it for a month."

Miss Webley swept us off in detachments to our various destinations. An awful lot of time was wasted simply hanging around waiting your turn to be interviewed, or measured for your uniform, or whatever it happened to be. The morning passed rather drearily. But after a meat-loaf lunch I went upstairs for my physical, and I enjoyed every minute of this because the doctor was so utterly charming. Her name was Elizabeth Schwartz. She was quite a young woman, with an exquisite face and prematurely white hair; and when she discovered that I enjoyed being talked to, she yakked away happily. She poked me and prodded me, she took the usual urine and blood samples, she weighed me, she took my blood pressure, she examined my eyes, my ears, my nose, my throat; and she talked constantly, in a very friendly but adult way, explaining why all this was so necessary. Blood, for example. You can't fly regularly if you're anemic because at high altitudes your blood won't be able to carry enough oxygen. In fact, hostesses weren't permitted to give blood donations fourteen days before a flight; and if a hostess simply *had* to give a blood donation for some urgent reason, she had to report it to the Medical Department and have a blood count and a hemoglobin determination before she could fly again. Of course, if you had diabetes you were out, and if your blood pressure was too high you were out, and in general the airline was dubious about taking you if you showed any indications that you might drop dead while you were handing a passenger a glass of milk. There was a personal examination, too; but it wasn't in any way grim because Dr. Schwartz conducted it under a sheet, and she merely disappeared from sight for a minute brandishing a flashlight, and one wasn't particularly aware of what she was doing. When it was all over and I was dressed she said, "You're in very good shape. Carol. Your pulse is a little fast, but that's nothing to worry about."

She was so nice that I couldn't help laughing. I said, "I'm not surprised that my pulse is fast. This is my first day here and the very first thing that happened when I arrived was that Mr. Garrison called me to his office and gave me an absolutely terrible bawling-out. I'm still shaking from it."

The news had already circulated. She said, "Are you one of the three girls who went down to dinner at the Charleroi wearing evening gowns?"

"Yes."

She said, "I hear you all looked so stunning, you caused a sensation."

This was a new angle. I was so surprised, I just stammered, "Really? All that Mr. Garrison said was that we'd brought eternal disgrace to the fair name of Magna International Airlines."

She doubled up, laughing to herself. She said, "Let me tell you in confidence. I was with Mr. Garrison at lunch today, and he was boasting to everybody within listening distance that you were the three best-looking girls that ever walked into the place. Why, he's so proud of you, he's clucking as if he hatched you out himself."

Well, the old son of a bitch, I thought; and I very nearly said it aloud.

We were all back in the classroom by three-thirty, and Miss Webley said, "We only have an hour left this afternoon, girls. Let's see if we can learn what the various parts of an airplane are called. After all, you'll be flying quite a lot, and you can't always go on referring to that thingemebob over there. Then, if we have a little time left over, we'll go on to airports and codes. Turn to page 5 of your Little Black Book, girls: terms and definitions."

During the course of the day we had each been given a huge volume weighing at least three pounds, officially entitled *Magna International Airlines Flight Service Manual For Hostesses*. It was just a fraction smaller than the New York telephone directory and it was known, briefly, as the Manual, or, affectionately, as the Little Black Book, because it was bound in black-paper boards. We were solemnly warned that we had to protect it with our lives, and if we ever managed to pass the training course and actually got to be hostesses we had to carry it with us on all flights as a reference and guide.

And this was when we began to discover Miss Webley's true character. She looked as if butter wouldn't melt in her mouth—a really sweet old-fashioned young lady, slim, graceful, modestly dressed, with soft golden hair and blue eyes and dimples, and the gentlest voice. Compared with the other instructress, Miss Pierce, who looked as if she had enough energy to launch a battleship single-handed every morning, our Miss Webley looked like an angel of mercy and compassion. Or, in other words, as Donna said later, a pushover.

Tread softly, because you tread on my dreams. Miss Webley looked like an angel, smiled like an angel, spoke like an angel, but she happened to have a will of iron. We whisked through airplane terms and definitions, and I have to admit that I enjoyed this thoroughly, having a junk-yard type of mind which adores collecting all sorts of scrap information. For example, I was delighted to learn that the part of a plane that I used to call the tail is actually called the empennage, and the part that goes up is the vertical stabilizer and the part that goes across is the horizontal stabilizer. Wings were still called wings, thank God, but they had all sorts of accessories on them, flaps and ailerons and trim tabs and rubber boot deicers and, on jets, spoilers and leading edge flaps, and they also carried the engines, which were never to be called motors.

Very interesting indeed. I don't know how much of this Alma took in: she sat at my side watching Miss Webley intently, practically looking down her throat at her tonsils; but Donna was rather at a loss. She whispered to me, "Carol, I'll never remember this stuff. A gizmo is just a gizmo as far as I'm concerned. I mean, we aren't expected to *pilot* the plane, are we?"

"Not as a rule," I said. "But suppose the captain orders you to climb out on the wing and clear the trim tab, you'll look like an idiot if you don't know what the trim tab is."

"You mean, the captain can order you to climb out on the wing and do *that!*"

"Certainly," I said.

Miss Webley said, "You two girls in the rear, please pay attention."

She covered airplane definitions in three quarters of an hour and then, as she'd promised, she went on to airports and codes for the remaining fifteen minutes. Now this was pretty fascinating material, too. It seems that every important airport has its own code letters; for example, the Allentown-Bethlehem-Easton airport, which is quite a mouthful, situated in Pennsylvania, is reduced in code simply to ABE. Say ABE to a pilot, and he instantly knows what you mean; and hostesses are expected to know, too. Los Angeles is LAX; Miami International Airport, where we were, is MIA; La Guardia is LGA, Idlewild is IDL, San Francisco is SFO. And so on. It made sense, and it was obviously useful, not only to pilots but in handling luggage. But like everything else that looks too easy, there were some hidden snags. You'd take it for granted, for instance, that the airport at Willow Run in Detroit would be WRD, or, maybe, DWR. Not on your life. It's YIP. Stifel Field, at Wheeling, West Virginia, is HLG.

Miss Webley carefully pointed out these hidden snags and admitted that they were confusing. However, she said, we'd soon get used to them, and find ourselves using these codes automatically. Then she said, "Well, that's all for today, girls. You'll find your bus waiting for you." And as we stood up with a collective sigh of relief, she added, "Oh, by the way: we'll have a written test of airplane terms and definitions and also on airport codes after your coffee break tomorrow morning."

I couldn't believe my own ears. Every girl in the classroom looked stupefied. There were some frantic screams of protest. "A *written* test! On all *this!* Tomorrow *morning!*"

"Why, yes, girls," Miss Webley said. "It isn't very much. And it's basic, you have to know it. And you have all evening to study." She laughed sweetly—such a darling laugh, all dimples and perfect white teeth. "If you think this is anything, wait until you get further on in the course." She stopped laughing. "Girls, sit down for a minute. Do you mind? I haven't really had a chance to talk to you seriously. Don't worry, that little old bus will wait for you."

We sat down silently.

She perched herself on the edge of her desk. "Now," she said. "One or two of you, not all of you, seem to feel I've given you too much work for your home study tonight. Any girl who feels this should go right upstairs to Mr. Garrison and ask for her plane voucher to return home. He'll let you have it, I assure you, without any hesitation or argument."

She paused, and seated herself a little more securely. "Girls, let's be honest about this. We think of you as a very special group. You aren't just any twenty girls whom we picked off the street. Every day our personnel offices are swamped with applications from girls who want to be Magna International Airlines hostesses." She paused again, to allow that vital statistic to sink in: "One, just *one* is selected for training out of every six hundred applicants."

Nobody even dared to move.

"Perhaps," she said, "you're wondering why we're so fussy. I'll tell you. It's simple. When you're flying as a hostess on one of our jet airliners, you have what is probably the most responsible job that any girl can have today. It isn't just putting a pillow behind a passenger's head; it isn't just serving coffee, tea, or milk; it isn't just giving everybody a pretty smile. You have far greater responsibilities, as you'll learn, responsibilities that might possibly mean life or death to many people. I'm not kidding you, girls, it's true. And we will not let a girl fly as a hostess on our planes unless we are absolutely sure that she is capable of living up to her responsibilities. We have to be sure of her intelligence. We have to be sure of her guts." Suddenly her voice became icy. "This may sound awfully corny. If it does, I'm sorry. But unless you measure up to these qualifications, we have no use for you. You'd be better off looking for another job."

She certainly could express herself in no uncertain terms. I waited for the next volley of cannonballs.

But she didn't go on. She slid off the edge of the desk and straightened herself gracefully and said, "Okay, girls. That's all. I won't keep you any longer. Good night."

"Good night," we said, although it was only a few minutes after five. And that's when Donna made her celebrated remark. "God," Donna said, "I thought she was a pushover." I said, "So did I." Oh, boy.

I rode back on the little old bus with another red-haired girl who was in our class, Julia something. She was one of those delicate red-haired girls, with fine white transparent skin—not the lusty type, like Donna, but in her own way very beautiful.

She said to me wistfully, "I'll never learn all the airport codes."

"Oh, sure you will. They're easy."

Julia said, "Do you know how many airports there are that we have to learn? I counted them. About sixty."

"So what?" I said.

"No," she said. "I'm fated. You know that trick one for Detroit—YIP?"

"Yes."

"It's just an omen," she said. "I come from Detroit."

I said, "Look, I believe in omens, but that's going a little bit too far. I mean, why do you have to think of it as a bad omen? Why not think of it as a good omen?"

"Nothing good ever happens to me."

Honest, I swear, there's nothing in this world as morbidly miserable as the average girl. Here they are, with life and love and happiness ahead of them, and what do they do? Welcome the future with outstretched arms? Hell, no. They just sit on their fannies patiently expecting the worst. Doom, destruction, slipped wombs, cancer, vitamin deficiency and desolation. I'm merely stating this as Paragraph One, Section One, of my Ph. D. thesis on Girls Through the Ages, under the subheading, Misery, the Normal Pattern of Girlhood. I don't mean any of this as criticism of poor Julia. Compared with me she was probably a screaming optimist. Who falls flat on her face in the mud at the drop of a hat? Thompson. Who's handpicked to be bawled out at the crack of dawn by Mr. Garrison, on her first morning at the training school? Thompson. Who is undoubtedly going to be the first girl kicked off the course? Naturally, Thompson. The only thing that surprised me to date was that Dr. Elizabeth Schwartz hadn't discovered that I had two hearts, or something, or no liver, which would mean that I'd have to be packed in cotton and sent home in an ambulance to Mother.

At five o'clock in the evening Miami Beach was still blazing with sunshine, the people were all gay, waving to us and wolf-whistling, the waterfront hotels were shining, the royal palms and the coconut palms and the date palms were all rustling in the breeze, the air was so rich and winy that I was a little surprised Mr. Garrison hadn't passed a rule forbidding us to breathe it. We descended from our chariot at the Charleroi, we walked in through the magnificent entrance, and lo and behold, about a thousand men turned to grin at us. Grin, grin, grin. Old men, young men, middle-aged men, hairy men, bald men, all grinning. Holy cow, what did they expect to *accomplish* grinning like that? You'd think this was how Western man displayed his virility—the bigger the grin, the bigger everything else.

The only way to treat these apes was as if they simply didn't exist, and all the girls, without any exception, did precisely this. They were wonderful. They didn't falter, they didn't stop chatting to their companions, they just walked across the lobby to the elevators with calm dignity, and the grinning men were left behind looking thoroughly stupid. I don't mind a man eying me with healthy interest. I hate being grinned at as if I'm a dirty joke.

I was still fuming when I walked into 1412. I dropped my Manual on my bed and said snappishly to Donna, "What are you planning to do now?"

"Baby, I'm going to get into a swimsuit and go right into that ocean."

I said, "Before you change, the first order of business is food."

"Food? I'm not hungry. That meat loaf we had for lunch is still with me—"

"I mean food for the meals we cook here. Jurgy says she doesn't mind fixing breakfast, and I'm prepared to fix dinner; but I have to know what you eat so that I can make up my list."

"Anything, honey," Donna said. "I'm happy to leave it in your hands."

I knocked at the door between the two rooms. A voice said, "Come in," but it was Annette, alone, stretched out on her bed with her Manual. She said, "Oh, God, Carol, do you know what? We have to learn the codes for about a million airports, and the names of all the parts of an airplane—"

"So do we. Where's Jurgy?"

"Oh, she went out."

"To the pool?"

"Maybe. Carol, she wasn't looking too good."

"What do you mean, she wasn't looking too good?"

Annette hesitated. "I don't know how to describe it. She looked kind of grim—you know, upset. Carol, I'm worried about her."

I sat down on Jurgy's bed. "Why?"

"Figure it out for yourself, Carol. I mean, look at her background. Carol, I'm not a *snob*, I like Jurgy, even though she isn't a specially warm person; but all she's ever been in her life is a waitress. She didn't even finish high school."

"So?"

"Well, look at the study assignment we have for tonight. Miss Pierce told us frankly, this is just the *beginning*. In a few days we'll be carrying a real load. That's why I'm worried about Jurgy. She may not be prepared for anything like this. Maybe that's why she went out looking so upset."

I said, "She doesn't have to be upset. We'll all help her as much as we can."

"Gee, Carol, I knew you'd say that."

I stood up and said, "Let's not kid ourselves. Jurgy might not be the only one to need help. My IQ isn't so high, either. We'll just have to shake all our brains together and hope for the best."

I went down to look for Jurgy. This business of food was on my mind and I wanted to get it settled. About a dozen of the girls were already draped around the pool looking thoroughly pleased with themselves. They had every right. The water was crystal clear; the air was divine; the sun was like gold; the palm trees and the gorgeous clumps of flowering bushes and the steel-and-glass architecture of the hotel made a fantastic background.

I asked a brunette stretched out on a chaise longue if she'd seen Mary Ruth Jurgens.

"Gee, I wouldn't know. There are so many girls here I haven't learned to tell them apart. Maybe she's on the beach."

I scouted around the beach, feeling an awful fool to be wearing shoes and a high-necked dress with thirty buttons down the front; and finally I spoke to another brunette who was sitting with her back against a palm tree, studying her Manual.

She said, "Wait a minute. I think I did see her—she was here a while ago. I believe she took a walk." She pointed. "Thataway."

"Thanks," I said. "I'll walk along to meet her.—Isn't there any swimming this evening? The water looks perfect."

She said sadly, "I know. But the lifeguard went off duty at five o'clock, so we aren't allowed to go in."

I took off my shoes and started to trek down the beach, and to my relief I'd only gone about a hundred yards when I saw Jurgy in the distance walking slowly toward me. She was wearing a cocoa-colored sunsuit and a straw hat rather like a small punchbowl, and she was completely out of this world, meandering along at the edge of the water and stooping down every few seconds to pick up sea shells which she examined with deep attention. She was so engrossed that she didn't notice me until I was practically on top of her.

I said, "Hi."

"Oh, hello, Carol."

She glanced at me and then, to my surprise, began to walk on as if she didn't want my company.

I said, "Hey! We were going to have a talk about laying in food."

She stopped. "That's right." She bent down and picked up a shell, and without looking at it threw it into the water. "I can't talk now, Carol. Let's leave it till tomorrow." She walked on again, kicking up little jets of spray with every step.

I caught up with her. "What's the matter with you, Jurgy?"

She said sullenly, "Just leave me alone."

"But what's the *matter?*"

"Carol, I told you to leave me alone."

I said, "Mary Ruth Jurgens, you may or may not like this, but you're living in a group with four other girls now, and you'll just have to act civilized."

She turned on me in a fury. "What does that mean, act civilized?"

I said, "I'm not trying to interfere with your privacy. Everybody's entitled to take a walk by themselves. I only came looking for you because I was worried about you, and you can't brush me off like this."

She couldn't have been more hostile. "Why are you worried about me?"

"I am, that's all. So is Annette. She told me you came back from class looking upset. So I came out to find you, and here you are. Annette was absolutely right."

"Why the hell don't you and Annette mind your own business?"

I said, "Jurgy. Be sensible. There are five of us in 1412. We're all in the same boat. We all want to pass this course, we're all scared that we'll flunk out, we all have exactly the same worries."

"We're all in the same boat," Jurgy said, and laughed. "We are, too."

She walked on a few paces, away from the edge of the water, and sat down cross-legged staring out at the horizon.

I sat down beside her. I said, "Jurgy, I'll be candid with you. *I'm* scared. I don't know what your Miss Pierce told you, but our Miss Webley put the fear of God into us. We'll just all have to work together every night. I mean, take these airports and codes—"

"I'm not worried about airports and codes."

"No?" I said.

"No." She scooped up a handful of sand and threw it in the air. I said, "Then what *are* you worried about?"

"Let's go," she said harshly. She made an effort to stand up, and sank back again. "What's the use, Carol? It's no good talking. They're going to send me home."

"Oh, no! Why?"

Her face was ashen. "I have an interview with Mrs. Montgomery at noon tomorrow. She's going to send me home."

"Jesus," I said. "Jurgy, honey: *why?*"

Words began to boil out of her. "You're lucky, Carol. Anyone only has to look at you, and they can see it right off, you had a home, you had an education. That big bitch you go with, Donna, she's the same. Remember last night, how she tossed that roll of bills around, and the two diamond rings? She makes damn sure you realize she has a background. Annette's a secretary in a bank—yeah. Her father's the assistant manager. You know what my father was? A night watchman. Whenever he had a job. That's some profession, eh? He was just a low-down drunken bum. And you know what I've been all my life, don't you? A waitress. I carried trays."

"Honey, *believe* me, nobody gives a damn what you were or what your father did. You're *here*. You're on the same level as everyone else."

The words went on boiling out of her. "Listen, Carol. I couldn't take it any more in Buffalo. I had it, right up to my neck. I'm a human being. I have a right to live. So I took a chance. I filled in an application form for a job with Magna International Airlines. Garrison came to Buffalo and interviewed me, and you know what he said? He said Miss Jurgens, you're the kind of girl we want. That's what he said—the first time anyone ever gave me a break. Life, that's what it meant. Life." She began to cry.

I said, "Honey, what went wrong today? Why do you have to see Mrs. Montgomery tomorrow?"

She brushed her tears away. Her voice became harsh again. She said, "You had a physical this morning, didn't you? Did that doctor go over you from top to bottom?"

"Oh, my God, Jurgy, did Dr. Schwartz find something wrong with you?"

"Nothing wrong. Just that I'd had a baby."

It was one of those crazy statements that leave you practically speechless. I said, "When did you have a baby?"

"Oh, I was a big girl, then," Jurgy said. "I was sixteen."

"Oh, Jurgy."

"It died," Jurgy said. "I never even got to see it. And my boy friend skipped town. And I couldn't face going back to school, so that's when I got my first job, in the diner."

"Oh, God, Jurgy."

"It's okay," she said. "The kind of background I come from, it happens all the time."

I said, "How did Dr. Schwartz find out?"

She laughed sourly. "You're innocent, aren't you?" She pulled back the skirt of her sunsuit and showed me the inside of her thigh. I couldn't see anything special, but she said, "See that?" Then she put one hand across her breasts. "And up here. You're never the same." She buried both her hands in the sand, as if she'd soiled them by touching herself. "The doctor was nice, but she explained—she had to include it in her report. I'm not blaming her. Everyone has to do their job. And then, at four o'clock I got this note to see Mrs. Montgomery."

"Listen, Jurgy. She'll understand. She's a swell person—"

"Carol, you may be a tramp, but no one can prove it. I was a tramp six years ago, and they have all the proof they need. You think Mrs. Montgomery or Mr. Garrison want tramps working as hostesses on their airplanes?"

I said, "Jurgy, forget it. Let's go get a cup of coffee or something."

Two hairy young apes came skittering over the sand toward us. "Hi," they called. "Hi, fly-girls. All by yourselves, fly-girls?" One of them had a camera, a nice new shiny Leica. He crouched down a couple of yards from where we were sitting and said, "Hold it, girls, hold it. This is a terrific picture. Just stay as you are."

Jurgy said, "Beat it."

The ape behind him grinned and said, "Smile at the little birdie, girls."

"Beat it," Jurgy said. "Do you hear me?"

The kid who was standing wagged a finger at her and said, "Now, now. No temper. Fly-girls must always smile."

85

"I'm telling you for the last time," Jurgy said. "Beat it."

I heard the camera click. The kid who had taken the picture began to wind the shutter of the Leica, preparing to take another.

Jurgy pushed herself to her feet. She strode across to the kid with the camera, and hit him across the ear with the flat of her hand so hard that he went flying over sideways. The Leica sailed about ten feet through the air and practically buried itself in the wet sand at the water's edge. It was as beautiful a smack on the ear as I've ever seen, delivered by an arm that was hard with bitterness, and it would have knocked a house over. The kid who'd been hit lay there too dazed even to move. The kid who was still standing pointed at the Leica being lapped by the Atlantic Ocean and said, "Hey! You've ruined his camera!"

Jurgy said, "If either of you two little monkeys ever comes near me again, I'll ruin the both of you, not only your camera."

She turned her back on them contemptuously. Then she said to me, "Ugh. I feel better now, Carol. Let's go for that coffee you were talking about."

I said, "Jurgy, that was absolutely sensational. Let me be your manager from now on."

"Bah, that was nothing," she said. "You should see me when I'm really mad."

We walked on. I said, "I'll tell you something, Jurgy. I have a mysterious feeling. Everything's going to turn out all right."

"Are you psychic?"

"Yes. Didn't you know?"

She said, "That's good," and smiled.

We grabbed some hamburgers in the cafeteria, and then all five of us sat on the beds in the big room until about one o'clock in the morning, learning those damned airports and codes, and airplane definitions. ALB, Albany; ABQ, Albuquerque—right through the two-page list ending with ICT which any fool can see is Wichita, Kansas; and AVP, which is Wilkes-Barre-Scranton. The genius who figured out these abbreviations, we decided unanimously, should get the Mud Medal with Bar of the Library of Congress, and a cast of his brain should be kept in a special case in the Museum of Natural History.

It was the darndest thing, though, to walk out into the

orridor of the fourteenth floor. There was a sustained sound oming from every room, like the buzzing of hives of bees. *WA, Fort Wayne, Indiana; IPT, Williamsport; EWR, Newark, New Jersey*. . . . And for hours girls were wandering from room to room, their hair in curlers, their faces covered with cold cream, mumbling those code letters to themselves, looking and sounding like poor Ophelia after a bad session with that utter bastard Hamlet.

I should have dreamed about those code letters, I suppose. Or about Jurgy. Or the school. Something immediate. But I didn't. For the second night in a row I dreamed about that plane crash in Tokyo, and it was as miserable as hell.

6

I don't know how Donna did it. Maybe she'd become ac
customed to going without sleep living all those years in
ski lodge; but I'd no sooner started my nightmare than some
body shook my shoulder and said, "Hey. *Hey*, Carol, hey.
I looked out from under one eyelid wondering who neede
me so badly, and there was this babe from New Hampshire
naked as the day she was born, leaning over me and shakin
her breasts in my face. I couldn't figure it out, and I close
my eye and tried to return to my fate in Tokyo. I didn'
want to return. I just *had* to return.

She shook me again. "Hey. *Carol*. Hey."

I said, "Wass up?"

"Don't you remember? We're going to take a swim. It'
the most beautiful morning you ever saw."

"Wass time?"

"Five-thirty."

I sat up and screamed, "You heartless bitch, we didn't ge
to bed until one-thirty. What are you trying to do to me?

"Ssssh," she whispered. "You'll wake the others. Come or
Crawl into a suit."

I said, "Holy God—"

"Stop that griping. Are you one in six hundred or aren'
you?"

I toppled out of bed and began to paw through my ches
of drawers for a black one-piece job that my dear old Lor
and Taylor had supplied (I should have charged them fo
publicity, really: I was just covered with Lord and Taylo
labels from head to foot); and on this particular occasion
was so mad with Donna, I didn't give a hoot for modesty
I tore my pajamas off, I slung my swimsuit on; and Donn
said, "Hey, Carol, you're built pretty good."

I snarled at her, "So what?"

"Boy, are you horrible in the morning."

I wished I had a right arm like Jurgy's. I'd have slugge
her.

She wasn't wearing a swimsuit like mine. Hers consiste
of two wisps of white satin, so sexy that Lord and Taylo

would have died rather than carry such a garment in their store, even under the counter.

I said, "Hah! Wait till Mr. Garrison gets an eyeful of you in *that* outfit."

"What's wrong? I'm covered, aren't I?"

"Yeah. And how."

We found our robes and crept out. Somebody had discovered the previous night that there was a special self-service elevator for swimming-type people like ourselves. The regular elevators took you down to the main lobby, and then you had to wend your way through all those herds of bug-eyed men; whereas this special elevator took you down to a palatial shower room which had a boardwalk leading out to the pool and beach.

Down we went, and out onto the sands, and it was so exquisitely beautiful that all my ill temper disappeared at once. There wasn't a soul around, the morning had scarcely begun, the sky was rosy pink and blue, the water was like a sheet of pale blue glass, and we might have been coming out on an absolutely new world.

Donna said, "Isn't it too gorgeous!"

"It's heaven."

We ran down to the water, and suddenly I was struck by a thought. The usual thought of law-abiding Thompson. I said, "My God, Donna, we aren't allowed to swim unless the lifeguard is on duty."

She said, "Carol, I swear, I'll never understand how your mind works. How the hell do you expect the lifeguard to be on duty at this hour of the morning?"

I said, "That's the whole point."

"What's the whole point?"

I said, "He isn't on duty."

"I *know* he isn't on duty," she said. "That's part of the charm of this situation. We don't have a big hairy gorilla looking down our necks."

"Donna—"

"Honestly, Carol, you're getting to be nothing but an old hag." She looked up and down the beach. "You know what? Nobody is going to be down here for hours. I don't need a swimsuit at all."

"Donna, be sensible—"

She took off her top and handed it to me. "Here. Hold this. There's nothing I love more than swimming raw."

She began to pull off her lower wisp, and I said, "You

keep that on, Donna." My voice must have been so threatening that she pulled it back up again, smiling.

"Okay," she said. "Are you coming in or not?"

"I don't have much choice, do I, with you naked like that. I'd better stay here and keep watch for prowlers."

"Nuts," she said.

She waded out until the water was waist-high and then dived neatly, without a splash, and came up about ten yards away. She was obviously an absolutely expert swimmer. I know something about this because one of my former beaus, Oswald, the boy with the changeable eyes, won about a dozen championships in his time, and he used to spend hours pointing out to me just how good swimmers swam. The great thing was, conserving your strength. You did *not* thrash your arms and legs about, no matter how impressive you thought this looked; you used your energy to carry you along, not to stir up foam. The best swimmers just *glide* through the water, hardly disturbing it.

Watching Donna, I saw that she had this pure style. Oswald would have been proud of her. She was flat on the water, and there was only the tiniest white splash as she paddled her feet, and her arms came curving up and over in slow and perfect rhythm. She was a joy to watch, as every good athlete is, and even though she seemed to be going out quite a way, I didn't worry.

Evidently she decided after a while that she'd gone far enough, and I saw her do a neat twist that carried her half out of the water; and then, evidently, she decided to give herself a workout. I used to do that occasionally, purely for show-off purposes: nearly everybody does. You swim a mile in utterly perfect and faultless style and not a soul gives you a second look. But then you turn on the heat and kick up as much foam as an outboard motor, and the whole world watches you in admiration and says, "Boy! Can she *swim!*" That's how Donna came back, at a mile a minute with her wake streaming behind her; and I stood admiring her for putting on such a beautiful show. These athletic New Hampshire girls, I thought: they've really got it.

The strange thing was that when she reached shallow water she kept right on going; and then, when she grounded, she stumbled to her feet and tore out of the water with her arms and her legs and her breasts going like windmills. She managed to get a few yards up the beach, and then she fell flat on her face, and I thought, My God, she's dead. It was an awe-inspiring sight.

For a moment I was too paralyzed to move. Then, waving her bra, I dashed over to her; and sure enough, she looked dead as mutton. I got astride her hips and began to give her artificial respiration, and suddenly she moved her head and said, "Stop it, you cow. Get off me, you're breaking my back."

I couldn't help sighing. All was well, this was the dear sweet Donna I knew and loved; and I rolled off her and sat beside her watching her.

She was deathly white and breathing heavily. She said, "You weigh a ton, Carol. You'd better start on a reducing diet as soon as—" She didn't complete the sentence and I saw that her head had slumped; and here she was dead again. So again I got astride her hips and began to pump air into her; and in a little while she was alive again and abusing me in unprintable language. Eventually she was alive enough to sit up, and I handed her the skimpy little white bra and said, "Here. Cover your shame."

She took it with a little growl, and as she was putting it on I said, "Now maybe you'll tell me. What the hell were you up to out there?"

"What was I up to?" she said. "Didn't you see?"

"All I saw was you swimming to beat the band."

She said, "You fool, I ran into a school of sharks. That's what happened. Dear God, sharks. At least ten of them."

"No!"

She began to wave her arms like a windmill once more. "Don't you believe me? I got out there, and there they were waiting for me with their mouths open, and I just turned and tore back without even knowing where I was going. Look me over, Carol. I bet they took a bite out of me somewhere."

I said, "How do you know they were sharks?"

"They were huge!" she cried. "Each one was over six feet long. What do you expect me to do—swim up to them and ask them what kind of fish they were? They were sharks, I tell you."

I said, "Okay, let's go and have breakfast." I didn't even mention the word lifeguard, but as we walked back to the elevator she said, "Oh, for God's sake, stop that goddam whistling."

Sure enough, trouble began as soon as we were assembled in the classroom. Ah, woe, woe, woe.

"Good morning, girls," Miss Webley said sweetly when we'd all squeezed ourselves into those strangulating seat-and-desk devices, our Iron Maidens.

"Good morning, Miss Webley," we sang out.

This morning her appearance was particularly angelic. She wore the prettiest gray silk dress, with a white collar and white cuffs. Her eyes were clear and blue and innocent. Her dimples were out in full strength. It's a strange thing: I've really been around long enough to know about these females with innocent blue eyes and dimples and white collars and cuffs. You can't trust them an inch, or as far as you can throw an elephant, whichever is the shorter distance of the two. But gazing up at Miss Webley, I melted. She was just adorable.

She gave us a long, fond look.

We all looked fondly back at her.

She loved us so much.

We loved her in return.

"Girls," she said. "How many of you suffer from curvature of the spine?"

Not a hand was raised.

She said, "I think perhaps we'd better spend a few minutes talking about posture and grooming."

Now everybody knows why we have so much trouble with our posture. It all stems from the fact that we evolved from ancestors who, when they weren't hanging from the branches of a tree, went clomping around on all-fours, and it's just the most natural thing in the world for us to revert to this position whenever we can. Indeed, I've heard some pretty plausible theories that if we reverted to this position all the time, a lot of the ills that beset mankind—and more specially womankind—would simply disappear. There wouldn't be any indigestion, varicose veins, headaches, etc., etc., and as for having babies, they'd pop out as easily as your morning toast.

Miss Webley didn't even bother to examine any of these theories. From here on in, she informed us, there would be no more slumping. We would walk erect, with our chins up and our shoulders back. We would sit erect, with our shoulders back and our knees together. "And," she said passionately, "for heaven's sake, when you're walking around don't have that *hunted* look in your eyes. I want you to look, as if you know *exactly* where you're going and, what's more, you know *exactly* what you're going to do when you get there. Is that clear?"

It may have been clear to the other nineteen girls, but it was a wildly new idea to me and I needed a little time to think about it. All my life I've walked around in a total daze, and I couldn't guarantee that I could make myself over as quickly as Miss Webley seemed to expect. It was rather like converting from the old type of cooking gas to the natural gas that's pumped up from Texas. I might need a lot of completely new plumbing; and my pressure would have to be readjusted—that for sure.

"Now," Miss Webley went on, "we come to grooming. That's really a special subject on its own, and we'll deal with it in detail later in the course. But what we have to do something about *immediately* is your hair. You can understand why. I'm sure you don't need to have it spelled out to you. Just imagine yourself working on one of our new jet liners. You're busy every minute serving meals or drinks, which of course have to be prepared in the galley; the passengers are constantly calling for you, not to mention the captain and the crew; and so on. And you simply don't have time to dash to the ladies' room and do your hair every half-hour. It isn't practical, girls. You simply must have a hair style that's neat and orderly. Furthermore, to conform to our rules, it must be its own true natural color —that is, it mustn't be altered by rinsing, bleaching, or dyeing—and it must be short enough so that it won't touch the collar of your uniform."

She waited for the shrieks to die down.

"I'll just do a preliminary survey," she said. "When we get down to grooming in detail we'll work out your most becoming hair styles. But in the meantime I'm afraid that some of you will have to visit a hairdresser tonight."

"*Tonight!*"

She smiled sympathetically, and began to inspect the first row of girls. The two French girls were there, and one of them had a cute blond ponytail. "No ponytails, Suzanne," Miss Webley said.

"But—"

Miss Webley turned to the other French girl, who'd obviously had her hair cut by a poodle expert. "I think you'll have to comb it out, Jacqueline."

"But—"

And so on down the next line, and the next; until she came to ours. Only three girls went scot-free out of the first fifteen.

She looked at the deep-red wavy mass of hair on Donna's head and asked gently, "Is that your natural color?"

"Oh, yes, Miss Webley."

"It's beautiful. But I'm sorry: it's too long in the back and there's also too much of it in front. Will you get it cut tonight, if possible?"

"But, Miss Webley—"

She turned to me. "Carol. Cut."

I didn't even have time to open my mouth. She passed right on to Alma. She looked at Alma's crowning glory, black and glossy and curling all around her face and throat, and she said, "Oh, dear."

Alma said with a modest laugh, "These is all my own, Miss Webley. It come all the way down to the middle of my back."

"Alma—"

"Yes. These is how in Italy the ladies wear the hair."

"I'm sorry, Alma—"

"Yes. These is how in Italy the men tell the ladies they must wear the hair."

"Alma, you see, the rules—"

"Ah! These rules are not for Italian girls. For American girls, yes. For French girls, yes—they have terrible hair anyway. For any other kind of girls, yes; but not for Italian girls. No."

Miss Webley said calmly, "You may be right, Alma. I'll ask the Director of Training."

"Good!" Alma said. "He is sensitive man. He will understand."

Miss Webley returned to her desk.

Donna said to me in a furious whisper, "My God, this is worse than the army. Why the hell don't they order us to go and have all our hair shaved off, and then issue us toupees?"

"Quiet down," I said.

"Don't tell me to quiet down. I'm ready to bust a gut."

"Now," Miss Webley said: "Let's talk for one minute about hygiene. Girls, I don't have to tell you about the importance of hygiene—"

She was interrupted again by Betty, the girl with glasses who worked for Mr. Garrison. Betty walked stiffly to the front of the classroom and handed her a folded slip of

aper; and I wondered idly which poor slob was being
alled to the Presence this time. And for what reason? Smil-
ng at one of the doormen at the Charleroi, maybe.

Miss Webley said, "Carol Thompson."

I couldn't believe my ears. Oh, no! Not Mudface again! It
ust wasn't possible. What had I done this time? Wasn't
here any justice in this world? And my heart began to
eat clompety-clomp because I knew I couldn't be hauled
efore Mr. Garrison on two successive mornings and escape
with my skin.

I stood up shaking like a leaf.

Miss Webley said, "Please go to Dr. Duer's office. Betty
will show you the way."

"Dr. who?"

"Dr. Duer, Dr. Ray Duer."

I said, "Miss Webley, I had my physical yesterday—I had
it in Dr. Schwartz's office."

"Oh, no. This is something quite different." Miss Webley
addressed the class. "Girls, I should explain this. Dr. Duer is
he psychiatrist attached to the school. He'll be talking to
each one of you at some time or another. Carol, will you
go with Betty? Don't keep Dr. Duer waiting."

I thought, Holy mackerel, this is the end. A *psychiatrist*.
What will they dream up next?

He was the man with the horn-rimmed glasses whom I'd
seen with Mr. Garrison on three separate occasions. Betty
left me outside his room, which was on the second floor,
and when I tapped at the door I hadn't the faintest idea
who to expect. But then the door opened, and there he was,
perfectly friendly but still electrical, wearing a neat blue
suit which was at the same time formal and informal. "Hello,
Miss Thompson," he said. "Nice to see you. Come right in."
He closed the door, motioned me to a comfortable chair with
a leather back and a leather seat, and said, "Make yourself
comfortable. Would you care for a cigarette?"

I thought: *cigarette*. H'm. Should I or shouldn't I? This
isn't a human being, Mudface. This is a psychiatrist. Be very
careful, now.

And then I thought: What the hell. If I'm old enough to
be psychoanalyzed, I'm old enough to smoke. I said, "Thank
you, sir. I'd love a cigarette."

"Good," he said. He offered me a Kent and gave me a
light, and when all this was accomplished he sat down in his

own chair and looked at me across his desk. I looked right back at him, square and fair in the eyes, without a trace of fear, the way you're supposed to look at a rattlesnake if you happen to come across one on your travels.

The trouble was, I'd been bitten too often in the past few days by people I'd decided were trustworthy. Mr. Garrison, who was as nice as nice could be, and who'd virtually destroyed my faith in human nature. And Dr. Schwartz, so sweet and charming, who'd reported Jurgy for having a baby umpteen years ago. Even our Miss Webley had done her bit, acting as if butter wouldn't melt in her mouth and then scaring us all out of our wits. And here was another of the same brood. Nice? Gad, he was nicer than that. He almost slayed me the moment he began to talk, his voice was so warm and easy. He was a sensible size, not too big and not too small, and his features were equally sensible—a reasonable quantity of dark hair, an interesting mouth, and a dimple in his chin which didn't quite belong. Sensible all over, except for those gray eyes with dark lashes (and not merely dark lashes, but those *thick* dark lashes, double lashes, probably, like Elizabeth Taylor's). I suppose he was about thirty, or thirty-two. All in all, he was a pleasant example of the scientific type that you see around more and more these days. And really and truly, he couldn't have been any nicer. Charming. Just charming. My mother would have adored him. So I puffed at my cigarette and looked him square and fair in the eyes fearlessly, the way you're supposed to look at a boa constrictor when you find one in the vicinity.

He said affably, "This is simply, oh, a friendly little chat, so that I can get acquainted with you. Purely informal. How are you getting along in class?"

I pointed out that I'd only had a little more than an hour in class. It was early to say how I was getting along.

"That's true." He looked down at a paper on his desk, and I realized that it was my application form, giving the story of my life. He said, "I see your father was Gregg Thompson, who wrote so many travel books."

That wasn't originally on my form. Mr. Garrison must have inserted it after our first interview. I said, "Yes, sir."

"You traveled with your father fairly extensively?"

"Yes, sir."

"I read his book on Brazil a few years ago. I thought it was excellent. Did you go to Brazil with him?"

"No, sir." Brazil was where he died.

"You enjoy traveling."

It wasn't a question: it was a statement. I said, "Yes."

"And, of course, when you're working for Magna International Airlines you'll have an opportunity to travel quite a lot."

It was another statement, and not wildly original. "I hope so."

"Tell me something, Miss Thompson. The day you arrived here, Monday, there was a crash at the Tokyo airport. You heard about this, I assume."

He'd changed direction so abruptly that I was startled. "Yes, sir."

"Has it troubled you at all?"

He was watching me in his friendly way, and I was afraid of him. He had the special kind of black magic that psychiatrists have, he could probably read my mind, and there wasn't any sense in even attempting to keep the truth from him. I said, "Dr. Duer, I guess it has troubled me."

"Oh."

He didn't ask me how or why: he waited for me to tell him.

I said, "I don't mean it's *troubled* me. I dreamed about it, that's all."

"Can you remember the dreams?"

"They were the usual confused stuff, sir. I was inside the plane, and outside the plane at the same time—you know how these things are."

"What were you doing *outside* the plane?"

"Just watching. It wasn't very nice."

"And *inside* the plane?"

"It was just stupid, handing out parachutes and telling people to put them on."

He looked startled, this time. He said, "We don't carry parachutes on passenger planes."

"I know. That's why I said it was stupid."

He watched me for a moment. He said, "Don't worry about your dreams. You're under a certain stress coming here, and it's apt to reflect itself subconsciously." Then he added in an offhand way, "Oh, incidentally, I'm staying at the Charleroi."

"Really?" It was just a casual piece of information, and I took it in that spirit.

He said, "Yes. I'm on the twelfth floor. Room 1208."

If he wanted to chitter-chatter, I was fully prepared to go along with him. I said, "Why! That's almost directly under us! You know, they don't have a thirteenth floor because it's supposed to be unlucky."

"I know," he said. "What were you and your friend doing on the beach at a quarter of six this morning?"

I sagged. There it was. I'd lowered my guard for one second, and he'd sunk his fangs into me. I had nobody to blame but myself.

"The beach?" I said faintly.

"I woke early, Miss Thompson. I looked out of my window, and there you were. Who was your companion?"

"*My companion?*" I said. "Was I *with* somebody? Oh, gee, she was just someone I picked up in the hotel. Just a girl."

"Donna Stewart?"

"Stewart?" I said. "*Stewart?*"

"Look," he said. "Take it easy. I'm not going to report you."

I sat back almost in tears. *Take it easy.* How could I take it easy? I was simply quivering with woe. And the worst of it was that I'd really begun to soften toward him because he was so masculine and nice and intelligent, and I couldn't help wanting him to like me. Instead, here he sat gazing at me reproachfully, as if I were a child. An aging juvenile delinquent. There's nothing more shattering to the female ego.

He said, "You know, it was sheer foolishness this morning. You might have gotten into very serious trouble. Except that in your case you're technically in the clear—you didn't actually enter the water to swim. What held you back?"

"I don't know, sir."

"Did some dim recollection come to your mind that we have a rule about not swimming if the lifeguard is off duty?"

"I don't know, sir."

"What happened to the girl you were with? Why did you have to give her artificial respiration?"

"She—she had a scare."

"What scared her?"

"She said she was chased by a—a fish."

"A shark?"

"Just a fish. She didn't know what kind."

"You might inform her—if she goes swimming in the nude she's liable to be chased by practically anything."

"Oh, my God," I said. "You saw *that?*"

"Of course. Did you and Donna Stewart think you were invisible?"

I said firmly, "Dr. Duer, she wasn't really nude."

"Nude enough," he said. "Personally, I don't mind. But Mrs. Montgomery might have been a little upset."

There was a little pause here, while we both became ruminative. I had a peculiar sensation: it was just as if, having seen Donna partially nude, he'd seen me partially nude, too. There wasn't any sense to this, it was just the sort of thing, I imagine, that happens all the time when you're with a psychiatrist.

He said, "Carol, I don't want to keep you from your class. I'd just like to talk to you for a minute. Another cigarette?"

I refused it, and then because I was so nervous I accepted. He came around his desk to light it for me, and I was awfully conscious of his hands and the closeness of his body and those knowing gray eyes with the double black lashes. No man should be allowed to have such demon eyes. It's too unfair. Then, to make matters worse, he went back to his chair and took his glasses off; and, gad, it was devastating.

He said, "I don't intend this to sound like a lecture. You're too adult to be lectured—"

Absolutely. Describe Thompson in twenty-five words or less. *Too adult to be lectured.*

"—I just want to try to explain our attitude here in the training school. Our rationale." He cleared his throat. "It probably seems harsh to you: so many rules, so many restrictions. But there's nothing mysterious about it. It's perfectly simple."

He didn't look at me as he spoke, and I was afraid to look at him. I watched his hands. They were very brown, and strong.

He said, "First of all, let me say this. Mrs. Montgomery and Mr. Garrison have grown up with the airline. When they interview a girl, they know exactly what they're looking for. But a single interview, or even two, or three, isn't adequate. We can't avoid making mistakes; and when we've made a mistake we have no alternative—we have to send the girl home."

My heart began to go clompety-clomp again.

He went on, still not looking at me, "The trouble is, we demand more from our girls than we can reasonably expect. We know it. That's always gnawing at us. And yet we can't help ourselves, we're forced to make these strict demands; and, in fact, these demands are becoming increasingly rigorous."

He looked at me earnestly, and I thought: Here it comes.

"Put yourself in our position," he said.

I knew that gambit. It was exactly what Mr. LeFebvre said to me when he was about to fire me from the job in the art gallery on Fifty-seventh Street.

He said, "Let's not talk about the future. Let's talk about today. We're now flying at speeds of six hundred miles and more, at about six miles above the earth. Have you any idea what our present jet airliners cost? Make a guess."

"Two million dollars."

"You're way off. Much nearer six million."

"Gee," I said. I had no idea what he was driving at.

He asked, "Do you know how many passengers these planes carry?"

"Over a hundred," I said.

"Right. So one of these planes, in the air, is a pretty big investment in terms of both human lives and money?"

"Yes," I said.

"Okay," he said. "I asked you to put yourself in our position. This is what you have to do: you have the job of selecting four girls—only four—who will be responsible for everything that happens in the cabin of one of these six-million-dollar airplanes, flying six miles above the earth at six hundred miles an hour, with more than a hundred people on board. These four girls will have complete responsibility for the welfare of all these people, for feeding them, for seeing that they are comfortable and at ease, and also for ensuring their safety in the event of an emergency. Do you get the picture?"

"Yes." I felt as if he'd hit me over the head with a baseball bat.

He said, "You'd select those four girls with care, wouldn't you?"

"Yes, sir."

He said, "Now do you begin to see why our demands are so stringent?" His face became moody. "That's *today*. *Tomorrow* is another story. Sometimes I think we'll have to wait while we breed a completely new type of human being."

I plucked up all my courage and said, "Dr. Duer, why are you telling me this?"

"I thought you ought to know."

"Do you feel I can't meet your demands, sir? Are you sending me home?"

He looked at me very seriously, and I looked right back at him, square and fair, but as a human being this time; and suddenly, to my utter astonishment, something seemed to pass between us, from my body to his, from his body to mine, a strange warmth, a strange recognition, a strange trembling wave of excitement. I knew it for myself, and I knew it for him, because he stood up and put his glasses on (trying to hide those devastating eyes from me) and said abruptly, "We have no intention of sending you home. I was merely trying to explain what our situation is here, why we have to be so strict. That's all."

I said, "I see. Thank you."

He said in the same brusque way, "I'm sorry I kept you so long. If you have any problems, don't hesitate to let me know. I'm available in this office every day, and in Room 1208 at the hotel most evenings—you can telephone me there."

He walked me to the door, and he seemed annoyed and upset. I wasn't upset—I was still purely astonished. I'd never in my entire life experienced anything like this sexual electrocution. He said, trying to smile. "Well, good-by now," and I looked up at him, at his eyes and his mouth, and thought, God, you're an amazing man. And so we parted.

The class was taking its coffee break. I caught up with the girls in the cafeteria. Donna was sitting alone, and I bought a cup of coffee and a doughnut and joined her, slopping most of my coffee over into the saucer. She looked at me with her eyebrows raised and said, "Boy! You were up with the psychiatrist for *hours*. What *happened*, all that time?"

"You know. Just the usual business."

"*What* usual business? I've never *been* to a psychiatrist. I don't have the faintest idea what goes on."

I was feeling light-headed, my heart was racing away

101

with itself, and I guess I was slightly crazy, temporarily. I said, "Be your age, Donna. Of course you know what happens when you go to see a psychiatrist."

"All I know is," she said, "he makes you lie down on a couch."

"What kind of couch?"

"A leather couch."

"There you are," I said. "You *do* know."

"And then what?" she asked.

"He asks you a lot of questions, you dope."

"What sort of questions did he ask *you?*"

"The usual questions."

"Honey, you keep stalling. I don't know the *usual* questions are. Like *what?*"

"Can't you guess?"

"About your love life?"

"Sure. All the sordid details about your love life."

"*Really?*" She seemed intrigued by this prospect.

I said, "What happened in class while I was out?"

She wrinkled her nose. "Miss Webley just talked about personal hygiene. Carol, tell me more about this psychiatrist."

"There's nothing to tell."

"I know one thing," she said. "When I lie down on a leather couch, my skirt rides up all the way. I've had experience of *that*, believe me. Did you have trouble with your skirt riding up?"

"You don't wear your skirt," I said. God knows why I said it: I was just unhinged.

She gave a wild screech.

I said, "You get completely undressed—"

"Oh, *no!*"

"Sure. You get completely undressed, and then you put on one of those hospital nightgown things."

"You do?" she whispered.

"A psychiatrist is like any other doctor."

"And you lie there, in a nightgown, telling him all about your love life? Doesn't he get ideas?"

"He's a *doctor*, you fool."

"But even so . . ." Her voice drifted away. Then she said, "You know, Carol, it sounds kind of a fascinating experience."

"Yeah, and you get it for free. Other people have to pay twenty-five bucks an hour."

"No kidding." She was impressed.

Miss Webley stood up to leave, and the class stood up with her. Everybody, I noticed, had taken a full step forward in evolution. They were erect, chins up, chests out. I gulped my coffee, and then Donna and I followed the crowd back to the classroom.

Donna said, "You know what's next on the agenda, don't you? That test."

"Oh, God, I'd forgotten."

But it wasn't too bad. We were each given a mimeographed sheet with twenty airport codes which we had to identify, and six aircraft terms which we merely had to associate with definitions; and as soon as we completed our answers we took them to Miss Webley, who sat quietly at her desk watching us. Donna was the first to hand in her paper, and I was surprised when Miss Webley called out, "That's very good, Donna. All your answers are correct. One hundred percent." Alma was only a little slower: a couple of the aircraft terms confused her, but she managed to make ninety percent. I lagged behind because my mind kept wandering away from the subject in hand, apparently preferring to meditate on Dr. Ray Duer. I scraped through with the required ninety percent, which didn't cheer me very much since almost everybody else scored the full one hundred percent, including both French girls. A brainy bunch, I realized. They had a lot more than good looks.

For the rest of the morning, Miss Webley chatted about the history and organization of Magna International Airlines, and wound up the session by giving us about five thousand more terms and definitions, not about aircraft in particular but about flying in general. Of course. This was a whole new world, with its own vocabulary which *had* to be learned. Words like deadheading and overfly and stacking and stopover and positive and holding. Not to mention a slew of abbreviations which we had to memorize so that we could decipher them at a moment's notice, such as OVWX, which means passed over a scheduled stop on account of weather, and RTN, which is a rather elaborate way of writing *routine*, and ETA and ETD, which mean, respectively, estimated time of arrival and departure. "I hope you'll remember all this, girls," Miss Webley said, "because it will come in a test." We gave a token groan, and she gave us a sweet smile.

We went to lunch at twelve-thirty, and I tore down to the cafeteria looking for Jurgy. It's ridiculous how the human brain works: I'd practically come out in a rash, worrying all morning about her interview with Mrs. Montgomery, and I just couldn't wait to find out what had happened. She was sitting alone at a table, with a cup of coffee and a doughnut in front of her; and for a moment I was scared out of my wits. She was *so* alone, and her face was *so* grim.

I hurried over to her and said in a whisper, "Hi, Jurgy. How did it go?"

She gave me a strange look, as if she couldn't understand why I was interested. "Okay."

"Really okay?"

"Yeah."

"Well, thank God," I said, and collapsed onto a chair beside her.

Getting any further information was like pulling a tooth. Most girls are ready to bare their souls at the drop of a hat, but not Jurgy. Finally she said in her flat, dry way, "I was only up there for a minute. Mrs. Montgomery explained, Dr. Schwartz has to report anything out of the usual to her, and it'll go on my medical record, and that's all."

"Oh, boy, what a relief," I said. "Didn't I tell you Mrs. Montgomery is a swell person?"

She gave me another strange look, and changed the subject abruptly. She said, "Miss Pierce went on a rampage in class this morning. We all have to get our hair cut tonight, or else."

"Miss Webley did the same to us."

She turned her head and stared into the middle distance. "I can cut hair. I'll do yours, if you like."

"Why, Jurgy! That's marvelous!"

She smiled grimly. "You trust me?"

"Sure. It'll save me having to go out looking for a hairdresser."

"Okay. Could you just trim mine at the back?"

"I can try."

She receded into the middle distance again, and I didn't press her any further. It was an odd little episode, and I couldn't quite figure out what it meant. I suppose she'd come to the conclusion that every man's hand wasn't turned against her, and this was how she expressed it.

After lunch we buckled down to work in earnest. Miss Webley gave us an outline of the various subjects we had to learn, and when she finished we were all rigid with shock. It was staggering. We had to be familiar, in absolute detail, with every type of plane the company operated; we had to know about all the passenger-service equipment and all the emergency equipment on each plane; we had to know about cabin management and preflight duties and dining service and liquor service; we had to know about all the forms that had to be filled out in triplicate or quadruplicate—zillions of forms that an airplane can't possibly fly without; we had to know first aid, we had to know emergency procedures (that is, in addition to knowing about emergency *equipment*); we had to know about hostess regulations and agreements and union regulations and how to bid for flights, and so on, practically forever.

"Now, girls," Miss Webley said, "we still have some itsy-bitsy little airplanes which we occasionally use on domestic routes where it obviously wouldn't be economical to use a larger airplane. The Martin 404, for example. It's possible you'll start your careers on these planes, and they really couldn't be more fun to fly in. The nicest thing about them is that they only carry one hostess, so you see, if *you're* the hostess you're in complete charge of the cabin during the entire flight, you're the queen bee. It's delightful, I assure you. There's nobody to interfere with you, you just do things your own sweet way."

So we began to learn the Martin 404, which had only two engines and carried a mere forty passengers. "My God," Donna whispered. "Did you hear that? One queen bee to take care of forty passengers, can you imagine?"

"Yeah," I said.

"And on your nuptial flight, what's more."

"Quiet, girls," Miss Webley said.

There was a cigar-shaped diagram in the Manual, representing the fuselage of the plane, and for two hours Miss Webley explained it in detail; and this was another staggering experience, because that itsy-bitsy airplane had so many *things*. The jump seat, where the hostess sat, was obvious enough; and the rows of seats, where the passengers sat; and the galley, up forward, where she prepared meals and refreshments for her little family of forty—all this you *expected*. But then there was the heating system, which the queen bee controlled, and the ventilating system, which she also controlled; and panels over the seats with reading lights and call buttons and vents and oxygen; and a public-address system; and lights for the galley and the companionway and the aft ramp and the baggage ramp, night lights and lavatory lights and a door warning light and emergency lights—a whole infinity of lights. Then there were fire extinguishers. A hand ax. An emergency chute; emergency exits with ropes; a first aid kit, and God knows what else. I swear, that plane was crammed with more things than you could shake a stick at.

"It's very simple, really," Miss Webley said. "You won't have any difficulty learning it. We'll have a little test on it tomorrow morning after your coffee break."

Somebody, braver than the rest of us, said in a weepy voice, "But, Miss Webley, you told us we had to get our hair cut tonight."

Miss Webley said gaily, "Well, that won't take you long, surely."

Another girl said, "Miss Webley, we also ought to get to a supermarket tonight to buy food and stuff."

"But, girls, marketing won't take you more than a few minutes. Come, come, now. You aren't afraid of a test on the little old Martin 404, are you? Why, I'm certain you'd all get one hundred percent if I gave you a test right this minute."

Nobody even murmured. Nobody even moved an eyelash.

She looked at her watch. "We still have half an hour left, so let's talk about passenger safety, the use of seat belts, and so on."

On we went to the use of seat belts.

By the end of the afternoon we were all exhausted—except, of course, Miss Webley, who continued to look as pretty and as bright and as unruffled as a daisy. Riding back in the pink-and-blue bus, scarcely anybody uttered a word; and in a left-handed way it was encouraging because at least I wasn't alone in feeling that the inside of my head was packed with nothing but sawdust. The next four weeks loomed ahead like the steppes of Central Asia, an extraordinary sensation to have while one is speeding through the sunny avenues of Miami Beach.

Donna said, as soon as we were in our room, "Well, I know what *I'm* going to do."

I said, "What?" She was a bright girl. She might have

106

dreamed up something brilliant to solve our problems, like mass hypnotism.

She was tearing off her clothes. She said, "Queen Bee, honey, I'm going to crawl into my swimsuit, and I'm going to crawl down to that pool, and I'm going to crawl into that water, and then I'm going to sit in that good old sun and relax. Boy! The way I feel now, I'm no good to man or beast."

I said, "Donna, you have the right idea. I think I'll join you."

"Okay. But make it snappy. Don't let's waste the precious moments."

She put on a fairly respectable green swimsuit, and I put on my black one-piece number, and just as we were about to leave, in our robes and slippers, the telephone rang. I nearly jumped out of my skin, I hadn't heard that sound for so long. There was a telephone in our room, near my bed, and another in Jurgy and Annette's room; but it hadn't occurred to me that they actually worked.

I said, "Now who can that be?"

"Answer it and find out," Donna said.

I picked up the receiver and said, "Hello," and a refined female voice said, "Is Miss Thompson there?"

"Yes. Speaking."

"Oh, Miss Thompson, I'm calling from Mr. Courtenay's office. Would you please come down to see Mr. Courtenay as soon as it's convenient?"

It sounded so ominous that I went numb at once. I said, "Why?"

"Mr. Courtenay will explain that when he sees you. Thank you, Miss Thompson."

I put the receiver back and sat down on my bed. Trouble. It could only mean trouble. Mudface had done it again. Donna said, "What's wrong?"

"I have to go to Courtenay's office."

"What does he want?"

"How do I know? I guess I've broken some damned rule and he's going to bawl me out."

"Oh, nuts. What rule can you have broken?"

"Your guess is as good as mine."

She said, "I'll come with you, Carol. We'll both go down to see him. If he wants to bawl you out he'll have to bawl me out, too."

I looked up at her gratefully. She was a pillar of strength.

I sighed and slid out of my robe, and pulled down one of the straps of my black swimsuit; and she said sharply, as if she thought I'd gone out of my mind, "What are you doing?"

"Changing."

"What on earth for?"

"Donna, we aren't allowed to go into the main part of the hotel unless we're properly dressed."

Her eyes popped open. "You mean, you're getting dressed again? You're going to put on a *dress*, and a *girdle*, and *stockings?*"

"We have to."

"And then you're going to come back, and take them all off again, and get into your swimsuit?"

"That's right."

"You're crazy!"

"I'm not crazy. The rules may be crazy. But I'm not crazy."

"Everything's crazy," she yelled at me. "I seem to have stepped into a crazy world." She took off her slippers and threw them at the wall, one by one. Then she calmly began to change.

We both put on white dresses, perhaps through some subconscious idea that we might appease Mr. Courtenay by slinking into his presence looking like a couple of lost Vestal virgins. But there was no need. We found him sitting in state at a vast blond desk in a vast blond room, decorated in simple splendor with blond furniture and a blond carpet and he greeted us with such enthusiasm that I began to wonder immediately what the hell was really going on.

"Miss Thompson! And Miss Stewart! What a pleasure! You *both* came down to see me! How delightful!" He beamed at me, but he practically blew a fuse over Donna.

She said, "Gee, Mr. Courtenay, I've felt so *terrible* about the other night. You were just so gracious to us, and we had such a divine dinner; and then when we were leaving we couldn't *find* you to *thank* you for your hospitality. Why, Mr. Courtenay, you must have thought we were the *rudest* people."

He and Donna stopped pelting each other with roses eventually, and at last he came to the point. "Now, Miss Thompson." He shook all over laughing. "I have a surprise for you."

I shook all over, but not with laughter. "Yes, Mr. Courtenay?"

"Would you be kind enough to come with me?"

Donna and I glanced at each other in wonderment and went out to the lobby with him. He led the way to the elevators; an elevator boy snapped to attention; Mr. Courtenay merely pointed to the floor when we entered; the elevator boy said, "Yes, *sir*," as the doors closed; and when the doors opened again we stepped out into a huge garage which I realized must be underneath the hotel. Not altogether a brilliant thought, but then my mind wasn't altogether at its brilliant best. I was in a complete fog.

Mr. Coutenay snapped his fingers at one of the attendants, pointed at me, and the attendant said, "*Yessir*," and sped away as if he'd been shot out of a catapult. This, apparently, was the big moment. Mr. Courtenay turned to me, took an envelope from a side pocket of his black jacket, handed it to me with a smile, and said, "This, my dear young lady, will explain all."

I opened the envelope; I took out the message inside. It had been scribbled with a red ballpoint pen on a sheet of Hotel Charleroi notepaper.

Dear Miss Thompson—I rented it for a month from the rental people—so you can get around and see Florida—and see the sights while you're here.—There's plenty to see that's really worth your while.—Remember?—Indian villages—sponge divers—and if you get a chance to—get down to see the Keys.

Kind regards,
N.B.

And, as I finished reading it, the garage attendant pulled up beside us in a brand-new cream-colored Chevrolet convertible.

"Oh, no!" Donna cried.

Mr. Courtenay said, "N.B.—you know, Mr. Brangwyn—felt you should have some means of transportation while you are here with us, Miss Thompson. Very considerate fellow, N.B. So, by courtesy of the rental people, he has placed this little car at your disposal. A charming gesture, in my opinion."

"Carol! From Mr. Brangwyn!" Donna was almost beside

herself. "Why, Mr. Courtenay, I never heard of anything so sweet!"

"I've known N.B. over a period of many years," Mr. Courtenay said, "and I have always found him most generous, generous in the extreme."

Donna cried, "It's an Impala, Carol! Did you ever see anything so pretty?"

It was so pretty that I wanted to cry. It had red-and-cream upholstery, and a red-leather dashboard, and white-wall tires, and it had Mr. Brangwyn's heart in it tied up in a bouquet of utter kindness; and even if it had been a Model T Ford I would still have wanted to cry.

"You lucky thing, you," Donna said.

Mr. Courtenay said, "Well, Miss Thompson?"

"I can't accept it."

Donna said, "What?"

"I can't accept it. Mr. Courtenay, I'm sorry, I can't accept it."

He was watching me with a cool smile.

Donna said, "Honestly, Carol—"

An attendant called, "Mr. Courtenay, sir: wanted on the telephone," and Mr. Courtenay excused himself politely and left us.

"You *idiot*," Donna said.

I said, "Listen, Donna, you haven't been through what I've been through. Donna, I never did anything like this in my life, I've never accepted gifts from strangers. I'd feel like the worst kind of gold-digger."

"Honey, you're just soft in the head—"

Mr. Courtenay reappeared and said, "I'm afraid I'll have to return up above, my dear young ladies. Some guests are departing, and I must speed them on their way. I shall see you later, I hope." He smiled at me again coolly, ever so coolly, and added, "Have no fears, Miss Thompson. There are no strings attached to this; you can accept with a clear conscience, I assure you. N.B. is not at all that sort of fellow."

He beamed at Donna, she beamed back at him; and when he left she returned to the attack. "Really, Carol, you surprise me. You're supposed to be sophisticated, and here you're acting as if you'd crawled out of some hole-in-the-ground in the Ozarks. You're acting like a real peasant."

"Donna, don't talk to me like that."

"I will, too. You don't seem to realize, a gesture like this,

110

renting a car for you for one month, means absolutely nothing to a man like Brangwyn. Why, my God, he probably does it all the time, he thinks no more of doing it than sending his friends a box of cigars. Don't you see?"

"No."

She sighed. "Look: if he gave you a present like, say, a gold wrist watch, or a gold bracelet, I'd be the first to say to you, *Carol, send it back*. But this is completely different. He's doing you a service. Honey, if you rode in a taxi with him, would you fight to the death when he paid the taxi driver?"

"Donna—"

"Just listen, don't argue with every word I say. Carol, this is Brangwyn's way of providing you with your own private taxi service, that's all. You heard what Courtenay said: there aren't any strings attached to it. It's a *taxi* service. And, boy! Do we need one! It's manna from heaven."

I said, "Oh, sure, it's fine for you to speak. You weren't on the carpet in front of Mr. Garrison and Mrs. Montgomery—"

"Who's going to know, Carol?" she said. "Just answer me that. Who's going to know this car came from Brangwyn?"

"It's no good, Donna. You can't talk me into accepting it."

She stamped her foot angrily. She glared and she swore. I said, "I'm sorry. That's how I feel."

"Okay," she said. "Okay. Okay, okay, okay. You win."

We stood looking at the pretty thing. I had to sigh. I love driving, and driving a convertible is like eating chocolate éclairs.

Donna said, "Carol."

"What?"

"Gee, honey, you're breaking my heart. I can't bear to leave it, it's such a dream. Let's use it just to do our marketing tonight. What do you say? Just this once, for the hell of it, to the supermarket and back."

She was nothing but a female Satan. I couldn't resist her any longer, all my resistance collapsed. I said weakly, "Will you drive?"

"You bet."

"We'll have to take Jurgy," I said. "I'll have to go and find her."

She said, "I knew you had some sense in that thick head of yours. I'll tell you what: I'll drive round to the main entrance and wait for you and Jurgy there." She called the attendant, who was looking in a puzzled way under the hood of a big Mercedes. "Hey, mister, does this jalopy have gas in it?"

"Yes, ma'am. She's filled up with gas."

"Thank you." Then she said to me, "Get going, baby, time's a-wasting," and she opened the door of the Impala, smiling as if she were on her way to Paradise.

I found Jurgy sitting by the pool, wearing the sunsuit and the rather odd punchbowl-shaped straw hat which were her usual beach costume. She was studying her Manual and scowling. I said, "Donna and I have the use of a car to go to the supermarket. Want to come along?"

"Sure."

"Fine. Get changed as fast as you can and meet me in the lobby."

She took off like a rocket, and I meandered back to the hotel and sat—shoulders back, knees together—in a straight-backed leather chair, watching the elevators. There must have been something very formidable about sitting like this: men kept looking at me, but instead of looking me over with care from top to toe they'd almost instantly look away, as if I were a nun, or a visiting midwife, or possibly a guy from the Central Intelligence Agency who'd dressed up in female garb in order to get his hands on them and whisk them away to headquarters for some intensive questioning. Miss Webley certainly knew how a girl should sit to discourage male attention.

Jurgy was down in about three minutes flat, wearing the same dress she'd worn to class; and off we went to the supermarket. We bought practically everything in sight from soapflakes to peanut butter, ending up with three huge packages and a bill that came to $23.37. It couldn't be helped because many of the things were basic. Housekeeping is like that: the first investment comes as a shock.

We began to drive back slowly, enjoying the dreamy Impala and the sunshine and the palms sprouting out of the sidewalks and the stares of the people on the streets who seemed to find the three of us kind of interesting; and suddenly Donna cried, "Hey! Look at the cute beauty shop!" She slammed on the brakes, and we were nearly rammed by the car behind us. It didn't bother her a bit.

We looked; and sure enough it was as elegant a beauty shop as I've seen anywhere.

She said, "I'm going to ask them if they can take me now."

I said, "Donna, we have to get back to the hotel."

"But, cream, you know what Miss Webley said: I have to get my hair cut tonight."

I repeated, "We have to get back to the hotel."

"Okay," she said. "Drop me off, then. You take the car and I'll grab a taxi back."

I said, "I don't want to drive the car."

"But why not?"

"You know why not," I said.

She said, "Okay, *you* take a taxi. I'll pay for it. And as soon as I'm through in the beauty shop I'll bring the car back with the groceries."

I was furious with her. I said, "All right, we'll do it that way. But we can pay for our own taxi, thanks." Jurgy and I climbed out, and some second sense made me say, "We'll take a couple of the packages with us, so at least we can get dinner started."

"Please yourself," Donna said.

We took a taxi back to the hotel, and Jurgy didn't even ask what the scene was all about. It was a relief. She knew when to hush up.

Donna returned a few minutes before ten-thirty. She didn't say where she'd been and nobody asked her. She'd had her hair cut and set, and she'd also had a manicure. She looked very pleased with herself, like the cat that's swallowed the cream, and the cream in her case was obviously gin. She wasn't drunk, but she stank of liquor.

We stayed up until one-thirty learning the Martin 404, and terms and definitions, and abbreviations like OVWX and RTN. Then, at five forty-five, Donna woke me gently and said, "Hey. How about a dip in the pool before breakfast?"

I stared at her. She was her usual morning self, naked as a newborn baby, beautiful and friendly and full of the devil.

I said, "Okay."

Going to class that morning, there was a strange silence in the bus. The girls hardly spoke to each other, and when they did they kept their voices low. This was only our third morning, and I wondered about it—in this short period of time we'd all changed. Even Donna had changed, though she was putting up a fight every inch of the way. The silence in the bus might have been due to the fact that we were all tired: I think every one of us had stayed up long past midnight to learn about the insides of the itsy-bitsy little old Martin 404. Or the silence might have been due to sheer nerves, wondering what new complications Miss Webley had dreamed up for this blessed new morn. But I think it was something more fundamental (I love that word and I intend to use it whenever I possibly can for the rest of my life). We were under pressure and we knew it, and we knew the pressure was going to get fiercer and fiercer and I suppose each of us was wondering exactly how much pressure she could take, how bad it would get, just where the breaking point would come, and what would happen then. I mean, I just couldn't contemplate being thrown off this training course. My ego absolutely would never survive such a disgrace.

Miss Webley gave us a cursory inspection when we arrived, commenting—fairly leniently, for her—on our haircuts. There was no comment on mine, good or bad, and I heaved a sigh of relief. Jurgy had done a very neat job. I wasn't going to win any beauty contests on the strength of it; but at least it was adequate. I'd rather butchered hers, in return, and with her usual calmness she hadn't uttered a word of protest—she didn't seem to care, as long as her appearance met Magna's standards. Donna was rebuked very gently: her hair was still too long and bushy. And it wouldn't do, Miss Webley pointed out, because the uniform hat wouldn't sit properly on that kind of hair-do. "Remember, girls," Miss Webley said, "you're only allowed one small, plain barette. No combs, no hair nets, no visible bobby pins." You could almost hear the rustling of small feathered wings as sex flew out of the window. Miss Webley gave Alma a sweet smile, but didn't say anything about those luscious black curls. Presumably the word hadn't come down from the Chief Prosecutor, brooding in his skull-lined study on the second floor.

We spent the first part of the morning on hostess regulations, and it became clearer and clearer that the roof could fall in on you at practically any minute. Magna International Airlines expected discipline, and how. When you were supposed to be on duty there weren't any two ways about it: you *were* on duty. If you failed to report for a flight assignment, you were a dead duck. And there was a situation called Involuntary Release from Duty Assignment, in which the captain of the airplane could suspend you for being stewed, or refusing to obey legal orders, or any other irregular conduct. It made sense to me. Even Donna agreed, with reservations. "Oh, sure. Imagine being served tomato soup in a thunderstorm by a pie-eyed stewardess. But it still smacks of the army."

After coffee break we had the dreaded test. And again I realized I was with a bunch of female geniuses—hundred percents popped up everywhere. It would have impressed even the Dean of M.I.T.—not that all these girls were ready for the Nobel Prize, but how often do brains and beauty go together? Hard-luck Thompson made her usual ninety, Donna stunned me by racking up ninety-five, proving that fundamentally she was quite a brain, since I'd expected her to get a nice fat zero after her stupid behavior the previous evening; and Alma, bless her heart, kept up to par with the same score as mine.

Then to kill the morning, we went on to the check list for Martin aircraft, all the things a hostess has to do (a) before the passengers board, (b) when and as they board, (c) in flight, and (d) on landing. There weren't any more than seventy *numbered* operations, and it actually didn't look any more complicated than the countdown for a three-stage rocket before it's fired from Cape Canaveral. One girl, one female with one head, was expected to do all that? Miss Webley, however, seemed to think it could be managed without difficulty by any normal three-year-old child; and the pressure was on again. Another test. "After your coffee break tomorrow, girls," Miss Webley said, reeking with sweetness and light. In the afternoon we began to learn how to use the galley on the Martin, a contraption which looked like a huge stainless-steel kitchen sink, except that it was actually a self-contained home from home. It was so complicated, with a huge electrical panel covered with switches and lights, and a six-drawer cabinet here, and a dozen doors there, that I was filled with panic. Even Donna looked shocked. How on earth could we expect to learn to operate this monster in four weeks?

"Girls," Miss Webley said, "it's really perfectly simple." She added, I suppose to help us relax, "It's really nothing, compared to the galleys on the larger planes, believe me."

For the remainder of the afternoon period she went on with safety hints. Everybody laughed when she said, "Now, girls, you have to be very careful not to walk into propellers," but nobody was laughing when she'd concluded her remarks on the subject. And we were all completely silent when she spoke about the engines on jets.

And then there was oxygen. I've always had a respect for oxygen because it's essential to life; but apparently the airline was mad for it. It, too, had its dangers. For example, if you were inhaling oxygen, you weren't allowed to smoke at the same time. If you were even merely sitting beside a passenger who was inhaling oxygen, you weren't allowed to smoke.

"Because," Miss Webley said, "oxygen is inflammable. You know that, don't you?"

"Yes," we said.

Then she said, after a little pause, "Girls: I think you're a wonderful group. I think every one of you can make it, if you really want to. Work hard. It's worth while." She turned away. "That's all. Good night."

"Good night, Miss Webley." Good night, sweet dreams to you.

Donna said, the moment we entered 1412, "Swim?"

I said, "Sure."

"All right. But make it snappy."

I said, "Donna, don't push me. I'm tired. Let me get changed in my own time."

"Honey, I have to be back at five-fifteen to see that psychiatrist man."

I'd forgotten. After lunch, Miss Webley had read out a list of appointments with Dr. Duer, with an explanation that Dr. Duer wished to chat with each of the girls as soon as possible and he would therefore continue his interviews throughout the evenings this week in his room at the Charleroi. Both Donna and Alma were seeing him after class today, and when Miss Webley completed reading the list I felt a little pang of misery because my name wasn't included. True, I'd had my brief moment of truth, but it somehow didn't seem enough. I wanted more, more; and since that weird electro-spiritual look passed between us I hadn't seen hide nor hair of him. The ghastly thought had occurred to me that the same thing might happen with all the girls he interviewed; the electrical treatment might be included at no extra cost. But no. Impossible. Unthinkable. He'd scowled, he'd been upset, he'd been annoyed and disturbed, as if by allowing it to take place he'd violated his Freudian Oath, or whatever psychiatrists swear to when they receive their diplomas and can go out into the world to practice their Black Art. In a way—thinking in purely female terms—this was the most interesting part of the whole business. The scowl, the brusque farewell. Why? What had I done to *his* psyche? I had a faint idea what he'd done to mine; but what devastation had I wrought in return?

Alma was lying on her bed staring at the ceiling. I said to her, "Are you coming down for a swim with us?"

"I rest."

"Tired?"

"Tired? I am never tired. I rest before I go to Dr. Duer."

For the fraction of a second I blacked out with pure jealousy. This sexy, bulgy, voluptuous, honey-eyed dame alone with poor innocent Dr. Duer—the scented Florida air drifting in through his window, the strains of Hawaiian dinner music lilting up from the terrace—no! I couldn't let it happen! And then sanity returned. He wasn't so innocent. He was hard-headed, a Magna man. He wouldn't be taken in by anything so obvious. Or would he?

"Come on," Donna said. "What's the matter with you, Carol? You're acting as if you're in a trance."

So in hardly more than a twinkling I was out of my dress and girdle and stockings and into my black swimsuit and robe and slippers and, of course, just as we were about to leave the telephone rang.

I said, "See? It never fails. You answer it this time, Donna."

She pounced on the receiver, said "Hello" violently, listened, glanced across at me as if to make sure I was still inhabiting this vale of tears, and said, "Oh. Are you speaking from Mr. Courtenay's office?—You are?—Well, this is Miss Stewart. Will you *please* tell Mr. Courtenay that Miss Thompson and I are on our way down to the swimming pool at this very moment, and would he be a dear, dear man and contact us there?—He will? How nice of him! Thank you so much."

She put the receiver down and said, "Courtenay. He wanted you to come to his office."

"Oh, God. What for this time?"

"Who knows? Maybe you're going to get a submarine for a month."

I said, "Yeah, and I know who'd be using it."

The pool area was crowded with young beauties. Jurgy was there, and most of her class, a few of them swimming and the rest frowning over their Manuals, obviously trying to memorize the seventy steps in the Martin check list, or perhaps trying to figure out what all the switches on the galley panel were supposed to do. A dozen or so hostess-hoppers were hanging around, young men and middle-aged men and older men, all agog at so much flesh and yet absolutely baffled by what this flesh was occupying itself with; and it was a glorious sight to see one of the guys make the supreme effort, walk over to one of the girls and shoot his line, and get either a frosty stare or a curt, "No, thanks." These girls were in earnest. I knew exactly how they felt.

Donna and I fooled around in the pool for about five minutes and then lay back in chaises longues soaking up that golden sun. We'd both begun to show the effects of Florida, as if we'd been lightly fried in Crisco, and my only regret was that when all my clothes were off I looked like a new and rather repulsive kind of zebra. But Donna had heard that there was a solarium on the roof of the hotel where we could legally expose the whole of ourselves; and we'd agreed to spend as many hours up there as we could in the coming weekend.

The early evening peace was shattered by a page bawling my name. He started bawling it about a mile away, and as he came nearer the noise was awful. I grabbed him as soon as I could locate him, and he gave me a sly up-and-down grin and said, "From Mr. Courtenay, miss," and handed me an envelope.

I opened it, and saw that red ballpoint scribble on a Hotel Charleroi letterhead. It had only come *via* Mr. Courtenay; not *from* Mr. Courtenay.

Dear Miss Thompson—Maxwell just tells me you can't accept the car. Too bad. Well, okay—if that's how you feel, that's how you feel.—But it's already been paid for, so why send it back?—Maybe the other girls can make use of it and if they can they're welcome.—A car is a must if you're going to see the Indian villages—sponge divers—etc.

Kind regards,
N.B.

I walked back to the pool, feeling like the worst heel in existence, and Donna said, "What's the bad news?"

I gave her the letter.

She read it, and read it again, and said, "Carol, you know what?"

"What?"

"This Brangwyn is one hell of a nice guy."

"I know he's a nice guy."

"You shouldn't treat him like dirt."

I could have killed her. "I'm not treating him like dirt."

"Cream, you really are."

I said, "What am I supposed to do? Mr. Garrison and Mrs. Montgomery warned me solemnly not to have anything to do with him. So what am I supposed to do?"

"Are you going to let Garrison and Mrs. Montgomery run your whole life?"

"They're running it this month."

"Oh, cream, show some guts."

I was so mad with her I couldn't speak. I turned and began to walk away.

She scrambled off her chaise longue and ran after me. "Hey! Carol!"

"What do you want?"

"Relax, relax. Tell me something. Are you going to use the car?"

"No."

"You're just going to let it sit there in the garage?"

"If I'm not allowed to associate with him, I can't accept gifts from him." Quite a word, *associate*. It sounded as if, in the State of Connecticut, it was punishable by a minimum of twelve ducks on the ducking stool.

Donna said, "In that case—" She stopped and dimpled.

"In that case, what?"

"Well, in that case, do you have any objections if I use

it now and then? I mean, Brangwyn says in his letter tha[t] any of the girls is welcome to it."

"Do whatever you like."

"Honey, don't be so snooty about it. I thought I'd *ask* you.—Coming upstairs?"

"No. I think I'll stay down here for a while."

She gave me an amused look and sauntered away. I joined Jurgy and some of her classmates and sat listening to their girlish chatter, but I was seething inside. Donna couldn't have upset me more. Nobody, ever, had accused me of lacking guts. All my life I've been too defiant of everything and everybody, which is precisely why I was fired from each of my three jobs. But what hurt most was that I knew Donna was fundamentally right. As a free human being I couldn't permit *anyone*, not even the President of the United States, to say to me, Thou shalt not speak to him, or her; thou shalt not be seen with him, or her; thou shalt not associate with him, or her; thou shalt not sleep, if thou wantest, with him, or her. So why had I allowed Mr. Garrison and Mrs. Montgomery to order me not to associate with a certain person? Why had I agreed? Because, I suppose, just as *I* had every right, *they* had every right, too. They didn't want the reputation of their precious training school besmirched, which seemed reasonable enough. But—

Oh, God. It was useless. One could go around in circles forever. They were right and I was right, and they were wrong and I was wrong; and what I really needed was Aristotle or Bertrand Russell or somebody to sit down beside me and get the whole mishmash straightened out.

Jurgy said to me, after a while, "You know the time? It's a quarter of seven. Don't you think we ought to go up and fix supper?"

"Gee, is it as late as that? No wonder I'm starving." I wasn't, really. I was just feeling sick and miserable.

We went up to 1412, and I'd no sooner entered the door than Donna leaped off her bed and pointed a finger at me and howled, "You! You! Carol Thompson, I ought to poke you right in the eye."

I looked at her in stupefaction. "What have I done now?"

She doubled up with laughter. She was so hysterical she couldn't say a word.

I said, "Donna, what's the matter?"

"Oh, God," she said, and wiped two large tears out of her eyes. "Oh, Carol. Boy! I have to hand it to you."

"What on earth are you talking about?"

"The psychiatrist."

"You mean Dr. Duer? What about him?" Clompety-clomp, went my heart. Clompety-clomp.

She said, "Don't you remember? You lying bitch. You told me at coffee break yesterday I'd have to take off all my clothes, and put on a hospital nightgown, and lie on a leather couch, and tell him all about my love life—"

Jurgy hooted; and I couldn't help myself, I began to giggle.

Donna said, "Goddammit, Carol, I believed every word. I went down there at five-fifteen expecting a real thrill."

I said, "What happened?"

"Hell, he sat in an armchair, and I sat in an armchair, and we smoked a couple of cigarettes, and talked about skiing, and that was just about that. My God, it was about as thrilling as going to the dentist and have him tell you you don't have any cavities."

I said, "Didn't he probe into your nasty character?"

"No. Honest. We just talked about skiing, and the Lodge, and how my father started the place from scratch thirty years ago—"

I said, "Baby, that's the kiss of death. As soon as you mention your father to a psychiatrist he has you by the short hairs."

She flushed. "No kidding, Carol."

"Ask Jurgy."

Jurgy became white, and said, "I wouldn't know." And suddenly and unexpectedly I realized that all three of us, in one way or another, had father trouble. But it didn't matter. Everybody has a father, everybody is influenced to some degree by his, or her, father, and I've never understood why it should cause such a fuss. It's the most natural thing in the whole wide world, having or not having a father complex.

I said, "Where's Alma? Is she down with Dr. Duer?"

Donna became hysterical again.

I said, "Stewart, what's the matter with you tonight? You're acting real nutty."

She choked. "Carol, I swear to you, I nearly had you paged to come up to the apartment. I almost *died*."

"Why? What happened?"

"Well, when I came back from seeing Duer, Alma asked me what the routine was, just as I asked you yesterday.

And, honey, I pulled the same gag. I told her she'd have to take off all her clothes, and crawl into this horrible white hospital nightgown that didn't fit anywhere and gaped all over the place, and lie down on a couch—"

I said, "You *didn't!* You *didn't* tell Alma that!"

The tears were pouring down Donna's face. "Honey, I did. But you'll never guess what happened next."

I said weakly, "What?"

"Carol, she took it all in. And then she went into her Maria Callas act and said, nevair, nevair would she allow a hospital nightgown to touch her skin; and she swished into the bathroom and locked the door and stayed there for an hour. When she came out she was made up to the eyes and smelling to high heaven of perfume and—" Donna's voice rose to a shriek.

I shook her. "Tell me. Tell me."

"You'll never believe it, Carol. She was wearing the sexiest black silk nightgown I ever saw in my life. Honest, it was enough to make your eyes pop out. Ballooning at the bosom, and pulled in tight across the belly—"

I said, "You mean she went down to Dr. Duer like *that?*"

"Just like that. With a little embroidered jacket over her shoulders, so she wouldn't be arrested on the way."

I said, "Oh, my God," and sat down on my bed.

Donna said, "I asked her what she thought she was doing, and she stuck her nose in the air and said, if she had to be interviewed in a nightgown she'd be interviewed in a *respectable* nightgown. Carol, it was absolutely *lewd.*"

I put both my hands over my face to shut out the sight.

Annette crept in from the next room and said in a sad little voice, "What's all the hilarity about?"

"Hey," Donna said. "Look at this little old Queen Bee."

I looked at Annette. She was pathetic. Her face was pale, her eyes were puffy.

She said, "I was trying to sleep, that's all."

"You've been crying," Donna said.

"Yes."

I said, "What's wrong, sweetie?"

"I'm just homesick, Carol. It's silly, isn't it?"

Poor kid. She was really low. We did our best to cheer her up, but without much success; and then Alma returned like a summer storm.

The embroidered bed jacket was a thing of beauty, but

it didn't exactly blot out the Alma that lay beneath. It was merely one of those exquisite trifles which a girl clutches to herself when a strange man enters the room, as a prelude to giving a piercing shriek. Underneath this piece of frippery was the black nightgown, which was breathtaking— just the sheerest black transparent nothingness, with lace attached. You see girls wearing them in magazines, but I never imagined that anybody wore anything of this kind in real life.

She strode over to Donna and snapped, "You lie to me."

Donna hardly flinched. "I did?"

"You tell me there is leather cooch. I will have to stretch out on leather cooch. There is *no* leather cooch. Just chair."

"That's funny," Donna said. "I could have sworn there was a leather cooch. How did Dr. Duer like your nightgown, Alma?"

"He was very gentleman."

"He was?"

"Certainly. Very gentleman person."

"Don't keep us palpitating!" Donna cried. "What did he say?"

"Ha-ha! You want to know?"

"Sure. What happened when you walked in wearing this outfit?"

Alma shrugged one shoulder. "I walk in, that is all. I take off my little coat. I put it down. I say to Dr. Duer, Please, Dr. Duer, you wish to have me wear hospital nightgown, but these cheap cotton stuff itch my skin, so if you like I wear these old nightgown of my own. And he say, Perfectly okay, sit down, have a cigarette. Then when I am sat, he say, Perhaps you better wear little coat otherwise you catch chill. And I laugh, ha-ha-ha, and say, Doctor, you are very amusing man. These is Florida, remember (I say to him), these is warm climate. And he say, That's right, pardon me."

I said helplessly, "What did he talk to you about?"

"Carola, you are intelligent girl. You know these is secret, between him and me. But a charming thing happen right in the middle of the examination—"

"Examination!" I screamed.

"The talk. The psychology. He examine my mind."

"Oh."

"Right in the middle of the examination—who walks in? Mr. Garrison! He take one look, turn red like a lobster, and run out again. Ho-ho-ho. What a joke."

I said, "Ho-ho-ho is just perfect. My God, that certainly takes care of Dr. Duer's career."

"Carola! These is Dr. Duer's profession, to examine women. He has sacred duty. He just laugh and say, Garrison learn to knock first, next time. Then, very gentleman, he apologize for interruption, and we go right on where we leave off."

"Well, you can say that for Dr. Duer," Donna said. "He sure has what the French call savoir faire."

I said in blind fury, "Donna, you know what you've done? I'll tell you what you've done. You've just cooked the poor bastard's goose, that's all."

There was utter silence. Donna stared at me. Alma stared at me. Jurgy and Annette stared at me.

Then Donna said, "What are you talking about? Which poor bastard's goose have I cooked?"

"Duer's."

"I cooked *Duer's* goose?"

"Yes. And how."

"Okay, you tell me, and how."

"Sending Alma down like this. Sending Alma down to his apartment practically stark naked. And Garrison finding her there. *That's* how you cooked his goose."

Alma said, "Ho-ho, Carola!"

I said, "Listen, you. Go cover your damned bulges."

She said, "But, Carola! These is wonderful! You are hixed on these Dr. Duer!"

"Hixed yourself," I said, and went to the kitchenette and began to prepare our evening hamburgers.

I ate about half of my hamburger and practically choked to death on it. The girls were just as nice as they could possibly be (except Alma, who went on chuckling to herself like a clogged drain), and they carefully avoided any mention of doctors or psychiatrists or love or sex (that was quite a strain for Donna) out of deference to my upset feelings. It was pretty clear that something utterly mad had happened to me—metaphorically, Dr. Duer was sticking out all over my face—and I was even shocked by it myself. Good God, I'd only *seen* the guy four times, I'd only *spoken* to him once; and why should my nerves get jangled

124

up about him like this? Screaming at Alma. Screaming at Donna. Love? This wasn't love. This was sheer unmitigated lunacy. Even to the extent of calling him a poor bastard at the top of my lungs. That, of course, was the giveaway. Any bunch of girls has a right to jump to conclusions when one of their number suddenly starts to refer to a man as a poor bastard with tears of passion in her voice.

We buckled down to work after supper, learning the Martin 404 and the rest of the stuff, and at about nine-thirty Donna stretched and yawned and said, "I'm going out. I need a breath of fresh air." It didn't require the brain of an IBM machine to figure out that she was going down to the garage to get the Chevrolet and then on to some bar for a few martinis. I wanted to stop her but I wasn't in any shape to start a fight.

About ten minutes later I found everything utterly impossible, I was suffocating with weltschmerz, and I closed my Little Black Book and said, "I'm going down to the pool for a swim."

Jurgy said, "Want me to come with you?"

I said, "No, thanks." I planned to do some energetic diving off the spring board to cast out my devil, and if I cracked my head wide open on the bottom I didn't want her diving in to save me.

The pool was lit up like fairyland. Music drifted through from the terrace, the air was so sweet that I wanted to eat chunks of it, people sat around laughing and drinking, a few were even clinging lovingly to each other in the pale blue water. Of course, any female who indulges in an orgy of fancy diving off a springboard at night, in an illuminated pool, with a couple of dozen people watching every move she makes, is only asking to be called an exhibitionist, but I didn't give a damn. I wanted to tire myself, I wanted to get rid of a lot of energy that was playing hell with my nervous system, and I went right on. Until I came to the surface, one time, and there was Ray Duer at the edge of the pool watching me. He was wearing swim trunks and smoking a pipe.

I stared at him, and he stared back at me with a faint smile.

He said something but I couldn't hear what it was because of my bathing cap. I pulled the rubber away from one ear and called up, "What did you say?" and he called back, "Mind if I join you?"

"Come right in," I called.

He took me at my word. He plunged in with a mighty splash and came up beside me with the pipe still in his mouth.

I pointed to it and began to laugh so idiotically that I swallowed half a gallon of water and began to sink, coughing my lungs up; and for a few blessed moments he had his arm around me, supporting me as I gasped for air, still with that ridiculous pipe in his mouth.

"Okay, now?" he asked.

"Yesh," I said; and I would have been, if the pool attendant hadn't shouted, "Hey, there! No smoking in the pool." That set me off again, and I nearly expired. It wasn't *so* funny, but it practically *killed* me, and Ray Duer had to help me to the side.

When we'd both recovered our equilibrium we sat down at a table, and he looked ruefully at his pipe and said, "Well, that's that." Fortunately, I'd brought a pack of cigarettes with me, together with book matches and lipstick and a couple of dollar bills, all wrapped in a little silk scarf; and as I offered him a cigarette he said, "Thanks, that's wonderful. Can I get you a drink?"

"Sir, we're not allowed to drink."

"That's *right*," he said. He had goofed quite genuinely. "My God, it's lucky my head is screwed on tonight." Then he said, "Don't call me sir any more."

I said, "I can't help myself. I was brought up to be horribly polite."

He said, "I don't greatly like being called sir, that's all. Particularly away from the school." He kept his eyes averted. "How about iced coffee?"

"I'd love that."

He ordered two iced coffees, and when the waiter trotted away I said, "Dr. Duer, I want to apologize for Alma di Lucca's visit to you this evening."

He looked surprised for a moment, and then he laughed. "Were you in on that?"

"It was all my fault," I said, and I explained why.

"Don't worry about it," he said. "I've had far worse things happen." He seemed amused, nothing else.

"But, Dr. Duer, I understand that Mr. Garrison walked in while Alma was with you."

"Honestly, don't worry about it."

"I was afraid it might cause trouble."

He glanced at me curiously. "Why should it cause trouble?"

"Well . . . Mr. Garrison finding a girl in a slinky black nightgown in your apartment at the hotel . . ."

"Mr. Garrison knows that's an occupational hazard."

"It is?" This time *I* was surprised. I was astounded, in fact. He was so calm, so unmoved. Girls in slinky black nightgowns—an occupational hazard. My God.

He said, laughing again, "We had a girl once who suffered from lunambulism. That's sleepwalking induced by the moon in some unexplained way. In her case, it was a full moon that caused mental disturbance." His gray eyes filled with mischief. "She came calling on me at three o'clock one morning, and she wasn't even wearing a nightgown."

That's the kind of man Thompson would naturally pick for herself, one who's chased by naked women whenever there's a full moon.

"Good gracious," I said. "What did your wife say?"

His eyes were still mischievous. "My wife didn't say anything. I'm not married."

Females are vile in this way, absolutely vile, but they can't help themselves. There are certain things that have to be established right at the start of a relationship, even though establishing them may have little effect on the future course of events. I'm ready to bet that Eve sneaked that question into her first conversation with Adam, simply because she *had* to know, and if he'd answered, "Well, as a matter of fact there does happen to be a little woman in the bushes down at the bottom of the garden," I doubt if it would have affected further events one scrap. He was the only guy in the whole world, the Ray Duer of B.C. 5000, and she had to grab him while the other little woman's head was turned —she had no alternative. I'm not saying I'd have acted like this in relation to Mrs. Ray Duer, if she had existed; I'm merely grateful to Providence that one horrible complication was absent.

I can't remember what we talked about while we drank our iced coffee. I think he mentioned the University of Southern California, where he'd done some of his research work, and I mentioned Bryn Mawr, and my father, and living in the Village. The person-to-person electricity just grew more and more intense, and I became so excited and so jittery that I smoked about eight cigarettes in a chain. I was excited simply being near him, seeing him, listening to him; everything inside me and outside me seemed to have flared up with excitement; and I was jittery because I didn't know how to control everything that was happening inside and outside me. He was smoking heavily too, and he sounded *almost* calm, *almost* collected, but he couldn't quite manage to stay remote. He didn't dare meet my eye; he didn't dare move his chair nearer to mine or even away from mine; he hardly dared to move his hands an inch. He *wanted* to break through the sound barrier of his responsibilities, his Freudian Oath and all that stuff, and he must have felt that I wanted him to; and he couldn't take the chance—here, anyway, by the side of the pool, with some of the girls sitting around, and a dozen or more hotel guests sloshing down Scotch. We were face to face, with thousands of volts of electricity about to explode between us, and he had to force himself to be a model citizen and I had to force myself to be just a thing in a one-piece black bathing suit. It was bad enough for me, but it must have been worse for him. What a blow, when you're an expert on psychology, suddenly to discover that the rival science of biology has you in its grip.

We finished my pack of cigarettes, and he called the waiter to bring two fresh packs, one for me and one for himself. At the Charleroi, naturally, cigarettes don't come as easily as that. They have to come in style, and in this case they were brought on a tray by a redhead attired as an eighteenth-century duchess. But he hardly noticed her. He gave her a vague look, and put some money on her tray, and said to me, "Would you care to walk down to the water for a minute?"

I nearly burst into tears as I answered him. "Dr. Duer, I think it's past ten-thirty and I ought to be back in my room."

"Just for a minute." His voice was grim.

"Yes, sir."

He said, "Don't call me sir."

My knees were knocking together. "No, sir."

We walked out of the pool area and through the sweet-smelling gardens that led to the beach, all hung with Chinese lanterns for my benefit because this was a gala night for me. Then we were on the cool sand, in silence and darkness, and the stars were unbelievable, a trillion million stars all shining for my benefit also. I'd forgotten my robe and he'd forgotten his—he'd even forgotten his glasses, which were lying on the table beside the stub-filled ash tray; and as we went down to the water his naked arm brushed against mine and I felt as if a great spark had flashed across the lower part of my insides. When we reached the water we stopped, although if he'd gone on walking, I would have remained beside him until we reached the coast of Africa. But we stopped, we stopped in silence, side by side, looking out over the glistening water; and he said in the same grim voice, "It's beautiful, isn't it?"

"Beautiful."

Then he said, without turning to me, "Carol."

"Yes, sir."

He swung round angrily. "I told you not to call me *sir.*"

I said, "Oh, God, I can't help myself. I'm so frightened."

"What are you frightened of?"

I could have said snakes, or crocodiles, but I said, "Myself."

"What do you mean? What do you mean, you're frightened of yourself?"

"I—I—I don't know."

He said, "God damn it. God *damn* it. It's too difficult. You know it's too difficult, don't you?"

"Yes, sir."

"*Don't call me sir.*"

"I don't know what to call you. Don't shout at me, please don't shout at me. I just don't know what to call you."

"My name is Ray."

"Ray."

"Call me Doctor in school, if you have to speak to me when Garrison's around. *Never* sir."

"Yes, sir. Yes, Ray."

"God *damn* it," he said. "God damn everything. We'd better go back."

I couldn't move a muscle.

"Did you hear me?" he said. "We'd better go back."

I'd turned to a block of ice, with a trillion million stars shining on my dead body.

He put his hand on my arm and said for the third time, "We'd better go back," as if he were warning me of something disastrous that might occur if I stayed. Then he said furiously, "I don't know what the hell is happening. I haven't stopped thinking of you since—" He didn't finish the sentence. He was filled with violence, just as I was filled with excitement and fear. And suddenly Magna International Airlines ceased to exist because of his violence, the Board of Directors ceased to exist, the Hostess Training School and Company Policy ceased to exist, even those trillion million stars were blotted out, and only Ray Duer and I remained, holding on to each other in an utter frenzy of passion. His arms were terribly hard, harder than I could ever have imagined, and his mouth was hard, and his hands were almost too strong; and I felt as if inside my body everything was drowning in an ocean of blood. I couldn't believe that love could be so hard and so fierce and so painful, and at the same time I wanted it to increase, to be harder and fiercer and more savage, until my heart became his heart and my mouth his mouth. *That* was what I wanted, to be utterly one with him, not myself separate, but utterly taken into his body and his existence. A kiss. A kiss from a man I scarcely knew, a stranger; and I wanted this total transformation.

Then all those stars returned, and Magna International Airlines, and he said, "Oh, my God, I'm mad."

"*Ray.*"

He looked at me in horror. "I'm mad, I tell you. I've gone completely insane."

"No, you haven't, Ray—"

"Don't you understand? I can't *do* this. I can't *do* it."

"But, Ray—"

He made a strange snorting noise, as if he were trying to laugh and at the same time trying not to laugh. "You thought Alma di Lucca's visit to my apartment might cause trouble. Good God! What sort of trouble do you think *this* would cause?"

I said, "Ray, don't be so upset—"

"I can't have a love affair with one of the trainees," he said in a rage. "It's *impossible*. It's an *impossible* situation."

I drew away from him. I said, "Dr. Duer, is that what I am? A little trainee you're starting an affair with?"

He snapped, "I told you, didn't I? I just *told* you. I haven't stopped thinking about you since I saw you in the restaurant the other night—since you were hauled up in front of Arnie Garrison—since I saw you in my office yesterday morning. You've been on my mind the whole time."

I said, "Please kiss me again."

"*What!*"

"Please kiss me again, please, please."

He gripped my arm, as if I were an escapee from a loony bin and said, "Come on. Let's get back."

I wanted to tell him in detail that I hadn't stopped thinking about *him*, that I loved him with all my heart, that I wanted his kiss again with all these trillions of stars shining down on us, that I couldn't live without his kiss and his body close to mine; but he strode across the sands so fast, still gripping my arm, that I had to run to keep up with him.

He stopped when he reached the gardens where the Chinese lanterns hung, and glowered at me and said, "Carol."

"Ray—"

"This mustn't happen again."

My heart sank. He spoke so harshly, so vehemently. I said, "Ray, you don't mean that."

"I do. For the time being, anyway. It mustn't happen again. It's too unfair to everybody concerned."

I said, "Very well, sir."

"Don't call me sir."

And suddenly I blew up. All my emotion poured out in bitterness against him. I said, "What the hell else can I call you? You're a great big psychiatrist who can't have an affair with a little worm of a trainee like me, so what the hell else can I call you? Sir?"

"Carol—"

I didn't wait. I tore back to the pool, and collected my robe and the rest of my belongings, and went up to 1412.

For the next three hours I buried myself, literally *buried* myself in the mysteries of the Martin 404. At least that was real. At least a fire extinguisher was real. At least a hand ax was real. Whereas Dr. Duer was merely a phantom. One kiss, and that was that.

8

In the morning we had our test (one hundred for Donna, ninety for Alma, a bleak eighty-five for me, which brought a hard stare from Miss Webley), and immediately afterwards we had our first lecture on fire fighting. Fires don't happen inside airplanes with any regularity; they're about the same kind of hazard as they are in the home. For example, some tired businessman might doze off while he's reading a newspaper and smoking a cigarette, and combustion might result, which could easily upset some of the other passengers. So a hostess has to know how to deal with little emergencies of this kind. She can't call the fire department. *She's* the fire department.

A nice elderly gentleman came and explained the procedure to us, the different kinds of fires and how to deal with them; then we all trooped out to a corner of the airfield (which very conveniently came up to the back door of the training school) and the man demonstrated exactly how a fire extinguisher should be used. He built a small fire, sloshing it with kerosene constantly to keep it blazing, and each of us took turns putting it out. There was a prankish wind which kept changing direction every few minutes, so that we had to maneuver around the fire to hit it from the right angle; but what the wind did most effectively to us was blow our skirts practically over our heads, making us look as if we were rehearsing for the cancan. "Girls," Miss Webley said, "in future you must keep a pair of slacks and a blouse in your lockers for these outdoor demonstrations. You'll wear them on your familiarization flights, too. After all, pilots are men like any other men, you know."

It was Friday, the end of our first week, and I had fish for lunch, not because of any special religious thing but because it was there and I hadn't even glanced at a fish since I last saw Tom Ritchie, nearly two months ago. Donna said, "Oh, *fish*," as if it were the greatest delicacy in the world, and Alma had to have it for religious reasons although she apparently loathed it; and all three of us sat at the same table with these queer browned-over hunks of stuff, wondering what kind of fish they were supposed to be. "Cod," Alma said, but both Donna and I were at a loss. This led to a quite aimless discussion, Donna saying to me, "By the way, do you fish?"

"You mean, go out with a pole to catch them?"

"That's one way of putting it."

I said, "I can't think of anything more horrible."

"It isn't horrible, honey. It's great fun."

"You mean to tell me, Donna Stewart, that putting a poor little worn on a nasty sharp hook is *fun?*"

"Not *that.* God, no. I used to do a lot of trout fishing with my old man. *That's* fun. You'd love it, Carol, honest."

"Why can't you let the poor little trout live? They haven't done you any harm, have they? Why do you have to murder them?"

"Oh, you're impossible," she said. Then she said casually, "Will you be using the Chevrolet over the weekend?"

"No."

"Do you mind if I take it?"

"You don't have to ask my permission, Donna. It's *there.*"

She said, "I spoke to Miss Webley about leaving the hotel for the weekend. She gave me an okay."

Alma said, "You are leaving these beautiful hotel? Why?"

"I have some cousins staying in Palm Beach. I haven't seen them in years. I thought I'd make the effort and look them up."

"Palm Beach?" I said.

She was just too casual. "Yeah. They're at The Breakers. You don't mind about the car?"

"No."

She said, "If you *did* happen to mind, you know, I could always go to the rental people and rent my own."

"Don't be so bitchy," I said.

We had a grueling time for the rest of the day, learning about the Crew Flight Time Log and how to get reimbursed for routine expenses, and various other formalities which came into the job; and when we arrived back at the hotel I was temporarily bushed as usual. I lay on my bed feeling terribly sorry for myself; Alma lay on her bed thinking her own fine Italian thoughts; and Donna swished around packing her weekend bag. The connecting door was open and I could hear Annette talking to Jurgy, but I couldn't hear what they were talking about and I didn't particularly care.

I'd almost dozed off when Donna came over to me hesitantly and said, "That's odd."

"What's odd?"

She had her big purse in her hand, open, and was peering into it and picking at the things inside as if she were trying to find something. She glanced at me queerly, and then sat down beside me and said in a low voice, "Carol, I had that roll of bills in this purse, didn't I?"

"You mean, the twelve hundred dollars?"

"Eleven hundred. I have the rest in my change purse—I broke a hundred for the groceries, remember?" She looked at me helplessly. "The eleven hundred isn't here."

"Oh, no."

"Forget it," she said, and stood up. "I can manage on what I have."

I stood up too. "Wait a minute. Where did you keep this bag?"

"In my closet. It's been there all week."

"Do you have your diamond rings?"

"Yes. Carol, don't worry. The money will turn up."

I was prickly-skinned. I called, "Annette. Jurgy. Could you come in here for a minute?"

Donna said, "What are you doing, Carol? Leave the kids alone."

Annette and Jurgy came in. I said, "Look, Donna's misplaced that roll of eleven hundred dollars."

Jurgy became stiff and white.

Annette cried, "Donna, the other night when the three of you dressed up and went down to dinner, remember, you left everything lying loose on your bed and I collected it together for you and put it all back in your handbag—that one, the one you're holding. And then I put the handbag away in your closet, as I promised."

Donna said, "I know. You see, I haven't been near this purse all week. Oh, hell, kids, forget about it. It'll turn up. I'm not worried."

I said, "Let's look in the closet. The money may have fallen out."

Donna laughed. "I've already looked through the closet."

"Have you gone through all your other handbags?"

"I only have the white one I've been taking to class, and a couple of others on the closet shelf."

"Let's look through those."

We looked. We looked through all her luggage. We looked through her chest of drawers. We looked through things until we were blue in the face—the three of us, Donna and Annette and myself. Jurgy stood with her back to the wall, watching us, and Alma lay on her bed, completely indifferent to the whole business.

Donna said, "Honestly, we're wasting our time, Carol. It was only in one place—this purse. If it isn't there, it isn't anywhere."

I said, "We'll have to report that it's missing, then."

"What do you mean, *report?* Who to?"

"Mr. Courtenay."

"For crying out loud, why?"

I said, "Somebody from the hotel must have come up here while we were in school."

"You're crazy," she said. "I'm not going to report anything to anyone. Forget it, will you?"

Jurgy hadn't said a word. At this point I caught her staring at me, and she lowered her eyes at once, and turned and went into her room. The expression on her face stayed with me, though. She was white and sulky and defiant, and it frightened me to death.

I said, "Okay, Donna. Do it your own way."

"What good will reporting it do? Courtenay will just have all the hired help searched, or something, and then what? Baby, it's only money."

"That's right," I said. "It's only money. God! You make me mad."

"Only *money!*" Annette cried. "Eleven hundred dollars! Why, that's a fortune!"

Alma yawned. She was sprawled on her bed with her hands behind her head like the Sultan's favorite wife. She said in a bored voice, "Please. What is all these commotion?"

Annette said excitedly, "Didn't you *hear?* My goodness, you must be *deaf.* Donna has lost eleven hundred dollars out of her handbag."

Alma yawned again.

I said, "Alma."

She ignored me.

"*Alma.*"

She looked at her fingernails.

I marched over to her and stared down at her. She continued to look at her fingernails. I said, "Alma, do you know anything about this money?"

She gave an indifferent sniff.

I said, "Alma: *where is it?*"

She did that damned yawning act again. Then she looked at her fingernails again. Then she shrugged one shoulder. God, how she overacted. Then she said, coldly, "Where it should be."

I yelled, "*Where?*"

She sprang off her bed like a tigress and yelled right back at me, "You want to know? I tell you! Where it should be!" She swung round on Donna. "You bloody goddam lousy rich American girl. You leave your goddam lousy money lying around like it is nothing, eh? Eleven hundred dollars! In Italy, a family of ten people live on these for five years. Shame! Shame! Shame on you, leaving such a temptation for girls who have to struggle and sweat! Shame on you!"

Donna said to me, "What the hell is she talking about?"

I looked at her; and then I looked at Alma, who'd turned almost black with rage; and I said, "Come on, Donna: help me roll up your mattress."

"Huh?" Donna said, stupefied; but I hustled her, and we rolled up her mattress; and the money was there.

"Well, what do you know?" Donna said.

Alma sneered, and arranged herself on her bed again, her rump thrust out in Donna's direction.

I said, "Let that be a lesson to you, Donna."

"But why?" Donna said. She was completely baffled.

I walked into the other room. Jurgy was staring out of the window. I said, "It's been found."

"Yeah. I heard the Italian screaming."

I waited. She remained as she was, staring at the Gulf Stream. Then I said, "What's the matter with you, Jurgy?"

"The matter?"

"Yes."

She turned very slowly. She said, "You known damn well. You thought I took it, didn't you?"

"You mean, the money?"

"Yeah. The money."

I said, "Jurgy, are you going on like this forever?"

"Who else would take it, except me? That's what you thought. I saw it in your eyes."

"Do you know something?" I said. "You're mad. You're

nuts. You're cuckoo. I ought to slap your ears back for you."

She said, "You don't trust me. Why should you?"

"Oh, hell," I said, and turned to leave her.

She said, "Carol," and when I looked at her there were tears in her eyes.

I said, "I'm going down for a swim. You coming?"

"It's an idea," she said. "It might cool me off."

We had no special assignments for the weekend, just a general instruction to read over everything we'd learned so far and be sure we could recite it blindfold, word for word. This really meant that we could practically relax: we could tour Miami Beach and visit the stores and sigh over all the gorgeous clothes we couldn't possibly afford, we could even go on a sightseeing-boat trip to an Indian village in the Everglades.

At about ten o'clock on this first Saturday morning, Jurgy and I decided we'd take a long walk: we'd cross Collins Avenue to Indian Creek and somehow find our way to Burdine's and then have a hamburger and carry on with a little window shopping until midafternoon. Then we'd come back to the hotel for a siesta, and then we'd see what the evening had to offer. By a coincidence we were wearing dresses of almost the same shade, ivory, and people might have taken us for sisters. We were about the same height and build, and about the same age and blondish, and the only real difference was in our expressions. Jurgy had this rather cold touch-me-not look—not surprising, in view of her Buffalo experiences, whereas I generally look like a carefree moron. My friends used to comment about it, in the past. They'd say, "Carol, you always look so *happy*," but what they really mean was that I looked as if I'd just been released from Bellevue on probation—a cheerful but harmless idiot girl.

Jurgy and I went down to the hotel lobby and began to walk to the entrance with slow dignity, when right out of nowhere a man loomed up in front of us and said in a loud voice, "Pardon me, young ladies. You happen to know if there's a good movie playing in town today?"

We couldn't ignore him. He blocked our path. And he happened to be huge, a sort of human dinosaur: a great big bony man, very very bony and ungainly, about six feet four. His face was bony, too, and curiously bumpy, and he wore gold-rimmed glasses. His suit was tan-color, with old-fashioned wide lapels; his tie was absolutely hideous, a cubist pattern in red and yellow and blue; and he carrried a Stetson hat in his hand. At the very least, he looked about sixty-five years old.

It was one hell of a subtle question for a prowling dinosaur to shoot at a couple of girls at ten o'clock in the morning, particularly when this prowling dinosaur was obviously old enough to be their grandfather and a damned sight homelier than a mud fence. But there he was, directly in front of us, and we had no alternative, we had to say someting. *We*. There wasn't any *we* about it, because Jurgy just stiffened like a lamppost in a snowstorm, and I had to do the honors. I said politely, "I'm sorry, sir, we don't know anything about the movies in town. I'm sure you could find out from the Miami newspapers."

It didn't deter him one little bit. He boomed, "Well, say! Ain't you two young ladies from the stewardesses training school that's staying in the hotel here?"

"Yes, sir."

The peculiar thing about this conversation was that I was answering his questions, but he hardly looked at me. His eyes were fixed on Jurgy. Her lip was curled, her eyes were narrow with disgust, her nostrils were pinched, and yet the old boy kept staring at her.

He said, "You know, I'll tell you something. I've done a whale of a lot of flying in my time, and I got to admit it—I learned to have a lot of respect for you girls. Yes, sir. A lot of respect. But you're only training, eh? Just training?"

"Yes, sir."

He went right on. My God, we couldn't get away from him. "Heard all about it, the other night. Met a fellow in the bar they have here, the Souvenir Bar—you visited that yet?"

"No, sir."

"Cute little bar. Serve a good daiquiri. You ought to try it. Where was I? Oh, yeah, that's right—met this fellow in the Souvenir Bar, he was telling me all about the training they give you girls. Fellow by the name of Harrison. Know him? Harrison?"

"Do you mean Mr. Garrison, sir?"

He was still staring at Jurgy. "Harrison, yep. Told me all about how they put you through the mill—a month, ain't it?"

It was a pretty boring situation. Even when the guy is approaching a hundred years old, you still expect him to at least glance at you while he's asking you a lot of questions. I said wearily, "Yes, we're here for a month."

"Put you through the mill, don't they?"

Some elderly men are so courteous, and so charming, and so plainly delighted to be in your company, and so fascinating, that it's a joy having them talk to you. But this one was nothing but a big bony noisy bore. So, to conclude the matter, I said, "You'll have to excuse us, sir. We're on our way out to do some shopping—"

"All day for that. Why don't you come into the Souvenir Bar and let me buy you one of them daiquiris? Eh? Too early for you, maybe? Okay, let's go in the coffee shop and have a cup of coffee."

"I'm sorry, sir. Some other time, perhaps."

"All right," he said. He turned to me slowly, at last. "Some other time. Give me a lot of pleasure to buy you two ladies a drink. My name's Lucas."

"Thank you, Mr. Lucas."

"Wait a minute," he said. "You mind if I ask your names? I'd like to tell this fellow Harrison, next time I see him, I met a couple of his girls. So he'll know which two I'm talking about."

I had to tell him. Public relations and all that. I couldn't have him go to Mr. Garrison and complain, *Met a couple of your girls the other morning, they were too damn snooty to say hello. You expect me to fly on your airline, Harrison, after they treat me like dirt?* So I said, "I'm Miss Thompson and my friend is Miss Jurgens, and it was awfully nice talking with you, Mr. Lucas, good-by."

"Miss Jurgens, did you say?"

"Yes, sir," I said. "Good-by."

"Ah-hah. Hope I'll see you around."

He watched us go. I didn't speak until we were outside the hotel, and then I said, "Well, my God, what a pain in the neck that was."

"He wasn't so bad."

I was simply flabbergasted. I said, "How can you even *say* that? He was at least a hundred years old, and the most crashing bore I've ever met."

We were in the sunshine, walking down the driveway under the magnificent Royal palms. She said flatly, "You expect too much."

"You mean you *liked* him?"

"I didn't say I liked him. I only said you expect too much. This is an old guy who's worked with his hands. Everyone can't be Cary Grant."

"Jurgy, don't kid yourself. I don't go around all the time with stars in my eyes. I'm pretty realistic about men."

"You are?" She gave me one of her cold, funny looks.

I said with a certain amount of annoyance, "Well, anyway, you certainly made a big hit with him. He thought you were the most."

"Oh? I didn't notice."

"In a pig's eye, you didn't notice."

"Let's get to the stores," she said. "I have to buy some orange sticks and emery boards."

"You can borrow my manicure set."

She said coldly, "I don't like to borrow."

We arrived back, according to plan, at three o'clock, and I put on pajamas and stretched out on my bed, hoping that sleep would come. This isn't the way any normal American girl acts, snoozing the hours away on a gorgeous afternoon in Miami Beach, but I'd been led to the conclusion that I wasn't in any sense normal, I was so abnormal that if the authorities every caught up with me I'd probably lose my citizenship. Here I was, twenty-two years of age and allegedly as strong as a horse, whereas in actual fact I was feeling physically exhausted after one week's work, and emotionally exhausted after one kiss from the staff psychiatrist. I kept thinking about him too, in an utterly morbid, disgusting, un-American way. His eyes, naturally, returned to my mind. And his chest. Why should that keep reappearing in my imagination? Great Scott, you only had to walk out on the beach and there were a thousand male chests, all looking like slabs of liverwurst. And his ears. Everybody has ears, so why all the excitement? Another kiss. I'd have given my life if he'd walked into 1412 and marched over to where I was lying and snapped, "Hold up your face." I wanted him desperately, damn him.

Donna was away. Alma was out, I had no idea where. Jurgy had retired to her room to do a manicure job. Annette was rarely visible, and she wasn't visible now. The air was filled with a soft, pleasant drone, and I feel asleep and dreamed about Dr. Duer. Nothing special happened—we just talked, entranced with each other in tropical darkness, fireflies dancing between us. It was so sweet and so beautiful and so perfect that when Alma woke me I wanted to cry. Reality was so drab and wretched.

She said virtuously, "Carola! You spend the whole day sleeping! You waste this nice sunshine?"

"What's the time?"

"Five o'clock."

I groaned.

She always swathed herself in peculiar gauzy garments when she went out in the sun, and she always wore a huge sun hat. She didn't want to get tanned, anywhere. The idea simply horrified her. She was proud of her smooth porcelain skin, she didn't want it altered in any way. She stood looking at me, dressed like Salome before she started the dance of the seven veils, and there was something so smug about her that I said, "What's the matter with you?"

"Nothing."

When she said "Nothing" in that coy way it meant she wanted to tell you the whole story from beginning to end but you weren't going to get it for free. She expected you to drag it out of her, inch by inch.

"Well?"

"Nothing, Carola. Nothing. Just . . ."

"Just what?"

"Oh, nothing. I meet someone. It is not important."

"A man?"

"A *man?* Oh, well. Yes. Perhaps. A kind of man. Yes."

It went on like this for twenty minutes. Put together, it was a man whose name was Sonny, Sonny Kee when everything was added up. He was about twenty-eight, and *strong* —"Carola! So strong! *Strong!*"—and he was handsome except that his nose was pushed in.

"What do you mean, Alma, *pushed in?*"

"From the box."

"What the hell is the box?"

"He is a box fighter."

"Oh, boy," I said.

"He is so nice. We talk together all these time. He buy me lunch. Tonight—" Her eyes sparkled.

"What about tonight?"

"Carola, I *told* him. *Please*, I told him, *please*, I must study my work. I cannot leave my work. I must study—"

What it amounted to was, she had a date with him for dinner.

"Good for you," I said.

"Yes."

"But watch your step now."

"Carola! He is just nice American guy. Just simple."

I thought I'd better nip this in the bud, fast. "Listen, Alma. Let me give you some advice. Some of these nice simple American guys know their technique. Don't fool yourself, baby."

She gave a hearty laugh.

"*Listen* to me, Alma."

"Carola, after Italian men, American men is only like children." She smiled pityingly. "Just nice. Very sweet, simple."

"As one who's learned the hard way, Alma, I tell you that's not true."

"You are silly. A boy like these Sonny, I twist him around my little finger." She stood up, chuckling. "Fun, eh? My first date in America. Now I take a bath."

I put on the old black swimsuit and went down to the pool. Life was certainly passing me by. Here it was, after five o'clock on a beautiful Saturday afternoon, and nobody had even offered to buy me a soda. Oh, well. There was always the springboard. And I could always go back to my Manual and study check lists.

Jurgy was sitting at a poolside table, wearing her cocoa-colored sun suit and her punchbowl straw hat. I might have guessed: she'd been cornered by bony old Mr. Lucas, who was wearing orange slacks and an utterly horrifying Hawaiian shirt. He was yattering away to her, gesturing with his hands, grinning, scratching the back of his leathery old neck, and—I couldn't believe my own eyes—she was actually smiling. She was actually enjoying sitting there and listening to him. It was one of the biggest surprises I've ever had in my entire life. Jurgy smiling. Not cold and suspicious. Smiling, and interested, and pretty.

I didn't know what to do. If I began to bounce on the diving board it would look as if I were trying to attract their attention, or trying to break up their little tête-à-tête. But Jurgy saw me as I stood there hesitating, and called, "Hey, Carol! Come on over."

I walked over reluctantly. The old man said, "Hello, little lady," and I said, "Hello, Mr. Lucas."

"Pull up a chair," Jurgy said. "Have a soda, or a coffee, or something."

"Thanks, Jurgy, but I'm just about to swim."

142

"Well, sit down and have a cigarette."

"I will, but let me have this swim first."

I dived in, and swam half a dozen lengths, and when I climbed out of the water I saw that Jurgy was alone. I joined her, shaking the water out of my left ear, and said, "How long have you been sitting with the old bird?"

"Oh, an hour, two hours, I don't know."

"You sure got trapped."

She stood up. Her face was sullen again. She said, "I'm going up to the apartment."

"Wait for me. I'll go with you. How about an early supper, Jurgy? I'm famished. We might go to a movie—"

She said, "I'm going out to dinner."

"You *are?*"

She looked at me bitterly. "Mr. Lucas invited me out."

"Well, good God."

"I knew you'd say that." She began to walk away.

I ran after her. "Hey, look—" But I had to seize her arm to hold her back. "*Wait* for me, will you? I'm coming up with you. Just hold your horses for one second."

She waited for me with grim reluctance. She didn't speak as we went up in the self-service elevator, and she still didn't speak as we entered the apartment. Alma was screeching Puccini in the bathroom with immense passion, and Jurgy banged on the bathroom door and shouted, "Hurry up in there."

"Who is these?"

"Me. Jurgy. Hurry up, will you? I have to use the bathroom too."

"Go away, please."

Jurgy shouted, "If you aren't out in five minutes I'm going to come in there and drag you out by the ears." She went to her room, and I followed her, and when she sat down on her bed I sat on Annette's bed, and we looked at each other. She was just blazing with hostility.

She said, "Maybe you didn't hear what I said about Mr. Lucas. *He invited me out to dinner.*"

"Jurgy, that's great—"

"I'm not going to *sleep* with him." She was really fighting mad. I'd never seen her so angry. She said, like a snapping turtle, "He wants to take me to some place called the Sun King Room, or something—"

I had to try to pacify her. "That's right here," I said.

143

"In the hotel. It's beautiful."

Unexpectedly, at those few words, all the fight went out of her. She slumped. "Oh, God," she said.

"What's the matter? It's a *beautiful* restaurant. You'll love it. And the food is out of this world."

She jumped up and went to the window and stood with her back to me. "It's fancy, eh?"

"Well, yes. It's the main restaurant of the Charleroi, and you know how fancy they can get."

She didn't speak for several moments. Then she said, "I can't go." She walked back stiffly. "I'll have to call Mr. Lucas." She reached for the telephone.

"What's the matter, Jurgy?"

"Nothing."

"Stop having kittens. *Tell* me."

Her eyes were pale at any time. They seemed to have no color at all now. She said, "I don't have an evening dress. I'm not going into that kind of place wearing one of my old rags. So it's off."

"Oh, for God's sake, is that all? You can wear mine. We're the same size—"

"No."

"Why not?"

"I won't borrow anything. I never borrow anything. From anybody."

I said, "Mary Ruth Jurgens, you'll wear my evening gown tonight, or I swear I'll never speak to you again as long as I live."

She sneered. She actually sneered. "That's some threat."

"I mean it."

She put her hands over her eyes, and I knew she was crying. I went to my closet, took out the gown, carried it into her room and laid it on the bed beside her. I said, "Here it is. I have the strapless bra that goes with it. Do you need that?"

She looked up at me. The tears were pouring down her face.

I said, "Do you need the bra or not?"

She nodded.

"Okay. Start getting ready. I'll yank Alma out of the bathroom and run a fresh bath for you. Okay?"

She nodded again.

All this stupid fuss. What did she *gain* by being so stubborn? But the most puzzling thing of all was, what the hell did she see in that big bony old geezer? It didn't make sense.

It was fun, in a way, watching the two girls getting dressed. Alma looked like the Queen of Sheba, wearing a red gown and some pearls in her hair. Jurgy couldn't match her for sheer lushness, Jurgy didn't have that kind of outswelling flesh. Jurgy had something else—hardness and strength and a fine clean line to her body, and she would stay like this for the next thousand years. She'd never lose the hardness. But the *harshness* had left her in all the excitement, she was breathless and bright-eyed and eager.

She wouldn't wear her own jewelry, realizing, maybe, that it wouldn't bear inspection in the Sun King Room. I offered her a pair of gold earrings which I'd inherited from my grandmother, and my necklace, my most prized possession, which my father brought me once from Madrid, but she shook her head. She had small, lovely ears, so why did she need earrings, anyway? She had the neck of a princess, smooth and long, so why did she need a necklace? Our only real problem was shoes. The gold slippers I'd bought at Lord and Taylor to go with the gown were too small, and there was no alternative at this late hour; we had to settle for black sandals.

Alma had a few spasms of hysterics before she left, which was only to be expected. Out she went, finally, giggling and panting over the prospect of meeting her box fighter, her first date in America. Jurgy, of course, couldn't have hysterics if her life depended on it; she was bottled up so tight inside that she couldn't even shed a few simple tears until she was in the last extremes of agony, just about at the point where you were beginning to wonder whether you should send for the priest. But there was a hint of mistiness in her eyes as she was ready to leave, and she said (like any normal girl, praise the Lord), "How do I look?"

"You know how you look. Stunning."

"Honest?"

"Honest. Miss Georgia Peach of 1965."

"God, I'm scared."

I knew she was scared. I said, "Don't be a dope. You're going to knock every gal in that restaurant dead as a dodo." Then—old Mother Thompson in her usual role—I added, "Just remember your deadline, Cinderella. Two o'clock."

"Okay."

Off she went, as stiff as a lamppost on a frosty morning, and I stood at the door watching her until she stepped into the elevator.

Annette had gone to a movie. I was all alone in the apartment, and I'd never in all my life felt *so* alone. The original Ugly Duckling on its worst day never felt one tenth of what I felt on my first free evening at the Luxurious Hotel Charleroi on Romantic Miami Beach. I might just as well have been in the isolation cell on Alcatraz.

I couldn't bear to fix food for myself; and I couldn't bear the thought of going to the coffee shop because it would undoubtedly be crowded with couples looking passionately into each other's eyes. There's a limit to what even Thompson can take in the way of punishment. So I made myself a pot of coffee, which turned out to be absolutely undrinkable, and then I said in a loud, clear voice, "Well, well, well! What a marvelous opportunity to catch up with my correspondence! Why, this is great!" I sat by the window, on Donna's bed, and wrote to my mother, and to my aunt and uncle in Philadelphia, and to a second cousin in Seattle whom I hadn't seen in five years; and then I started on an epistle to Tom Ritchie which was obviously going to be at least as long as *War and Peace* before I was through. After all, I had every right as a wronged woman to demand that he share my woes. And as I poured them out, page after page, I began to amaze even myself with the number of woes I had. Apparently, until tonight, I just hadn't begun to realize how miserable I was, how vilely life had been treating me. It was enough to break the heart of a brass monkey; and when I'd written nineteen pages, exactly at the stroke of midnight, I tore them all up, feeling quite a lot better. I stood up and shook myself like a wet dog, and tore up the other letters I'd written, and thought, Okay, kid. You've had Saturday. Now go to bed. And, just as I was undressing, Jurgy opened the apartment door and walked in, looking like a ghost.

I didn't dare speak. She said, "Hi," weakly, and stumbled across the room and sat down in a chair, looking at me dumbly. The funny thing was, she was *acting* as if she'd been raped, but she didn't bear any *signs* of being raped. My dress was intact.

Somebody had to speak sooner or later. I said, "Well, how did you like the Sun King Room?"

"Gee, it's beautiful."

That stumped me for a moment. I said, "How was the food?"

"Gee, it was delicious."

That stumped me even more. "What did you have?"

"Steak."

I couldn't figure her out. She honestly *behaved* raped, but she didn't *talk* raped. I mean, my God, you don't get lyrical about how good the steak was before you give out with the gory details of how the guy lured you behind the bushes. So I put the decisive question to her, in an attempt to get some clue as to why she'd returned in this alarming condition. I said, "Did you have a good time, Jurgy?"

She answered, vaguely, "Yeah. Pretty good."

Some clue. I was more baffled than before. So I tried another tack. "What brings you back so early? I mean, you could have sayed out till two."

She answered in the same vague, dazed way, "Luke thought I shouldn't stay up after midnight."

"You shouldn't *what?*"

"Stay up after midnight."

"For crying out loud: why?"

"He wants me to be up at six tomorrow morning."

I said, "Wait a minute, Jurgy. Just hold it right there. Let me find a pack of cigarettes and get myself comfortably settled. I want to hear about this in detail."

She said, "No. I have to go to bed."

"Why do you?"

"Because I have to be up at six in the morning."

I said, "If you say that again I'm going to scream. Tomorrow's *Sunday*. Why do you have to be up at six in the morning?"

"Luke wants to go and inspect some Brahman cattle."

She wasn't raped, she wasn't even drunk. She was simply and purely in a daze. I said, "Luke is Mr. Lucas?"

"Yeah. That's his name. Luke Lucas."

"Did you say Brahman cattle?"

"That's right."

"Why does he want to inspect them?"

"That's his business, you see."

"Honey, I don't see one goddam thing. What is he? A butcher? Does he have to inspect these cattle before he slaughters them, or something?"

"No. He breeds cattle."

147

"What the hell are Brahman cattle, anyway? They sound Indian to me."

"That's right. They come from India." She suddenly became lucid. "They've been raising these Brahman cattle here in Florida, see? And Luke wants to drive out and look them over, see? And he wants me to drive out with him, and he wants to make an early start. That's all."

I was still baffled. "Anyway, you had a good time."

"Not bad." She walked to the connecting door, and said, "Well, good night."

"Good night. Sleep tight."

She hesitated, her hand on the doorknob. "Carol."

"What?"

"This isn't a one-way street."

"What do you mean?"

"You helped me out tonight. The other day, too. If I can help you out any time, I will."

"Oh, Jurgy—"

"Wait a second. Let me finish. About Luke. Carol, I want you to believe me, this is a pretty good guy. That's all. And I'm asking you for just one last thing: don't make any more cracks about him."

I stared at her. "Jurgy!"

"I'm telling you: he's a good decent guy, Carol."

"For God's sake, Jurgy, be sensible. He's three times as old as you are—"

"He's fifty-six, that's right. And I'm twenty-three. And he talks in a loud voice, and I don't give a good goddam." Then she said, "Come and unzip me, will you? I might as well take the dress off in here."

I unzipped her, and she stepped out of the gown and handed it to me. Then she went into the bathroom and came out a moment later wearing her robe and carrying the strapless bra. As she gave it to me she said, "Thanks for the loan."

"You're welcome."

Quite unexpectedly, she leaned forward and pecked me on the cheek. It was like a bird's peck, as if she'd never learned how to kiss. She went into her room and shut the door firmly, without another word.

I thought, Lord! What on earth has happened to her? I tried to figure it out in bed, but nothing clicked because I couldn't even begin to imagine what had taken place between her and that big bony old lug in the Sun King Room.

Then I fell asleep, and I didn't wake when Alma came in, which was my only break that entire day.

I just slept on and on and on, that Sunday morning. I not only didn't hear Alma come in, I didn't hear Jurgy leave at six o'clock, and Alma didn't disturb me when she woke at nine o'clock and dressed and went out. Annette went out at about the same time, and when I finally woke at ten I was all alone in the apartment once again. It was puzzling, looking around the big, sunny room, to see two empty beds; and then, walking into the other room, seeing two empty beds there. But everything became clear when I looked at my watch. *Ten o'clock!* Oh, brother!

I felt marvelous, though. All my miseries had drizzled away in my sleep, all my juices seemed to have renewed themselves, I felt practically young again. I ran an ice-cold shower, and I put on the absolute minimum of make-up because after all that sleep I hardly needed any, and I wore my best dress, a really choice number in gray linen; and then, feeling right on top of the world and as hungry as a hunter, I swished down to the Salon de Fragonard for a slap-bang breakfast. Thompson, I told myself, you're a growing girl, you need sustenance, so to hell with the expense: just eat. If it comes to $1.50, so what? That's the kind of mood I was in—ready to throw away $1.50 on breakfast without practically a second thought. So in I went to the Salon de Fragonard, and there, sitting at an almost deserted counter, was Herr Doktor Ray Duer, psychiatrist-in-waiting to Magna International Airlines, that fine upstanding honorable clean-living decent guy who'd given me an emotional hemorrhage a couple of nights back.

He saw me at the same moment I saw him. He stared, he frowned, and then he pulled himself together and smiled.

"Hi. Good morning."

"Good morning, sir."

"Just coming down for breakfast?"

"Yes, sir."

"Will you join me?"

"Thank you, sir."

I climbed on the stool on his left, and he said, "You look pretty chipper this morning."

"Just full of piss and vinegar, Doctor, sir," I said.

"What's that?" He jerked upright.

I gave him my village-idiot smile and said, "That's just

a good old New England expression, sir. Miss—bacon, two fried eggs, French fries on the side, and toast, please. Oh, and coffee."

She frowned at me. I guess I was in the kind of Christmas mood where everybody would be frowning at me for a while. She said, "You don't want the hostesses' breakfast?"

"Gad, no. Don't even suggest such a thing."

She shrugged and turned to her grill.

I'll say this for the Herr Doktor. He *tried* to make conversation. He did his best. But I didn't give him a chance. I chomped away on my toast, I juggled with my fried eggs, I jabbed at my French fries, I crunched my bacon, and every few minutes I asked the waitress to replenish my coffee cup—I must have had at least five cups of that delicious brew—and I offered Ray Duer no encouragement at all. Why should I? Why, indeed. I'd offered him all the encouragement in the world the other night, and he'd flinched. He'd turned away. He'd been a true servant of Magna International Airlines. And I couldn't give him another chance. It wasn't a case of Hell hath no fury like a student hostess scorned; it was simply that my insides are too soft, far, far softer than my outside, and I didn't want them torn apart and left, as they'd been left on Friday night, flapping in the wind, so to speak.

He said quietly, as I finished my meal, "I have to go over to Arnie Garrison's house for a conference in half an hour."

"Well," I said. "Isn't that nice."

He ignored my tone of voice. "I was thinking of taking a stroll along the beach first. Would you care to come along?"

My heart turned over, but I pretended not to care, I left it where it was, upside down. "No, sir. I'm sorry."

"Do you have other plans?"

"No, sir."

"I asked you not to call me *sir*, Carol."

"It's hard for me not to, sir."

"I want to talk to you."

"Sir, I'd rather not talk. Besides, it's Sunday morning."

"What does that have to do with it?"

"Dr. Duer, you know quite well that I have to rest up on Sunday so that I'm in fit condition for next week's work."

That shook him. He said, "Oh." Then he said to the waitress, "My check, please. And this young lady's check."

"Oh, no," I said. "Oh, *no*."

We swung around on our stools, staring at each other; and perhaps because we weren't properly grounded, sitting up so high, the electricity was so violent that it nearly knocked both of us over. All the breath went out of my lungs, and I saw his lips turn white.

We didn't speak. He stepped down, grounding himself presumably, took both checks, and said, "Well, good-by."

" 'By."

He went, damn him, leaving me alone there; and when he went out the door my stomach turned over, in addition to my heart. I felt horribly sick, bubbling with acidity inside, and I said to the woman behind the counter, "I guess I drank too much coffee. Give me a Bromo Seltzer, please."

She made no comment. I guess love didn't mean a thing to her. The Bromo saved my life.

I had the morning to kill, and I thought, Well, I might as well do something about my stripes, and I asked the clerk at the hotel desk how one reached the solarium. He said, "Self-service elevator, all the way. You can't miss it." Back I went to 1412, and hung away my gray linen dress—a lot of good it had done me—and then I wondered what on earth one wore to go up to the solarium. There was only one way to find out: I picked up the telephone, asked for the women's solarium, and put my problem to the first person who answered. I suppose she was the attendant up there.

She seemed a little perplexed. "Why, madam, you come up in your robe."

"Nothing underneath?"

"Madam, you're coming up to sunbathe, aren't you?"

"Yes."

"Then why do you want to wear anything under your robe?"

She had me there, cold. I hate these situations where you ask somebody an utterly simple question and they turn the tables on you and ask you the same question right back to your face, and make you feel like a complete imbecile. I had to admit, though, that her logic was fault-less. Just the same, going up to the solarium, clutching my terry-cloth robe tightly to my bare person, I felt practically shameless. True, a robe hides you from sight much more effectively than, say, a swimsuit; but it hardly seems the right thing to wear in a public elevator even if you're alone.

Entering the solarium I had another spasm of modesty. About a dozen women of various shapes and sizes were draped on mattresses, some dozing, some being massaged by white-uniformed attendants, some just chewing the cud, and I crept among them as if I were intruding on their privacy. They were *so* nude, and glistening with sun-tan oil which simply highlighted their bareness.

But I've always found that nudity stops being embarrassing after a couple of minutes, you just forget about it. In 1412 somebody was always in the porcess of dressing or undressing, and it didn't mean a thing. Females are made in pretty much the same general way, once you've seen one you've practically seen all the rest; and once I'd metaphorically become used to the glare in the solarium I found myself quite at ease.

On my right there was a big buxom platinum blonde sunburned to a chocolate color, who gave me a slightly hostile look as I lowered myself beside her and turned every now and then to give me another scowl. It may have been because she was about thirty-five, to judge from her face, and she was getting to be heavy in some places and droopy in others—I couldn't think of any other explanation. Mother Nature is sort of brutal, allowing the female of the species to show signs of crumbling so early; and I've felt the pangs of it myself, at the ripe old age of twenty-two, looking with envy at some exquisite, dewy, breath-taking young thing of eighteen, and realizing I was just an old hag by comparison.

I didn't want to spoil the morning for the platinum blonde, though, and I smiled across at her in a fairly friendly way, hoping she'd relax. She didn't. She continued to snarl under her breath. Apparently she despised me from the bottom of her heart; so, for once, I showed discretion and avoided catching her eye.

That didn't help. Maybe she took it for a sign of guilt. She said, suddenly and curtly, "Are you one of those airline girls?"

"Yes, I am."

"H'm." She said it with deep loathing.

I tried to win her over with another small friendly smile.

"Airline girls," she said. "Phooey. Homebreakers."

"Pardon me?" I was really puzzled. I thought she meant housebreakers, people who enter through a window and steal alarm clocks and candlesticks.

"Homebreakers," she repeated."

"I'm sorry, I'm afraid I don't understand."

"All of you. You're all the same. Just a bunch of home-breakers."

I guessed what she meant at last. I said, "Oh, no. We aren't really."

"I know it from my own experience."

"Oh," I said. "Oh, dear."

"One of my own husband's brothers left his wife and children and ran off with an airline girl. A disgrace. Nothing but a disgrace. I told Joanie she should sue the company. *Sue* them. Get *damages*. That would teach them a lesson."

I said, "Now, honestly. You can't blame all airline girls for that, you can't blame the airline company. What about blaming your brother-in-law?"

"Let me tell you something, miss. Bill was a nice quiet home-loving fellow until he met up with this girl. He was crazy about his wife and his beautiful children."

"Well, if he was so crazy about them, he sure sounds like a guy with an awfully weak character."

"I've heard of other cases, too."

"You have?"

"I have. Airline girls. Ugh. They're all the same."

"Well, if it comes to that," I said, "one of my uncles left his wife and seven lovely children to run off with a platinum blonde. You ought to hear what they say about platinum blondes in my family."

She gave me a glare to end all glares, and turned her back on me. Mr. Garrison might have been distressed, since she probably flew hither and thither in jet liners constantly, and one shouldn't offend potential customers. Perhaps I should have turned the other cheek and said, "Hit me again." But not today, in the mood I was in. I was missing Dr. Duer pretty badly, recalling that I might have been walking beside him on the beach if I hadn't been so arrogant, walking and talking and walking and talking, instead of displaying my nakedness to a lot of equally naked dames who couldn't have cared less.

The sun was fairly concentrated on the roof of the hotel, and I'd decided I'd had about enough when three girls appeared with a portable phonograph and some striped beach bags. All three were tall and strongly built, and for a moment I looked at them with interest. Then I looked away—they were just females like the rest of us, and why should their muscles mean a thing to me? As it turned out, though, they weren't females like the rest of us, because one of them said in a loud croaking voice, "Hey, ladies. You mind if we rehearse our routine for a few minutes?"

Somebody asked, "Routine for what?"

"We have an engagement for a private party in the Supper Club tonight, see?"

"Well, sure," the same somebody said. "Don't let us stop you."

It was fascinating. Frankly, I'd never seen anything like it. It was so fascinating, in fact, that all the women in the solarium including the attendants and the masseuses gathered in front of these three girls, and we might have been an audience in a theater. Two of the girls were dancers—I assume that's what they called themselves—who did grinds and bumps in unison. They must have been good because the women in the audience laughed and clapped and showed immense enthusiasm; but to be perfectly honest, after the first few minutes I rather lost interest because it didn't amount to anything much more than dislocating your pelvis in time to Ravel's *Bolero,* a rather monotonous way to publicize sex.

The third girl, though, *really* fascinated me. Gad, it was a compelling performance. I nearly went blind watching her. She was a tassel twirler. Maybe she was billed as a dancer, but she hardly moved a leg in any direction. She merely twirled tassels, and when I say *merely* I don't mean to sound like Brooks Atkinson. It was one of the most fantastic things in my whole experience. She twirled these tassels with *herself.* She attached the things—they were about four inches long and they came in several different styles—she attached the tassels to various parts of her anatomy (where I, for one, don't have any control that I know of) and they *twirled.* The performance that intrigued me most was when she attached a tassel to each breast, smack over the nipple, and began to twirl them like a couple of egg beaters; and if I hadn't seen this with my own eyes I wouldn't have believed it. As everybody knows, or should know, the female breast is a globby thing designed primarily for the feeding and comforting of the newborn. It just isn't intended for any muscular exertion. Over the past few years poets and public relations guys have gone to town giving the female breast an absolutely underserved reputation, completely fooling the public on the subject, building up the bosom to a ridiculous point; whereas the truth is, bosoms—considered as glamour accessories—might just as well be packed in cardboard boxes and hidden on a top shelf until you have some actual use of them. When you're in your teens they embarrass you to death, because they're either too damned small and nonexistent, or too damned huge and bulky; and as you get older they just get more and more droopy, like the globs on the platinum blonde who despised me so much; and all in all, as most girls will admit, they're just a pain in the neck because (a) the only thing you can do with them is sling them out of the way, and (b) you're constantly forced into wrestling matches with fellows who are intoxicated with the idea of grabbing hold of them in their fat greasy hands, God knows for what purpose.

This is a subject on which I can get pretty heated, but I have to admit the tassel twirler gave me cause to revise my thinking. She could twirl those two tassels fast, she could twirl them slow. She could twirl them in different directions, she could twirl them in the same direction, and she could stop them in midair and set them twirling in opposite directions without a pause. I couldn't see that it had any application to the business of nourishing the newborn—most likely you'd give the baby gas or colic with all those gyrations—but it sure impressed me to death as an art. Most critics, I feel, would agree. It didn't represent anything, it didn't have any functional purpose; it was just pure abstract art. And it added a completely new dimension to Ravel's *Bolero*. I sat there watching her with my mouth wide open.

I couldn't bear it when she stopped. I was trying to figure out how in heaven's name she made her nipples twirl, because if she was built like me the thing was impossible. And yet it wasn't impossible, because there she was, right in front of my nose, twirling away so smoothly that I'm sure that Ravel, not to mention the Timken roller-bearing people, would have been proud of her. So when she stopped at last, I glanced around hastily to see that none of the brass from Magna International Airlines was in sight (it wouldn't have surprised me in the least to discover Mr. Garrison watching me grimly from a corner, wrapped in a Turkish towel), and I went over to the girl and spoke to her. She was just as sweet and nice and unassuming as she could possibly be; and after we'd been talking for some time, and she'd discovered how interested I was, she said, "Would you like to try them yourself, honey?" That, of course, was practically beyond my wildest dreams; but she went to her striped beach bag and brought out a red plastic box and found a pair of tassels and pressed them in place on me —they had some magic goo, like Scotch tape has. I looked down at them, and *groaned*, and *grunted*, and tried to *will* them to twirl; but, of course, nothing happened. They just hung there like two lead weights on a windless day. I couldn't even get them to swing from side to side, like a pendulum.

I said, "How long did it take you to learn to twirl them?" She laughed. "About twelve years."

I said, "I suppose fifteen minutes every evening wouldn't be enough?"

"No, honey."

The tassels made a little plop, plop, as she took them off me. I was sorry when she put them away. But let's face it. Twelve years is an awful long time. By then, I figured, Ray Duer would have lost interest.

Anyway, it all helped the morning to pass, and it kept me out of mischief.

About midafternoon I began to realize that I might have to do something really drastic to improve my popularity rating. To all intents and purposes I was left high and dry in the Hotel Charleroi—a bitter blow to one who in the past always had more dates during the weekend than she could possibly handle. Alma had disappeared without a trace; Donna was in Palm Beach; Jurgy was inspecting Brahman cattle; Annette had gone off on a sightseeing tour. I was left with a bunch of California girls who were nursing a collective grievance against Magna International Airlines for bringing them to this ghastly slum, Florida. Finally I left them and sat by the pool with my Little Black Book, reading about the Martin 404 and the duties of a queen bee.

I was immersed in emergency exits when I felt somebody staring at me. I looked up and saw Nat Brangwyn about ten yards away, with three big, rather fleshy men. They were all smoking cigars, and they all had that strange, unmistakable aura of prosperity that some men have, even though by Tom Ritchie's standards they weren't by any means well dressed. I don't know how one instantly recognizes these things, but they were the kind of men who only have to snap their fingers in an expensive restaurant, and six waiters fall dead trying to break the speed record to their table. I've seen it happen often.

N.B. waved at me, and I couldn't pretend he wasn't there; I had to give him a little smile in return. He spoke to the others and then came over to me with the friendliest grin, and said, "Hi, Miss Thompson, haven't seen you in days, how have you been?"

"Fine." What else could I answer? "How are you, Mr. Brangwyn?"

"Great, just great. You having a good time?"

"Very good, thank you."

Then he said, "Mind if I sit down for a minute?"

It wasn't my hotel. And I couldn't say to him outright, *Sir, I have been forbidden to associate with you.* I had to act like a human being. I said, "Please do."

He pulled up a chair and sat down. He was suddenly nervous, as if he didn't know what to say next. He clasped his hands together and stared at them, and then he smiled at me again and said, "Sorry about the car."

"So am I." I couldn't think of a vaguer answer. It was a subject I couldn't discuss.

And, as usual, he couldn't have been nicer. He laughed and said, "If I'd given it a minute's thought, I would have known you aren't that kind of girl." Then he stopped laughing, his eyes became serious, he stared down at his clasped hands, and said, "That isn't what I wanted to talk to you about, Miss Thompson."

I waited.

He said, "I saw one of your friends last night, that Italian kid. The good-looking brunette you introduced me to in the Sun King Room."

"Alma."

"Yeah. I saw her in a nightclub last night with a character called Sonny Kee. You know Sonny Kee?"

I shook my head.

"Look, Miss Thompson, it's none of my business, but do me a favor. Tell your friend this Sonny Kee isn't a particularly nice guy. Okay? She shouldn't go around with him."

I said, "Why?"

He shook his head. "I don't want to go into details. Just believe me. This isn't a guy with a nice character, he isn't right for a girl like that."

"She told me he's a boxer."

"Yeah, he used to be in the fight game. He isn't fighting any more—that gives you a hint, doesn't it? Honest, someone like this friend of yours can find someone a whole lot better than Sonny Kee."

"Thank you very much, Mr. Brangwyn. I'll tell her."

"Yeah, just tell her. That's all. I'm sure she'll listen to you." He smiled. "You're still calling me Mr. Brangwyn. I thought we were old friends. Couldn't you call me Nat, or N.B., like everyone else?"

I laughed, to hide my embarrassment.

He glanced at his watch. "Hey. It's the cocktail hour. How about dropping into the Souvenir Bar for a little refreshment?"

"I told you the other evening, Mr. Brangwyn—N.B.—we aren't *allowed* to. We aren't allowed to drink while we're in training."

"Oh."

"I'm sorry."

"Well," he said: "How about meeting me a little later for dinner? What about that? We could go along to a little club I know—"

I held up the Little Black Book. "Mr. Brangwyn—I mean, N.B.—I just couldn't do it. I have to learn all *this*. We have tests on it every morning. I'm terribly sorry."

"Okay," he said. He stood up. "Tell your friend about Sonny Kee, won't you. Mention it to her. And I guess I'll be bumping into you again soon, eh?"

"Oh, yes."

He looked hurt. He looked repulsed. "Well, good-by, now," he said, and I said, "Good-by," and he walked away quickly.

Ray Duer was sitting at a table on the other side of the pool.

I might have known. I might have known I wasn't safe for one single minute from the spying minions of Magna International Airlines, I might have known they kept a tail on me twenty-four hours a day. I lit a cigarette and smoked it for five minutes; then I stubbed it out, picked up my Manual, and walked around the pool to Ray Duer's table.

He said genially, "Hello, Carol."

"Dr. Duer. Do you know who that was—the man I was just talking to?"

He didn't reply.

"Dr. Duer, that was Nat Brangwyn, the notorious gambler, who owes the federal government a hundred and fifty thousand dollars income tax."

"Yes, I recognized him."

"Dr. Duer, Mr. Brangwyn just invited me to have a drink in the Souvenir Bar. He asked me to have dinner with him. He asked me to go to a nightclub with him. I haven't had a date all weekend, but I remembered that I must not bring disgrace on the Hostess Training School by associating with him, so I refused. Don't you think I'm a good girl, Dr. Duer, sir?"

"Carol—"

"Just let me finish, sir, please. I didn't approach Mr. Brangwyn. He approached me. I was just sitting over there minding my own business—studying my Manual, in fact—when he came over and asked me to carouse with him. Now, what I want to know is this: what am I supposed to do all weekend to avoid being seen with Mr. Brangwyn? Lock myself in my room, like a nun? Or wear a mask? Or what? Sir?"

"Carol, we realize—"

"Dr. Duer, as long as you *realize*. That's all I want to know. Thank you. Good-by, sir."

He jumped up. "Carol. Listen to me."

I wouldn't listen to him. I wanted him to take me in his arms and kiss me and love me, and all he was doing was talk, talk, talk. Talk, talk, talk, talk, talk, talk. I strode away with dignity, and went up to 1412. There wasn't a soul in it, so I could hurl myself on my bed and have a good cry without disturbing anybody. Then I opened the can of tuna fish and made a cup of tea to wash the tuna fish down. I began to think of those happy, carefree days in Greenwich, Conn., what fun it had been to go out with young Tom Ritchie, riding in his Thunderbird, dancing with him at the Country Club, and how sweet and solicitous he'd been that night when he led me out into the garden because I had hiccups; and I wished I were dead.

Annette was the first to get back. She was breathless about her sightseeing tour. I couldn't have cared less.

Jurgy was the next to arrive. She looked very white.

I said, "Jurgy, what happened?"

"What happened?"

"You're looking so pale—"

"I'm okay."

That old buzzard, I thought, he made a pass at her. I said, "Did you see those Brahman cattle?"

"Yeah."

"Were they interesting?"

"Yeah."

"You had a good time?"

"Yeah."

That's all I could drag out of her. But it didn't require the brain of an Einstein to figure out that she'd had to fight the old buzzard off. Poor Jurgy. Life was nearly as tough for her as it was for me.

Then came Alma, at ten o'clock, not a hair out of place and a five-cent smile on her lips, like the Mona Lisa. I wanted to pass on N.B.'s warning at once, but I couldn't with the other girls around. I said, "Hi, Alma. How was your date?"

"Very nice boy. Very gentleman."

"Did you have a good time?"

"Every minute, charming."

"Are you going to see him again?"

That smile of hers murdered me. She said. "Maybe. Perhaps."

And, finally, after one o'clock, Donna tottered in. We were all in bed by this time, but I'd left her light on so she'd know where she was.

She tiptoed over to me, weaving. "Carol. You awake?"

"Hi, Donna."

"H-hi, cream."

"Did you have a good time with your cousins?"

"P-perfect."

I said, "It's late, you know. You'd better get to bed."

"Okay. Wanna swim in the morning?"

"Sure."

"Good old Carol," she said: "Good old faithful pal," and she staggered away. I was surprised she didn't toss me a dog biscuit.

9

Miss Webley lit into us mercilessly the following morning. As soon as we were assembled, and firmly in the embrace of our Iron Maidens, she stood looking us over, and then pursed her lips. "Boy!" she said. "Some of you sure had a jazzy weekend. Elizabeth: did you iron that dress before you put it on this morning?"

Elizabeth, a cute brunette from Nevada, said, "Gee, Miss Webley, I didn't think it needed ironing—"

"You will *never* come to class again in a dress that isn't freshly ironed. Do you understand that?"

"Y-yes, Miss Webley."

"Joan, what happened to your hair?"

"Gee, Miss Webley, I was swimming in the ocean yesterday—"

"Without a cap?"

"I guess I forgot to put it on—"

"Lisa, did you get any sleep at all in the weekend?"

"Miss Webley, why, certainly—"

"How many hours?"

"I couldn't say exactly—"

"You look as if you can't keep your eyes open."

And so on, and so on. Finally, when she'd bawled out about a dozen individuals, she bawled us out collectively. She stood in front of us, very erect, her hands behind her back, and said, "Now, girls. Let's get this straight before we go any further. Miami Beach is a wonderful place for a vacation. You can really have a ball—sunshine all day, and dancing and entertainment all night. Unfortunately, girls, you aren't here on vacation. You're here to work. Nobody has any objection to your enjoying yourselves on the weekends—of course not. You need rest and recreation. But we simply cannot tolerate any abuse of weekend privileges. Why, just look at yourselves! Barely half of you are awake! We simply can't get through this course if every Monday is going to be like this—just a day on which you recover from your weekend frolics. Girls, I expect you to come to class

161

on Monday morning in future, not *exhausted*, but *refreshed*. Is that clear?"

"Yes, Miss Webley."

Now, I was just beginning to dig this chick. She hadn't said a word about weekend debauchery when class ended on Friday afternoon. Logically she should have warned us then, in her sweet, calm way, that she wanted us starched and pressed on Monday morning, or else. And I'm ready to bet ten cents that she had this speech prepared to the last comma before she even set foot in the classroom, before she even cast an eye over us. She knew we'd be looking like the wreck of the Hesperus; and she'd staged this little scene so that the iron entered deep into each girlish soul, and she could be darned sure that every one of us was fully aware what kind of woe was in store for us if we dared to arrive bedraggled next weekend. I had to admire her.

"Now, girls. Sit up straight. Make an effort to be alert."

We made an effort. Then, without any pause, we plunged into work. Last week we'd learned how to be a queen bee on the one-hostess Martin. I suppose the idea was to give us a broad picture of a hostess's general duties. Now we went on to the two-hostess and three-hostess planes like the Constellations. When we'd learned these, we'd go on to the four-hostess jets. Very simple. All we had to do was digest and learn by heart were the thousand pages of the Little Black Book. But this only dealt with piston-driven planes. *Then*, if we lived so long, we'd switch to an entirely new Manual, of approximately the same size and weight, covering jet-liners. Quite a program.

The day passed incredibly quickly. Everything was so new, everything was so complicated, that there wasn't a chance to feel bored. Whole areas of my brain, which had just been inert swamps of soggy gray matter, were being forced into action, and by the end of the afternoon my head was actually hurting. I guess it was rather like tennis elbow, which you can get from being too energetic at tennis, or bursitis, which you can get from being too energetic at swimming. Bursitis of the brain, that's what I had.

When we arrived back in 1412, we were all three of us pretty low. Donna and I agreed that a dip in the pool might help, but before I could even get my dress off, Jurgy called me from the other room. "Hey, Carol."

I went in to see her. She was sitting on her bed looking green—really green. I said, "What's wrong?"

"Annette."

"What's the matter with Annette?"

"She's gone."

I said, "Gone? Gone where?"

"Home, I guess. All her things are missing. Her clothes. Her luggage. Everything."

I said, "But, why? What happened?"

Jurgy said, "She was called out of class this morning. She didn't come back. I guess she saw Mr. Garrison, or Mrs. Montgomery."

"Oh, no! You mean she's been *fired?*"

Jurgy nodded miserably.

It seemed impossible. And yet, in a way, it made sense. Annette was a sweet, gentle kid; but once or twice I'd wondered whether she was tough enough to take the kind of life we were heading for. She was just too gentle, too soft.

Jurgy said, "There were three other girls called out at the same time."

I remembered suddenly. "My God, there were three girls called out of our class this morning. I wondered about them —they didn't come back."

"Let's find out," Jurgy said.

We went from room to room, and we found out. The score was exactly seven. Seven girls had quit, or been sent home. None of them had left any message. I could understand why—I wouldn't have left a message either. My pride would have been busted to smithereens. And then I remembered something else—Ray Duer in the Salon de Fragonard yesterday morning, telling me he was going to a conference with Mr. Garrison. Probably that's when the final decision was made, that's when they weeded out the names. Whether that was true or not, here, anyway, was the living proof that Mr. G., Dr. D., Mrs. Montgomery, Miss Webley, Miss Pierce, representing Magna International Airlines, were in deadly earnest, and there was consternation in our hen coops on the fourteenth floor.

We sat around discussing it, practically in whispers, and after a while Jurgy left us. She was still looking green, a very strange, alarming color, and I followed her into her room and said, "Jurgy, are you all right?"

"Sure." She was hunched up on her bed.

"Do you mind being alone in here, without a roommate?"

"No. I don't mind."

I stood watching her. She sat quite motionless, sickly green, staring at nothing.

Then she said, "Shut the door, Carol."

I closed it.

She said, "*Lock* it."

"Lock it?"

"Yeah."

I locked it.

She said, "When I got back here this afternoon, I found this waiting for me." She twisted her body and pulled a gaily decorated box from under her pillow.

"What is it, Jurgy?"

"See for yourself."

She held it out to me. I walked over and took it from her hand, and opened it. There was a blue velvet case inside.

She said, "Go on. *Open* it."

I took the blue velvet case out and opened it and said, "Oh, my God." The velvet case contained a gold bracelet, in the heavy modern design that I've always admired and coveted.

"Well?" Jurgy said coldly.

"Who's it *from?* Who *sent* it?"

"Luke."

"You mean that old Mr. Lucas?"

"Yeah."

"Jurgy!"

"It's gold, isn't it?" she said.

"My God, I don't know." I took the bracelet out of the case. "My God, it weighs a ton. My God, Jurgy, it must be gold."

"We can soon find out," she said. "You see the name inside the case?"

The name was in Gothic lettering on the white silk lining inside the lid: *The Jewel Box. Hotel Charleroi. Miami Beach, Fla.* I said, "That's the chic little jewelry store in the lobby. My God, they're more expensive than Tiffany's."

"They'd tell us if it's gold or not, wouldn't they?"

"I guess so."

She said, "Why waste our time. It's gold. I know it's gold."

She seemed to be getting paler and greener and more rigid.

I said, "Jurgy, what are you going to do with it? Are you going to *keep* it, or what? My God, it must be worth a thousand dollars."

"He flew back to Kansas today, so I can't give it back to him. He'll be here again for the weekend, Friday night." She turned her head and stared at me. "You think I ought to give it back to him?"

She was testing me in some way, feeling me out, trying to get me to pronounce judgment. I said, "That's for you to decide. You're going to see him next weekend?"

"Yeah."

"Looking at Brahman cattle again?"

"No," she said. "He wants me to go on a boat with him. The whole weekend." She smiled grimly. "Don't look so scared. There'll be other people on the boat." She began to rock to and fro. "I don't know what the hell to do. This never happened to me before. What the hell should I do, Carol?"

"You mean, about the bracelet?"

"The bracelet, the weekend, everything."

"It's up to you to decide."

She looked at me again, bitterly. "He's an old man, fifty-six. A girl shouldn't take gifts from an old man, eh?"

I didn't answer.

She said, "The only trouble is—" She stopped, and stared at nothing for a few moments. Then she sighed painfully. "I guess I'll have to think about it, that's all. Thanks, Carol. Don't mention this to the other girls."

I said, "Of course not," and left her.

That night Donna forgot about going out for her nine-o'clock martini. She was more shaken up than any of us by the quiet ruthlessness of Magna International Airlines. I'd misjudged her. I thought she was kind of slaphappy, she couldn't care less, she didn't give a damn about anything, etc. But this wasn't so. We had a talk about it the following night, when we simply had to take an hour's breather from pages and pages of Constellation emergency equipment, and we went down to the pool for a dip just before the boom was lowered on us at ten-thirty. We were in the water at ten-ten, which gave us time for a cigarette before we scooted back to the apartment. I'd said something flip about the way she was giving her all to Magna, and she made quite a speech in reply, in a very serious tone of voice. She said, "Look, cream, it's okay for you. You've been around, you've had different kinds of jobs, and if Garrison canned you, well, you'd find some other job you could get a bang out of. It's

different with me. All I've ever had is the Lodge. I can'
type. I don't know the first goddam thing about office work
I'd die if I had to go to work behind a counter in a depart
ment store, I just can't imagine what the hell I'd do.
guess I'd have to sell my body, or something."

"You could go back to the Lodge, Donna."

She said sharply, "If my old man marries that bitch
Marion? No. Boy, that's out. Dad and I had a pretty good
relationship all these years, and if she's to be the new boss
I'm not going to hang around like an unwanted doughnut
No, sir." She sat brooding. "And I can't go to my old man
for any more money. I mean, he'd give me the shirt off his
back, he's the most generous guy in the whole wide world
but I know the situation. He has some big expenses coming
up—a new cable for the ski tow, and things like that. So
hell, I just have to make my own way from now on in."

"Don't worry. You'll pass the course in a breeze."

"I *am* worried," she said. "It's no good telling me not to
worry. And there's this, too, Carol. You've seen the world
You've traveled. I haven't been anywhere, but *anywhere*
God, this is my big chance. I mean, I'm ready to wear my
feet down to the bone if that's the only way I can get to see
London and Paris and Rome. Imagine it! A weekend in Paris
To me that's heaven."

I said, "Talking about weekends, are you planning another
little trip to Palm Beach to visit your alleged cousins?"

She laughed, and then said, pouting, "No. I guess I'd better
stick with my damned Manual."

She'd changed. She'd changed quite a lot. I remembered
how indignant she'd been after my battle with Mr. Garrison
on our first morning, when she said, "They aren't going to
treat *me* like Little Orphan Annie." She was toeing the line
now. I have a theory that secretly she admired the discipline
at the training school: it was a new experience, and I think
she'd made up her mind she was going to take it simply to
prove to herself she *could* take it.

As for Alma, she practically built a nest for herself in
side her Little Black Book and she couldn't be dislodged
Another surprise. She was physically such a total sexpot that
the only reasonable assumption anybody could make was that
she'd spend every minute displaying her bulges to an admir
ing public. Not at all. She worked like a dog. She hardly
went out. She just sat on her bed, scowling at diagrams of
Constellation galleys and exit handles, trying to soak them in

I have a theory about her, too: that she came from a poor family in Rome, and in spite of all her romances with "friends" she wanted to make something of herself *by* herself. This could be a really big stepping stone, flying as an international hostess. It might lead anywhere. She'd meet diplomats, lawyers, big-game hunters, jewel thieves, all sorts of fascinating characters, whereas at home she'd most likely end up as the discarded mistress of an automobile salesman. In the circumstances, there didn't seem to be much point in passing on N.B.'s warning about Sonny Kee. She acted as if she wouldn't recognize a man if she saw one.

On Thursday afternoon we had the detailed grooming instruction which Miss Webley had promised at the beginning of the course; and for the first time in my life I felt like a Zulu warrior. A curious experience.

We changed into slacks and shirts after lunch, and returned to the classroom for a brief lecture in deportment. Sitting in a chair—we'd been through that. But there was also *getting up* from a chair, which surprised me. You don't just unglue your behind from the seat and hurl yourself out into space, hoping you'll end up standing on your two feet. Oh, no. You *rise*, gracefully. And you do it from the abdomen, so-o-o. Then, shaking hands. You don't grab and pump. You *offer* your hand, and *accept* the other person's hand. And so on, and so on.

Then Miss Webley set up hand mirrors for each of us on our desks, and we removed all our make-up with cold cream. This in itself was kind of traumatic—all these girls who'd been looking as cute as the dickens a minute earlier suddenly looked like typhoid cases. Some of them had no eyes; some of them had no mouths; some of them seemed to have no faces at all. God, we were a repulsive bunch without our ten cents' worth of make-up.

"Now, girls," Miss Webley said, "the whole point is this. Flying at high altitudes causes dryness of the skin. Also, since you're in an airplane during your working day, you don't get out into the sun. As a result, your skin tends to fade, and that's what we have to compensate for."

She didn't seem at all put out by our hideousness. She just went on talking in her sweet natural way, explaining that we must always work the cold cream *up*, so as not to get wrinkles, and remove it in the same way, *up*, with tissues; and immediately after de-creaming ourselves we always had to use an astringent. Then, she said, we had to use a base make-up with loose powder, and the base make-up had to be the liquid kind.

There were screams, there were shrieks, there were groans. I was alarmed, because I'd never used this kind of base make-up before—in fact, I'd never greatly bothered with any kind of make-up except lipstick and a few pats of powder. But Miss Webley handed out cotton pads, and bottles of liquid base, quite unperturbed by her screaming pupils, and explained how the goo was to be applied. "Merely dot it on your forehead, the tip of your nose, your cheeks and your chin," she said; and Thompson, obedient as ever, went ahead exactly as instructed, working it around in circles, getting blinder and blinder as the stuff crawled into her eyes.

I guess I must have used about ten thousand times as much as I should, because when I eventually managed to catch sight of myself in my mirror I had the shock of my life. Thompson! Where was Thompson? This wasn't Thompson, this was Chief Wa-wa-wawa, pride of the Zulus and terror of the veld, and I didn't like him, and I screamed for Donna.

"Oh, God," she said. "Give me your face," and she rubbed the stuff off me with hands that felt like an electric floor waxer, and made me start again from the beginning. There were screams all around the classroom, because half the girls had never used the stuff, and they were scared out of their wits at suddenly finding themselves transformed into bloodthirsty Africans on the warpath.

Then, when we'd dried off, we had to put on rouge. "Never," Miss Webley said, "*never* use lipstick instead of rouge on your face. *Rouge*. And take it right up to the eyes."

On it went.

"Donna!" I screamed.

"Honey, you don't have to use a *pound* of the stuff," she said. "Oh, God, give me your face again."

I was practically in tears by this time, but Miss Webley wasn't affected one little bit. We brushed powder on. We fiddled with eyebrow pencils. We lined our eyes. We put on mascara—on the upper lashes only. "Never," Miss Webley said, "on the lower lashes." Then we did our lips. "Girls," Miss Webley said, "the secret is to build up your upper lip so that it's a little fuller than your lower lip. The reason is your lower lip is naturally fuller so we build the upper lip to match. And use a lipstick brush, that's by far the best way."

When I'd finished I sat studying myself in my mirror for a long time. I'd stopped looking like a Zulu warrior. Instead I looked as if I'd just stepped out of a Shanghai whorehouse. It was a change, anyway.

Some creature came over to me and screeched. "Carol! You're *beautiful!*"

I said, "Huh?"

"Your eyes are so *expressive!*"

I said, "Who are you?"

"I'm Shirley. I'm in the next apartment to yours at the hotel. Don't you recognize me?"

I said, "Baby, your own mother wouldn't recognize you."

She laughed hysterically.

I turned to the girl beside me, who used to be Donna. "Hey."

"Hey what?"

"Is that you?"

"It's me," she said. She looked utterly stunning.

On my other side, Alma had been working away without saying a word. I could understand why. She'd simply removed her old make-up and put on exactly the same kind. She hadn't changed a fraction of an inch.

Miss Webley wandered around offering advice and making little comments. She said to Donna, "Well, really! Our passengers are going to be awfully pleased when they see *you!*"

"Thank you, Miss Webley." Donna blushed to the roots of her hair, except that it was masked by all the goo on her face.

Miss Webley said to me, "Why, Carol! You have the most kissable lips in the world."

"*Me?*" I said, and nearly fainted.

She looked at Alma for a few moments, perplexed by the lack of change. She made no comment about it, but she said, "Oh, by the way, Alma, I spoke to the Director of Training about your hair. I'm sorry. He says you'll have to obey the regulations, like everybody else. It mustn't touch the collar. I'm *very* sorry."

"I understand, Miss Webley."

"Will you have it cut tonight?"

"Miss Webley, when I finish here I fly on international flights, do I not?"

"Well, yes. I imagine so."

"Ah. In these case, I take the hair to my own hairdresser in Rome, Giuseppe, and he cut it for me. Okay?"

"Alma—"

"Yes. Giuseppe understand the way my hair grow. American hairdressers, they never understand it. Italian hair, these is something different. Okay?"

"I don't know, Alma. I'll have to ask Mr. Garrison again."

"You ask him. Very sensitive man. He won't mind."

Miss Webley walked back to her desk. "Girls: may I have your attention, please."

We sat up. Chests out, knees together, etc.

"Girls: you all look perfectly lovely. I never guessed I had a class full of such raving beauties. From now on, this is the make-up you will use every day."

"Every *day!* To come to *class!* But it takes *hours!* We'll have to get up at *four o'clock* in the *morning* to do it! Oh, Miss Webley! Not every *day!*"

We were just wasting our breath. "Now, girls," Miss Webley said. "Let's talk about your diet."

Diet. On we went to diet.

My face was literally squeaking, as we went back in the bus. It's the most curious sound in the world, your face squeaking like a pair of new shoes. I said to Donna, "I'm never going to leave the hotel without a veil."

"For God's sake, why?"

"You think I want anybody to see me like this? I'm going to get me a black veil, and I'm going to cut two holes for my eyes, and I'm going to wear it night and day."

"Carol, honestly, you look fine."

"Yeah? I expect to be branded with a scarlet letter any minute."

Jurgy was in the apartment, looking absolutely radiant. I said, "Wow! What happened to you today?"

"We had our grooming class, too."

"Gee, it really suits you, Jurgy. Wow, wow."

"Wow, wow, yourself."

"No," I said. I was still squeaking. "I'll never get used to it."

She said, "Carol, when you're free can I speak to you?"

"Sure. What's wrong with now? I'm free as the wind."

We went into her room, and she sat down on her bed in her usual hunched-up position; and as usual she didn't say a word for about an hour. She just stared into space while I waited. Eventually she turned and gave me a long, searching look and said, "Carol. Do you know anything about fishing?"

170

"Fishing! Is that what you got me in here to talk about! I despise fishing! I think it's the most cruel thing anybody can possibly do—"

She said, "This boat I'm going on with Luke next weekend. He wants to go deep-sea fishing."

"Deep-sea fishing! But that's different. Oh, boy! It's supposed to be fabulous."

"I wouldn't know." She smiled sourly. "We didn't do anything like that in Buffalo. I don't even know what to wear."

"You're really going?"

"Why not? What do I have to lose? I thought you might be able to tell me what clothes to take."

"Gee, Jurgy, that's outside my province. Wait a minute. I'll ask Donna—"

"No!" Jurgy said violently. "I don't want her in on this."

"Don't worry. I'll be tactful. But she's the great fishing expert around here. She used to go fishing with her father all the time."

I slipped out. Donna was changing into her swimsuit. I said, "Hey, Donna, tell me something. What did you wear when you went fishing with your old man?"

She stared at me. "That's a hell of a question. Why?"

"Just *tell* me."

"Hip boots," she said.

"*Hip boots?* What are they?"

"They're rubber. They come all the way above your hips so you don't get wet when you're wading."

"Gad, they sure sound glamorous. You have them here with you?"

"Are you crazy? They weigh a ton. What on earth do you want with hip boots?"

"Oh, we're just having a discussion. Is that what you wear when you go deep-sea fishing too?"

"My God, Carol, use your imagination! You don't *wade* when you're deep-sea fishing. It's *deep sea*, honey, *deep sea*."

"You don't have to shout. What do you wear for *deep sea*, then? Water wings?"

"Honey, you don't go *in* the water at all. You fish off the boat. You wear anything that's sporty—slacks and a sweater, that sort of thing. Why?"

"I told you, we're just having a discussion."

I went back to Jurgy and gave my report.

She said, "I'll have to go to Burdine's tomorrow, after we get our pay checks. Will you come with me?"

Tomorrow was Friday, payday. I said, "Your pay check isn't going to go very far. Don't you have anything casual you can wear?"

"Nothing good enough. Luke's friends will be on the boat."

"Don't worry. I have lots of stuff."

"I can't borrow from you any more."

"Oh, shut up, Jurgy. Stop acting so goddamned independent all the time. You make me sick. Every minute of the day, you act as if you have this chip on your shoulder. Always picking a fight, always arguing. We all have to live together, you know."

That silenced her temporarily, and as soon as Donna left the apartment we went and rummaged around in my closet. We found a pair of really cute pedal pushers, with gay up-and-down stripes; a pair of slinky blue slacks—very nautical, with slanted pockets in front; a couple of good-looking shirts; and a gay silk scarf that was practically designed for flapping in an offshore breeze. Good old Lord and Taylor. They think of everything to grease the skids of romance.

Jurgy said, "Carol—"

"Let's move this stuff into your room before Alma comes out of the bathroom and starts getting nosy."

We carried the things into her room and put them on her bed. Then I remembered something else, she'd need a weekend bag; and I rushed back and yanked out the smallest of my three suitcases, a white pigskin job which was really quite elegant. I said, "Here. And anything else you want, just come and ask for it. Understand?"

"Carol—"

"Oh, forget it. One of these days you can do me a favor in return."

I don't know what happened to her. She went clean out of her mind. She tore over to her chest of drawers, scrabbled around wildly, snatched something out, tore back to me, and tried to force it into my hand. It was the blue velvet case which contained the heavy gold bracelet.

We nearly came to blows. I said, "What the hell are you doing?"

"I want you to have this. I want you to have this. Take it, Carol. Take it."

"Are you crazy?"

"Take it. Please take it."

"You dope. Put it away."

"*Take it.*"

172

I said, "Mary Ruth Jurgens, be your age, will you?"

She bit her lip and put the blue velvet case back in the chest of drawers without another word. She turned her face away from me and stared out of the window, and after a few seconds I returned to the other room and settled down with my Manual.

Friday was fine except that I still hated the goo on my face. We spent the morning on dining service, actually preparing meals in the galley and serving each other. Three pairs of airplane seats had been set up in the classroom, so that six girls could act as passengers while two girls went through the routine of being the "A" and "B" hostesses. In real life, the "A" hostess does the serving, carrying the trays, giving everybody pretty smiles and so on, while the "B" hostess sets up the galley, gets out supplies and heats everything that has to be heated; and, if it happens to be a three-hostess plane, the "C" hostess helps "A" with the general serving. In practice we departed somewhat from the real-life script—"A" poking her nose into what "B" was doing in the galley, and "B" leaving her coffee-maker to ask the passengers if they desired champagne (which is the "C" hostess' duty), and it all sounded and looked rather like a Mexican revolution, with lots of giggles. Miss Webley said calmly, "Don't worry, girls, you'll soon get into the swing of it," but frankly, I didn't believe her. If any two girls in our class ever flew together, there was going to be sheer chaos.

After lunch we changed into slacks, and all of us, including the girls in Miss Pierce's class, went out to the airport and climbed aboard a Constellation, and after about an hour on the ground going over the general layout we took off and zoomed all over the sky on the first of our familiarization flights. The fascinating thing about this was that the minute we entered the cabin we felt practically at home. Everything was right there, exactly as we'd learned it, except that it was *real*, in three dimensions. The galley, the magazine racks, the card tables, the fire extinguishers, the Jacob's ladder, even the first-aid kit, precisely as advertised. No groping around. I felt as if I'd been born in one of these planes. And it was wonderful, absolutely wonderful, to be flying again. Subconsciously I'd begun to wonder if we'd ever get out of the classroom, and this first flight renewed my confidence. It might yet come about, if I could stay out of Mr. Garrison's clutches.

So, another weekend started. On Saturday morning Jurgy left the apartment at seven-thirty with a curt, "So long, every one," and when Donna demanded—after the door was closed —"Where's *she* going?" the natural answer came readily to my lips: "Oh, just visiting cousins in Palm Beach." Alma was behaving in a highly suspicious manner, humming to herself and smiling her mysterious little smile as she ironed some wisps of lace and silk which she had the nerve to call underwear, and I said to her, "Do you have again an as-signation with your friend the box fighter?" Donna was in the room, so I spoke Italian. Box fighter was rather tough, but I rendered it as *pugiliste*, and it seemed to register.

She said loftily, "Why do you ask this question? Is it any concern of yours with whom I have assignations?"

The art of conversation may be dying in this country, but in Italy it's on the same level as opera, and often you can't tell which is which. I said, "Please listen to me, Alma, dear one. I have no desire to concern myself with your assigna-tions, but I have heard that this box fighter is a man of whom one should be careful. It is said by those who know him that his character is not of the best."

She ironed two pairs of so-called panties and a so-called slip while she answered this. It was a complete discourse on minding your own business, with references to the secret police, and being surrounded by spies who were nothing but jealous virgins. *That* certainly struck home, although it wasn't literally true, and I interrupted with a loud scream of protest which she didn't even bother to hear. She wrapped the whole thing up by saying more or less finally, "If you were not so blind with jealousy you would realize that I can guard myself well. I do not need these warnings. Be-sides, he is a simple American boy, without great technique."

"Fool not yourself, dear one, there are plenty of bambinos in Italy that were brought about by simple American boys. They had enough technique for what they wanted, and some to spare."

"Pooh. This is a boy of the best class. He owns an Italian car. Do you wish more proof than this? A Lancia. Even in Rome, only people of the very best class can own a Lancia, with only two seats for the sport."

"Listen to me, Alma. In Miami Beach such a car is prac-tically an admission of guilt."

But she was pigheaded as usual, and I had to admit that I really didn't have a leg to stand on. I mean, if anybody had

174

come to me a year ago and said, "Listen, Carol, beware of Tom Ritchie; underneath that crew cut he's nothing but a fiend in human form," I'd have answered in much the same way. Not at quite such length, maybe, but with much the same kind of argument. In fact, when I come to think about it, I'm surprised Alma was so tolerant. I'd done my best, though, and when she flounced out shortly before noon all I could do was utter a sigh.

Another aspect of this whole business was, she looked so sumptuous, and her eyes were glittering with such anticipation, that both Donna and I were convulsed with jealousy because *we* didn't have dates; and the minute she left we began to show all the symptoms of going stir-crazy. That was the great occupational hazard on the fourteenth floor; one minute you were worrying about heating beef stew in the galley, and the next minute you were wondering hysterically whether you'd ever smell a man again. There was a complete and utter and total *absence* of the creatures. I remember one evening one of the elevator boys, a pimply creature just growing a mustache, stepped out of his car to deliver a birthday telegram to one of the girls. Did she thank him? No. She screamed, "Do you realize you're taking your life in your hands coming up here?" and the little monster was so scared he tore back to his elevator and dived right down to the basement and wasn't seen again for a week.

Eventually, about half an hour after Alma left, Donna said, "Listen, if we don't get out of this place soon I'm going to start busting up the furniture," and I said, "Donna, strangely enough, I feel exactly the same way." I probably felt worse, because Ray Duer was to all intents and purposes underfoot, and I was growing more and more heated because he didn't have the simple decency to pick up the telephone and call me. Just to hear him say, "Carol, we mustn't go on" (as if we'd ever started), or "Carol, we must never see each other again," would have been balm to my lonely heart. But there wasn't a peep out of him, and I took it hard.

Donna said, "Stop looking like a ghost, slap some clothes on and let's get out." So I slapped on a rather cute little flowered number, and Donna slapped on another piece of greenery, and out we went, looking rather like the Hanging Gardens of Babylon. As we walked to the elevator, Donna said, "Let's take the car," but I was prepared for that. "If you take the car," I said, "you're on your own." She said, "My God, sometimes you sound like George Washington," and I said, "Nuts. The car is out, as far as I'm concerned, and you know it." So we took a taxi and asked to be dropped at Burdine's, which is a sort of central dropping station for girls; and as we were climbing out of the taxi two tall young handsome Air Force boys strolled by, and whistled long and low. I hate to admit this, but that sound was music to my ears. I blushed. Donna smiled with secret satisfaction, and I could actually feel her having the same sensation that I was having—Mon Dieu, I'm a girl again. Out of the corner of my eye, I managed to observe that one was a captain and the other a full lieutenant, but Donna didn't even turn her head one one-thousandth of an inch. She gripped my arm, and to my consternation led me into the store; but as soon as she was inside she stopped short, as if she were wondering where the ladies' room was. Two seconds later both Air Force boys practically crashed into us—Donna had calculated it to the millimeter, they couldn't possibly *miss* crashing into us—and she sang out, "Why, fellows! I don't mind being loved to death, but I sure hate the idea of being trampled to death," and there we all stood, laughing like idiots.

The captain, whose name turned out to be Elliott Ewing, and the lieutenant, whose name was Bob Keeler, weren't any slouches, either. Almost before I knew what was happening we were being led away to some elegant restaurant where Elliott thought we might have a spot of lunch, as he called it. Befitting his rank, too, he had first pick of the loot, and he very sensibly chose Donna, leaving the dregs to his subordinate. I didn't mind—there wasn't anything I could do about it, and actually, of the two men I preferred Bob Keeler. On close inspection, Elliott was a rather tough guy, heavily built and very sure of himself. Bob was quieter and nicer —maybe that's why he was only a lieutenant. He was fair in his coloring, with brown eyes, and hair like cut straw; and possibly this was what made our association safe, because my heart had been sliced in two by a character with gray eyes and dark hair, a psychiatrist by trade.

The strange part of the situation was that I remained embarrassed and tongue-tied for an incredibly long time. At Bryn Mawr, for example, you might go in to Philadelphia and be picked up by a boy from Haverford or Swarthmore; and it didn't mean a thing because those boys were in a way like your own brother. In the Village there was a sort of unwritten law that if you lived there and dressed and acted like a Villager, then you belonged to the human race. But this thing with the Air Force was different, for reasons I couldn't figure out. I suppose it had something to do with age. I was a mature old lady of twenty-two, and when you reach that mountain peak, being picked up is a little undignified. Or that's my theory.

It became easier as the afternoon progressed. Elliott was amusing, Donna was funny as hell, Bob was rather cute, and we laughed a lot. That helped. Laughter is the great ice-breaker. And then I realized that, after all, these two boys were in much the same fix as Donna and I. You could tell from the way they talked that we were doing them an enormous favor sitting in an expensive restaurant with them and absorbing pounds and pounds of stone crab Thermidor. As far as I could make out, they were both pretty desperate. They were confined most of the time to some mysterious installation where their job was to keep guard over the liquor stores of their commanding officer, a certain General Wuzzy Goof, and they were also supposed to maintain friendly relations with the draftees to prevent mutiny. "Really!" Donna and I said; but I guessed they were from Cape Canaveral or one of those other rocket places, and later I found that Donna had guessed the same. We couldn't blame them for being cagey. From the way we ambushed them they'd have been fully justified in assuming we'd just stepped ashore from a Russian submarine.

Elliott had a shiny new Dodge, and after lunch he insisted on driving us over to see Fort Lauderdale; and Bob Keeler and I sat in the back and began to get acquainted. It turned out that he was an intellectual type, and of all things in the world for an Air Force lieutenant, he was wild about all that old Beat Generation stuff. You never can tell with people: I'm always being surprised. As far as I could make out, his only ambition, apart from sending a rocket to Mars or somewhere, was to get his immortal words printed in some lousy San Francisco anthology. Of course, I didn't mention that I'd lived in Greenwich Village for six months, and that I'd sat around for days and nights on end with some of those slobs; I just let on, very casually, that I'd read this and read that, and the boy looked as if he'd been *bombed*. He couldn't believe his ears. He'd met a human *girl* who'd heard of Sartre! Who'd heard of Zen! "You *have!*" he kept saying, "you *have!*" just as if it were a major miracle.

I should have kept my big mouth shut. By the time we reached Fort Lauderdale he'd fallen head over heels in love with me—not with *me*, but this soulmate who'd been sent straight into his arms by Destiny. There he was, probably dreaming of the day when he could get out of uniform and start growing a beard, and suddenly *I* appear in his life, practically fresh from the Overnite Café. It just sent him into a frenzy. And all I could think was, there's the proof: never let yourself be picked up by strange men. First N.B. Now Bob Keeler.

Fort Lauderdale reminded me of Venice, with all those waterways: a souped-up, jazzed-up, flattened-out Venice jammed with forty-thousand-dollar Chris-Craft and hundred-and-fifty-thousand-dollar waterfront homes. Donna was enchanted by it, and her enthusiasm led Elliott to announce another project. "Listen, kids. How about going to the jai-alai game tonight? Eh?"

It left me speechless because I had no idea what he was talking about, but Donna found out. "Gee! That sounds wonderful!" she cried at the top of her lungs. "What is it?"

He explained that it was a bit like handball, but the players wore things like baskets on their arm which they used instead of their hands, and it was the hardest, fastest, toughest game known to man. It sounded lively. First, though, we went to another huge and elegant restaurant where Elliott said we could have a spot of dinner; but before anything was ordered, Donna and I slid away to the ladies' room for a dab of powder and a conference.

"How do you like these boys?" she asked. "Cute, aren't they?"

"Yes. Cute."

"You seem to be making out pretty well with the lieutenant."

"He's okay."

"What's this Zen stuff I hear him talking about?"

"Zen?" I said.

"Yes, Zen. It sounds like one of these new underarm deodorants they're always plugging on TV. Zen first, zen romance." She giggled. "Oh, Carol. Isn't it great to feel alive again? Isn't it?"

I didn't answer. I needed electricity to make me feel really alive, and there wasn't any electricity around. Why am I so hixed on that confounded man, I asked myself; and I couldn't answer. I was just hixed, and hixed good.

He was at the jai-alai game, with Mr. Garrison, Mrs. Garrison, and Peg Webley. Naturally. If I'd only stopped to think for one minute, once Donna and I had listened to fate's wolf whistle, and been picked up by Elliott and Bob, there probably was no place on this planet where we could have gone that night without running into Ray Duer and Arnie Garrison. I should have *known*. Mrs. Garrison and Peg Webley were just a bonus.

Just as inevitably, we had seats three rows in front of them. And I was so paralyzed by the way fate was treating me that I sat there as rigid as a lamppost in a snowstorm, knees together, chin up, chest out, etc. In any other circumstances I could have been regarded as a credit to Miss Webley's training. In these circumstances I was nothing but a prowling bitch who'd picked up a fine upstanding innocent young American boy with intent to disgrace both him and his uniform; and I could feel four pairs of eyes fixed disgustedly on the back of my neck. There was absolute pandemonium around us while the players smashed at the ball with those baskets on their hands: people were shouting and yelling and making bets, and getting up from their seats and crawling out, and then crawling back, and eating hot dogs; but I hardly saw or heard a thing. To make matters worse—as if they could get worse than they already were—Bob was seized with overwhelming affection for me as the game progressed. Wasn't I his soulmate? Wasn't I the girl from the limberlost? Every time he thought of Zen he tenderly reached for my hand. He must have read Norman Mailer, too, because now and then he'd drop his hand, purely by accident, and finger the hem of my skirt and edge his way inward to my kneecap. Or he'd light a cigarette and, purely by accident, hold the cigarette so that his knuckles rubbed against my left bosom. Or he'd put his program down on my lap and a minute later scrabble around to find the program again. *Now* I understood why Magna was so insistent on our wearing girdles whenever we went out. My God, they should have issued us spiked chastity belts—it was the least they could do for us in this mad jungle called Life. The final hell of it was that I had to fend Bob off without *appearing* to fend him off: I couldn't, under the scrutiny of those four pairs of eyes, turn to him and say with authority, Cut it out. They'd have seen. All I could do was growl at him out of the corner of my mouth, which he seemed to think showed that I was getting whipped up into a lather of sexual excitement, and as a result he just redoubled his efforts.

At half-time, or whatever the break was called, we trooped out into the milling crowds to meet fate head-on. We had to. Donna and I figured it out simultaneously. We'd be in a better position if we were brazen than if we remained cowering in our seats covered with a mantle of guilt.

They were waiting for us, not in anger but with mild interest, no doubt wondering in which direction we'd wriggle first. Mr. G. wore a benign smile; Mrs. G., a lovely woman of about thirty-five, wore a fairly welcoming smile, as if to say she'd been a girl once herself; Miss Webley wore her "Now, children," smile; Ray Duer wore a regular psychiatric smile: he'd experienced everything, nothing could surprise him any more.

Donna rushed in, seizing the bull by the horns. "Why, hello! Mr. Garrison and Mrs.—?"

"Mrs. Garrison," Mrs. Garrison said.

"How nice to meet you," Donna said sweetly. "And Miss Webley! And Dr. Duer! What a surprise! Isn't the game *exciting!*"

It was a fine effort. They were taken aback.

"Miss Webley," she continued, with the same wild abandon, "do you remember I went to Palm Beach last weekend to visit my cousin? Well, isn't it darling of him, this weekend Cousin Elliott came to visit little old me! May I introduce him? Captain . . . Glug."

The martinis she'd had before dinner had done their dirty work. She'd forgotten his name. So had I. I couldn't remember it for the life of me. Something to do with sheep.

"How do, Captain Glug," Mr. Garrison said. So did Mrs. Garrison. So did Miss Webley and Dr. Duer.

He said faintly, "How do."

Donna remembered Bob's name. And as she introduced him, Ray Duer and I saw each other, we saw each other with a million volts of pure electricity illuminating the scene, he saw clear through to my heart which he'd cut into two neat slices, and I saw clear through to his heart and knew that I'd done the same to him. He wasn't handsome, he wasn't huge and strong, he wasn't anything except the man I'd fallen in love with, God knows why; and I wanted to hear one word from him, just one word so that I could have the joy of hearing his wonderful voice.

He said, "Are you enjoying the game?" He said it to me.

"No," I said. "Are you?"

He said, "It's fast."

"It's too fast," I said. "It makes me dizzy." There was communion between us. Miraculously, he understood what I meant; the words inside me, unspoken, reached him through the foolish words I spoke. For a moment he was grave, and then he smiled gently and nodded.

"Is it really too fast for you, Carol?" Miss Webley asked.

"I like the action to be a little slower."

He said, "It's that kind of game."

Nobody else could have guessed, but we were conversing in a language which was untranslatable and known only to each other. What I had said to him was, I love you, I miss you; and what he had said was, I love you too, but wait, please wait. I was ready to wait forever, now that he'd put it so clearly; and for the rest of the evening poor Bob couldn't understand what had happened. I was there, smiling, but I wasn't there. He seemed completely bewildered as we said good night in the lobby of the Charleroi: I existed, but I'd ceased to exist.

The time was a quarter of twelve. I'd pleaded a sick headache to get back, so that I could contemplate Ray Duer and me in privacy. Donna was still out with Elliott Glug.

I said, "Well, good-by, Lieutenant Bob Keeler, thank you for a perfectly lovely evening. It was swell."

He said, "Am I going to see you again, Carol?"

I said, not unkindly, "Why spoil a good relationship?"

"By George," he said, "you sure know all the answers. Does that mean you have a boy friend, or something?"

I just looked at him.

"Okay," he said. "And so long."

"So long."

He was cute in his way, but it wasn't enough. I was getting to be pretty choosy in my old age. If anybody was going to finger the hem of my skirt, I knew exactly who that somebody was going to be; and he lived practically underfoot. For that's the surest sign of love I know, when the man you love encounters you with another man, and can talk to you in an untranslatable language, fully aware that your love belongs entirely to him. Bliss, bliss.

The next morning Donna was rewarded with a genuine old-fashioned hangover, the kind Mother used to make, in which you feel your head has been left in the Mixmaster all night, and you were baked at the wrong temperature, and the dough rose too high. I could sympathize with her, because

181

I've had a couple of those vintage hangovers myself. So I fixed her a couple of prairie oysters and forced them down her throat, and I planted an ice pack on her head, and left her to groan in misery while I took care of the household chores. With Jurgy away, and Alma acting mysterious, and Donna hors de combat, there was plenty for one pair of hands to do. We were expected to keep 1412 immaculate, and when I finished it didn't look too bad.

Donna had half a slice of toast for lunch, averting her eyes as I ravenously consumed a hamburger; and then she decided she might as well die in peace, and took a Nembutal. I waited until she was decently laid out, changed into my good old black swimsuit, and went down to the pool with my Manual. There, swathed in gauze and wearing a picture hat to keep the sun off her, was Alma, fanning herself with a magazine; and with her was the guy with the pushed-in nose who was obviously Sonny Kee.

It was the only time I ever saw him, and he didn't look obnoxious. He wasn't very big, only about five feet eight, but he was all muscle. Big Top Charlie was all muscle, too, but his muscles were purely for decoration—they were useless for anything else. Sonny Kee's muscles were for use. They weren't pretty. They were distributed in clumps across his back and at the top of his arms and down his belly. His skin was covered with black hair. There wasn't anything beautiful about him: he was even slightly bowlegged. His face had no meaning. The pushed-in nose had robbed him of all expression, and he actually reminded me a little of a Boston bull terrier—he had some of the same difficulty with his breathing. The only way I can describe his face is, bland and beady-eyed. And the only other thing I noticed about him was that he seemed to have a permanent thirst. While I was down there he must have gone to the water fountain about a dozen times. He couldn't get enough water into his blood stream, and what this means is beyond me. It could mean, of course, that he was plain thirsty—he might have had ham for lunch. I was struck by it, though: the way he kept returning to the water fountain, and the way the muscles of his throat moved up and down as he gulped the water.

He was obviously crazy about Alma. He hung around her, just yearning to serve. Naturally, she lapped it up, she encouraged him to the hilt. She was coy, she was flirtatious, she was fluttery; and if this is European sex they can keep it in Europe, all of it. Furthermore, she wasn't sharing him with anybody. He was all hers. She must have seen me swimming, she knew I was in the immediate vicinity, but she didn't give me a look.

This was the only time I saw the box fighter. I didn't speak to him. I didn't even get to say hello. I didn't have a chance to feel anything about him, pro or con.

She came up to change at six-thirty, looking as smug as a pregnant bedbug. She was going out to dinner with him. So I opened my eyes as wide as I could and said breathlessly, "Alma! Who was that man I saw you with at the pool?"

"Man?" she said. "At the pool?"

"The pocket Hercules."

She trilled with laughter. "Oh, these is my friend, Sonny. You saw him?"

"Just out of the corner of my eye, Alma. You're going to be careful with him, now, aren't you?"

"Carola! You are so funn-ee! He licks my fingers."

"Just be careful."

She said, "Oh, Carola, you are the big clown. Now, please excuse. I must use the bathroom."

He must have waited for her at least an hour. She was looking just like Carmen when she left, only more so. "Remember," I said. "Be careful." She shrugged one shoulder.

Donna slept on; and at nine-thirty Jurgy telephoned.

I thought the call might be from Ray Duer, and I snatched up the receiver shaking in every limb. But it was only Jurgy, so husky-voiced that I didn't know for a moment who was speaking.

"Carol?"

"Yes?"

"This is Jurgy—Mary Ruth Jurgens."

"Oh, hi, Jurgy. Where are you?"

"Down in the basement. Outside the shower room."

"Did you catch any fish?"

"Yeah. A sailfish. About six foot long."

"Jurgy! Do you have it with you?" It was the only reason I could think of for a telephone call from outside the shower room.

"No. We threw it back. Carol, listen. Are you doing anything?"

"Nothing important."

"Do me a big favor, will you? Come down for a minute. I'll be on the beach, right in front of the hotel."

"Now?"

"Yes. Carol, I can't face the apartment, I can't face the other girls."

"Okay."

"Thanks, Carol."

She was where she said she'd be, on the beach in front of the hotel. I couldn't have failed to recognize her. She was wearing my striped pedal pushers and one of my Lord and Taylor blouses. There was still a little daylight left, the tail end of dusk, and I knew from previous experience that the night sky was plenty bright enough for any tête-à-tête.

"Hi, Carol."

"Hi, Jurgy."

She led me down to the water, away from the hotel, where a couple of palm trees sprouted up out of the sand at a sharp angle to each other. I said, "Well, what is it, Jurgy?" but she didn't answer. She began to pace back and forth, back and forth, her head bent forward; and she was so trapped in her thoughts that she seemed to forget my presence. At last she stopped and stood facing me, rocking on her heels.

She said, "I have news for you, Carol."

"Good news?"

"I don't know. I can't figure out any answers."

"Tell me then."

She sniffed several times. She rubbed the tip of her nose with the back of her hand. Then she said, "He wants me to marry him."

"Mr. Lucas!"

"Yeah, Mr. Luke Lucas. He asked me to marry him." She came close to me and said, "Look." There was a ring on the fourth finger of her right hand, a plain white band which might have been platinum. But then she turned her hand slowly so that it was palm up, and I saw the stone, a huge white stone, sparkling in the stray light coming out of the dark sky.

I said, "Oh, my God, what is it?"

"A square-cut diamond. That's what he told me."

"Oh, my God, Jurgy, if it's real it must be worth a fortune."

Her voice was cold. "It's real."

Tears were streaming out of my eyes. I couldn't help myself. I was so sorry for her, my heart was ready to break. I wanted to sit down and weep and wail and rend my garments and rub ashes in my hair. I said, "Jurgy, no. You aren't going to marry him."

"Yes."

"Jurgy, are you crazy? You're a beautiful girl, you have everything ahead of you, you can't throw yourself away on this old man. Jurgy, you can't do it."

"He's fifty-six."

I cried, "My God, is that supposed to be *young*, or something?"

She said bitterly, "You don't trust me."

"I *trust* you. Of course I trust you. But this is *wicked*, it's a *crime*, there ought to be a law against it—"

"Look, Carol. I have to talk to somebody, I've *got* to talk to somebody. You're the only person I know." She cried passionately, "Carol, *listen* to me, will you?"

We had to calm ourselves, we had to try to face this ghastly situation with quieter minds, we couldn't stand out here screaming at each other. I said, "Would you like a cigarette?"

"I smoked a pack and a half today already."

"Jurgy, you'll have to cut down. You can get cancer, smoking as heavily as that."

"I know it."

She took one, though, and the brief interval helped us both. We were both practically over the edge.

I said, "Who else was on the boat for the weekend?"

"A cattleman from Texas, a guy named Harry Winnaker; and his wife Alice Bce; and the crew, Big Joe and Little Joe —I didn't find out their full names. That's what everyone called them: Big Joe and Little Joe."

"Did you catch lots of fish?"

"Harry Winnaker got a sailfish. And I got one. That's supposed to be tremendous. We ran up two sailfish flags."

"What are they?"

"When you catch a sailfish you run up one of these flags with a sailfish painted on it, so everyone will know. If you catch a marlin, you run up a marlin flag, Carol."

"Okay, go on, I'm listening."

She did the pacing bit for a few moments, her head down; then she came back to me. "It's like this. He has three kids. One's eleven, one nine, one three. That's when he lost his wife, when she had this last baby. He needs someone to take care of the kids and run a home for them and for him, and so on."

"But, *Jurgy*—"

She made a gesture with her hand. "I know what you're

going to say. He doesn't need a wife. He needs a nurse or something, a housekeeper, and why pick on me? Eh?"

I cried, "That's absolutely right! Why pick on a beautiful young girl, why ruin her life? All he needs is trained help."

She said, "He's in love with me, that's all."

"Oh, yeah? Nuts."

She said, "Carol, just listen, will you? Stop shooting off your mouth about him."

"Okay," I said. "Okay. Go on."

She said, "I'll tell you just what he told me. Right?"

"Right."

"He told me, he was in the lobby the evening we all arrived from New York. He picked me out right then—"

"That *first* evening!"

"Yeah. That first evening, when we walked into the Charleroi, he picked me out. He kept looking for me all week—and I know that's true because I'd noticed this big lug eying me. Last night, on the boat, I asked him what he saw in me that took his fancy so much. You know what he said? He said, he can judge a woman the same way he can judge a steer, in one minute."

"Oh, boy!" I cried. "That's some compliment. My God, if any man said that to me I'd slap his goddam face."

"It wasn't meant to be a compliment. Listen, Carol, we had quite a talk last night. I told him what I'd been: a waitress. He said he used to sling hash for the cattlemen. I told him my father's been to jail. He said, what the hell, he'd been in jail a dozen times, once for killing a guy. I told him about how I had this baby, and he said too bad it didn't live, he'd like to have another kid around."

My eyes had become wet. I said, "Jurgy, he sounds nicer than I thought. But he's still fifty-six—"

"Carol, you don't know what you're talking about. This guy won't let up even when he's a hundred. You know why he comes to Miami Beach so much?"

"I can guess."

"Number one, for the fishing. Number two, for the call girls. That's how he put it, last night when we had this long talk. I told him he was a stinking old liar, it was number one for the call girls, number two for the fishing. He admitted maybe I was right, but what the hell could he do about it, that's how nature made him."

"Jesus," I said. "An old man like that! It's kind of sickening to think of, Jurgy."

"Is it?"

I couldn't answer honestly. She had somehow given him quite a build-up, he sounded a bit more human than the usual run of old men who go around sniffing at girls' bicycle seats.

I said, "Jurgy. I'll be honest with you. I don't know what to say. I'm just in a state of shock."

She cried, bitterly and passionately, "What state do you think I'm in? I just came here to be an airline hostess. I thought *that* was something. And now *this* happens to me."

"Are you in love with him?"

She bit her lip. "I don't know. I respect him. I never met a man like Luke in the whole of my life. I *respect* him. That's something I never expected to happen."

I used the butt of my cigarette to light another. She said, "Let me have one, Carol," and we stood smoking, without speaking, for a couple of minutes. The branches of the palm trees were creaking overhead, the water was hissing gently just a few feet away, and the South American music from the hotel terrace drifted across the soft air.

I said, "Why are you wearing your ring on your right hand?"

"I told Luke: I don't want to be engaged until the course is over. He made me take the ring anyway."

"You mean, you're going to stay on with Magna?"

"Yeah. I want to fly for six months before I get married."

"But why?"

She raged at me. "I *need* it, Carol, I *need* it. You don't realize, just in this little time they've practically made me over at the training school. You don't know what Miss Pierce already did for me. I need some polish before I can take over a home, Luke's or anybody's."

I said, "You know something, Jurgy?"

"What?"

"I've changed my mind."

"What about?"

"You and Mr. Lucas."

Her voice was suspicious. "You have?"

"I think it's going to work out."

"You do?" Her voice was still suspicious.

"I think maybe it will."

"Thanks, Carol."

We finished our cigarettes, and began to trudge back to the hotel. She took the ring off and put it carefully in her handbag, and I said, merely as an idle statement, a comment on the news, "He must have some money stashed away to be able to buy you a ring like that, and that gold bracelet."

She said, "Yeah. He's worth about thirty-five million."

The sky came down and hit me on the top of the head. The beach rose up and hit me under the chin. I stopped, and I clutched at her arm because I was suddenly so dizzy. I gasped, "Are you *kidding?*"

"Alice Bee Winnaker told me this morning."

"Jurgy! You're *kidding!*"

"That's what she told me, Carol. I don't have any way of checking on it. She said he's one of the biggest cattle breeders in the country."

"Oh, my God," I said. "Thirty-five *million!* It's impossible."

"I'm only repeating what Alice Bee said."

I was still dizzy with shock. The night sky was whirling around my head in circles. I said, "Holy smoke, Jurgy, you'll be able to *buy* Magna International Airlines. You'll be able to have your own private Boeing 707."

She said violently, "I don't want to buy *anything.* I just hope to God if I marry him I can be a good wife to him, and have some peace in my life for the first time." She burst into tears and threw herself into my arms, sobbing on my shoulder. "That dirty old son of a bitch, if he goes with another call girl I'll break his neck. I will. I swear I will."

I said, "Did you tell him, honey?"

"You bet I told him. I scared the bejeesus out of him." She laughed hoarsely through her tears, like a crow. "He turned white as a sheet."

I held her while she had a good cry, and then she released herself and dried her eyes. She said, "Don't mention this to any of the others," and I said, "You can trust me." Then she said, "Thirty-five million dollars—it doesn't make sense, does it?" I said, "Well, I guess it will give you a sense of security." She said, "No. That's the funny thing. It isn't important. Luke's all that's important. All the rest, it's just icing on the cake."

I knew what she meant; and in a way I envied her.

10

They doubled up on us the following week. They doubled the pressure, and how. Miss Webley made the situation clear as soon as we were assembled in class on Monday morning. "Now, girls," she said, "we have a lot of ground to cover in the next few days, and I want to warn you—one or two afternoons we may have to stay after four-thirty, our usual dismissal time."

Somebody groaned.

"Also," she said, "I want to tell you this well in advance so that you don't make any commitments: we'll be working on Saturday until three o'clock. I'm afraid this means a rather short weekend."

Everybody groaned.

Miss Webley continued calmly, "The first order of business, girls, is uniforms. We must get this out of the way by noon. Mrs. Sharpless is here to give you your fittings, so let's hurry over to Room 15. And, please. No lingering."

Not all of us went to Room 15. She gently detained two girls, whom we never saw again; and we learned later that two girls in Miss Pierce's class had also been released from the course. They were still whittling us down. We were only twenty-nine now.

Trying on the uniforms was a wild experience. Mrs. Sharpless was a busy little woman who'd been with Magna ever since they started flying balloons, and she didn't go wrong. Those russet skirts and jackets fitted like gloves. There we were, jazzed up in all our war paint and attired in our uniforms for the first time, and I was suddenly struck right between the eyes by the realization that every one of us had changed. Boy, we'd changed. I mean—excepting myself for a moment—we'd come together at the Charleroi just two weeks ago, a fairly good-looking bunch of girls with reasonably good proportions, full of vim and vigor; and now here we were, a mere two weeks later, quite different. We'd added some magic ingredient, and we were practically unrecognizable. I don't know what the magic ingredient was. But everybody looked a little taller and a little straighter, and a little more serious, and a little more dignified. I said to Miss Webley, "You ought to take a bow," and she said, "Why, Carol?" and I said, "Just look around you." She laughed and said, "Oh, this is only the beginning. You still have another ten days to go." I thought, Lord! How much *can* one change without nature striking back?

After lunch we were handed our jet Manuals. We remained in class until five o'clock. The following day was tougher: we stayed until five-thirty. On Wednesday we stayed until five again. We had tests roughly every three hours. We stayed up at night almost until dawn, doing our home study. Miss Webley's manner became sharper and sharper; she was less indulgent, she simply wouldn't stand for any nonsense. "Don't forget," Miss Webley said. "In the event of an accident, the Civil Aeronautics Board will call for all your papers, to make sure you knew your stuff when you became a hostess. You can't weasel your way out of that." Mr. Garrison lectured us, engineers lectured us, and nice Dr. Elizabeth Schwartz began to give us a series of lectures on first-aid. As far as I could see, we had to be able to do *everything*, short of navigating by radar and starting up the engines. We had to be cooks, barmaids, geisha girls, ticket inspectors, baby sitters, waitresses, lavatory attendants, and medical experts into the bargain. We had to know what to do about airsickness (a natural hazard), nosebleed, hiccups (why hadn't I been told about this before?), pains in the abdomen, foreign bodies in the eye, heart attacks, epileptic fits, all the way through to delivering a baby. When Dr. Schwartz referred to this last calamity, during her introductory lecture when she was merely outlining the subjects she intended to deal with, the girls nearly fainted en masse. She put on the mildly surprised look which Miss Webley pulled on us so often, and said, "But, girls, it has happened often enough in the past. It's only too possible that a woman might go into labor on *your* plane, flying over the Atlantic, and you'd look awfully silly if you didn't know what were the first steps you should take. You couldn't just leave her in a corner to handle it by herself, could you? That might be tantamount to murder. Don't you agree?"

Frankly, I didn't. The more I thought about it—all that mess, and all that blood, and the female bellowing at the top of her lungs—the more I began to feel that no woman ought to be allowed to fly if there was even a suspicion that she might be with child. Certainly not on *my* plane. But Alma wasn't dismayed. She said loudly, "Delivering a baby, these is not hard."

"There you are, girls," Dr. Schwartz said. "I hope Alma has reassured you."

"First," Alma said, "you must have many pails of boiling water—" She was ready to expound the whole routine on the spot.

Dr. Schwartz said, "Alma, we'll be going into this in detail later."

"But it is simple," Alma said. "You lay the woman down with pillows under her back, and find her a rope to pull on—"

"Alma, we'll go into that next week."

"Yes, but you must tie the rope—"

"Alma," Dr. Schwartz said: "Our technique is a little different nowadays. But *you* know it isn't alarming, and *I* know it isn't, and we'll convince the rest of the class one week from today. Right?"

"Okay."

On Thursday morning, one of the girls in our class went to see Mr. Garrison and resigned. Twenty-eight. That afternoon, one of the girls in Jurgy's class was called to the Medical Department and told that it would be unwise for her to fly on regular schedule because she had an anemic condition. Dr. Schwartz had discovered it right at the beginning and had tried to improve things by giving the poor kid pills, but no go. Twenty-seven.

And that night, Thursday night, Donna cracked slightly. She'd been a model citizen all week. Most of the week before, too. She'd adjusted marvelously to life on the fourteenth floor, all things considered; and she was way ahead of me in class. I used to think I was a fairly bright kid, until I came to Miami Beach; but I hardly *clung* to my ninety percent average, whereas Donna hit a bull's-eye nearly every time. She was one of those people with what you might call concealed brains. I wouldn't go out on a limb and say she was the greatest female genius since Madame Curie. She was just naturally brilliant and, what irritated me to death, it didn't mean a thing to her.

On Thursday, then, at about nine o'clock, when we were all sweating away at our Manuals, she suddenly stood up and said, "Kids, I've had it."

I said unsympathetically, "Who hasn't?"

"Want to come out for a breath of fresh air?"

She had a glint in her eyes. I said, "Where's *out?*"

"Oh, I just thought I'd drive around for a while."

"No," I said. I still wouldn't go in N.B.'s Impala.

She sounded relieved. "Okay. I'll see you anon."

She changed from slacks to a dress, put on a pair of gold earrings and a gold charm bracelet, and went out swinging her hips. Jurgy and Alma and I continued to sweat over the treatment of epilepsy, and preflight procedures, and the mechanism of escape hatches; and I have to admit we were fraying around the edges. The pressure was beginning to show its effects. We were drinking quarts of black coffee to keep ourselves awake, but it only kept us awake at the expense of our nerves.

So when Donna returned, after midnight, I didn't exactly flap my wings with joy. In fact, I didn't say a word. I just looked her up and down with utter contempt, and went on studying nosebleeds.

"Hey!" she said, leaning against the door and laughing. "Why the look?"

She'd been drinking, of course. She was flushed and happy and beautiful. I said in freezing tones, "Do you know how late it is?"

She tried to focus her eyes on her wrist watch, and couldn't. She shook the damned thing and held it to her ear and listened intently; then she took the earring off that ear, and shook the watch again, and then she said in a husky whisper, "You know what? My watch has stopped."

"Is that so?"

"Oh, hell, cream," she said. "Don't bawl me out."

I said, "Listen, Stewart. I couldn't care less. If you want to bitch up everything for yourself at this stage of the game, that's your affair, not mine."

She tottered across the room and sat down beside me. "Sugar, don't be mean to Donna. Please."

I said, "Get the hell off my bed. I'm trying to work."

She giggled, "Carol. You know what I did?"

"No. And I don't give a damn."

She said, "I have a confession to make, Carol."

"Go and confess somewhere else, will you? Leave me alone."

"Carol, you're not going to like this, Carol, baby."

"Why don't you let me concentrate? Get your can out of here. Beat it."

"I banged up the car, Carol."

"Oh, no," I said. "Oh, *no*."

"Yep." She began to make motions in the air with her arms. "You know that turn at the bottom of the driveway, into the garage? It's just crazy, it's the craziest thing. Why, you're coming down this steep incline, and then you have practically this two-hundred-and-forty-degree turn, and honestly it's a menace. You can't *help* crashing into something—"

I said, "My God, Donna, you didn't. You *didn't*."

"Yep. I did."

I just stared at her in speechless horror.

She laughed. "Don't look like that. I just banged up a fender. It won't be any trouble to get it fixed."

Somehow everything, but everything, was involved in this accident: my feelings for Ray Duer, my feelings about N.B., my feelings about the training course—my feelings about the whole world. I ended up simply one great mass of blind, helpless rage. I *stormed* at Donna. I *raved* at her.

She said, "Look, you don't have to have hysterics. It's only a fender, Carol. My God, anybody can bump a *fender*."

"You're damned right they can," I said. "Specially when they've had a few drinks."

She stood up with icy dignity, staggered into the bathroom, and took a shower. I guess she felt I'd betrayed our friendship. She just couldn't get it into her head that I had such deep emotions about this car, I couldn't bear to have it bumped even by a raindrop. She didn't speak to me, and I didn't speak to her, until noon the following day. Then, in the cafeteria, we made it up, with a minimum of words, and by evening we were on more or less our old terms. She said, "Don't worry, honey, I'll speak to the garage man and have the bump ironed out, I promise," and I tried to forget the whole unhappy business.

By three o'clock on Saturday afternoon even Miss Webley looked as if she were going to crumple at any moment. There were shadows under her eyes. Her cheeks seemed to have fallen in. But she still held herself straight when she dismissed us, she still managed to smile and speak in a sweet voice. She said, "Girls: it's been quite a week, hasn't it? Really, I'm surprised to find myself standing on my feet; and I can just imagine how all of you must be feeling. But next week, I promise you, is going to be a lot easier. Just four days of work, and then on Friday you have your graduation ceremony." She looked down at a paper on her desk. "Incidentally, the graduation ceremony will be held in the Empress Room at the Charleroi, where you're staying. Anybody who wishes to do so may invite relatives and friends. We'll be delighted to see them. Are there any questions?"

We were too exhausted to ask questions.

She said, "Girls: I'm very proud of you. You've all done wonderfully. It proves—" She faltered. I suppose she was going to say, It proves you can do it if you want to, or something of that kind, and decided it was a little corny. She went on, "Let me give you one last piece of advice, if I may. Rest up this weekend. You've been under tremendous strain, so just take it easy. You'll have all the opportunities in the world to celebrate next weekend, when all this is behind you. Okay?"

"Yes, Miss Webley."

We began to crawl away, and she laughed and said, "Oh, come now! Straighten up, straighten up! You can't go out slumping like this, girls! Think of your dignity!"

So each of us thought of our dignity (the last thing any of us would have thought of normally) and went out to Harry and the pink-and-blue bus. We made an effort as we rode through Miami Beach, we made an effort as we walked through the hotel foyer; but as soon as we reached 1412 I collapsed face down on my bed, Donna sat down sighing, and Alma sat muttering to herself in Italian. I guess the same thing happened in all the other apartments.

We didn't have a chance. There must have been a zillion men waiting for the girls to get back, and all at once telephones began to ring like mad. I could hear them ringing up and down the fourteenth floor. The damned thing rang five times for Donna, no less, and once for Jurgy, who was curled up on her bed in the other room, and once for Alma: and I was just fit to be tied, *I* had to answer each call because I was nearest to the phone. And not only were my weary bones dragged out of the grave by each call, but once again I was alone, unloved, undated, Miss Leprous Personality herself. I wanted to lie back and howl. It was even more unbearable because I just felt lousier and lousier each time I said, "One moment, please," whereas each of the other girls perked up like crazy as she took the telphone from me, just as if it contained an inexhaustible supply of vitamins, or Benzedrine, or hormones. God, I needed vitamins, or Benzedrine, or hormones, just as much as they did. I needed all three.

Finally the confounded thing rang once too often, and I screamed at Donna, "Answer it, it's sure to be for you." She answered it, and then let it dangle from her fingers like a dead rat. "Anybody seen Thompson around?" she asked.

I said, "Are you on the level?"

"The party on the other end is inquiring for a party by the name of Thompson. You Thompson?"

I grabbed the receiver from her and said, "*Hello!*"

"Miss Thompson? Hi. How's things? This is N.B."

I could have died. I could have wept an ocean of tears and drowned the entire Charleroi. I could have cut my throat on the spot. I said, "Oh—oh, hello! How nice of you to call."

"It's great to hear your voice again, Miss Thompson. I haven't seen you around all week. I was hoping we'd bump into each other."

"Well, you know, we've been working so hard, none of us has had a minute to call her own."

"They're treating you real rough, eh?"

"They're certainly making us work."

"Yeah." He took a deep breath. "Look, in that case, couldn't you use a few hours' relaxation? Eh? How about it? Maybe you could have dinner with me tonight, we could go along to a little club I know—"

There, in a few words, was Thompson's life history. Who invited her out on a date? The man she wasn't allowed to see. Who didn't invite her out on a date? The man who wasn't allowed to see her. Oh God, oh God, oh God.

I said, "Mr. Brangwyn—I'm sorry, I'm so sorry—"

He waited.

I said, "I appreciate your invitation a lot, I'd love it any other time, when I'm free; but I'm so *tired*, I just couldn't face going out tonight. I'm terribly sorry."

"Okay. How about tomorrow night?"

I was ready to commit hara-kiri with my blunt old manicure scissors. "Gee, tomorrow night—I'm awfully sorry—tomorrow night I have a date that I made earlier in the week."

"I see."

"I feel awful about it—"

"Don't feel awful about it, Miss Thompson. Some other time, maybe. Eh?"

"Yes. I hope so."

"Take care of yourself, now," he said.

"I will. Thank you for calling. Thank you very much."

He rang off. I put the receiver down and turned my face

to the wall. It was just a battle to the death between Fate and myself, and I knew who was going to come out on top.

Donna said, "Brangwyn?"

"Yes."

"You damn fool."

"Shut up, Donna."

"What harm would it do anybody if you went out with him? You can take care of yourself, can't you?"

"Donna, shut up."

"I don't understand you, cream. I don't understand how your mind works."

I walked out of the apartment in pure despair. It was impossible in there anyway, with the three girls preparing for their dates. Each one was in a sweat to get bathed and dressed, but Alma had commandeered the bathroom, as usual, and open warfare might start at any minute. I went down to the lobby, muttering to myself over and over again, *Saturday night, no date. Saturday night, no date;* and suddenly I discovered that I was promenading around the lobby peering at the men, and they were peering (and leering) right back at me. My God! What a shock!

It's amazing, what one's subconscious can drive one into, just because one is entering one's third weekend in a row without a date with a man one cares for. And at this point, when I realized how desperate my subconscious was, I thought, Okay, kid, there's only one way to settle this matter realistically; and I went to a telephone booth, and shut the door with a thump, and said coldly to the operator, "Give me Apartment 1208, please," and waited.

He said, after five seconds had passed, "Hello?"

"Dr. Duer?"

"Yes?"

"This is Miss Thompson."

He was certainly taken aback. "Well, well, well," he said.

"I hope you don't mind my calling you on a Saturday afternoon?"

"Carol, I was just about to pick up my phone and ask for your number."

"Is that true?"

"Absolutely."

I said, "I'm calling from the lobby. The number of the phone here is 26," and I put the receiver down.

It rang a couple of moments later. I let it ring six times times and then I picked it up and said, "Hello?"

"Carol—"

"Excuse me. Who is this?"

"Ray Duer."

"Why, Dr. Duer! What a surprise! How nice of you to call! And what can I do for you, Dr. Duer?"

"Carol, will you believe me? I've wanted to call you every night this week, every night."

"Dr. Duer, you say the sweetest things."

"I'm not lying to you."

"Why, Dr. Duer, I'd never for one instant think you were lying to me."

"Carol—"

I couldn't keep my voice in check. "Ray, oh, Ray, I'm almost dead with loneliness. Ray, I'm so lonely and miserable, I wish I were dead."

"You're in the lobby?"

"I'm still in the lobby, Ray, I'm still at phone number 26."

"I'll be right down. I'll meet you in the coffee shop."

I didn't say good-by or thank you. I replaced the receiver and went to the coffee shop, and sat at a table looking at the paintings of disheveled shepherdesses; and sure enough, he arrived within a couple of minutes and sat down facing me. He wore gray slacks and a gray shirt and a narrow solid-color pale yellow tie and a gray sports jacket; and behind his horn-rimmed glasses his gray eyes were hard but anxious.

"Hello," I said.

"Hello."

"Do you want me to apologize for calling you?"

"Of course not."

"I've never telephoned a man like this before. I'm ashamed of myself. Dr. Duer, are psychiatrists taught how to be cruel?"

"No, don't say that."

"The fourth night I was here, you took me down to the beach and kissed me. Do you remember that laughable incident?"

"Yes."

"Since then—"

He interrupted acidly, "Since then I've been in love with you. Do you want a notarized statement?"

"Oh, my God," I said. Then I said, "Order some coffee for me, please. With cream."

He turned and beckoned to a waitress, and we didn't speak until she brought coffee for both of us, in small silver pots with a silver cream pitcher to match and a silver sugar bowl.

"Do you know how I feel?" I said as soon as we were alone. "I feel exactly like that poor girl with the moon trouble who came to see you at three o'clock in the morning without any clothes on. But I did it in broad daylight."

"I'm sorry."

"I'm glad you're sorry, Ray."

He said, "I thought I'd made it clear to you. I thought you understood."

"What, Ray, dear?"

"It's impossible for me to have an affair with a girl who's a trainee at the school."

"I remember, Ray. You told me that. I asked you if I was just an affair, but you never fully explained. Can you have an affair with me when I graduate?"

He said, in the bitterest, harshest voice, "Arnie Garrison knows I'm in love with you."

"Oh! I'm so awfully glad you told him before you told me."

He brought his hand down on the table, *smack!* "Will you be *quiet?* Will you stop being so *brilliant* at my expense?"

"But, really, I'm delighted that Mr. Garrison was the first to know. I couldn't be any happier."

"The whole school knows!" he said violently. "Everybody in the whole world knows!"

"How fascinating. Did you have it printed in the Miami *Herald,* or something?"

"To all intents and purposes," he said. He glared at me with real anger. "It was printed all over my face when I met you at the jai-alai game last week, that's all. Arnie Garrison, Caroline Garrison, Peg Webley—hell!—they couldn't miss it. Arnie said it was the funniest sight he ever saw in the whole of his life. He said I just sat there the whole evening mooning over the back of your neck. And then, when you spoke to me later—" He stopped and took his horn-rimmed glasses off and breathed on them heavily.

I said in a small voice, "Oh. Miss Webley guessed?"

"You bet she did."

"Was she upset?"

"Why should she be?"

"I thought perhaps—"

"It's time you stopped thinking perhaps. She's getting married shortly to one of our pilots. If you really want the facts,

I had dinner with her a couple of evenings ago and she spent three hours singing your praises."

"Oh, Ray." I began to cry.

He put his glasses back on and handed me a freshly laundered hankerchief. As a trained expert, he probably knew that I was going to shed a tear or two during this get-together. "Here," he said.

"Thank you." I mopped my eyes and blew my nose.

He said, "Arnie's arranged for you to stay in Miami after you graduate. This is going to be your home base. He didn't mention it to me until last night. He just went ahead and fixed it so that you and I—" His glasses were bothering him again. He took them off and stared at them grimly. "We won't be separated. That's the important thing."

I stood up without a word and tore into the ladies' room. I blubbed there for nearly ten minutes. He said, as soon as I returned, "I'm having dinner with the director of flight training tonight. I can't get out of it. And I won't be back until late. Will you have lunch with me tomorrow?"

"Yes, Ray."

"Will you meet me in here at eight-thirty?"

I said, "Ray, isn't that a little early for lunch?"

"We can start with breakfast."

"Yes, Ray."

"Then we can drive out some place and be alone. That's what I was going to call you about. I'd been trying to fight the urge down, but I couldn't, I had to see you. But you called first."

I said, "Ray, I was just ready to cut my throat."

"After you graduate next Friday we can—" He looked at me.

"We can what?"

"Make it official."

"What does that mean, Ray, make it official? Tell Mrs. Montgomery?"

"Get engaged," he said. "Get married. Something like that. Whatever you say."

"Oh, God."

He reached across the table, and I reached, too, and met his hand and held onto it. I said, "This is an idiotic question, but can I call you darling between now and next Friday? It's a terrible urge. I've never called anybody darling before."

"Not in the classroom," he said. "You'll have to be discreet. I'm talking to your class next Tuesday, and it might look—" His hand became very tight and hard. He said, "I'm crazy about you. Do you know that? I'm blind and stupid and crazy about you."

"It's all that electricity," I said.

"Electricity?"

"Yes. Millions of volts."

"No. In my case it was adrenalin."

"I don't even know what adrenalin is, Ray. Isn't that something you take for a cold?"

"We'll get it straight tomorrow," he said. "I have to go now."

"Now?"

"Yes, I'm having dinner with the director of flight training. I just told you."

"I remember." Tears gushed out of my imbecile eyes. "Ray, must you go? Must you?" But before he could answer I said, "All right. Go. Go. Goddammit, I won't come between you and your duty." I blew my nose in his handkerchief again and mopped away the new torrent. "I'm sorry I'm such a pain in the ass, Ray. It's just terrible, that's all. I've only just gotten my claws into you, and you're going to leave me for somebody else."

He said, "Don't make me feel worse than I do already."

"All right, darling. All right."

"What are your plans for tonight?"

"Plans!" I cried. "Who has plans? Are you mad? All I want is love and all I've got is a lick and a promise—"

He looked utterly miserable.

I said, "I guess I'll go and bury myself in a movie. Don't worry about me, Ray. I'll have gobs of fun."

"Just bear in mind what I told you."

"About the director of flight training?"

"No. That I love you, with all my heart."

"Oh, darling—"

"And," he said, "stay away from Air Force officers. Understand?"

"Ray! Were you jealous last week? Were you?"

"I wanted to strangle the guy with my bare hands."

"You did!"

He said gloomily, "That's a fine reaction from somebody in my profession."

"Oh, God, you're jealous! How wonderful!"

It was odd, because I'd always despised jealousy as the most contemptible of all emotions. Now I welcomed it. My cup of happiness overflowed.

We'd scarcely touched our coffee, but he had to pay all the same. We walked out side by side, and I suddenly noticed that the coffee shop was crowded with men and women and children and poodles, and somebody even had a blue Persian cat on a yellow leather leash. Strange; because while Ray and I were talking there wasn't a human being within miles of us. It wasn't really an ideal setting for a love scene, I realized, and it must have cramped Ray's style to a certain extent. I mean, when you've finally succeeded in nagging a man into admitting he loves you, something more than a few well-chosen words ought to follow; but Ray couldn't exactly have gone to town in the Salon de Fragonard, it was a little too much to expect him to get madly passionate and start ripping off my blouse, etc. After all, he did have a tremendously responsible job with Magna International Airlines, and when a man has that kind of tremendously responsible and important job, he has to safeguard his reputation. Any fool knows that.

Outside the coffee shop he said, "I'm going to leave you here. I'm sorry. But I have to. Okay?"

"Okay, darling. But go quickly."

I intended to turn my back as he left me but I couldn't. I just stood and watched his nice strong body, and the easy way he walked, until he stepped into one of the elevators and I lost him. Then I mooned around the lobby for a while, feeling as if a hydrant of tears had opened inside my belly and was drowning me, and I went to another ladies' room—the Charleroi was full of them—and cried until I felt better. Then I wandered out into the lobby again and found Suzanne, the blonde who'd had to have her pony tail chopped off, staring into the window of the Jewel Box, the miniature Tiffany's where Luke Lucas had bought Jurgy's gold bracelet and very likely her engagement ring, too. I said, "Hi, Suzanne," and she said, "Allo, Carol," and we stood mournfully looking at diamond necklaces which probably cost the earth. We chatted in a desultory way, and I discovered that she was without a date for the evening, too—her friend Jacqueline had met up with a South American gentleman who was in the nut business, selling bushels of Brazil nuts all over the place. The upshot, though, was that I suggested to Suzanne that we might have dinner together and take in a movie, and she was as pleased as punch. We agreed to meet again in half an hour, right here in front of the Jewel Box, and we went back to our respective abodes to freshen up.

Jurgy had already left, obviously to meet Luke. Donna had also left, but I had no idea who her date was—she seemed to have collected quite a retinue in the past three weeks. I didn't even know whether she'd taken N.B.'s Impala, and I was past caring. Alma was in the bathroom as usual, but she was merely putting the finishing touches to her front curls, and the door was open, so she could scream at me.

"Carola!"

"Yeah?"

"Ah, it is you. You are staying in tonight, Carola?"

"No, I'm going to a movie."

She came bustling out of the bathroom and, as usual, she was a dream, in a gorgeous white dress cut low at the neck and embroidered with a huge yellow rose over her left hip. Her hair was lusher than ever, tumbling down her back. The moment she saw me she said, "*Carola!*" In italics, like that.

"Now what?"

She peered at my face. "You have been crying."

"Who, me?"

"Ho ho, Carola! You are different. Ha ha, Carola!"

"For Pete's sake, stop making those noises. *Ho ho. Ha ha.* You sound like feeding time at the zoo."

She said, still chortling, "You know what we say in Italy? She have been to the fiesta, her voice have change. Which mean, she is no longer girl. Virgin."

"Alma, honest to God, you have a mind like a sewer."

"The doctor?" she asked, beaming at me. "I do not mean you have slept with him, but he make you happy? Huh?"

"Be a good girl, honey. Pipe down."

"Okay, you want to keep these secret, I do not interfere."

"What time is your date?"

She looked at her watch. "Twenty minutes ago."

"That sounds reasonable enough."

"Sonny is nice sweet boy. He like to wait."

"Where are you going?"

"He has big plans tonight. Some place very special."

"Alma—"

202

She came close to me and laughed in my face. "Oh, Carola! Carola! You are my mother again?"

"Honey, I'm not one little bit your mother, but just be careful with this guy, will you?"

"*Careful, careful,*" she mimicked in a deep bass voice. "You think I am not careful?"

I said, "There's no harm in being careful. Just remember."

"My mother always speak like these." She put on the deep bass voice again. "*Alma. Be careful. Just remember. Be careful.*" She chuckled. "Carola, you know what? No man ever touch me. True. No man—ever."

I stared at her.

She looked at me calmly, with those big beautiful honey-colored eyes, and to my utter astonishment I knew she wasn't lying. She turned away, saying, "Tonight is cool, yes?"

"No, warm."

"I better take coat. In the car it is cool."

Suzanne was somewhat tardy, also, and she'd been crying, too—because she was homesick, she explained later. I could understand, and sympathize. She came from Paris, and any girl who comes from Paris is ready to commit suicide if she's away from Paris for even a few hours; and, let's face it, Paris and Miami Beach are slightly different in tone and atmosphere. We had dinner in a Chinese restaurant, and she told me the story of her life from beginning to end. People are so fascinating, I can listen to them for hours. Her boy friend was named Jacques (she showed me a snapshot of him, and her eyes became misty. He had a long, thin face, and wavy hair that was about six inches high, and an enormous Adam's apple, and a hideous necktie, and a terribly intense look); and her problem was that Jacques was studying medicine, and he couldn't possibly afford to marry her for years to come. In addition, he was extremely puritanical, and he wouldn't even dream of sleeping with her in any circumstances, though he slept with other girls regularly; because, after all, she was the girl he was going to marry, and defiling her was just out of the question. The French are utterly darling about things of this sort. I mean, they're so wildly logical, one can't help admiring them. In the meantime, Suzanne was saving every cent she earned so that she could set him up in practice when he was fully qualified, which was going to happen (as far as I could gather) about the middle of 1999.

She was crazy about seeing a Western movie, and we

managed to catch a double feature showing two. They were gruesome, I thought, but Suzanne was absolutely and completely bugeyed over them. They seemed to arouse something very primitive in her sophisticated bosom, and if this isn't existentialist I don't know what is. Later, we had a hamburger and coffee—she was crazy about hamburgers, too, another existentialist bit—and then we meandered back to the hotel. At least the evening had passed. It wasn't the best and fairest evening of my life, but it had passed. I'd be seeing Ray for breakfast in a few hours, we'd begin in earnest the joyous business of learning about each other and loving each other; and as I went up in the elevator I shivered.

The apartment was dark and cool and sweet-smelling when I walked in. None of the girls was back yet—the time was only about ten minutes past one and I didn't expect to see hide nor hair of them until two o'clock, our Saturday deadline. I put on my pajamas and sat looking out of the picture window for a while, listening to the quietness outside, and occasionally seeing a shooting star streak across the velvety sky, getting drowsier and drowsier and loving it—loving that exquisite sensation of slipping away into the softest kind of nothingness—and occasionally I'd become wide awake and think about Ray, and about Jurgy and Luke Lucas and how fantastic everything was; and then I'd slip away into the foam-rubber nothingness again and go floating away into the infinite. And then, suddenly, when I was so lost that I wasn't even in this universe, the telephone rang. It scared me almost out of my skin; and as I dashed over to answer it I was shaky and breathless.

"Hello?"

A woman's voice said, "Ah. Is this Miss Thompson?"

"Yes, speaking."

"Ah. This is the Homestead General Hospital."

"The *what?*"

"The, ah, Homestead General Hospital."

"Yes?"

She didn't want to tell me. She hesitated. I clutched the telephone to my ear, and tiny cold shivers began to creep up and down my back. At last she said, "Miss Thompson—ah—a Miss di Lucca has just been admitted here. She gave us your name and asked us to contact you."

"Miss di Lucca! Alma di Lucca! Oh, no! What happened to her?"

"I'm sorry. She was involved in an automobile accident."

I said in a whisper, "Is she hurt?"

"She has suffered, ah, certain injuries. Do you happen to be a relative?"

"No—"

"Does she have any, ah, relatives here whom we can contact?"

"I don't think so, she's never mentioned any. Please, is she seriously injured?"

"She is resting as comfortably as can be expected. . . . Ah—Miss Thompson, do you think you could come to the hospital?"

"Now? Yes, of course. At once. I'll be right over. Will you please tell me where it is?"

She told me, and added without any emphasis, "Come to the Emergency entrance and ask for Mrs. McQueen."

"Are you Mrs. McQueen?"

"Yes. I'm the night supervisor."

"Please, Mrs. McQueen, please: is she badly hurt?"

"Just come as soon as you can. Good-by."

She hung up.

I put the receiver down and tried to catch my breath. It wasn't true, it was part of some horrible dream. Then I picked the receiver up again and kept jiggling the switch bar until the operator answered. I said, "Room 1208. It's urgent."

He was there, thank God. He answered after the second ring.

I said, "Ray, this is Carol. Something terrible has happened. There's been an automobile accident, my roommate Alma is in the hospital, they just called me to say she's been hurt. I have to get over there immediately."

His voice was like Mrs. McQueen's, without emphasis. "Which hospital is she in?"

"Homestead General Hospital."

"Who called you? One of the doctors?"

"No, a Mrs. McQueen, the night supervisor in Emergency. Darling, I'm sorry to worry you with this—"

"It's my job," he said. "All right. Meet me in front of the hotel as soon as you can. I'll be down there."

I put on my blue slacks and a patterned shirt, and searched around frantically until I found my gray cashmere sweater. I brushed my hair in two seconds and made up my mouth in three seconds; then I dragged out my white pigskin bag and packed Alma's black nightgown because I remembered too well that she couldn't bear the itch of a hospital nightgown. I added her toilet accessories, a small bottle of perfume, and a package of facial tissues.

I stood shivering in front of the hotel for a couple of minutes until Ray drove up. He had a shiny red sports car, an MG, which was a surprise and showed a new facet of his personality. He was very formally dressed, in a dark blue light-weight suit and a dark blue bow tie.

As we zoomed down the driveway I said, "Do you know where the hospital is?"

"Yes. I spoke with Mrs. McQueen."

"Did she tell you—" I couldn't finish the question.

He answered brusquely, "We'll find out when we get there. Mrs. McQueen was reluctant to give any specific information."

"What about the boy Alma was with, Sonny Kee?"

"He was killed."

"Oh, my God."

I hunched down in the seat. Overhead, the fronds of the palm trees made a swishing noise, and everything in front of us was golden green in the headlights.

Ray said, "Did you know this boy?"

"I didn't *know* him. I saw him, just once."

"What's his name again?"

"Sonny Kee."

Ray said, after a moment, "That's a familiar name."

"He was a boxer, Ray. He used to be a boxer."

"Yeah. I guess that's why it's familiar. How did Alma get mixed up with him?"

"She met him in the hotel."

Ray grunted.

I said, "Ray, I did my best. The last thing I said to her before she went out tonight was, be careful. I *warned* her about him."

"Why?"

"He was a bad character. I warned her. She laughed at me."

Ray said sharply, "How did you know he was a bad character? What's all this about?"

"You see, Nat Brangwyn told me—you know, the gambler, the one I'm not allowed to associate with?"

"What did Brangwyn tell you?"

"That Sonny Kee was a bad character and that Alma shouldn't have anything to do with him."

"And you told Alma?"

"Yes."

"Then what?"

"She wouldn't listen to me, Ray. She just laughed. She said she could take care of herself."

We stopped for a traffic light. Ray said, "Why didn't you pass this information on to me, or to Arnie Garrison, or Peg Webley?" He sounded furious.

I said, "Darling!"

"I'm asking you, Carol: why didn't you pass this information on?"

"Ray, how can you even expect me to do such a thing?"

"It was your duty to report it."

"But, Ray, be reasonable. I can't report to you, or anybody else, about each of my roommates, I can't come to you and tell you about the men they're going out with."

He brooded for a while, and then said, "I'm sorry. I shouldn't have said that. We might have been able to avert this mess, that's all."

We hardly said anything more to each other until we reached the hospital. We hurried into the Emergency entrance and asked for Mrs. McQueen; and, after waiting a couple of minutes, she came out, a big heavily built woman in supervisor's uniform. As she approached, Ray said, "Let me do the talking."

"Yes, darling."

He said to her, "Hello, Mrs. McQueen. This is Miss Thompson. I'm Dr. Duer."

She didn't even glance at me. "Ah, Doctor. Ah, yes."

He drew her aside, and they talked in low tones. This was his special province, I realized: he could ask all the questions in the world, and I couldn't—I was nobody. Then they began to walk away, as if they'd forgotten my presence completely; but at the last moment Ray remembered. He strode back to me and said, "Sit down and make yourself comfortable. I'll be with you as soon as I can. I'm just going to have a word with Dr. Walker, who's in charge of this case."

It's always the same in hospitals. They tell you to rush over as fast as you can, and then you wait and you wait and you wait and nothing happens—you see nothing, you hear nothing, the nurses and interns who pass by you seem to act as if you're invisible. The room I waited in was quite pleasant, and nicely furnished; but I wasn't interested in hospital furniture, I was only interested in Alma. I just wanted to be assured that she would be all right, and that she wasn't suffering any pain.

Eventually, after about forty minutes, Ray returned with a small, plump young intern. A police sergeant, red-faced and sweaty, hovered in the background. The intern was one of these people afflicted with a nervous smile. He grinned at me unhappily as Ray introduced us. "Miss Thompson. Dr. Walker."

"How do, Miss Thompson."

"How do you do, Dr. Walker. How is she?"

He looked blank.

Ray said, "She's under heavy sedation."

"But *how* is she?"

Ray said, "I told you. She's sleeping."

"Can I see her?"

Dr. Walker said, "Well, there really isn't much point, Miss Thompson. She's *sleeping*, you understand, she's under sedation. You wouldn't be able to talk to her."

"Is she dead?"

"No," Ray said.

I said, "Please, won't somebody tell me how she *is?*"

Dr. Walker glanced at Ray. Then he said gently, "She's suffered injuries, but we don't know as yet how extensive these are. Not until we get some X-rays taken—that's what we're just preparing to do. She's as comfortable as we can make her, and we all hope for the best."

"I want to see her. She asked for me. I'm her friend. I want her to know that I came."

Ray said, "Carol, she's *asleep*. She's been given heavy sedation. And they're just preparing to move her into the X-ray room."

"I'll wait until she wakes up. Ray, I must be here when she wakes up. She's a stranger here, Ray, I have to be around."

Dr. Walker said, "I'm afraid, Miss Thompson, she'll sleep through at least until morning."

"Then why was I told to come over here as soon as possible?"

Ray said, "There are certain formalities, in a case of this kind. I've already taken care of all that."

"Ray—"

"Relax," he said kindly. "Just relax."

I bit my lip and blinked back some tears. I said to Dr. Walker, "I brought over a few things for her—a nightgown, and make-up, and so on. Would you please see that she gets them?"

"Certainly." He took the white pigskin bag as if he were afraid it might explode in his hands.

I said, "If she wakes up, Doctor, will you tell her I was here and I'll be back to see her first thing in the morning?"

"Sure, sure. You can trust me, Miss Thompson."

"Let's go," Ray said. He shook hands with Dr. Walker and said, "I'll be in touch with you." Then he called to the police sergeant in the background, "Good-by, sergeant. Thanks for your help."

"You're most welcome, sir."

Dr. Walker smiled at me timidly, and Ray led me out.

When we were in the little red car I said, "Ray, tell me the truth. How is she?"

He was about to start the motor, but he drew his hand back. His voice was very flat and neutral. He said, "Carol, I'm sorry. Her condition isn't good."

"What do you mean, Ray? What do you mean, her condition isn't good?"

"They don't know yet how extensive her injuries are. She has a crushed pelvis, and there appears to be some functional damage."

"Oh, my God, what does *that* mean?"

"At present she's unable to move her legs. They'll know more about that when they see the X-rays."

"Oh, how terrible."

He started the motor, but he didn't put the car into gear. We sat. He said, "She was conscious when she was brought in. She told Dr. Walker that the man had attacked her on some beach, he'd raped her."

"Ray!"

"I guess he had some sort of guilt feelings afterwards. Sergeant Hadley estimates the car was traveling at well over a hundred miles an hour when the accident occurred."

I was crying helplessly. "Where was this, Ray?"

"On the Overseas Highway. The car hit a curb, the man lost control, and they overturned. He was killed instantly."

"Ray: tell me. Did you see her?"

"Yes, for a few moments."

"How does she look?"

"She was under sedation. I told you."

"No, I mean, was her face hurt?"

"The car went into a skid before it rolled over. Apparently she had time to cover her face. Her hands were cut, and she has some scalp injuries, but these aren't as serious as the rest."

"Thank God her face isn't hurt, Ray. She's such a beautiful girl, so beautiful."

He put the car into gear and we drove off.

We didn't talk all the way back. He left me alone to brood —maybe he was brooding, too—and I thought of poor Alma, hurt and unconscious, beautiful and selfish and grasping and irritating, and yet, for some reason, close and warm to me, a person I'd grown to love. Without reason. That's the thing about love, I suppose. It doesn't need reasons to happen.

When we reached the Charleroi, Ray left the MG to be parked by one of the doormen. As we walked to the elevators he said, "I want you to come to my apartment. I'll give you something to help you sleep tonight."

"I don't need anything, really."

He didn't argue. He said to the elevator boy, "Twelfth floor," and when we stopped he took me by the hand and led me to the apartment. Inside, he said, "Sit down," but I couldn't sit down. I stood looking at him, and he knew that I desperately needed his comfort. He took me in his arms and I felt, only for the second time, the hardness of his mouth and his body. I began to cry again, and he led me to an armchair and, very tenderly but expertly, deposited me there. Then he left me for a little while, blubbing into my fists.

When he returned he said, "Here," and handed me a glass filled with ice cubes and some yellow liquid.

I said, "What is it?"

"Whiskey."

"I'm not allowed—"

"Yes, you are. It's purely medicinal. And take this, too." He handed me a small green capsule.

"Must I take it?"

"Yes."

I choked over the whiskey, and while I was choking I looked around the room so that I'd know in future, when I was away from him, what his surroundings were like. It was a big room, like ours upstairs, with a smaller room attached which he used as his bedroom. I was glad it was all rather untidy. There were books strewn everywhere, and untidy piles of papers on a desk, and a couple of shirts hanging over a chair.

I said, as soon as I had any voice, "You need a woman round here."

"Do I?"

"For sure. I never imagined you were so sloppy. I thought you were neat and precise."

"Where did you pick up that idea?"

"I just imagined. You know how girls are. Full of fantasies."

"Have you taken that capsule yet?"

"I'm holding it in my hand."

"Take it."

"No, Ray, I'm not going to."

"Why not?"

"I'm afraid I'll oversleep. I must get to the hospital first thing in the morning." Then something that was bothering me came to the surface of my mind. I said, "Ray—those scalp injuries. Are they bad?"

"Walker told me he didn't think there was any serious damage."

"Is her head bandaged?"

"There are dressings on the wounds, naturally."

"Did they have to cut her hair?"

"Yes, of course."

He let me cry a little longer; then he coaxed me into drinking more of the whiskey. "Take the capsule," he said, but I still refused. He said, "Okay. When you wake in the morning, call me. I'll drive you to the hospital."

"Thank you, Ray."

"Now I'll see you to your apartment."

"You don't have to—"

"Don't argue with me."

"But men aren't allowed on that floor."

"I'm not men. I'm the medical staff."

"You're men to me," I said. "All the men in the world." I stood up and kissed his mouth. "Oh, Ray, I love you so much."

A few minutes later he took me upstairs, and left me, quietly, outside 1412. The lights were on inside the apartment, but only Jurgy was back. I knew, because her door was closed. I couldn't bear to wake her to tell her about the accident. Donna wasn't home yet, and there was only a piece of black velvet ribbon on Alma's bed. I picked it up to put it away, and then I dropped it where it had been.

211

11

I woke in a panic at eight o'clock. It had been one of those awful nights when you hate being asleep, you fight against it every minute, you feel as if there's a huge weight pressing down on your chest. I knew, all the time, that I had to be awake early to go to the hospital but I couldn't get away from my nightmares, I couldn't open my eyelids. Horrible

Donna's bed hadn't been slept in, which was none of my business. Alma's black velvet ribbon was still where I'd left it. The connecting door was open, but Jurgy had already made up her bed and left. I guessed she'd gone off with Luke again.

I called Ray but he didn't answer. I showered in a hurry sluicing off the nasty night sweat, and dabbed on a lot of eau de cologne, and put on a white dress and white shoes because today was Sunday. I called Ray a second time but he still didn't answer; and I completed myself by putting on a little white hat and carrying a white handbag, and went down to the coffee shop to see if he was there. He was; with his glasses off, drinking orange juice at the counter.

I went over to him and said into his unsuspecting ear "Good morning, Ray."

He turned, startled. "Well! Good morning."

"Are you having breakfast?" I asked.

"No, only a glass of juice. What will you have?"

I sat down beside him. "Just coffee, please."

He ordered it, and then sat looking at me in a vague way. His eyes were rather strange; he seemed unable to focus them; and I said, "Are you tired, Ray?"

"A little."

"Darling, would you prefer to rest? I can go to the hospital by myself."

"Oh, no."

I said, "I overslept. I meant to be up at seven, at the latest. Ray, I'm so anxious to get going."

"Okay," he said. "As soon as you have your coffee."

We left within ten minutes. His shiny red MG was parked

outside, on the driveway; and before he climbed into it he took off the light cinnamon-colored jacket he was wearing. Underneath the jacket he was wearing a white short-sleeved shirt and a brown tie; his slacks were light gray. He clashed a trifle with the color scheme of the car, but he didn't clash with me one iota.

We turned into Collins Drive, then along Indian Creek and across one of the bridges to the mainland. We hardly spoke. Then, after we'd been driving for about twenty minutes, I suddenly said to him, "Is this the right road?"

"You mean to the hospital? No."

"Ray! Where are we going?"

He said, very quietly and gently, "There's no point in going to the hospital. She died at five o'clock this morning."

"Ray!"

"Dr. Walker called me at about three-thirty. I went over at once. She had a massive internal hemorrhage, there wasn't a thing they could do to save her. I'm sorry, Carol."

He drove on and on, slowly and carefully, along an endless road that seemed to have been cut through a dense green jungle. Few cars passed us; hardly anybody could see my face; and I simply cried until there were no more tears left, until I was so exhausted that I couldn't continue crying. I sat helplessly and stared at the jungle, and at the brightly colored birds screeching down at us; and eventually I asked, "Ray, where are we?"

"We're in the Everglades."

It was a good place to be because it was so utterly unreal, and it could somehow contain the unreality of Alma dead, and that man with the squashed-in face dead, and an overturned car with its wheels spinning in the air.

"Was she in pain, Ray?"

"No. Walker is a good guy. He knows his job. He took care of her."

"I wish you'd let me visit her last night."

"I thought it would be better if you didn't."

"I can't believe it. I'll never see her again. Oh, God. . . . What happens now, Ray?"

"I've spoken to Arnie Garrison. He and Mrs. Montgomery will do everything that's necessary."

The birds were fantastic, so gaudy, so active. Alma would never see them. There were trees that seemed to be covered entirely by white egrets, which Alma would never see; and birds that looked like eagles, perched on tree stumps, but which were only turkey buzzards, according to Ray. All along the roadside there were small herds of wild pigs rooting in the grass, grayish, tough-looking creatures with miniatures of themselves squealing underfoot. Mother pigs and father pigs and baby pigs. "Razorbacks," Ray said. "We stay away from them. They're dangerous, particularly at this season." We had to slow down to avoid snakes which had been run over by other cars, blacksnakes and rattlesnakes, and Ray explained that they couldn't escape on a road like this, that a rattlesnake (for example) can only move at about four miles an hour even at top speed. I always thought a snake could outstrip a race horse, but apparently not.

I don't know how long we drove. I was just helpless with misery. Every time I thought I had control of myself at last, I'd burst into tears again. Ray was utterly kind and gentle, but he couldn't do anything about the thoughts and pictures that came into my mind. I remembered her in the dress she had worn last night, and wept. I remembered all sorts of incidents that had seemed amusing at the time, like her argument with Dr. Schwartz about how to deliver babies; and another shower of tears started. Why should such a terrible, senseless thing happen to her, why?

Eventually we came out to the water again. I said to Ray, "Where are we now?"

"Cape Sable."

"What a pretty name. Where is it?"

"On the Gulf of Mexico."

We had lunch there, on the terrace of a restaurant overlooking the water, and gradually I managed to get a grip on myself. Then, when we were ready to leave, at about half-past two, I noticed how tired Ray looked. Of course. He'd been up most of the night. So I persuaded him to let me drive, and after watching me at the wheel for a few minutes to make sure that I knew how to handle the MG he relaxed and fell asleep. I felt very responsible for him and I drove with great care. He woke and took over just before we reached Miami.

He parked the car, again, on the hotel driveway. Before we climbed out he looked at his watch and said, "It's a quarter after six. What do you want to do with yourself this evening?"

"I just want to stay with you. May I?"

"You ought to take a sedative and go to bed."

"No. I want to stay with you."

He gave in, finally. He said, "Okay. But I have to go up to my apartment and make some telephone calls. Suppose you meet me in the lobby at six-thirty?"

"Yes, darling." I'd be away from him for three quarters of an hour, but it couldn't be helped.

As we entered the hotel he said, "I have to get some cigarettes, and I want to stop by the desk to see if there've been any messages for me. Do you want to go on up?"

"No." I just wanted to stay with him permanently, I never wanted to be away from his side. So I remained with him while he went to the little kiosk where they sold cigarettes; and I remained with him while he inquired at the desk for his messages.

The clerk said, "Dr. Duer? Oh, yes," and took about half a dozen white slips of paper out of a pigeonhole and handed them to him. Ray glanced through them, and then looked at me as if he were about to say something; but he didn't speak. I saw his face harden, and his eyes suddenly become bitter; and when I turned I saw Donna and Elliott Ewing walking arm in arm across the lobby. Elliott was in his captain's uniform, and Donna was wearing her Schiaparelli cobwebs with a little white jacket trailing from one shoulder; and they were both drunk.

There couldn't be any mistake about it. They were high as kites. I couldn't say to Ray, Ignore them, they're just happy, they're just feeling gay. They were drunk, damn them, they were drunk as lords, they were staggering and sniggering. Everybody in the hotel was watching them.

I said, "Ray—" but he wasn't listening to me. He stood there, hard-faced and silent, staring at them as they came lurching toward us. Then Donna saw me, and it was obvious how pie-eyed she was. Instead of swinging Elliott around, and getting out of sight as fast as she could, she began to screech, "Carol! Carol! Hey, Carol! Wheeee!" and tottered toward me as fast as she could, with Elliott in tow.

I said, "Ray—" again, beginning a sentence I couldn't hope to finish. He didn't hear me, and I froze.

She was flushed; her red hair was a mess, and yet it was still enchanting; and she breathed liquor all over me. "H-hi, Carol," she laughed. "Little ole cream. Little ole queen bee. And Dr. Duer. Nice ole Dr. Duer. H-hi. You remember little ole Captain Glug, don't you? H-hey, Cap'n Glug, precious. Come say hello to Carol and nice little ole Dr. Duer."

"Well, hi, there," Elliott said, blinking at us. "Great. Great. Running in. To you."

Ray said to me, very quietly, "I think you'd better take Miss Stewart up to her room."

"Now, wait a minute," Elliott said, blinking stupidly. "Just gonna have drink. See? Souvenir Bar. Wanna come? Okay. Everyone come."

Donna gave a mad shriek. "Wheeee! Come on, everyone. Let's have a party, let's celebrate."

Ray's voice was flat. "Miss Stewart, I think you'd better go up to your room."

"Now, feller," Elliott said. "Now, just a minute. Just wait a minute." He lurched between Donna and Ray, suddenly aggressive. He was a couple of inches taller than Ray, and much heavier.

Ray said to him, in the same flat voice, "Please stay out of this, Captain."

Elliott shouted, "Lady. With me. Understand? With me, feller. Gonna have drink. Souvenir Bar."

"Miss Stewart," Ray said.

"Listen, you," Elliott said. "My girl. You can't order her around, like that." He reared up and put his big fat hand over Ray's face, and pushed with all his strength.

Ray couldn't save himself, I couldn't save him. He was blinded and thrown completely off balance. He staggered a few steps back, until his legs gave way under him, and he collapsed. He lost his glasses. The cigarettes and the message slips he had been holding were scattered, and when I rushed over to him he seemed to have turned to stone.

"Ray! Are you hurt? Ray!"

He didn't answer, he didn't look at me. His eyes were fixed on Elliott, who was roaring with laughter. There was a crowd around us by this time, about thirty or forty people gaping at the scene; and out of the crowd came big bony old Luke Lucas, wearing his fawn-colored Stetson hat. "Okay, little lady," he said to me, and he began to help Ray up. "Everything's okay, son," he said. "Just take it easy, son—"

Ray didn't listen to Luke, either. He shook free of Luke's restraining hands, walked, almost on tiptoe, over to Elliott, said in a high, sour voice, "You goddam stupid fool," hit him with his left fist in the belly, and as Elliott lowered his arms, hit him with a great looping right fist so hard on the side of the jaw that I thought Elliott's head would be torn completely off his neck. Elliott threw up his arms as if he were going to turn a cartwheel, but he fell on his face just where he had been standing. His legs gave a couple of twitches, and then he was still.

"Jesus Christ," somebody said in profound admiration; and I guess then and there Magna International Airlines stock rose fifteen points.

Nobody moved, though. Then, very abruptly, Ray leaned down, rolled Elliott over and raised one of his eyelids. God knows what he saw there, but after two or three seconds he stood up, breathing heavily, and swung round and walked over to where I was standing. He said, as if he were talking to some dumb chambermaid, "Take Miss Stewart up to her room and see that she starts packing her bags immediately. There's a plane out of her to New York at midnight, and I want her on that plane without fail."

He didn't wait for me to say, "Yes, sir," or even, "No, sir." He began to walk away. Luke handed him his horn-rimmed glasses and said happily, "Is he daid, son?" and Ray answered, "No, he isn't dead," and edged his way through the crowd to the elevators. He was holding his right wrist as if he had sprained it. Mr. Courtenay and a couple of panting doormen appeared out of nowhere and stared down at Elliott's body; and I assumed they would take care of him, and return him in one piece to General Wuzzy Goof.

I said to Donna, "Coming?"

She hesitated.

I said, "Do you want to kiss Elliott good-by?"

She shuddered. "No. Not in public."

"Let's go, then."

She seemed to have sobered up completely. As we walked through the crowd she said, "It was kind of exciting there for one minute, wasn't it?"

I said, "Exciting as hell, that's all."

The people in the crowd moved aside to let us pass. She stood with her head lowered as we went up in the elevator, kicking at the thick carpet with the pointed toe of her shoe.

Jurgy was in the apartment when we walked in, trying to close the lid of a big suitcase which was bulging with clothes. She said, "Well, thank God you're here. You can help me shut this damn thing. I've been wrestling with it for twenty minutes."

Donna said, "Whose is that?"

"Alma's," Jurgy said.

Donna laughed. "Don't tell me she's been ordered off the premises, too."

Jurgy looked at me. I said, "Tell her."

Jurgy said, "Alma was killed in an automobile crash last night."

"Oh, no!" Donna cried. She looked, suddenly, like an old woman.

I said, "Okay, Jurgy, I'll kneel down on the lid, you try to snap the locks."

We accomplished it.

Jurgy said, "Boy, that practically gave me a hernia."

I lugged the suitcase over to a corner to get it out of the way. Donna was standing by her bed, undressing, her back to us. I said, "Do you want me to unhook you?"

"Thanks. I can manage."

Jurgy looked at me inquiringly. I said, "Donna's been sent home." Then I began to cry again. "Jurgy, this is the most beautiful weekend of my life, I swear to you, this is the most beautiful weekend of my life. What's going to happen next, that's what I keep asking myself, what's going to happen next?"

Donna said, "Carol, be a good kid and shut up."

I was quivering like a jelly. "You moron. You big stupid red-haired moron. You knew you were drunk. You knew you were high as a kite. Why didn't you stay some place until you sobered up?"

"For God's sake, honey, stop having hysterics."

"I could kill you," I said. "You only had four more days to go. Why did you have to louse up everything?"

Jurgy said, "Here, Carol, sit down. I'll make some coffee."

"I don't want any goddam coffee."

"Stop acting like this," Donna said. "It's only a job. There are plenty of other jobs. Forget it." She started for the bathroom, and stopped. "Jurgy, is that true about Alma?"

"Yeah."

"How did it happen?"

I said, "I'll tell you how it happened. She went out with this bastard she picked up in the hotel, and he got her onto some beach and raped her. Then he drove back at more than a hundred miles an hour and the stinking car rolled over. That's how it happened."

Jurgy said, "Where did you hear this?"

"I was at the hospital last night," I said. "And do you want to know what else? The poor bitch. They had to cut her hair off because she had scalp injuries. Her hair!"

"Oh, hell," Donna said.

Jurgy said, "I didn't know all that. I thought it was just a car crash."

"*Just*," I said. "There isn't anything like *just* any more. It's never simple. You ought to know that."

Donna went into the bathroom and closed the door, and I heard the shower begin to run. Jurgy said, "Carol, come and sit down. You're white as a ghost. Let me fix you a cup of coffee."

"I'm all right."

"You're *not* all right. What happened with Donna?"

I told her as best I could.

When I finished she said icily, "Yeah. I figured it was going to happen sooner or later."

"Don't say that, Jurgy. It isn't true."

"It is, you know."

"Jurgy, if she'd scraped through the next few days, if she'd only passed this fiendish course, she'd have become a different person. Jurgy, when you're actually *flying* you have to live up to your responsibilities, you have to. She wouldn't act like this if she were actually *flying*—don't you see?"

"Honey, it's no use blowing your top now. Come and sit down for a minute—"

"No," I said, and walked out of the apartment. There was still something I could do about this situation, and how. I took the self-service elevator and went down to 1208. I tapped at the door, and Ray bawled from somewhere inside, "It's open. Come in."

The door was unlatched. I walked in, but he wasn't in his living room. I found him in the bathroom, standing there with his right hand in the basin. He was running cold water over his wrist and fingers.

"Ray! Have you hurt your hand?"

"It's nothing serious."

"Let me see."

"Don't worry. Betty Schwartz is coming over: she'll take care of it." He gave me a quick reassuring smile.

My God, what a weekend. Nothing but calamities. I was all set for hysterics. But first I had to straighten out this trouble with Donna. I said, "Darling, may I talk to you for a minute, please?"

"Sure. Let's get out of here first, though." He turned off the cold water faucet and began to dry his hand, dabbing at it with a towel; then he led me into the living room. "What's on your mind?"

I was shaking. "It's about my roommate, Donna Stewart."

He said calmly, "What about her?"

He was a wonderful man. That's why I loved him. He'd listen to reason. I said, "Darling, please, I want you to give her another chance."

His lips tightened. "I'm afraid it's too late."

"Ray, it can't be too late, she's still here, in the hotel."

"I'm sorry. I've already spoken to Arnie Garrison and Mrs. Montgomery. They've confirmed her dismissal. She has a seat reserved on the midnight plane."

"Ray, will you listen to me for a minute?"

"It's no use, Carol."

"Will you please *listen?*"

"Okay." He sat on the arm of one of his armchairs watching me. He was pale: I suppose he was in pain. But I had to get him to understand about Donna, I had to save her.

I said, "Ray, I know she acted terribly in the lobby. That fool Elliott Ewing must have taken her to lunch and forced her to have a drink too many—"

"*Forced* her?" Ray asked.

"Darling, it can happen to anybody. You know that."

"Carol—"

"Wait a minute, let me finish. Ray, it's ridiculous to fire her for just this one slip. You have to admit, she's *perfect* for the job. She's beautiful. She looks stunning in uniform. Even Miss Webley said the other day that she'd make a lot of passengers happy. And she's one of the brightest girls in the group, she's really on the ball. Doesn't all that count?"

"No. I'm sorry—"

"Just let me explain. There's a reason for her behavior, Ray. You can't possibly imagine what this past week has been like in class. Miss Webley pushed us until we were ready to drop. There wasn't any letup, not for a second. Do you realize we were working until two and three and even four o'clock in the morning? But every night, Ray! It was ghastly. By Saturday afternoon we were in a complete daze. Darling, after a week like that you can't blame a girl if she goes out on a little binge, can you?"

"I know all about last week," he said. "I know all about the pressure. It was roughly double what it is normally."

"Well, there you are!"

He said, "That's how we planned it."

"You *planned* it?"

"That's right. We have to know how each girl reacts under pressure. You took it. Your other roommate took it. All the other girls took it. Donna Stewart couldn't. That's why we're sending her home."

"But it's so unfair! It's so unjust! To send her home just for slipping once!"

"Once?" He gave me a sharp look. "She'd been drinking before the jai-alai game last weekend. She was seen in a bar on another occasion. We gave her the benefit of the doubt those times. This time was once too many." He stood up and put his arm around me. "Carol, I'm as sorry about this as you are. It doesn't make us happy when we have to send a girl home, but our responsibilities are just too great. We can't take any chances."

"She's my friend, Ray."

"I know. But that doesn't alter the facts."

I was practically in tears. "I'm only asking this one thing of you, darling. Give her another chance."

He released me and walked away, in utter fury. "Carol, you have to leave this to my judgment. It's my job. What do you expect me to do now? Call Arnie Garrison and say I've changed my mind? This girl wasn't drunk this afternoon? She isn't an incipient alcoholic? Is that what you want?"

"Ray, if you give her just one more chance, I promise you, I'll stand over her with a whip if necessary."

"I can't do it."

I said, "Darling, last night Alma was killed. Today you're sending another of my friends home in disgrace. It's more than I can bear. For my sake—"

"You're asking something that's impossible."

The tears were pouring down my face. I said, "Do you know what you're doing, Ray? She isn't an alcoholic now. But if you send her away she'll turn into one, and that's for sure. Darling, we can't let it happen."

"My responsibility doesn't extend so far."

I said, "No? Well let me tell you something. That little

statement sums you up. You don't have a heart, Ray, you don't have human blood in your veins, you can't think and feel like a human being any more. It doesn't matter to you that you're destroying Donna Stewart. You know what you are? You're just another of Magna International Airlines' mechanical contraptions. My God, they ought to roll you out into a hangar every night and cover you with a tarpaulin so you don't collect dust."

"Carol, you'd better go and lie down."

"Do you think I'm hysterical?"

"Yes, you've had a bad time."

"You bet I'm hysterical. You bet I've had a bad time. Ray, I don't love you any more, I don't want to see you as long as I live."

He tried to put his arms around me, but I slapped at him wildly and walked out.

I made a few attempts to help Donna with her packing, but she lost patience with me in due course and said, "Look, sweetie, go sit down somewhere and stop getting underfoot all the time." Jurgy was magnificent. She and Donna didn't greatly care for each other in normal circumstances, but in this hour of trial they made a great team. Possibly it was Jurgy's past training, or possibly it was built into her nature; she was as strong as a horse and fabulously neat. She had the knack of folding things perfectly, which doesn't sound important but is without doubt one of the most important knacks any woman can possess. She could fold literally anything so that it fitted exactly into a suitcase—skirts, dresses, even jackets. Give me a jacket to pack, and when it's unpacked all it's good for is the Salvation Army. I began to feel great respect for Luke Lucas. It might very well be true that he could judge a woman the same way he could judge a steer, in one minute. He sure hadn't made any mistake picking out Mary Ruth Jurgens. He'd gotten himself a treasure. Gad, I bet she could even fold one of his prize bulls for him, any time he needed to take one some place and wanted to travel light with just one bag. I figured Magna could save themselves a million dollars a year merely by hiring Luke to process all their hostesses. They didn't need Mr. Garrison and a mechanical psychiatrist and all the rest. All they needed was this one old bird.

God, I felt lousy. I only had to look at Alma's bed, and I began to cry; I only had to look at Donna, and I began to cry; I only had to look at my feet and remember that Ray Duer was downstairs, and I began to cry. I didn't know that any living thing could be so blue and still go on living. Jurgy made me coffee, really strong, but it didn't help; she made me a hamburger, and it not only didn't help, it started me vomiting; and at last I realized that I was just adding misery to misery, and I went into Jurgy's room and shut the door, and slumped down on the bed Annette used to sleep on and let myself go.

I don't know how long I'd been in there when the door opened and Dr. Elizabeth Schwartz walked in, with Miss Webley. I saw them in a rather dim way, but I recognized them, and I wondered why they'd come. This was a hell of a time to drop in on a social call.

"Hello, Carol," Dr. Schwartz said. She was carrying a black leather bag, a regular doctor's bag, but looking very pretty and feminine just the same.

"Hello, Dr. Schwartz."

"Hi," Miss Webley said, and I said, "Hi."

Dr. Schwartz sat down on Annette's bed beside me and looked at me with a sympathetic smile. "How are you feeling, Carol?"

"Oh, fine. Just fine."

"That's good. I've just come from Dr. Duer's apartment. He thought I might drop by to see you."

"How's his hand?"

"Nothing serious. Just a couple of bones broken. I've sent him to the hospital to have it X-rayed. Men are foolish, aren't they? They don't seem to understand that the human hand is a delicate instrument and wasn't made for combat. He'll be all right in a couple of weeks."

I began to cry again.

Dr. Schwartz said, "My dear child, you've had a very difficult time, you're completely exhausted, and you can't possibly go on like this. I want to give you a sedative to calm you down, and I also want you to get a full night's sleep—"

"But I don't *need* a sedative."

Miss Webley said, "Please, Carol. Listen to Dr. Schwartz." She was looking down at me and crying too. Jesus, the whole goddam world seemed to be crying.

Dr. Schwartz said, "Peg, bring me a glass of water, please." Miss Webley slipped out.

I said, "Dr. Schwartz, why do things happen like this?"

"I don't know, Carol. I wish I did. It happens to everybody, though. It's happened to me, if that's any consolation."

Miss Webley came back with a glass of water. Dr. Schwartz gave me two small green pills, and as I swallowed them I felt exactly like Socrates swallowing the hemlock. I knew Dr. Schwartz was acting kindly, I knew she was doing this to put me out of my misery; and I honestly didn't expect to wake again, ever.

I slept for about fifteen hours, still on Annette's bed. I didn't immediately recognize myself when I opened my eyes. I was just nobody definite, just five feet seven of female without identity. Gradually, though, I drifted back to myself, but when I climbed off the bed and stood up I realized what Dr. Schwartz must have done—she'd taken my brain out to give it an airing, or to have new linings fitted: my head felt as light as a feather. It was a weird feeling, my head trying to float away by itself.

There were two notes on the chest of drawers beside Annette's bed, folded and standing up like Christmas cards. One was from Jurgy: *Dear Carol, Dr. Swartz says not to come to class if you don't feel like it. Miss Webley too. Take it easy. See you later. Mary Ruth (Jurgy).* The second was from Donna: *So long, cream. Good luck. D.S.*

I went to the kitchenette and had a glass of milk and an apple, and I knew I couldn't possibly go to class this morning and sit in my Iron Maiden while my head bobbed gently all over the ceiling. Apart from anything else, it would disturb the other girls. And besides, when I looked at my watch, I found the time was eleven-thirty—half the day had already gone. So I put on my old black swimsuit and my robe and sandals, and vacuumed down in the self-service elevator, and clomped out to the pool. Fresh air, that's what I needed. Not sun. Sun would be a little too much. I stretched out on a chaise longue under a huge sun umbrella, my cigarettes and matches and change purse in a silk scarf on a table by my side; and I lay there with my eyes closed, not quite asleep and not quite awake, letting the world whizz by me. I felt as if I'd been trapped just above the drain of a bath that was emptying itself—caught exactly at the point where the water swirls clockwise in a frantic manner; and every now and then I'd be transported to Australia where the water swirls counterclockwise. Gad, there must have been dynamite in those sleeping pills.

224

Gradually I became aware that somebody was addressing me, and when I opened my eyes and focused carefully I saw that it was my old and trusted friend, N.B. Dear old Nat Brangwyn in person, wearing a gray suit and a yellow bow tie, as neat and clean and well-groomed as a prize canary.

I said, "Well, hi," and gave him a weak, sleepy smile.

"Gee, I woke you up."

"Wasn't asleep," I explained: "Shnoozhing." A beautiful word. I tried it again. "Shnoozhing, that's all. And how you?"

"Fine, fine." He was beaming at me, and at the same time he seemed uneasy.

"Siddown, Mr. Brangwyn," I said. "You don't wanna stand out there in that hot old sun. Siddown. Take a load off your feet."

"But you're trying to sleep," he said.

"Tisn't that, Mr. Brangwyn. Doctor gave me coupla sleeping pills last night, and the effect hasn't worn off. Sorry impolite. Do siddown."

He sat down.

I suddenly discovered my mouth. It felt like an unemptied ash tray. I said, "Gee, I'm thirsty," and began to search for water. I could see it in the pool, and I could see it in the ocean, but I couldn't reach it.

N.B. said, "Don't move. Just stay there, Miss Thompson." He disappeared, just like a canary in a rosebush; and when he reappeared he was carrying a huge glass pitcher filled with ice cubes and liquid and floating slices of lime, and a big solid carved highball glass. He filled the glass and handed it to me, and as I took it I said, "Mr. Brangwyn, there isn't any alcol in this, is there? I just have a regular thirst, I guess I'm dehydrated to death, but I don't want any alcol."

He said, "Miss Thompson, I guarantee there isn't a drop of alcohol in the entire jug. It's pure limeade. Just what you should drink in your condition."

"Please siddown, Mr. Brangwyn."

He sat down and said, "Give me a break. Stop calling me Mr. Brangwyn. Nat. Or N.B."

"Okay. I'm not Miss Thompson either. Okay? I'm Carol."

"That's great. Drink the limeade, Carol."

I gulped down half of the glassful. Then I took a deep breath and gulped down the half that was left. I put the

225

glass on the table with a sigh, and he refilled it at once. I said, "Boy, that tasted good. Now I need a cigarette."

I groped around for my own but he was a million light-years ahead of me. There was a Tareyton under my nose and the flame of his gold-plated Zippo lighter.

I smoked for a while, and then I said, "N.B., I've come to a very important conclusion about you. Very important. You mind if I tell you?"

"I don't mind," he said. But he did. He smiled nervously.

"*I* think," I said, "*I* think, you're an awful nice guy."

"Well, thanks, Carol." It pleased him enormously, and he stopped being nervous at once.

I said, "N.B., tell me on the level, now. This is something's been bothering me. Is it true you're a notorious gambler?"

He laughed. "You want an answer to that?"

"If you care to give me an answer, N.B. Don't upset yourself, now. You wanna answer that rude question, you answer it."

He said, "Well, Carol, I do a lot of things. I have real estate. I have a part share in an automobile agency. I got investments in three restaurants, also a couple of nightclubs. Et cetera. And also I like to speculate. Some guys speculate on stocks, I speculate in what *I'm* interested in. There's no difference. It's all the same thing. Only my kind of speculation is called gambling. Get it?"

"N.B., I not only get it. It's exactly what I thought. Exactly. Speculate, that's the exact word."

"Okay?"

"Sure it's okay. And I admire you for it, N.B. A free country. You wanna speculate your way, you go right ahead and do it. Don't let anybody stop you."

"You don't think I'm some kind of a outlaw?"

"No, sir. Not me, N.B."

"Well, that's great. That's a step forward."

"N.B., tell me something else. Do you mind if I get personal?"

"First, ask. Then we'll see if I mind."

"Okay. Here goes. Is it true you owe the federal government a hundred and fifty thousand dollars income tax?"

He opened his mouth and roared with laughter. "Where did you pick up all this stuff?"

"Just picked it up, N.B. You know how these things get around."

"All right. I'll tell you. That a hundred and fifty is purely

226

or the birds. Every week the figure doubles itself. I don't mind. Put it this way, Carol. It's public relations, see?"

"Oh, sure. Everything's public relations these days."

"You said it. It doesn't do me no harm. Everyone has this idea, N.B. owes a hundred and fifty grand, he must be an important guy. So why not? Actually, I owe maybe forty grand. This is all a lot of fog. There's nothing can be pinned down. My lawyers argue with the tax people, everyone argues back and forth, and in the end I'll maybe settle for twenty-five. Okay?"

"Okay."

I drank more of the limeade, and again he refilled my glass.

"Feeling better?" he asked.

"Lots better, thank you."

I lay back looking at him. It was true. He just purely and precisely fitted his description: a nice guy. And of all the people I'd met and trusted, practically since the year dot, he'd done me the least harm. The whole span of time, from the moment he offered me a cigarette on the plane to this moment when he refilled my glass with limeade, he'd been kind and gentle and thoughtful and self-effacing. When I refused his generosity, like the offer of the car, like his offer of dates, he'd behaved with nice quiet dignity. He hadn't been a pest once. When he saw that one of my friends was heading toward the edge of a cliff, he came and warned me about it. He was at least human.

He said, "Just sit back, Carol, take it easy. You aren't going in to the airline school today?"

"No."

"I don't blame you. You had a rough weekend."

I nodded.

"Too bad about that Sonny Kee business. He was a louse, that's all. A terrible thing about the girl. Terrible. It hurt me, Carol. You know what I mean? A sweet girl like that. Really sweet, pretty as a picture."

"Yes. She was beautiful."

"Maxwell tells me your redhead girl friend was in some kind of trouble, too."

"Yes. She's gone back home."

"Rough, eh? Everything happening at once." He sighed and shook his head. "That's life for you. It never fails. Trouble? Brother! It always comes by the dozen. . . . Look, Carol."

227

"Yes?"

He frowned. "Wouldn't you like to get out for a while? Get away from this hotel, get away from your depressing memories, get away from airline companies—purely get out and enjoy yourself for a few hours? Get out and see a different world? You don't want to sit here all day and be miserable. Eh?"

I didn't answer. I looked at him and listened.

He said, "Come on. Let me take you to lunch. What about it?"

I said, "N.B., you're really so sweet."

He stiffened.

I said, "Thank you for asking me. I can't imagine anything nicer than to have lunch with you."

He sat back, with a huge happy smile. "Well, boy! Isn't that great!"

"I'll go up and change."

"Listen. Don't rush. There's no hurry. Just do it in your own good time. I'll be right here, waiting."

I took another sip of limeade, and said, "I'll be down as soon as I can, N.B.," and went up to the apartment.

Perhaps the limeade reactivated the sleeping pills or something, but as I took off my black swimsuit a portion of my wooziness returned, together with a slice of last night's anger. That goddam apartment was so *empty*. It was like a de luxe graveyard. Sure, Jurgy would be returning tonight (unless they decided to can *her* on the spot); but look at the rest of the apartment! Annette's bed, vacant. Donna's bed, vacant. Alma's bed, vacant permanently. It roused me to such an extent that I began to walk up and down, up and down, without a stitch of clothing on, blind with rage and woozy with sleeping pills, muttering and raving at Mr Garrison and Dr. Ray Duer and all the rest of that motley crew, until I collapsed on Donna's bed by the window because I had no more breath left. Then, when my breath and my strength returned, I began to dress, still muttering and raving and occasionally crying; and I chose to put on a number I hadn't dared to wear up to now because it seemed a little too daring for Magna International Airlines' lofty standards—a strapless job in a soft, deep rose. But before I slid into it I clomped to the bathroom in my panties and high-heeled shoes (which seemed to be a very appropriate costume for the occasion) and put on my war paint. At least I'd learned something useful, in these three weeks of endeavor: how to make myself up like a Shanghai whore. I slapped on the works. Miss Webley would have been proud of me, though she might have disapproved of my language. Liquid base. Rouge up to the eyes. Powder. Brushed-on lipstick. Eyeshadow. Mascara. Eyebrows. And, expressly for N.B.'s benefit, perfume. I was fairly expert at this routine by now, and the final effect was pretty exotic.

Then I hoisted myself into the strapless dress. Yeah, man, yeah. Those sunburned shoulders, those bronzed arms—me? Thompson? That golden thatch—Thompson? That bulging chest—Thompson? It was apparently so. A matching stole came with the dress, and I slung it around me; and before I left, I paused for a moment to look again at those blank beds. I said, loudly and firmly, "To hell with you Mr. Garrison, to hell with you Magna International Airlines, TO HELL WITH YOU DOCTOR RAY DUER," and I clanked out. Dignified, ladylike, erect, and as dizzy as if I'd just come out of a Waring Blendor.

N.B. was so surprised that he said, "Miss Thompson, I'll have to call you Carol again." It was meant to be a compliment to my ladylike appearance, but in his confusion he said it the wrong way round, which actually made it a double compliment. His car was something to behold, a metallic-gray Lincoln convertible, and when I said, "Wow!" he explained that since he was partly in the automobile business he had to keep up a front. He was a tremendously good driver—just one finger on the steering wheel was enough—and in addition he seemed to have periscope vision—he didn't have to look at the road, he looked at me, and the Lincoln still zipped in and out of the traffic with the utmost ease.

The next thing I knew, we were at the racetrack. When N.B. said, get out and see a different world, he certainly meant it. I was still too dizzy to take everything in, I simply had a blinding impression of sunshine and hordes of people in dazzling clothes and a loud upswelling noise that made me very excited. We didn't go anywhere near any horses; N.B. took my arm and led me into the clubhouse, and I found myself sitting in a huge glass enclosure, with a balcony around it, the same upswelling noise buzzing in my ears and the excitement getting wilder every moment. The glass enclosure was filled with people having lunch—the men dressed very much like N.B., all the women dressed absolutely to the teeth. There was an awful lot of movement, characters weaving between the tables constantly, and now and then everybody would make a dash for the balcony to see the finish of a race and there would be pandemonium. My God, Donna and Alma would have loved it, it was just their cup of tea: pandemonium, and flowers, and flamingos clomping everywhere, and horses foaming at the mouth in the distance, and music, and women smothered in mink, and those smooth men coming over to N.B. and saying politely, "Hi, N.B.," and N.B. saying politely, "Hi, Joey. Hi, Sam. How's things?"

According to N.B. the horses could wait, the first order of the day was lunch. I actually wanted to watch the horses but he assured me on his word of honor that they'd still be there after we'd eaten; and so we had champagne cocktails to begin, and then another round of champagne cocktails while our stone crabs Thermidor were being prepared; and N.B. took a sheet of paper from somewhere and wrote across the top in large print.

IG

and then drew a line under it.

I said, "What does that mean, ig?"

He said, "That isn't ig. It's one grand. That's your credit."

"Boy," I said, "I'm glad I have some credit. But where did it come from?"

"From me," he said. "I'm backing you."

I said, "What do you mean, I have one grand credit, you're backing me? How?"

"How yourself," he said; and he explained, this one grand, in other words, a thousand dollars, was there at my disposal to bet with for the afternoon. I could bet just any way I pleased, but if I wanted his advice he'd be only too glad to give me a tip now and then. "Like the race coming up," he said. "If I were you I'd bet a hundred on Number Six."

I said, "N.B., you've gone out of your mind, dear. I don't know the first thing about betting. Don't be ridiculous."

"It's only a game, honey. That's all."

"But suppose I lose the one grand? What then?"

"Look," he said, "it's only on paper, isn't it?"

He snapped his fingers, and a man came hurrying over and N.B. whispered in his ear, and I thought, Well, if we're going to play games on paper, well, why not? It seemed a perfectly harmless occupation, particularly when washed down by another round of champagne cocktails followed by stone crabs Thermidor. Boy, I thought, these notorious gamblers sure know how to live.

The afternoon just became more and more fantastic, with all the pandemonium getting louder and the excitement getting wilder, and these mad dashes to the balcony to see which horse was winning the race. There were flags and flowers and flamingos and the sun shining and utter panic; and I'd shout, "Come on, Lochinvar, come on," or whatever the name of my horse was, even though I couldn't tell Lochinvar from a hole in the ground—all the horses looked exactly alike. But the thrill! My God! It was stupendous! Then when the race was over we'd go back to our table, and N.B. would carefully make an entry under IG; and apparently I was a genius. At the end of the afternoon he turned to me with a pleased look on his face and said, "Honey. You did pretty good."

"I did?"

"Yessir, you sure did. You made a neat twenty-two hundred."

"Who, me?"

"Yessir, you, Miss Thompson. Wait a minute, we'll collect it, and then we'll get out of here."

I screamed, "You mean, this is real money!"

"Why certainly it's real money. What did you think it was? Russian rubles?"

"But you said it was only a game, it was only on paper—"

He laughed. "You're cute. You know that? You're real cute."

The next thing I knew, we were back in the Lincoln convertible, going somewhere at sixty-five miles an hour, and I had this enormous roll of bills in my handbag.

I said to N.B., "What time is it?"

"About twenty after six."

"Where are we going?"

"A little club I know."

"I ought to be getting back."

"For what? Forget it. You had a rough weekend, a little relaxation will do you good."

The little club turned out to be perfectly charming, like the prettiest indoor garden. It was cool and pleasant, with attractive little white iron tables and white iron chairs, and a flagstoned floor, a fountain splashing in the center, and off in one corner a trio playing in practically a whisper.

"Like it?" N.B. asked.

"It's beautiful."

"What will you drink?"

I was still swimming in champagne cocktails, except that I was as sober as a judge, and I said, "N.B., I think I'd just like some limeade."

"Okay."

That was the wonderful thing about N.B. No pressure. Never any effort to force you to do what you didn't want to do. Complete friendliness and co-operation. It required a special kind of character, really very strong in its own way, and I admired him for it.

"Care to dance?" N.B. asked.

"Why, I'd love to."

There were about six square feet of dance floor in front of the trio. That, again, is another giveaway of character, because some men will carry you onto a floor of this size and begin to act as if they're in the last quarter of the Army-Navy football game and the fate of the nation rests on their brawny shoulders. Not so my friend N.B. We just stood fairly closely together letting the music drift over us, and the bandleader called, "Hi, N.B.," and N.B. called back, "Hi, Johnny." It was delightful. I mean, dancing to a trio at the cocktail hour isn't meant to be a great big soul-shattering experience like Beethoven's Ninth Symphony conducted by Bruno Walter; it's just meant to be a few moments of friendliness before dinner; and that's how N.B. kept it.

We stayed about half an hour, while I finished my limeade and he drank a vodka martini, and then we were in the Lincoln again. I said, "Are you taking me back to the hotel now?" and he said nicely, "Why?" I said, "I ought to be back," and he said, "You have to eat, don't you?" I said, "Yes. Thank you."

Fair is fair, as my father used to say. Here was a man who'd treated me as decently and generously as any man could treat any girl; he liked my company (all right, let's not mince words, he had a yen for me); and I couldn't act coy with him. If it would give him pleasure to have me around for a couple of hours longer, I was ready and willing to give him that pleasure.

We had dinner in another club, much bigger and livelier and noisier than the first. The band here was a seven-man combination, and they sure had a beat, they were really the wildest. We had a table way up front, almost on the dance

232

floor, and the noise was so loud that I could hardly hear myself think. Noise, and flashing lights, and hundreds of people—fun.

The champagne cocktails had worn off by now, of course, and I was as sober as a judge; but I hung back a little when N.B. asked me what I would drink before dinner was served. For once, he pressed me; proving that although he was kind and gentle, he was no Milquetoast. He said, "Have a vodka martini, that couldn't harm a baby." I said, "All right," and as soon as he gave the order to the waiter he asked me to dance. "Before the floor show starts," he explained. I said, "Is there a floor show?" and he said, "Why sure. They have a dinner floor show, and a supper floor show, and a three-o'clock-in-the-morning floor show. You want to stay and see all of them?" I said, "Gee, I'd love to, but I have to be back at the hotel by ten-thirty at the latest." The band leader called out to him, "Hi, N.B., how you doing?" and N.B. called back, "Hi, Billy boy, what's new?"

The vodka martini at least tasted as if it wouldn't harm a baby, and I had a second. I ordered shrimp cocktail Rubens and lamb chops Florentine, which turned out to be double lamb chops from a lamb about the size of an elephant, flavored a trifle too sweetly with rosemary. N.B. insisted on a bottle of red wine, and he must have been something of a connoisseur, because he and Gaston, the wine waiter, had a learned conversation about the various kinds and the various years, and Gaston finally said, "Mr. Brangwyn, you are as usual most discerning, sir." It tasted fine, like high-class red ink, and it was probably loaded with alcohol, because by the time the floor show started I was feeling no pain although I was still as sober as a judge. I was actually in that state of sublime well-being that the Zen boys just crave—nothingness and somethingness combined. It took one queer form: my strapless dress kept sliding down me. I'd only tried it on once at Lord and Taylor and it had fitted like a glove then. At the race track it had behaved itself perfectly well, and so it had at the little club with the little white tables earlier. But the minute Zen came into the picture, bingo!— it began to lead a life of its own, slipping down in a carefree manner and exposing altogether too much of my charms to the multitude. At any moment I expected to find myself bare to the waist, like an Arab woman going to the well with a water pitcher on her head.

Apart from this, the world was in a splendid state of happiness. Everything was gay, everything was bright and noisy, everything was just plain wonderful. The first act of the floor show was a girl singer who sang some sad but sexy torch songs; and then a jittery youngish guy in a tuxedo with the widest shoulders did a patter act and told some semi-dirty stories like the story about the zebra's honeymoon and the story about the two goldfish, all of which I'd heard before in various versions. Gad, he should have spent a couple of evenings with the girls on the fourteenth floor; his back teeth would have been floating.

And then, to round everything off, the house lights were lowered, the band began to play *Scheherazade,* the dance floor was illuminated with red and blue spotlights, and out came the three girls I'd seen rehearsing on the roof of the Charleroi, the two girls who did grinds and bumps, and the tassel twirler. It was just like running into old friends at a watering hole in Central Africa. In actual fact I'd seen everything they had to offer, except that it all took place to *Scheherazade* and not Ravel's *Bolero,* and the red and blue spotlights added drama of a kind. But that tassel twirler still sent me. The finale was absolutely spectacular. She came forward, and all the lights began to revolve furiously; and between gyrating spotlights and gyrating tassels and gyrating bosoms and gyrating buttocks and even a gyrating navel, I began to feel Zennier than Zen. It was incredible.

I said to N.B., "Isn't she great?" and he seemed somewhat surprised. He said, "You like that stuff?" as if he couldn't believe I had such a low cultural level. So I explained that she was almost a friend of mine, and how I'd had a long chat with her in the solarium; and the upshot of my mentioning this to N.B. was amazing. When the act was over, and the girls were taking their bows, he called out in a low voice, "Hey, Ernestine," and she peered at our table and smiled. He pointed at one of the spare chairs at our table, and she nodded; and as soon as she'd collected a robe backstage she reappeared and joined us. The robe was a robe in name only. It covered the back of her shoulders but it had nothing at all to do with her front; and I guess she was so accustomed to being seen in public like this that she was scarcely aware of her muscular bosom resting on the tablecloth, with the tassels oscillating as she breathed.

"Well, gee, N.B.," she said cheerfully. "Sure is nice seeing you again. How have you been keeping yourself?"

234

"Oh, fair," he said. "Ernestine, remember my friend Miss Thompson?"

She looked at me in a puzzled way, and then threw back her head and roared with laughter. "Why, honey, sure I remember you! How are you, honey? And, boy, are you a beautiful color! And that dress! You look like a million dollars, honey. Why, N.B., you're a real lucky feller."

"You're telling me," he said. "How about having some brandy with us, Ernestine?"

"Delighted, N.B."

He snapped his fingers for the waiter and ordered three brandies. I protested, but he said, "Pooh, a brandy won't hurt you," and I sat back resigned to my fate. Thank God, I had this tremendous resistance to liquor. I was still as sober as a judge.

N.B. and Ernestine seemed to have known each other since birth, and they chatted away about people and places in the way old acquaintances do: How's Ted, how's Bosco, seen Gwen lately, what's new in Chicago, and so on and so on. I sat nursing my brandy, fascinated by those two dangling tassels; and I must have been so fascinated that N.B. suddenly broke into my thoughts, saying, "Hey, Carol, what are you dreaming about?"

I couldn't lie to him. I said, "The tassels."

He said, "Are you kidding?"

"N.B., they're just fascinating."

"You mean it?"

"Of course I mean it. They're just absolutely fascinating."

He said, "Ernestine, give them to her."

"Okay. I'll slip back to my dressing room—"

"Give them to her here."

"Here?" she cried.

"Sure, here. Why not?"

"Are you crazy or something, N.B. You want to have me arrested for indecent exposure?"

He took out his wallet, extracted two twenty-dollar bills and laid them on the table in front of her. "Cover yourself with these."

She howled with laughter. "N.B., you're a riot."

"Come on, now."

"Don't rush me, sugar, don't rush me."

I was so bugeyed, I couldn't utter a word. She took the two bills, arranged them across herself carefully, holding them with one outstretched hand; and then she pulled the tassels off, one after the other. Plop. Plop. She was giggling as she held them out to me. "Here, honey. They're all yours."

I stammered, "Well, gee. Thanks."

N.B. said, "Don't those things have to be disinfected, or something, before anyone else wears them?"

"Whiskey," Ernestine said. "That's all. Shake 'em off in whiskey."

She gave a loud whoop, pushed back her chair, and rushed away.

We were in the big luxurious Lincoln again, and I said, "Are you taking me to the hotel now, N.B.?"

"It's still early, baby. I thought you ought to sit by the water for a while and relax. This time of evening it's beautiful down there. Okay?"

Why not? "Okay," I said.

"Look at all the stars," he said.

"Yes."

"Smell the jasmine?"

"Yes."

"Happy?"

"Yes." Except for Donna, except for Alma, except for Duer.

"You'd have gone out of your mind staying in the Charleyroy all day by yourself."

"I guess I would."

We'd driven onto the Venetian Causeway, and suddenly he swung to the right and began to go down a smooth, curving road.

I said, "I didn't know you could go down here."

"It's private. For residents only."

"N.B., where are we going?"

"I have an apartment down here."

"You do?"

"Right on the water. You'll like it."

I sighed.

He said, "Why the big sigh?"

"Nothing. You don't live at the Charleroi?"

"Me? No, sir. I like privacy too much."

I understood what he meant when I entered his apartment. I looked and gasped. The lights were on in the living room, and he stood beside me watching my reaction, a little smile on his lips. It was a low-ceilinged room, about forty feet square—enormous and yet not enormous because there

236

was so much furniture in it, perfectly arranged. There were low, comfortable armchairs and low, comfortable settees, a huge divan piled with cushions, a big television set, long low cabinets, and over to one side a Steinway grand piano. There were magnificent flower arrangements everywhere; but there was just one picture on the wall which served as a centerpiece, bringing everything into focus.

He asked, "Like my picture?"

"Yes."

"Know who painted it?"

"Picasso."

"That's my girl!"

He took my hand and led me all the way across the room to a big window. The curtains were drawn, but he pressed a button and opened them partway and said, "Look out here."

I looked. There were shielded lights illuminating a long sloping lawn, and water glistening beyond. I said, "Is that the ocean?"

He drew the curtains again. "No. Biscayne Bay."

I said, "N.B., it's fabulous."

"Is it?"

He came close to me, and I made one weak effort to protect myself, I said, "N.B., please—" but he wasn't deterred. He took me in his arms, whispering, "Do you know I'm crazy about you, do you, do you know I'm crazy about you?" I couldn't fight. All my grief, all my hopelessness, all the liquor I'd drunk, all the day's excitement, seemed to drown me, I was weak all over, I had no bones, I couldn't resist him and I didn't want to resist him. He kissed every inch of skin he could reach, and I let him do what he wanted because I was so weak and also because he had been so utterly kind and so utterly generous with me ever since our paths crossed. Then, as I stood there quaking and being adored, that damned strapless dress gave up the ghost completely, I just seemed unable to keep myself within it, I felt just like a banana sliding out of its skin. I thought furiously, "My God, Lord and Taylor will hear about this," and I clutched at it and tried to wriggle myself back into a state of decency but I couldn't. N.B. led me to the divan and said, "Take that rag off," and I said, "It isn't a rag," and he said, virtually tearing it off me, "Carol, Carol, I'm going to dress you like a queen, that's the only way you should be dressed, like a queen, don't you understand? Why do you want to sell yourself to that lousy airline, just to be a glorified waitress, when you can live like a queen? Jesus, I'm crazy about you, you've been alive in front of me—*alive!*—day and night, night and day, all these weeks. Oh, Jesus, I'm so crazy about you, I'll give you the sun and the moon and the stars and anything you want. You're so clean, Jesus, you're so clean, I want you near me forever. And those eyes. Oh, Jesus, those ever-loving sweet level eyes, I dream about them."

Well, there I was, back again where I started, Level-Eyed Thompson. With a difference, though, because I was lost. From the very beginning, I was right about this man. He'd missed his vocation. He would have made the world's greatest surgeon, he would have been a legend on Park Avenue. He scarcely touched me with those gentle hands of his, and yet gradually he reached and awakened every nerve, the long-secret hidden woman nerves, the nerves that sleep most of one's life but can become a mad tumult at unexpected moments. He whispered to me, he kissed me, and I was utterly lost. It was this incredible subtlety that almost killed me—scarcely touching me and sending the long-hidden nerves into a frenzy, scarcely touching me with those delicate fingers and creating a piercing agony over my entire body, until there were a thousand voices screaming all over me for deliverance, a deliverance that only he could bring me. He was too cunning, he was too masterful, he went on and on kissing me and whispering to me and searching out more of those hidden nerves, until I couldn't bear another second of being apart from him. My body couldn't go on living without him, but my brain, curiously enough, was deathly afraid of him, and I screamed, "No! No! No!" as if I wanted him to go away from me, and at the same time I held onto him with all my strength for fear he'd go. I began to shudder as if I were going to die, and I couldn't hold him tightly enough; and then everything became altogether mad, and he laughed, and choked, trying to say something; and then we began to drift away from each other, he to his darkness, I to mine.

For a time it was like lying on the surface of a hot sea, with a black sun overhead, and the sound of singing far away, sickening and frightening and nightmarish. Then all feeling began to subside, and I saw the great bowls filled with flowers close by; I saw the solemn black Steinway

238

piano and I kept my eyes fixed on it, expecting music to come out of it; I saw the white ceiling watching me as I watched it; I saw a white furry rug spread on the floor—I saw all these real things but they weren't quite real, they had a new and different kind of reality, as if they'd only just this moment come into existence. And as the heaving of my body stopped, as my heart slowed down to a beat I could tolerate, he turned to me again.

God, he was insatiable. But the most terrifying thing now, when he sought me out, was that I'd become insatiable too. My brain revolted against him, but the devils inside me craved him, rejoiced at the first agonizing spasm of shuddering, craved and cried and took more and more. I yelled "No!" at him a hundred times, I clawed the skin on his back; and he laughed. He was seized with such a violence that I thought he was going to tear me to pieces, he was rough and sharp and careless with me, and I couldn't stop him. I was helpless, completely at his mercy in those mounting spasms of agony and ecstasy; and I thought it would go on forever. But finally he gave a shout of laughter and rolled away.

A few moments later he scrambled off the divan and left me. I didn't see him go. I only felt the disjointed movement and sway of the divan. I sat up eventually, my head in my hands, my hair hanging over my face, wondering what had become of him and what would become of me. Holy mackerel, I thought, it's lucky I was sober—God knows what would have happened if I'd been drunk.

Then, minutes later, I saw him—it seemed miles away across that huge room—returning with a tray. He was all bones and ribs, like an unfinished ship in a dry dock; and when he sat down beside me he was smiling contentedly. Of all the strange things in this world, he'd come back with two huge bowls of cornflakes, a bottle of champagne, and two champagne glasses; and he put one of the bowls of cornflakes on my lap.

I said, "What's this, N.B.?"

"Go ahead, sweetface. Eat up. It's good for you."

"But, mon Dieu, it isn't time for breakfast, is it?"

"Don't ask so many questions. Eat." He poured the champagne. "You know where I got this tip?"

"Which tip?"

"Chump, the tip about cornflakes."

"At the racing stables?"

He laughed as if I'd said something madly funny. Then he told me, almost in a whisper.

One lives and learns. I said, "Is that true?"

"Yes, *sir*. And, you know something? I'm even beginning to croon in that sleepy way."

Cornflakes. I'd been eating them for years and hadn't noticed any special effects, but they certainly worked for N.B. Almost as soon as he'd finished his bowl he was seized with the pangs of love for the third time, but I pushed him away. Every nerve in my poor worn-out old body had gone into a coma, and enough is enough. I said, "N.B., I have to get back to the hotel. Please."

"You aren't going back to the hotel. You're staying here."

I said, "No. It's impossible."

"Forget this stupid airline stuff. You're staying here from tonight on."

"No," I said. "I'm sorry. I can't."

He grabbed my arms. "Listen. I told you, didn't I? I'll dress you like a queen, I'll give you everything you want—"

"It's utterly impossible, N.B."

"Why?"

"It just is. Where's the bathroom? I have to get dressed and leave."

"Carol, listen to me. Just listen—" Then he stopped, and scowled. "Okay. *Okay.* The bathroom's back there, on the left."

It was a magnificent bathroom, all black and white. The walls were covered with Piranesi's engravings of the ruins of Rome, under some kind of protective glaze, and they couldn't have been more appropriate. Piranesi could have used me for a whole new set, the ruins of Greenwich, Connecticut. I was suddenly feeling like death. I felt as if I'd been ravished by a Caterpillar tractor.

When I'd showered I found an elaborate make-up bar, fitted with practically every shade of Elizabeth Arden lipsticks and eye shadow and all the rest of the paraphernalia, just what you'd expect to find in any bachelor's apartment. It was a thoughtful touch. Any girl, no matter if she was a blonde, a redhead, or a brunette, could make herself look as good as new, if she survived the cornflakes routine.

I put on a dab of lipstick, a dab of powder, slid into that treacherous strapless job, combed my hair, and went back to N.B. I said, "Will you call a taxi, please?"

"Taxi? Hell, I'll drive you there."

"There's no need—"

He said, "Don't be ridiculous, now."

I said, as we were leaving, "What's the time, N.B.?"

He looked at his watch. "A quarter of one."

"Thank you."

The night was soft and quiet and peaceful as we drove to the Charleroi. We didn't speak to each other. I thought, God, how funny everything is. How weird, how comic, how senseless, the way things happen. If Magna International Airlines hadn't ordered me not to associate with this man, he and I might, between us, have been able to save Alma's life. If, only yesterday afternoon, Herr Doktor Duer and I had merely arrived back at the hotel ten minutes earlier, he would have missed Donna, he would have missed getting into a fight with Elliott, I wouldn't have had to go down to his apartment to plead with him for Donna's life, I wouldn't have had that crying jag, I wouldn't have needed Dr. Schwartz's sleeping pills, I wouldn't have missed class today, I wouldn't have met N.B. at the pool, and I wouldn't be what I am now, a tramp. Probably pregnant, too. That was a sudden inspiration: it hit me like a bucket of ice water. Probably pregnant, too. How ducky.

We rolled up to the entrance of the Charleroi, and just as we were stopping I picked up my handbag in readiness to get out, and realized—another sudden inspiration—what was inside. I opened the bag, took out the bills, and put them on the seat at N.B.'s side.

He said, "What's this?"

"The money you won at the race track."

"It's your money. I didn't win it. You won it."

"I can't take it, N.B. I simply can't."

He said, "What's the matter with you, kid? The money didn't come from me, it came from the race track. It's found money. You could have finished not winning a cent. For Pete's sake, honey, don't be such a dumbkopf."

He put the roll of bills in my purse; and that's when I first heard the name that suited me best.

As the doorman opened the car door for me, N.B. said, "When am I going to see you again?"

I said, "I'm sorry, I won't be free any night this week. We have a very heavy schedule in class."

He pursed his lips. Then he said, "How about the week-end?"

"I can't say at present."

"Okay."

"Thank you for a very enjoyable day."

"Don't mention it."

I went slowly into the lobby, a rather dizzy Cinderella; vacuumed up to the fourteenth floor and crawled into 1412. Jurgy and Miss Webley were waiting for me.

Miss Webley said, "Well, glory be, here you are."

Jurgy just stared.

I said in a weak vague way, "I'm sorry I'm late."

Miss Webley's beautiful blue eyes were wet with tears. "We were just about to call the police. What happened to you, Carol?"

"I couldn't bear to stay in the hotel."

She understood. There were no arguments. She came over to me and put her arms around me. "Here you are, that's the important thing. Mary Ruth and I were beginning to imagine all sorts of terrible things." She had the most delicious fragrance.

"I'm all right," I said; but I wasn't in the least. The room was going around my head in circles.

She looked at me with pity. "You're worn-out, poor child. Mary Ruth, will you see that she gets to bed? Perhaps she ought to have a glass of warm milk."

"Yes, Miss Webley."

After a few minutes, Miss Webley left. Jurgy said, "She came of her own account. I didn't call her, or anything. She dropped by at ten o'clock to see how you were. When you didn't turn up we got kind of scared."

"Why should you get scared?"

"No reason. Want a glass of warm milk?"

I shook my head. It hurt. Then I said, "Yes, perhaps I would. Don't bother, Jurgy. I'll fix it for myself."

"Get to bed," she growled. "You look like the wrath of God."

I put my pajamas on in the bathroom and drizzled into bed; and she sat with me, smoking a cigarette while I sipped the milk.

She said, "I can sleep in here, if you like."

"No. Don't worry about me."

Then she said, "We were told our bases today. Where we're all going."

"Where are you going?"

"I'm staying here in Miami. You are, too."

"Oh."

"Show a little enthusiasm. You'll be near your boy friend."

"Which boy friend?"

"Dr. Duer."

"Who told you he's my boy friend?"

"But—" she began. Then she became indignant. "Hell, Carol, everyone knows about it. My God—when was it? Saturday. Half a dozen of the girls saw you in the coffee shop together, holding hands, no less. Even Miss Webley kind of hinted at it. You're supposed to be the big romance of the training school."

"Ray Duer doesn't mean a damn thing to me."

She was utterly baffled. "No?"

"And I don't want his name mentioned again."

"Okay." She'd recovered her normal calmness. She stood up, preparing to leave. "Incidentally, you have any plans where you want to live after we graduate?"

"Jurgy, I don't have an idea in my head."

"How about you and me sharing an apartment?"

"Fine. Why not?"

"Luke is staying here all week. I can ask him to scout round and try to find a place."

"Luke has better things to do."

She said coldly, "No, he hasn't."

She went to her own bed. But about two hours later I crawled into her room and wakened her. She sat up instantly and switched on her bedside lamp. She said, "What's the matter? Why you crying?"

"Jurgy—" I was ready to die.

"*Tell* me, for God's sake, if you're going to tell me."

"Jurgy, I was with a man tonight. I didn't know what to do—"

She groaned. "I figured that's where you were. God Almighty, it happens every time. Someone kicks the bucket and every dame in the neighborhood goes crazy with sex." Her voice became sharp. "What do you mean, you didn't know what to do? Didn't you take care of things?"

"No."

She said, "Baby, you know what you do first? This very minute?"

"What?"

"Get down on your knees and pray."

"Jurgy—"

She scrambled out of bed, opened the bottom drawer of her chest of drawers, and brought out a dangle bag. "Then use this. You know how to use it?"

"I think so."

"You *think* so? You *think* so?" She nearly struck me. "Where the hell were you educated? Finish your prayers and come with me."

The world became solid again the next morning. Returning to class was like returning home. As I climbed down into my Iron Maiden, Miss Webley said, "Carol, would you like to come and sit up front?" But there was no need. I sat where I'd sat previously, with the ghost of Alma on one side of me and the ghost of Donna on the other. They weren't the scary kind of ghost, they weren't malevolent, they just seemed to go about their business as I went about mine, turning the pages of their invisible Manuals, muttering to themselves, cursing with fine Italian or New Hampshire curses, trying to absorb all the information that was being hurled at our heads; and once or twice they were so real, so close, so warm, that I gave a little hiccup of grief. Everybody in the class heard me. Everybody in the class pretended they hadn't.

Jurgy was so right. There's something seriously wrong with American education. How can a female reach the mature age of twenty-two without knowing the facts about dangle bags? What every girl needed, I realized as I listened to Miss Webley, was a month of relentless study, being informed with Miss Webley's lucidity and eloquence about human affairs, with special emphasis on female affairs. What we needed, in addition to our Jet Manual, was a Girl Manual; what we needed to learn in harsh detail, without any beating about the bush, were the facts about us. That's all. Us. And I mean the facts in no uncertain language. I just didn't know any of these facts. For example, assume you had one of these things called an orgasm. It could happen to anybody who drank champagne cocktails, vodka martinis and brandy on top of sleeping pills. Well: what happened next? Were you automatically pregnant? And in that case how the hell did you *prevent* yourself from having one, if you were in the clutches of somebody like N.B.? Dammit, if we knew how to put out a fire on an airplane, we ought to know how to put out an orgasm. The future of the race de

244

pended on it. True, some of the girls talked as if they'd graduated summa cum laude from the Harvard School of Special Obstetrics, but it was just hot air. And I know, because I've talked that way myself on occasions. I once gave Tom Ritchie conniptions by talking about Fallopian tubes in a loud voice in a Schrafft's restaurant, and he never forgot it. Sheer bravado. I wouldn't know a Fallopian tube if somebody held one right under my nose.

As it happened, for about two and a half days we learned nothing except how to cope with emergencies; but these were airplane emergencies, not common female emergencies. Dr. Elizabeth Schwartz gave her celebrated lecture on how to be a midwife in mid-Atlantic and this, I had to admit, was to the point, and I had good reason to listen with care. But even so, she referred to oxygen. She spoke to us several times, and she *always* referred to oxygen. Oxygen was apparently so important that after Dr. Schwartz's lectures, Miss Webley recapitulated everything she'd said about oxygen, and then engineers came and lectured us and recapitulated what Miss Webley had said. Oxygen, oxygen, oxygen.

The whole point seemed to be that on an airplane flying above 5,000 feet, people are liable to get a condition called hypoxia, which means, roughly, oxygen deficiency. This can be pretty serious. At 5,000 feet the effect isn't bad, because only one's night vision is affected. Up to 10,000 feet, your body compensates for the lack of oxygen by forcing you to breathe more rapidly. But the higher you fly, the thinner the atmosphere becomes, which means that there is less pressure, which means in turn that less and less oxygen gets into your blood stream; and without oxygen your brain just gives up the ghost. At 18,000 feet you lose consciousness in about thirty minutes. At 25,000 feet, the pressure of the atmosphere is so low that you lose consciousness in two minutes; and at 35,000 feet the pressure is so ridiculously low that you're a cooked goose in a mere thirty seconds. Naturally, the airlines don't want this to happen to their dear passengers; it isn't the kind of thing you can plug in full-page advertisements in the *New York Times*—"Enjoy thirty seconds of carefree vacation over Sunny Bermuda"; and consequently airplanes manufacture their own atmospheric pressure right inside themselves. So no matter how high you fly you're perfectly safe because the flight engineer takes care of the pressure and you get all the oxygen any reasonable person can ask for, just as if you were walking in Central

245

Park. If, however, you suddenly decided to do some space exploration outside the plane at, say, 30,000 feet, you'd be unconscious in one minute, and you'd croak pretty damn quick thereafter. *But,* if you were supplied with oxygen before you got to the croaking stage, you'd be as good as new in a mere fifteen seconds. That's the amazing thing about oxygen, known to the cognoscenti as O_2. A few whiffs of it, and your brain takes up again just where it left off. You can go on being just as much of a dumbkopf as you were before.

We had to know the whole oxygen routine in absolute detail because one of our important duties, if we ever got onto an airplane, was to keep an eye on the passengers for any symptoms of hypoxia. We weren't exactly expected to dash madly up and down the cabin thrusting thermometers in the passengers' mouths and taking their pulse; as long as the flight engineer had the pressurization set according to the book, you could be confident everything was fine. But you had to keep your eyes open because some people were by nature more susceptible to hypoxia than others. Persons with heart trouble, for example, might become cyanotic which means turning blue; and if you saw anybody turning blue you just had to fight off the feeling of panic and yank down one of the oxygen masks, let him or her inhale, and hey presto!—he or she turned pink again. Babies might become cyanotic too, which they do anyway at the drop of a hat, but it's enough with a baby just to hold the oxygen mask an inch or so from its nose, otherwise it might be scared out of its little wits. Some people might act intoxicated without ever having had a drink: hypoxia. Some people might be unnaturally drowsy: hypoxia. It could happen to the flight hostesses themselves, of course; and the answer was that magic word, oxygen. Every time.

On Wednesday morning, Ray Duer gave us a lecture about various psychological aspects of flying. He needn't have been afraid that I'd call him darling in front of the other girls: I couldn't bear to look at him, I couldn't bear to meet his eyes. His right hand was splinted and bandaged, and I wept inwardly, wondering how badly he had been hurt. Apparently some odd myths had begun to circulate about jet flying, such as that it would make you deaf in due course, and that it would gradually disintegrate your insides because of supersonic sound; and he took each myth and analyzed it out of existence. He even dealt in the most

246

matter-of-fact way with the mental difficulties some girls seemed to have about flying during their menstrual periods: dysmenorrhea, he said, had been found to be less severe when flying than when staying at home. A great word. It meant, he explained, cramps. When he finished his lecture he stayed for a few moments to chat with Miss Webley; then, on his way out, he glanced at me. That's all I needed. I developed acute dysmenorrhea on the spot, and couldn't eat any lunch. God, I'd made a mess of my life.

The next morning we spent a couple of hours on board a Boeing 707. We didn't fly. Miss Webley explained, "Girls, before you actually work on jetliners, you'll come back here for an additional four-day course. You'll then get a more thorough briefing on safety and emergency procedures, and so on." I thought we'd already done all that thoroughly, but apparently not. "Look at these cabins," she said, and we looked at the vast expanse of the forward cabin and the aft cabin, stretching ahead of us and behind us. "That's quite some responsibility, isn't it?" Every girl on board caught her breath.

The afternoon was easy, as she'd promised: our last afternoon. We went upstairs to sign our contracts with Magna International Airlines. Then we went to Room 15 to collect our uniforms from Mrs. Sharpless. And then we had a small party in the classroom. Earlier in the week we'd taken up a collection to buy Miss Webley a gift; and since she was getting married shortly it had been decided that what she needed more than anything else was a negligee; and since she was marrying a pilot it was further decided that this negligee had better be so sexy it could practically walk by itself.

Miss Webley laughed when it was presented to her, and also wept a couple of tears. She said, holding it up, "Oh, girls, you shouldn't have done it. Thank you so much. But how can I *wear* it? What will Peter say? Oh, dear."

Then she looked at us. She looked at us very intently. She said, "Girls, I'm awfully proud of you. I really am. You've worked hard and you've proven yourselves. From now on you're no longer my students, you're my friends and fellow workers. Please don't call me Miss Webley any more. My name is Peg." She laughed. "It's a silly name, isn't it? But that's what it is and that's what I'd like you to call me."

"Yes, Miss Webley," we said. It was all as hilarious as

the dickens, and I merely wanted to creep away in a corner and hide. Not only for Donna's sake, or Alma's, but my own.

The graduation ceremony was set to take place at 11:00 A.M. in the Empress Room at the Charleroi.

We assembled, all twenty-five of us, in an adjoining room. For the first time we were wearing our uniforms in public; but they weren't quite complete. They lacked the little symbol which I guess was our badge of office, the bright silver wing which was pinned to the side of the hat like a cockade. This, really, was the purpose and the heart of the ceremony, the presentation of wings.

Miss Pierce and Miss Webley—our friends Janet and Peg —inspected us one by one, straightened the collars of our white blouslips, tucked away wisps of hair, pulled our jackets down, whispered advice and encouragement and instructions. We were divided into two groups as we'd been for our classes, which meant that I couldn't sit beside Jurgy.

We didn't talk much. We stood and waited. Twenty-five girls, waiting quietly to be presented with a bright little silver symbol. It seemed ridiculous, and yet it wasn't ridiculous; and it also wasn't particularly exciting. I may be wrong, but I think we all felt much the same way, that we'd done nothing but arrive at the starting line. I could remember four weeks ago, those forty tall lively beautiful kids in a mad hubbub on the fourteenth floor, all so fresh, all so excited, all so eager to prove themselves—forty, including Annette, and Alma, and Donna, and the rest. A bunch of slobs. We'd been whittled down without mercy, we'd been pulled into shape, we'd been made over into different human beings: calm, collected, dignified, ladylike. No hubbub—that told the story. Twenty-five girls, and no hubbub.

At ten-thirty the side door was opened and we marched in. Each class had been allotted three rows of chairs, and for a minute, thank God, there was utter confusion, which cheered me up. I'm not sold on any kind of marching-in routine; I daresay it looks effective, but for my money it belongs on Broadway or Czechoslovakia. Mrs. Montgomery, Mr. Garrison, Dr. Schwartz, and Dr. Duer were sitting on a dais, and we stood facing them until Peg and Janet said, "Take your seats, girls." Naturally enough, as I sat down one of my stockings developed a run, and I swore under my breath and one of the girls beside me sniggered. Trust

Thompson to turn a solemn occasion into a farce. God, I bet I'll wow them at my own funeral.

As soon as we were settled, Mr. Garrison rose genially and began to make a speech. He said, "It is my privilege to welcome you into the family of Magna International Airlines, a family that numbers some twenty-two thousand men and women. You are the newest members of our family; and if you'll allow me to do so I'd like to say just a few words to you."

That always slays me, when you're practically bound hand and foot and somebody announces *If you'll allow me to do so I'd like to say a few million words to you*. In any case, I have a block about speeches, I just can't hear them; and in this case it was a lot worse because I couldn't even look at Mr. Garrison and read his lips because I'd see Dr. Duer, and I literally couldn't bear to see Dr. Duer. His hand was still splinted and bandaged, his gray eyes were somber, he made everything inside me turn over as usual; but everything also turned over inside me when I thought of Alma and Donna. If you can't expect the man you love to be humane, what the hell *can* you expect of him? An orgasm once a week? Nuts. Sex is only a small part of the story. For my money, anyway.

Mr. Garrison was chatting away about our futures. "You will make mistakes," he said. "We all do. But I want you to believe me, that you know more than you think you know. You've proved it to us. What you have to do now is realize that you are responsible human beings and take hold of your responsibility with both hands." Yes, I thought. Okay. Okay. But at this point something else distracted my attention: the visitors.

Peg Webley had told us that we could invite friends and relatives to the graduation ceremony, they'd be welcome. I hadn't even bothered to write to Mother—she was probably having an affair with somebody's butler or whooping it up in San Francisco, and anyway, the only thing that interested her was that I wasn't drawing any money from the estate. I'd crossed Tom Ritchie off for good, and it would have been a little outré to say the least if I'd invited Big Top Charlie or Eena or Angel—they belonged only on Mac-Dougal Street. So I hadn't invited anybody. I was starting a new life, and I didn't feel the need of witnesses thereto. I was the cat that walks by itself. An independent bitch.

There were exactly two visitors: a nice-looking middle-aged lady, and old Luke Lucas. They sat to one side of the dais, where about thirty chairs had been carefully arranged. And, I think for the first time, the realization hit me right between the eyes like a cannonball, that I wasn't the only independent bitch in the world; I was surrounded by them. Practically all these girls were like me—they didn't need their families any more, they'd cut the cord, they'd qualified to make a new life for themselves. Some of them had pulled themselves up by their own bootstraps, but they'd made it. I remembered one of the kids saying to me while we were on our first familiarization flight, "Carol, you know what I'd be doing if I were home right now? I'd be out in the fields with my dad, shucking corn." There was the kid from Alabama who'd been assigned to New York; and only yesterday, in the cafeteria, I'd heard her being razzed by some of the other kids because now she'd have to wait on Negroes and be damned polite to them to boot. And suddenly she turned and said in a rage, "So what? You think I can't take it? I can take *anything*." There was a girl from Wisconsin whose boy friend had written to her that he was going to shoot himself if she didn't return and marry him; she'd torn the letter up and said, "Okay, let him shoot himself," and, by golly, a week later a telegram came for her saying he'd fired a shotgun into his belly, and she still didn't turn a hair. They wanted something, these kids, they wanted it real bad, they wanted it like crazy, and that's all that counted with them. Two visitors. My God, it suddenly gave me cold shivers.

Mr. Garrison concluded his few words, Mrs. Montgomery said a few words, and when she concluded the ceremony began in earnest. Peg Webley and Janet Pierce took up their positions in front of the class for which each was responsible; names were called; and, in pairs, the girls stood up and marched forward. Off came their hats, the silver wing was pinned on, the hats were replaced, and the girls passed down the line on the dais to shake hands and to receive their diplomas from Mr. Garrison. "Good luck, Carol," Peg Webley whispered to me when my turn came; and I smiled, and went on to shake Mrs. Montgomery's hand, Mr. Garrison's hand, Dr. Schwartz's hand, Dr. Duer's—but he had no hand to shake. He was hors de combat. He said quietly, "Congratulations, Carol," and I had to look at him. The electricity went in a great jolt up and down my spine, and I said, "Thank you, sir," and returned to my place.

That was all. The ceremony was over when the last wing was pinned on, except for some group photographs, and we could break ranks. Jurgy came over to me and said, "Hey, Carol, come say hello to Luke," and I noticed that at last she had slipped the Rock of Gibraltar onto the third finger of her left hand, where it belonged. I went over to Luke, and he loomed over me, gurgling in his bony throat, "Hello, little lady, hel-lo. My, oh, my, don't we look purty today, hey? A sight for sore eyes." Then Mr. Garrison arrived, rather puzzled: I suppose he felt it was his duty to greet the visitors (all two of them) and he could guess who the nice middle-aged lady was but he couldn't quite make out what this old buzzard was doing here.

Jurgy said, "Mr. Garrison I'd like to have you meet my fiancé, Mr. Luke Lucas."

Mr. Garrison went white, then he went pink, and his mouth opened but no word came out.

"Well, Harrison—" Luke began enthusiastically.

"Mr. *Garrison*, dear," Jurgy corrected him.

"I know, I know," Luke boomed. "Harrison: let me tell you something. I've been around in my time, and I've seen a lot of young girls, but I never in all my born days seen a purtier bunch than the bunch you have here, and I mean it. Yessir. Purty as a picture, every blessed one of 'em. Does you a lot of credit, Harrison."

"Thanks, Mr. Lucas. Glad. Glad to have your appreciation."

"How 'bout coming down to the bar and having a drink with us to celebrate? Hey, Harrison? How 'bout it?"

"Wish I could," Mr. Garrison said in a shaky voice. "Busy. Lots of things, another class coming in, another forty girls, no sleep for the wicked. Take a rain check."

"You bet," Luke said. "Well, Harrison, be seeing you."

Mr. Garrison drew me aside. His voice had stopped shaking; it had become hoarse. He said, "Carol, how long this been going on, Lucas-Jurgens?" I said, "Why, Mr. Garrison, I thought you knew. Mr. Lucas fell in love with her the minute he saw her, the first day she arrived here." He said, "Godalmighty, you realize who this feller is?" I said, "I realize he's a very sweet, gentle person." Mr. Garrison said, "Sweet, gentle, my eye. Feller's millionaire. Cattle. Millionaire, I tell you." I said, "You mean he's sweet and gentle and *rich*, too?" He said, "Multimillionaire. Didn't you see ring she's wearing? Big as duck's egg. I'd better let Public Relations know about this right away. God, who'll they be marrying next?" He turned to go and then turned back to me, his eyes popping out. "Mary Ruth Jurgens!" he said, and I said, "It couldn't have happened to a nicer kid, could it?" He thought about this for a moment and said, "You know, I think you're right." He hurried off, and the instant he left, Ray took his place.

He said, "Carol."

My heart was ready to burst. I couldn't meet his eyes.

"I was wondering," he said. "Have you arranged where you're going to live?"

"Mary Ruth Jurgens is making the arrangements."

"You're sharing an apartment with her?"

"Yes, sir."

"I'm glad of that. She's a fine girl. When do you report for duty?"

"On Monday morning, sir."

"Will you have dinner with me tonight?"

"No, sir. I'm sorry."

He waited a moment. "May I see you during the weekend?"

"No, sir. I'm sorry."

"Carol!"

I still couldn't bear to look at him. He turned and walked out.

Luke insisted on buying us lunch. We wouldn't go with him in our uniforms, they were too new and I suppose we felt too conspicuous in them. As we were changing in 1412 Jurgy said, "Carol, I think Luke is up to something," I said. "Like what?" She said, "I can't say for sure. But I'm getting to know that old son of a gun, and I can tell when he's got something cooking. Maybe he found an apartment." I said, "God, wouldn't that be wonderful." She said, "That's only my guess. Whenever that innocent look comes over his face I'm pretty sure he's up to mischief. You getting to like him any better?" I said, "I am, Jurgy." She said, "That's good. I saw you talking with Dr. Duer. Anything new in that direction?" I said, "No." She grunted.

Luke was waiting for us in the lobby. He beamed when he saw us and said, "Got to be honest with you, girls. Purtiest pair of females in Miami Beach. I'm proud to know you. How 'bout a daiquiri in that little Souvenir Bar before we go out?"

"We're going *out?*" Jurgy asked suspiciously.

"That's what I figured, Mary Ruth. Kind of fed up with all this fancy French food they serve here. Figured we might look around and find some little place where they serve a plain-cooked meal. I'm getting to have stomach problems."

"If we're going *out*," Jurgy said, "let's go. I don't want a drink. Do you, Carol?"

"Not really."

"Okay, Mary Ruth," Luke said. "Got the car waiting right outside."

I knew what Jurgy meant. He was just too meek and mild. It was a joke, and in a way exciting, because I couldn't guess what was behind those innocent eyes and the gold-rimmed glasses. There was plenty of life in this old bird, without any question, all the life that even Jurgy could handle.

He had a big gray Cadillac parked almost exactly in the spot where Ray had parked the MG last weekend, and as we approached I felt breathless and a little angry—I hoped to God Luke wasn't playing any tricks on me. He wasn't. Ray Duer wasn't concealed anywhere. But just as Luke opened the door of the Cadillac for us to enter, he said, "Good Lord, I nearly forgot. Here, girls, come and look at this."

Parked behind the Cadillac was a brand-new Corvette, blue-gray and silver, the prettiest thing I've ever seen.

Jurgy said in a quiet grim voice, "What about it?"

He answered her humbly, "It's for you, Mary Ruth."

"For me!" she cried. "For me!—What do you mean, it's for me? Did I ask you for it? What's the big idea, Luke Lucas, what do you think you're doing?"

He said, "Mary Ruth, you graduated today, didn't you?"

"So what?"

"Mary Ruth, I never in all my life had the chance to buy a graduating gift for someone I loved. You're the first such person."

She began to cry. God! What a bunch we were. The fountains of Miami Beach. She said, "You big old fool. If I didn't love you, I'd slug you."

"Now, now, Mary Ruth."

"What do I want with a car?" she wept. "I can't drive."

"Mary Ruth, honey, that's soon arranged. That's the easiest thing in the world to learn, lamb. And when you come to live in Kansas, why, you'll be needing your car every single day of the week. It ain't like the city there Mary Ruth."

She sobbed at me, "I told you he was up to something didn't I?"

"You certainly did."

"Do you drive?"

"Sure."

"Will you teach me?"

"You bet."

She said to Luke, "You big stiff, bend your face down." He did, and she kissed him on the cheek. "You damn fool I swear I'll kill you one of these days if you keep on thi way."

He straightened up, beaming. Then he said, "Carol honey."

"Yes, Luke?"

"You wouldn't slug a poor old feller like me, would you?"

I laughed at him. "Of course not."

"Okay, then," he said. "I guess it's safe to give you this Just a little remembrance from Mary Ruth and me, for grad uation day."

"Oh, no!" I said. It was a gold Omega wrist watch, with gold band.

So I blubbed, too, right there in front of the Charleroi and after I'd put the watch on, and we'd inspected the Cor vette from top to bottom, and Jurgy had sobbed a little more, we went to a steak house for lunch. They were very cute together, Jurgy and Luke. Anybody could see that he was just crazy about her, she could do no wrong as far as he was concerned. On the other hand, she was rather stern with him, as she was with everybody including me. She wa particularly stern, for example, when he wanted to orde his fourth bourbon. She said, "Now, listen to me, Luke Lucas I don't mind what you do when you're out with the boys But you're not going to get stewed when you're with Caro and me, understand? When you're with us you're a gentle man, and you got to act like a gentleman." He scratched hi chin and said, "Yes, Mary Ruth, you have a point there honey, and I have to admit you're right. Yep, I guess you'r one hundred percent right." He wasn't *convinced*, but he tried to act convinced. Every now and then, though, she for got about being Dracula, she became gay and light-hearte and bubbly with laughter; and Luke nearly fell out of hi

254

chair with yearning for her. It was the love affair of the century.

When we finished lunch I asked Luke please to take me back to the hotel. No use pretending. I was feeling a little down in the mouth, partly because the training course was over and my balloon was naturally deflated, partly because of Dr. Duer, partly because I didn't know if I was pregnant, partly for a million other reasons including the vile reason that I envied Luke and Jurgy. Envied is maybe the wrong word, because Jurgy had earned every inch of her happiness, and I daresay Luke had, too, and it wasn't this that I envied at all. I envied them having each other, because I had nobody. There are times when being the cat that walks by itself isn't all it's cracked up to be.

We'd been given instructions that the entire fourteenth floor had to be vacated by Saturday noon—tomorrow, in other words—to receive the new batch of forty slobs for the next course. It wasn't unreasonable, because the hotel staff had to do a thorough cleaning job, and furthermore, although most of the girls were due to arrive on Monday, several would be arriving early Sunday as a result of transportation problems. Jurgy and I had given this situation a little thought, and we'd finally decided that if worse came to worse we'd simply move out to a cheap hotel tomorrow and live there until we found a permanent place. We couldn't possibly afford to pay the rates at the Charleroi on the salary we were getting from Magna International Airlines.

That gave me something to do on this rather blue Friday afternoon. Pack. Of course, it was a farce for me even to think of doing anything of the kind; I mean, I can get less into an average suitcase than anybody in the whole world; and if there was any occasion when I really needed Jurgy this was it. At the same time, there's nothing like packing a suitcase for helping you out of an attack of weltschmerz. You just can't worry about your soul or your busted heart when you're holding your best gray linen dress and wondering how the hell you're going to boil it down so that it fits into a space that's roughly eighteen by twenty-one inches. You know it *can* be done and you also know it *can't* be done; and I can go quietly nutty over a problem like this for hours, with the result that my weltschmerz gradually recedes into the middle distance.

I stripped down to my bra and half-slip, hauled out a suit-

255

case, opened it on my bed, grabbed an armful of clothes from my closet, and set to. Quel business. Back in the Village, before the Great Flood of 1888, or whenever it was that I'd begun to prepare for my new life with Magna International Airlines, Eena had done my packing, woofing away all the time like an old bulldog; and I tried to recall what her procedure had been, and what Jurgy's procedure had been last Sunday when she helped Donna. I couldn't remember a thing, except that you always try to cross the sleeves across the front, or maybe the back—you get nowhere if you just leave the sleeves hanging down limp. But even with this professional know-how, I *still* got nowhere. After about an hour I had roughly one suitcase half-filled with stuff, and I'd just decided to sit down and calm my nerves with a cigarette when the telephone rang.

Ray! I thought. *Thank God!*

But it wasn't Ray. It was N.B.

"Hi, Carol," he said cheerily. "How's things?"

I said, "Oh, hello, N.B. Everything's terrible. I'm just packing. We have to be out of here by noon tomorrow."

"Yeah, so I understand from Maxwell. How about taking a breather and meeting me for a drink or a limeade or a cup of coffee, or something?"

"Oh, N.B., I'm awfully sorry. I absolutely and positively must get this packing done." Boy, he couldn't pull that gag on me twice. I knew exactly where a limeade could lead, but exactly.

"Look, Carol, you can surely take a break for ten minutes."

"N.B., I simply can't. I'm sorry."

I was so cold and firm that he desisted. He said glumly, "Okay. When will I see you?"

"I'm sorry, I don't know."

"I'll call this evening, maybe."

"Yes. Do that."

We hung up.

The brief conversation was upsetting. I lit another cigarette and sat brooding; and before I finished the cigarette he called again.

His voice was harder. "Carol. I want to see you."

"N.B., I just explained—"

"Ten minutes won't kill you."

"I'm not dressed—"

"Get dressed. You heard what I said. Just ten minutes."

I closed my eyes. I clenched my fists. I mentally said some

256

terrible words. Then I thought, Okay. Okay, we'll settle this business once and for all. If that's what he wants, that's what he'll get. I said, "Where are you?"

"In the lobby.

"I don't want to meet you in the lobby. There are too many people around."

"So. How about the Souvenir Bar?"

"Is that quiet?"

"The quietest place I know."

"Very well, N.B. I'll be there as soon as I can."

"How soon is that?"

"Fifteen minutes."

I took a quick shower, put on the unfoldable gray linen dress since it was lying right in front of me, tucked my pocketbook firmly under my arm, and stalked out to the elevators. I'd timed myself by Luke's watch—fifteen minutes right on the nose. The elevator boy directed me to the Souvenir Bar, and I walked in with confidence. Magna International Airlines now recognized me as an adult: bars were open to me as long as I wasn't in uniform.

It was a charming place, with masses of flowers everywhere as usual. The lighting was nice and dim, the carpet felt as if it were bottomless, the tables were widely spaced, there were cozy little chairs and loveseats all over the place, and it was startlingly quiet. N.B. was waiting at a corner table, and as I approached he stood up, smiling. He was wearing a black sports jacket with silver buttons, silver-gray pants, and a black and white tie.

"Carol."

"Hello, N.B."

"Sit down, honey. What will you have to drink?"

"Coffee."

"Okay. How about a cognac with same?"

I shook my head. He beckoned to a waiter and gave the order, a vodka martini for himself, coffee for me; and when the waiter left, he folded his arms on the table, looked at me closely for a few moments, sighed and smiled, and said, "Carol, you certainly are a sight for sore eyes."

"Thank you."

"It's not a compliment, it's the truth. Baby, I've missed you all week something awful."

"N.B., I want to tell you—"

"Wait a minute, wait a minute, let me finish. I have to explain why I had to see you so bad. Maxwell tells me you had quite a little ceremony here this morning in the Empress Room."

"Yes, we had our graduation ceremony."

"That's wonderful. You all graduated, all the girls? You're full-blown stewardesses, now?"

"Yes."

"And now you'll actually be flying in airplanes, walking up and down the aisle handing out coffee, tea, and milk?"

"Yes."

"Where they sending you? To live, I mean."

"I'm staying here, in Miami."

"*No* kidding! Oh, boy!"

"N.B.—"

"Wait a minute. I haven't finished yet."

We were interrupted by the waiter bringing the coffee and the vodka martini. N.B.'s face became blank. Then, as soon as we were alone again, he went on in the same cheery voice, "Well, you graduated at last, today's the day. I wouldn't even have known about it if Maxwell didn't tell me. That's why I had to see you, hon."

It was a puzzling remark. I said, "I don't follow, N.B."

"Sure. It's graduation day, isn't it?"

"Yes."

"So, naturally, you get a graduation present."

"N.B., no, please—"

He put a long, narrow, gift-wrapped box in front of me. "There it is. With love to sugar from N.B. Open it."

I said, "I can't."

"Go ahead, go ahead."

I said in despair, "N.B., I can't. That's the point. That's why I came down to see you—"

"You want me to unwrap it? Okay."

Those fingers were so deft. He took the little package and unwrapped it with a few effortless flicks, revealing a long white velvet case. Then he put it in front of me again and said, "There you are. From N.B. to sugar, with oodles of love. Open it, baby, take a look inside."

"I—please, N.B., I have to tell you—"

He raised the velvet lid. Inside, on white satin, lay a gold Omega wrist watch with a gold band, almost the duplicate of the one Luke had given me.

I laughed. I couldn't help myself. I laughed.

"What's so funny?" he asked.

I held my arm out, showing him Luke's watch.

He said incredulously, "You got that today?"

I nodded.

"Well, what do you know! Hell, it doesn't make any difference. We'll go right to the Jewel Box and change it for something else—"

I said, "No, N.B., I couldn't take it, I can't take any present from you. N.B., I'm sorry. I can't see you again after today. Ever."

He leaned forward. "What's that?"

I said it more decisively this time. "I don't love you. I can't see you any more."

He laughed. "Come on, kid."

"It's true."

He suddenly began to talk very rapidly and passionately. "Now, come on, come on. The other night—remember the time we had? Oh, hell, *you* remember. That's something a girl never forgets, do you know that? It's a fact. And listen, it doesn't happen every day of the week, hell no. You have to be crazy about someone, you have to have real feeling for them, it's the truth, Carol. You have to think—I want *her* to be happy, not me, I want *her* to be happy. That's the feeling I had about you—"

I cried, "Stop it, N.B.! Please stop it!"

He wouldn't stop. "Listen, sweetface—now, listen, I'm dead serious. Give up this crazy idea about being a stewardess—*give it up.* It's dangerous—Jesus, don't you realize that?—it's *dangerous!* I'll go nuts thinking about you—flying every day, flying, flying—serving hash, serving lousy beef stew, serving lousy highballs. Give it up! Didn't I tell you? I'll dress you like a queen, you'll have everything a queen has, because you *are* a queen. You can have your own apartment, you can have a dog and a maid and an automobile, anything you ask for. Honey, we're a *team,* we fit together good, we're made for each other—"

I said, "N.B., I'm in love with another man."

All the breath seemed to go out of his lungs. He leaned back, his mouth open, gasping slightly. Then he said, "Is that true?"

"Yes."

He sat staring at me.

I put my pocketbook on the table and took out the roll of twenty-two hundred dollars. "I want to give this back to you, N.B. You won it. I didn't. It's yours." I placed the bills beside the white velvet box.

He said quietly, "And that's really true, eh? That's really true? You're in love with some other guy?"

"Yes."

He said, "You twat. You don't even know what love is. You goddam stupid little twat."

"N.B.—"

He stood up. I expected to feel the weight of his hand at any moment. His face was tight. He didn't speak. He wasn't able to speak. He picked up his vodka martini and drank it at a gulp. Then he took out his wallet, extracted a five-dollar bill, and put it under his empty martini glass. Then he reached for the white velvet case and the big roll of bills, and stuffed them contemptuously back into my pocket-book. He said, "With the compliments of the house, baby," and walked out.

I went back to my packing feeling as if I'd been whipped. I sat down beside my half-empty suitcase, in that excruciatingly empty room, and I thought, Well, anyway, that's over. It's over with Ray Duer, it's over with Nat N.B. Brangwyn. What was the old saying? Everything comes in twos. It sure seemed to work out in practice. In the brief span of four weeks (a couple of days less, to be precise) not only had two girl friends come and gone into my life, and two male friends, but I'd also accumulated

> two gold Omega wrist watches
> two thousand, two hundred dollars
> two nipple tassels

and, if everything ran true to form, there were probably two utterly cute little embryos burping at each other inside me.

Some loot. Any girl would be proud. I didn't cry because I was much, much too old to cry. I just waited for Jurgy to come back.

12

urgy did all the packing that night without turning a hair. She was grimmer than usual, though, and absolutely uncommunicative, and it worried me sick. Finally I asked her if anything was wrong, and she nearly snapped my head off. "*Wrong?* Why the hell should anything be *wrong?*" About ten minutes later she added grumpily, "We saw an apartment."

"You did! Where?"

"Near the Seventy-ninth Street Bridge."

"You think it might do?"

"Maybe. You have to look it over."

"How many rooms? Is the furniture nice? How much is the rent?"

She turned on me in a rage. She cried, "Cut it out, will you? All these damn questions. I told you, you'll have to see the place for yourself. We have an appointment, nine-thirty tomorrow morning, with the renting agent. That's all."

I said, "Jurgy, have you and Luke had a fight?"

"If we have, what about it?"

She didn't wait for me to answer. She went to her room and slammed the door.

In the morning she was still surly. But it was queer, because she also looked prettier than ever. The corners of her mouth were turned down, and yet her eyes were bright; and I didn't have a clue to what was going on in her mind. After breakfast she said sourly, "Hey, Carol."

"Yes?"

"Want to drive over to see the apartment in the car?"

"Which car?"

"Jesus, what the hell has gotten into you? Why are you acting so dumb? The car Luke gave me."

Then, before we left I said, "I'd better take some money. If this apartment is any good, we can leave a deposit."

She flared up again. "What's the matter with you today? You don't have to take money. I have money."

God, she was impossible. And I couldn't tell her she was

impossible, I couldn't argue with her because I knew she'
only fly into more of a rage. That was the kind of signal sh
was giving off. Touch me not. Stay away. No salesmen. Be
ware of the dog. It just confirmed my belief that there isn'
any such thing as a rational female. All females ought to b
kept under lock and key.

She directed me to the apartment, watching everything
did out of the corner of her eye; and as we slowed down t
make the turn onto Indian Creek she said, "Is the car har
to drive?"

"It's new, Jurgy, so I'm driving slowly. You have to b
careful with it for the first few thousand miles. That's wha
they call breaking it in."

She said, "I asked you, *is the car hard to drive?*"

"Of course not. It's easy."

"You think I'll be able to manage it?"

"Certainly. If I can, you can."

"Huh."

We trickled along Indian Creek and then, very abruptly
she said, "Turn here." I swung into a square courtyard.

I said, "Is this it?"

"Yeah."

"Why, my God, Jurgy, it looks *beautiful*."

There were two-story apartments on three sides of th
square courtyard, built in a pleasant Spanish fashion, wit
white walls and round arches and ironwork trellises. Th
roof, running round the three sides, was red tile. Bougain
villaea grew everywhere, and hibiscus, and jasmine, an
shrimp plants; and in the morning sunshine, patterned wit
soft shadows, it was perfectly charming.

"Come on," Jurgy snarled. "Let's get up there."

"Is it an upstairs apartment?"

"Yeah."

"That's marvelous."

"What the hell difference does it make, upstairs or down
stairs? Stop being so goddam picky."

Luke was already here, and I parked beside his gray Cadil
lac. Jurgy led the way to the first unit, nearest the street, an
I followed her, still wondering why she was in this fou
mood. We went up two flights of stone steps, and Jurg
pushed open the apartment door, which was marked 2 B
and we walked in. First impressions are important. The ai
was clean and fresh, the outside surroundings were delightful
and the inside of the apartment was delightful too—com

262

fortably furnished, and friendly, and immaculate. I felt at home immediately. My God, I thought, this is wonderful, what a lucky find.

Luke was standing in the living room, his gray Stetson tilted back on his head, talking to a good-looking blonde who was wearing a plain white dress that must have cost at least $350 even in a sale. Her name was Miss Carter, and she was the real-estate agent. She had the most startling corn-flower-blue eyes I've ever seen—the rest of her was about thirty-six years old but her eyes were only about eight years old, and when she looked at me I was just dazzled.

Luke chuckled and boomed and made his usual bony noises, and said, "Mary Ruth, show Carol around. See how she likes it."

"Come on, Carol," Jurgy snapped.

I was practically speechless with excitement. The living-room windows looked right across Indian Creek, so that any time I had an attack of weltschmerz I could stare at the smooth blue water and the palm trees and watch the little boats go by; the furniture was as good as new and in perfect taste—not too modern and not too antique, not too heavy and not too light. Leading off the living room was a hall, with two charming bedrooms on one side, and a really mod-ern kitchen and bathroom on the other side. There were plenty of closets, there were lots of bookshelves filled with books—books!—and there was even a hi-fi installation.

I said to Jurgy, "My God, it's a dream."

"You think so?"

"Jurgy! Admit it! It's real swan."

She shrugged her shoulders.

We went back to the living room, and Miss Carter beamed at me with those blue blue eyes. "Well, honey. How do you like it?"

I suppose one ought to restrain one's enthusiasm when one's talking to real-estate agents—a single unguarded word of praise and they're apt to jack the price up ten dollars. But in this case I couldn't control myself. I said, "Gee, it's beautiful, it's really beautiful."

"It is, too," she said. "It's the cutest little apartment I've had to offer in many a moon."

I asked timidly, "How much is the rent?"

"Six hundred and fifty a month, honey," she said. "And a steal at the price."

Everything went black in front of me. Six hundred and

fifty a *month!* Why, holy smoke, that was more than Jurgy's salary and mine *combined.* No wonder the apartment was so attractive. For that money you could probably rent the Taj Mahal, with ninety-nine handmaidens to do your laundry.

I tried to swallow my disappointment, but it stuck in my throat. Bitter, bitter, a bitter blow. I said, "Oh, Lord. I'm afraid that's out of the question. It's a little more than we can pay."

Luke said, "Carol, child: it's been took."

I said, "*What?*"

"It's been took."

I glanced across at Jurgy. She was no help. She was scowling at the floor. I said, "What do you mean, it's been took?"

He said with a chuckle, "We rented it, little lady."

I cried, "But how can we have rented it? We can't possibly afford it. My God, after we paid the rent we wouldn't have enough money left over to buy a can of chicken noodle soup."

He said courteously, taking off his hat, "Miss Carter, I sure hate to ask this, but would you be kind enough to leave us for a few minutes, so I can have a word with Miss Carol?"

She smiled up at him. "Surely."

We waited until she left. Then I said furiously, "Jurgy, it isn't true! You haven't rented this place! At six hundred and fifty a *month!* Jurgy! Are you out of your mind, or something? How can we possibly afford it?"

She blazed back at me. "*I* didn't rent it. *He* rented it."

Luke said, "Now, girls, girls—"

I screamed at Jurgy, "What do you mean, *he* rented it?"

She screamed right back, "*He* paid six months' rent, that's what I mean. *Six months' rent.*"

"*He* paid it?"

"Yeah. *He* paid it."

"Oh, no," I said, and I began to walk out.

Jurgy ran after me and grabbed my arm. She screamed at Luke. "I *told* you she'd walk out, didn't I? I *told* you."

I said, "Jurgy, let me go. He's your man, and if he wants to rent an apartment for you at six hundred and fifty dollars a month, that's great. But he isn't renting an apartment for me, and that's final. Let me go."

She shrieked at Luke, "See what you've done? Do you see?"

Luke said, "Let go of her, Mary Ruth."

She released my arm.

He said, "Carol, honey. Come and sit down a minute, will you? Will you, honey? Just so I can say one word to you."

Jurgy laughed. "Huh! Try to sweet-talk her into it, that's right, Luke Lucas. See how far that will get you."

He said, "I ain't going to try to sweet-talk her into anything. I'm going to be just simply honest with her, that's all. —Carol: come here, will you?"

I walked over to him.

"Sit down, honey. Make yourself comfortable."

"I don't want to sit down."

"Okay. Please yourself." He peered at me through his gold-rimmed glasses as if he couldn't see me clearly. "Honey, why are you kicking up so much dust?"

I said, "Luke, I don't want to be under an obligation to you."

"Is that what you think you'd be, Carol?"

"This is why I came to Miami Beach in the first place. I want to live my own life. I want to make my own way. And I don't want to be under an obligation to anybody in this whole wide world."

"Honey," he said, "that's just the way I feel about things, too. I'd almost rather cut my throat than be under an obligation to any living soul."

"Okay," I said. "You understand. I think you're a swell guy, but I can't pay the rent for this apartment, and I can't live here."

He said, "Yep. I see your point. Only thing is, you have it all arsey-turvey, honey. If you come and live here, you ain't putting yourself under no obligation to me. It's the other way around. I'll be putting myself under an obligation to you."

"Sweet-talk," I said. "Boy! You sound like an expert."

Jurgy laughed harshly. She was sitting in an armchair, biting her nails.

Very gently, Luke took my hand. He said, "Carol, just listen to me for a minute, and then you tell me if it's sweet-talk. Give me your honest opinion: I won't mind.—Honey, you know, maybe, I have a few dollars in the bank; you know that, don't you? I mean, it's no great hardship on me paying this six months' rent. Eh?"

"What you have in the bank isn't my concern."

"Sugar, I'm every little bit as independent as you are,

maybe more so. But just get it firmly in your head: I ain't offering you charity. I'm asking charity from you."

Jurgy had stopped biting her nails. She'd turned her head away, but I could see that she was crying, the muscles of her throat were convulsed.

Luke said, "Carol: that sweet darling child sitting there, Mary Ruth, she's done me the honor to say she'll be my wife. I'm no bargain, Carol, honey: you know it. I'm just an old roughneck, beaten up, not much good no more for anything—"

Jurgy cried, "Don't you say that!"

He smiled. "Listen to her! But it's the truth. Now: this is how it stands between Mary Ruth and me, Carol. You judge for yourself. I didn't have any easy life; and Mary Ruth didn't have any easy life, either. She told me all about it. She had to work damned hard, with her hands, to make a living. And when she did me the honor to say she'd be my wife, she laid down one condition—that I'd wait at least six months before we got hitched."

Jurgy cried, "Why don't you shut up, Luke Lucas? She don't want to hear all that crap."

He said to me, "You want to hear it or not, honey?"

"Go on."

He said, "Well, I told Mary Ruth, okay, I'd wait six months. I understood her feelings. She's no different than you, Carol, she came here for the selfsame reasons, to make a new life for herself, to get out in the world—"

Jurgy cried, "I told you to cut out all this crap, didn't I?"

He said, "Mary Ruth, my love, I don't give a fart in hell what you told me. Just let me say my piece."

"Don't you dare use that kind of language in front of Carol! She isn't used to it."

"You offended, Carol?" he asked.

"No."

"Okay. I'll go on. That's what we agreed: we'd wait six months, so my darling beautiful girl could do these things she dreamed about all her life, so she could travel around and see a bit of the world, and get some polish, and work up some confidence in herself. Now, Carol, I'm asking you with my hat in my hand, don't you think my Mary Ruth deserves a break? Just one little break?"

"Of course I do—"

"Don't you think, these six months to come, she deserves a little comfort, a place to live that ain't a pigsty, a place to

266

live where she won't be ashamed if anyone comes to call? Is that wrong for my lovely young Mary Ruth, even if it costs a few lousy dollars?"

"Of course not—"

"Carol, honey, maybe you don't know this, but I do. She loves you an awful lot, deep down in her big soft heart. You showed her a heap of kindness. You're her friend! She won't move in here unless you move in too. I don't like asking a favor of any human being on this earth, but I'm asking a favor of you. Will you come and keep my Mary Ruth company?"

I burst into tears.

Jurgy cried, "You've upset her with all this crap you talk, you sweet-talking bastard," and she burst into tears.

Luke snuffled, and took off his glasses, and he burst into tears.

The fountains of Miami Beach. We moved in at noon.

At eight o'clock Monday morning we reported for duty to the supervisor of hostesses at the airport, Miss Duprez. We'd heard about her—she was one of the first hostesses to fly with Magna International Airlines, way back in the year dot. She was rather petite, with delicate pale skin and the kind of shrewd eyes that make you feel guilty even though you know you're innocent. There was a weighing machine in her office, and, first off, she weighed us and jotted the figures in a little black book. A great start: I was five pounds overweight, Jurgy was seven pounds overweight. Next she sat us down and gave us a brief lecture on responsibility, and made it clear to us that any slackening in our personal appearance would meet with her instant disapproval. Then she went on to explain that for the next week or so we were just a couple of bodies at her complete disposal: we'd be flying as "C" hostesses but actually we'd just be learning the ropes. She consulted a big wall chart and gave us our first assignments for the following day. I was on a flight leaving at seven-thirty to Tampa and New Orleans. Jurgy was on a flight at eight-ten to Jacksonville, Savannah, Charleston and Washington. We both had layovers for the night, and we'd return on the same routes Wednesday. We'd have Thursday off, and we'd switch flights Friday and Saturday—Jurgy to New Orleans, me to Washington.

Then, to my consternation, she called Dr. Elizabeth Schwartz and said, "Betty, I have a couple of girls here, re-

porting in for the first time. Carol Thompson and M. R
Jurgens . . . Thanks, Betty." She turned to us and said crisply
"Dr. Schwartz is up to her eyes with the new girls, but she'l
squeeze you in somehow after lunch. Be in her office at one
thirty."

I said in an offhand way, "Miss Duprez, what is this for?
mean, why do we have to see Dr. Schwartz?"

"Physicals."

My God, they seemed to be crazy about physicals. Oh
well. There went everything in a big cloud of blue smoke.
had a strong suspicion that radiant motherhood lay ahea
of me, nine months from last Monday night, and D
Schwartz would undoubtedly know all about it the minut
she set eyes on me.

New jobs always seem to start in the same way: you han
around, all hands and feet, wondering what on earth you'r
supposed to do with yourself. After Miss Duprez dismisse
us, we had about three and a half hours to kill before see
ing Dr. Schwartz; and Jurgy was just as vague as I was. W
had coffee in the airport restaurant; and then, right out o
the blue, I was hit by an utterly brilliant idea. We'd brough
the Corvette, because it looked so dashing, and on the wa
in I'd pointed out the various gadgets and explained rough
what they were supposed to do. Now, with so much tim
on our hands, I suggested to Jurgy that we might ride ove
to the Motor Vehicle License Bureau, or whatever it wa
called, and pick up a learner's permit so that I could begi
to give her driving lessons. She hung back at first, reluctar
to take the plunge but I coaxed her into being sensible, an
off we went into Miami, causing quite a commotion amon
the citizens, who seemed impressed by our general appea
ance and the splendor of our blue-and-gray chariot.
cheered us up a lot. Jurgy became very bright-eyed an
dimply again and it was all I could do to remain impassiv
and dignified when kids wolf-whistled at us. Not only kid
either. We even wowed the cops on traffic duty, which au
gured well for the future. Frankly, I don't dig it. What's s
sexy about a couple of airline hostesses driving a Corvett
I mean, where's the actual *sex*?

We picked up the learner's permit, had a green salad, an
arrived back just in time to be in Dr. Schwartz's office
one-thirty. She took me first, chatting in the friendliest wa
as she went through her routine, and to my surprise she ga
me a big smile and said, "You're fine, Carol." I guess it ha

just skipped her notice that I was a full six and a half days pregnant; and I didn't feel any special urge to bring it to her attention. I waited outside in the ante-room while Jurgy went through the ordeal; and this was another odd experience, because four girls from the new course (which was starting today) were waiting their turn to say ah. They stared at me with wide-eyed admiration, as if I were Ingrid Bergman or Greta Garbo or some other legendary figure, because, after all, I was the real McCoy, in uniform and all the rest. Any female is apt to act a little snotty in circumstances like these, and I just gave them a sort of condescending smile—a curl of the lip, actually—and looked nonchalantly out the window as if I were figuring out flying conditions for a nonstop flight around the world. All four of them were beauties; they had the right proportions; and their eyes bore definite signs of intelligence; but otherwise they were pathetic. They were practically hunchbacked, their hair needed a tree surgeon, they just seemed to *drip* all over the place. No snap. No sparkle. I laughed rather bitterly at the thought— *Just wait, kids. You'll snap, don't worry.* Three weeks from now they would be wondering why they'd ever been born.

As soon as Jurgy reappeared we drove off once again in the Corvette and found some fairly deserted little roads where we wouldn't be in anybody's way; and I launched forth on what makes a car tick. She was scared to death at first and the sulky look came over her face, but by dinnertime she was cruising along the Tamiami Trail at forty-five miles an hour, grinning like a hyena, holding the steering wheel in a grip of iron as all beginners do, and having a heart attack every time she saw a truck coming or going. But she was driving, at least. Of course. She was absolutely a natural at this sort of thing. I said, "Well, how is it?" and she laughed madly and said, "Oh boy, this is real living."

I was at the airport at six-thirty sharp the next morning, trembling in every limb; and at seven-thirty on the nose our plane waddled away from its ramp to the runway. The "A" hostess was a stunning blonde named Nan Burnham, the "B" hostess was a lively brunette named Jill Kerrigan, and they were both pretty tolerant about having me aboard. I couldn't expect much more than that. Fortunately we had a fairly light load, so there wouldn't be too much of a mad rush; the weather report was good, too, so—according to Nan—we could anticipate a comfortable flight without much turbulence. But it was staggering to see how efficient she and Jill were. They went through all the routine without turning a hair, Nan checking ticket envelopes, taking the passenger count, welcoming the passengers over the public address system, while Jill directed the passengers to their seats, checked their seat belts, and, as soon as we were airborne, set up the galley. I was in the forward part of the main cabin, handing out magazines, checking the overhead racks and so on—just helping things along as best I could and trying not to fall over my big feet.

We'd been flying about twenty-five minutes, and I was simply overwhelming the passengers with my magazine service—it was clear from the look in their eyes they'd never *seen* so many magazines—when Jill came to me and said in a whisper, "Carol, the Captain wants to see you."

"Oh, my God, what have I done wrong?"

She said, "He'll tell you."

I'd met the Captain before take-off, with the rest of the crew. He was one of those Apollo-like creatures, lean and bronzed, with hawklike blue eyes and a clean-cut mouth, just one of those divine beings who, before my faith in men was destroyed, used to drain the blood from my cheeks. According to an unwritten law the crew and the hostesses are supposed to be one big happy family when they're working a plane, and only first names are used from the moment you all meet. The Captain is supposed to say with a welcoming smile, "Hello, I'm Joe Blow," and you're supposed to answer, "Hello, Joe, I'm Betsy Crumbbun," and you shake hands and from then on you're always Joe and Betsy to each other.

But I couldn't do it. I couldn't call my first captain by his first name, which happened to be Willard. I practically couldn't call anybody Willard, and certainly not this Greek god who was piloting my first airplane. I slithered into the cockpit and said, "You sent for me, sir?"

He turned and inspected me from top to bottom. "Oh, hi Carol. Yeah. I sent for you." He was chewing gum, and he chewed steadily for about a minute while he tried to figure out how to break the news to me. "Fact is, Carol, we're having a spot of trouble."

"Oh, no!" I caught my breath. *They* wouldn't know it but *I* knew it. I'd jinxed the plane. The plane was doomed from the moment I stepped aboard. I whispered, "Is it serious?"

The Captain shrugged his shoulders. It was one of those you-want-to-live-forever gestures that Captains are always making. He said laconically, "Tell her what it is, Lew."

Lew was the flight engineer. Clean-cut, but not as clean-cut as the Captain. He said, staring at his zillions of dials and flipping a couple of switches, "Carol, seems like the hydraulic system is acting up. You know what the hydraulic system is, don't you?"

I said, "Sure." It was the hydraulic system. All planes had them. You buy an airliner and you get a free hydraulic system thrown in.

"Well," he said, "seems like the pipes are clogging up some place. Far as I can locate the trouble, it's down in the tail section—"

The Captain interrupted. "That's where you locate it, eh? The tail section?"

"Yeah," Lew said. "See here, Willard?" He pointed to a dial. "That's where the pressure's gone flooey. It's those darned toilets acting up."

"The toilets, eh?" the Captain said.

Lew's voice was rising in pitch. "That's right, Willard. These lousy toilets are cavitating the branch line." He turned to me. "You know what the branch line is?"

"Gee, I'm sorry. We didn't really go into the hydraulic system on our course."

"God Almighty!" Lew cried. "What are they teaching these girls now? What are they teaching them!"

"Don't get hysterical, Lew, old chap," the Captain said quietly. "We can fix it, with Carol's help." He sat chewing his gum, deep in thought. The copilot was at the controls, thank God, but I could see that his jaw was clenched.

The Captain said, "Listen, Carol."

"Yes, sir."

"We're going to have to rely on you to keep the pressure moving in those toilets. You understand?"

My heart was pounding. "What do you want me to do?"

"Tell her, Lew."

"It's dropping!" Lew shrieked. "My God, it's dropping below twenty—"

The Captain's voice was sharp. "Pull yourself together, man! We've lived through worse things than this before! Give Carol her instructions. Carol: listen to Lew."

"Yes, sir, I'm listening."

Lew said shakily, "Get back to the rear, Carol. Flush the

271

women's john. Do that *first*. The order is important—the women's john *first*."

"Yes, sir."

"Then," he said, "go into the men's john and flush that. You understand? The idea is to control the cavitation in the branch line. Get it?"

"Yes, sir."

"It's a Y-shaped branch line. See?"

"Yes, I think I see."

"Right. Now then: when you've completed the first cycle, stand by the Interphone. I'll be checking the branch-line meter. As soon as the cavitation starts up again I'll give you a signal—what signal shall I give her, Willard?"

"Five bells. That's the unassigned signal. We'll assign it to Carol."

"Okay," Lew said. "As soon as you hear your five-bell signal, Carol, hit those toilets and repeat the cycle. But *fast*. And remember, for God's sake, the order is *vital*. If you flush the men's toilet first we'll cavitate in reverse. Then we're really sunk."

I said, "I'll remember. The women's john first, the men's second.—Holy smoke, suppose somebody's occupying the men's john?"

The Captain said gravely, "Carol, this is no time for false modesty.—Lew, is there anything else?"

Lew said in a thin voice, "Willard. She's a new kid. She hasn't had to face anything like this before. Can we trust her?"

"We *have* to trust her," Willard snapped. "The other girls will be circulating among the passengers, won't they? We *have* to rely on Carol, she's our only hope.—Honey, you can manage this, can't you?"

"I'll do my best, sir."

"Good girl. Okay, there's no more time to waste. Jump to it."

I hurried down to the rear section. Nan and Jill were in the galley. Jill said, "What's the trouble, Carol?"

I answered in a low voice, "The branch pipes are cavitating."

"Oh, no!"

I hurried on to the toilets. The women's john was unoccupied. I flushed it. The men's toilet was occupied. I waited impatiently. The man who came out gave me a surprised look and I explained cheerfully, "We're just having a touch

272

of cavitation, sir, nothing serious." I flushed the men's toilet. Was it my imagination, or did the engines immediately sound a little smoother?

I went to the Interphone and stood by. One minute later the five-bell signal chimed out. I dashed to the toilets and started the second cycle. All this flushing was beginning to affect *my* insides, but there was no time for that. I hurried back to the Interphone, and waited five full minutes. God! It had worked! We had the cavitation under control! The Y-shaped branch pipe was normal again! I decided I'd help Nan Burnham hand out beverages and just as I was passing my first cup of coffee to a sweet old gentleman with a white mustache the signal chimed for the third time. Back to the toilets. Back to the Interphone. Back to the toilets.

That damned Y-shaped branch pipe was cavitating all the way to Tampa, but at least we made it. None of the passengers, as far as I could tell, had the slightest intimation of the terrible ordeal we had passed through. It was only when we were coming in for the landing, and we all had our seat belts fastened, that I noticed Jill had her hand over her face and was peering at me with one bright tear-filled eye. Then she took her hand away from her face and doubled up with silent laughter; and I realized that I had been had.

The girls were very sweet to me for the rest of the trip, and told me how they'd been had in their time, and how practically every hostess they knew had been had—and generally in some way connected with the toilets. Boys will be boys, Nan and Jill informed me: as true a maxim as I ever heard. And that night in New Orleans, Willard and Lew took me out to dinner in a fabulous French restaurant, and each of them presented me with an orchid. Willard told me I was okay, and he loved me; and Lew told me he loved me, and I was okay; and I told them they were sons of bitches, but I loved them both because all my life I'd only loved men who were sons of bitches; and they each held one of my hands and patted me affectionately and said, "There, there, everything's going to be all right." We had a smooth trip back to Miami the following day, Wednesday; and on the whole I didn't feel badly about the experience— I'd made some new friends. I needed some new friends, by golly, the way my old friends were disappearing into Limbo.

Jurgy arrived back at the apartment a couple of hours after I did. Her trip had been uneventful, except that a couple of male passengers tried to date her. They must have been traveling without their Seeing Eye dogs. On the other hand, the Captain and the merry crew of her plane hadn't attempted any boyish pranks such as had been played on me. I guess *they* knew when to be discreet.

Thursday was a day off, which was lucky because that morning I discovered I wasn't going to be a mother. Gad, I never had such a morning in my entire life—Jurgy was so alarmed that she wanted to call Dr. Schwartz. It was worth it, though. I felt terrible, but I felt wonderful at the same time. At least, if Dr. Ray Duer ever reappeared on the scene, I wouldn't have to explain away the blue-eyed little brat doing card tricks in the baby carriage.

We flew piston-driven planes for six weeks, alternating over the Washington and New Orleans routes, and slowly but surely some kind of maturity came. Jurgy was way ahead of me in this matter of maturity, but I began to catch up with her. I found myself walking out to a great big airliner in a brisk but unhurried manner, knowing exactly what to do once I was aboard, from the moment I stowed my kit to the moment I dragged my kit out again before deplaning. The most fascinating part of the whole business was trying to relate the Carol Thompson that I'd been a mere two and a half months ago to the Carol Thompson I'd now become. It wasn't a moral question. I mean, it had nothing to do with goodness, or betterness. I don't quite know how to say it, and yet this is the only way it can be said: Thompson's internal structure had been shored up, somehow. It had developed muscles. Which, again, doesn't mean that today's Thompson was finer or holier than yesterday's MacDougal Street Thompson. I hadn't developed muscles on the outside of my edifice, thank God: I seemed to have developed them inside like a lobster. The result was that I didn't die on myself so easily, I didn't give up the ghost at the drop of a hat. I'm not implying that whizzing about in the sky seventy-five hours a month is the answer to everything. I wasn't madly, madly happy, and I sure as hell wasn't complete because no woman is complete without a man around her neck, and I didn't have a man around my neck. Furthermore, it looked as if any chance of having a man around my neck had vanished forevermore, because one evening Jurgy came back to the apartment and reported that Mr. Garrison had been aboard her flight that day, and he'd told her that Ray Duer had gone back to the University of Southern California to do some research on training crews for supersonic flying. That night, I have to admit, my internal structure collapsed, and I had a crying jag when I got to bed. I was still in love with Duer, apparently, but I still couldn't forgive him for what he'd done to Donna.

Otherwise, life was pretty good. It was great having the apartment overlooking Indian Creek, and being able to cook and listen to music and have people drop by for a drink; the Florida sun was great and so was the Florida ocean; and, of course, there was the supreme joy of flying. It was a joy every time.

Then, after our six weeks on piston-driven planes we returned to the Training School to sweat through four packed days of jet training.

We'd learned the 707 in the last ten days of our basic training, but by Magna standards that wasn't enough. We had to go through the whole business again in detail: galley management, cabin service, and—over and over again—emergency procedures. Hypoxia, decompression, oxygen, oxygen, oxygen. We had a new instructor, a wonderful dark-haired girl named Ann Shearer who'd been flying jets for the past two years; and she made it plenty clear to us that flying jets at 30,000 feet was a lot different from flying piston-driven planes at 18,000 feet. It was marvelous for the passengers, but it was a lot tougher on the crews. The jets flew so fast that you had all your work keeping up, so to speak, with their speed. For example, the New York—Miami run was a mere two and a half hours, and in that space of time four girls had to prepare and serve meals for a hundred and twelve passengers, supply them with drinks and other beverages, hand out magazines, answer questions, pacify babies, rebuff amorous advances, and keep an eye out for anybody who was turning bright blue. As I said to Jurgy, "I bet it wasn't anything like this in the old Thripp Hotel in Buffalo," to which she replied, "You bet your boots it wasn't."

Betty Schwartz gave us a long talk about medical aspects of high-altitude flying; and before she plunged into her talk she mentioned that some of the matters she was going to cover were normally dealt with by Dr. Duer, but unfortunately he was away in Southern California doing special research. It was involuntary, I'm sure, but as she said this her eyes turned to me for a fraction of a second, and I felt myself turning brick red and breaking out into a cold sweat. Anybody who wasn't blind could have seen then and there that I was still hixed on that damned man; but what percentage is there in being hixed on a man with whom you've broken finally and irrevocably?

A couple of days after the course ended we went to work on jets. They were a dream. The work was grueling, as we'd been told, but it didn't matter so much because, for one thing we could handle it more easily, we were really beginning to know the job; and for another thing, Jurgy and I could fly together. The jets we were flying were essentially two-cabin affairs—that's how we thought of them: a forward and an aft cabin, each with its own separate galley and lavatories and its own two hostesses. "A" and "B" served the forward compartment, which was usually first class, while "C" and "D" served the aft compartment, which was usually coach. The routine varied occasionally, for example, when the flight was all first class; but this was how we flew generally. Jurgy and I, naturally, were the junior hostesses, "B" and "D."

We were on the Miami—New York run, and the arrangement suited us beautifully. At the New York end we could see the Broadway shows and shop in the big department stores; at the Miami end we had our apartment, and sunshine, and the ocean, and our friends. I guess it was the first real home Jurgy'd ever had, and she went absolutely cuckoo over it, just as she did over her Corvette. When she wasn't breaking every speed law in Florida she'd be at home baking cakes and making the most elaborate pies and roasting enormous slabs of beef; and it was sometimes a problem to find enough mouths to consume all the stuff she cooked. Miami Beach isn't exactly a place where the sidewalks are crowded with starving people, and you rarely see anybody you can hand a six-pound roast rib and say, "Here, buddy, maybe this will help." We could rely on Luke in the weekends, if we were home: he ate enough for ten. Occasionally he'd bring over some of his friends, huge men, all in the cattle business; and, my God, it was always a sight—they'd devour *everything*, right down to the legs of the table. We had the Garrisons over for dinner a couple of times, and Peg Webley and her fiancé—a charming guy, just right for her. We had Janet Pierce and Ann Shearer over, and Betty Schwartz, who was becoming one of my best friends; and so on. It was fun for me, but it was more than fun for Jurgy—it was a dream come true, she really had a ball for herself.

People kept turning up here and there. Bob Keeler, the

handsome young Air Force lieutenant with whom I'd gone to the jai-alai game, was on our flight one morning. Jurgy and I had coffee with him at Idlewild, and he told us that Elliott Ewing had seen Donna in New York several times after she left the Charleroi, but then she'd dropped him for some other man (or men). She was living at the Sherry Netherland, the last Bob heard of her, and that was as much as he knew. He sounded rather bitter. For example (he said) she'd gotten Elliott into a fight with some goon in Miami Beach, and Elliott had nearly been killed—at least, half his teeth had to be wired afterwards. I held my peace about this. There was no point in reviving that ancient battle. When I called the Sherry Netherland that afternoon they said they had no Donna Stewart staying there; then they looked up their records and found she'd checked out a couple of months ago without leaving any forwarding address. They sounded disapproving; and I could have wept.

I hadn't lost my appeal for Bob, it seemed. He asked if he could see me again, and I said unenthusiastically, "Some time." Something strange was happening to the world, from where I stood: the boys were getting younger and younger, and I was getting older and older, and I seemed unable to meet a boy of my own age. Bob was definitely too young, the minute he began to yap about literature.

But, on the whole, I was having fun, and I couldn't imagine myself doing any other kind of job. The only trouble was this absence of males, which could be summed up in a few words, the absence of Duer; and I figured time would heal that. Maybe.

At the beginning of April, when we'd been flying jets for about four months, I began to notice that Jurgy was acting in a rather weird manner. Nothing alarming. It was merely that she kept going into a trance at odd moments. For example, she'd be sitting in the living room drinking a cup of coffee at eleven o'clock in the morning, and suddenly, with the cup halfway to her mouth, she'd freeze, her eyes would glaze over, and she'd be away somewhere on the back of the moon. I watched this funny business for a few days, and then the answer dawned on me. April. Of course! The coming of spring. I should have thought of it sooner, but in Florida you aren't specially aware of the winter ending and spring taking its place, there aren't any little buds sprouting on the bare branches of the trees—everything in sight is sprouting like mad day in and day out all year round, which can get to be a trifle exhausting for a character like me, born and bred in the North.

That, anyway, was what I decided was afflicting Jurgy. Florida or no Florida, a woman feels the coming of spring in her blood stream, she has the unquenchable urge to start knocking a nest together, she can hear the cries of her young ones yet unborn, etc. And one evening, when she was supposed to be sewing a button on her uniform and instead was sitting there like a stuffed ostrich, her mouth open, her eyes glazed, the needle and thread stuck in midair, I said to her gently, "Look, Jurgy. Why don't you quit?"

She snapped out of her trance and said, "Huh?"

"Why don't you quit flying, and get married, and settle down with Luke?"

She nearly bit my head off. "Why the hell should I?"

"It's about time, that's all. You told Luke you wanted to fly for six months. You've been flying five and a half, already."

"Luke and I had a talk about it—we settled that I'll quit in June, and we'll get married early in August."

"Jurgy, honestly, you've had this dreamy expression on your face for days now—"

"Dreamy expression?"

"Yes. You've been acting real goofy."

"I have?"

"Come on. Give. What have you been dreaming about?"

She pursed her lips. "You really want to know?"

"I'm dying to know."

She looked around the room to see that there weren't any Russian spies listening. Then she said, "The North Southeastern Cattlebreeders' annual convention."

I nearly dropped in my tracks. I said, "Would you mind repeating that?"

"Yeah," she said. "But keep it quiet. I don't want it spread around. The North Southeastern Cattlebreeders' annual convention."

"For crying out loud," I said, "what makes you think I'd spread that mouthful around?"

She gave me a fishy stare. Obviously I'd proved myself to be nothing but an utter moron. She'd confided her glorious dream to me, and all I'd done was look stupid.

"Well?" I said.

Her voice was icy. "It's being held at the Charleroi this

year. It starts the twenty-eighth of April. It lasts three days."

I said, "Jurgy, that's the most stunning piece of news I've heard since Lincoln's dog died. I'm practically hysterical."

"There's going to be seventy delegates."

"Stop! Stop! I can't take it all at once."

She went on in the same icy way, "It so happens that Luke is secretary of the entertainment committee."

"Now, wait a minute," I said. "You aren't planning to entertain seventy cattlemen here, are you?"

"No."

"Well, what's causing all those stars in your eyes?"

She didn't answer.

I said, "If Luke is having trouble finding talent, I might be prevailed upon to do a tassel dance, maybe."

She still didn't speak.

"Jurgy!" I said.

And then, as if she couldn't keep up that fishiness any longer, she began to laugh. She laughed so hard that she had to cover her face with her hands. When she was able to catch her breath she sat there giggling, her eyes shining, her cheeks flushed and dimply like an ecstatic little girl. She said, "Oh, Carol! It's so crazy! It's just plain mad."

"What is?"

"Come here," she whispered.

I walked over to her.

"Listen, Carol. Honest to God, I mean it. Don't tell a soul. You *have* to keep it quiet.—Luke is planning a big junket when the convention is over."

"What do you mean, a big junket?"

"A weekend in Paris for all the delegates. A *long* weekend, Friday through Monday."

"Jurgy! Oh, Jurgy! Are you going with them?"

She took a deep breath. "Honey, *we* are going with them."

"We? What do you mean, *we?*"

Stars had begun to float over my head.

She said, "Luke is chartering a jet from Magna, see?" She couldn't help laughing. "It's a de luxe flight. There'll be four hostesses. You and I will be two of the four."

Comets were shooting all over the ceiling. "My God, Jurgy! Jurgy, is this true?"

"It's true," she said. Her face was wreathed in a big fat smug smile.

I tried not to exult, I tried to be sensible for a moment. "But how can Luke do this? We haven't flown international."

"Don't worry. Luke will fix it. Luke can fix anything." She beamed at me. "You want to come along?"

"Are you kidding?"

"Exciting, eh?"

"You bet it's exciting. I can hardly wait. When will Luke know for sure?"

"In a couple of days. He has to settle all the details with some feller from Magna."

I said, "I still don't see how Luke can pull this stunt."

"Carol, Luke can pull *any* stunt. Once he makes up his mind, there's nothing in this world can stop him."

"Well, my God," I said. "And I thought it was the spring."

"What was the spring?"

"The look in your eyes you've had all week."

"Nuts." Then she said, "You been to Paris?"

"A couple of times."

"Tell me something," she said. "Is that a good place to buy curtain material?"

"Gee, I wouldn't know, Jurgy. I guess so. Why?"

She suddenly became very heated. "This house of Luke's in Kansas. It has more than sixty windows. Do you hear? More than sixty. And I told him flat, when I marry him and move into that house, I'm not going to live with somebody else's curtains, I want my own curtains. That's the only thing I insist on: my own curtains. Is that too much to ask? So I was thinking, maybe we could pick up the material in Paris and save a few bucks. Get nicer patterns, too. What do you say, Carol?"

I couldn't say anything. I sat down and howled. She was very offended.

Luke fixed it. He dropped by the apartment, grinning all over his long bony face, to tell us how. "Yep," he said. "It was a cinch. I had to settle all the arrangements with this feller, name of Barker, see? Not a bad feller, the district sales manager, that's what he calls himself. You know how it is with all these fellers, they got to make their sales quotas and all that stuff, and this was kind of a tidy little deal to fall into Barker's hands. Well, we had the contract drawn up, and I pulled out my checkbook, and I opened it flat on the table, and I wrote in, where it says Pay to the Order of, *Magna International Airlines*. Then I wrote in the amount. Then I wrote my first name, *Luke*. Then I just kind of stopped. This feller Barker was watching me, and when he seen me hesitating he got all concerned 'cause he couldn't figure what was on my mind. So I said to him, 'Mr. Barker,' I said, 'something just occurred to me regarding the service on this little trip to Paris, and I'd like to have your co-operation, sir, if that's at all possible.' Well, he jumps about a foot in the air, and he says, 'Certainly, certainly, anything I can do for you, Mr. Lucas, I'll be only too happy to do it, just you name what it is.' So I said, 'Mr. Barker, it ain't any of my business who you get to pilot this plane, 'cause I'm sure in my mind you'll give us a good man. The navigator, he's none of my business either, 'cause I'm sure you'll give us someone who'll be able to find his way to where we're going. But it just so happens, Mr. Barker, there's two little girls I know, who in my humble opinion, sir, will help to make this a happier occasion, and I'd be mighty grateful if you could arrange for these two young ladies to fly along with us as official hostesses. You think that would be possible, Mr. Barker?' Well, he was kind of distressed by this, he hummed and hawed, he wanted to know if you'd ever flown out of the country before and stuff like that; and then he come right out with it. I'll give the feller credit. He didn't mince words, no, sir. He said, 'Mr. Lucas, I'm going to ask you straight. Is this for immoral purposes?' Just like that. And I said, 'Mr. Barker, I'm glad you asked me that question 'cause I'm only too happy to set your mind at rest. One of the girls is my fiancée, my own sweet Mary Ruth Jurgens, the loveliest girl in this whole wide world, bar none. And the other gal is her dearest friend, Miss Carol Thompson, the purest little lady that ever drew breath; and I'd kill the man that tried to lay a finger on either one of them. Does that satisfy you, Mr. Barker?' I guess it did, at that, 'cause he kind of took a deep breath and gave a sickly smile and said, 'Okay. I'll see what I can arrange.' I said, 'You won't fall down on this, will you?' and he said, 'I won't fall down on it, leave it to me,' and so I went ahead and wrote the rest of my name, *Lucas*. He sure was glad to see me do that."

Three days later, coming in from a flight from New York, we found a notice on the bulletin board in the Hostess Room requesting us to report to Miss Duprez, the supervisor of hostesses. "I guess this is it," Jurgy said out of the corner of her mouth, and I said, "Boy, I *hope*." We tidied ourselves as well as we could, but without any real success—the moment Miss Duprez laid eyes on us she said faintly,

"Mary Ruth! Carol! For heaven's sake! You're both so *bedraggled!* What *happened?*" We explained that we'd just come in with a full load of slaphappy vacationers, including eighteen babies; but this was no excuse. Then she said, "While you're here, let's see how you're maintaining your weight," and apparently we were maintaining it just fine—I was five pounds overweight, as usual, and Jurgy was seven pounds overweight, as usual. I swear those scales were rigged. Miss Duprez clucked disapprovingly and entered the figures in her little black notebook. It was all an act, of course, and we all knew it was an act, and yet it worked. When somebody like Miss Duprez, who was flying practically before you were born, tells you you're a fat untidy slob, you can't help feeling slightly ashamed of yourself.

She lectured us on the importance of weight and appearance for five minutes, and once this was out of the way she came to the point. "Now, girls, I have some very interesting news for you. You're flying to Paris on May one, returning May four. It's a charter flight, with four hostesses, and you will naturally be the two juniors, 'B' and 'D.' Does this meet with your approval?" She was sitting at her desk, her hands loosely clasped, watching us.

"Why, Miss Duprez!" we said. "It's wonderful!"

She glanced at me. She stared hard at Jurgy. Her voice fell several degrees. "Let me say frankly, girls, it doesn't meet with *my* approval. As you know, these flights are open to bids from all hostesses, and are awarded on the basis of seniority. In addition, on flights to Europe, for obvious reasons, we only use girls who have had considerable experience in international flying. But your fiancé is a very persuasive man, Mary Ruth."

Jurgy was silent. I daresay she was as startled as I was by Miss Duprez' bluntness. We'd underrated this little woman.

She continued, "Mr. Barker, our district sales manager, would probably be most unhappy to hear me talking to you like this—after all, it's his job to make sales for the airline. My job is quite different. As it happens, I have a lot of faith in both of you, otherwise I would never permit such an arrangement to go through, even if it meant losing this particular charter flight. However, I want to make this clear to you right from the outset: despite any relationship you may have to any of the passengers, you will not depart from our normal rules. I will expect from you the very highest standards of service and conduct, otherwise you will be subject to disciplinary action when you return. You will obey implicitly the senior hostesses who are assigned to this flight. There will be no slackening of the regulations pertaining to safety, and so on. Is this understood?"

Jurgy said, "Yes, Miss Duprez."

"Very good. As soon as I have further information I'll let you know. That is all, girls."

I thought Jurgy would explode with wrath as we drove back to the apartment. She didn't. She only said, in a kind of admiring grunt, "That sure is one tough little cookie." I said, "She sure is."

We flew our regular schedule until a couple of days before the charter flight. But for the last week of this period, Jurgy was in a wild mood that had me baffled again. I just couldn't figure out what was going on in her mind. Luke had arrived early for the convention because he had so much planning to do; he was staying as usual at the Charleroi; and she spent a lot of time with him over there. It suited me fine, because I enjoyed being alone; I could read, and play music, and really relax. The only trouble was, her weird behavior when she returned from seeing Luke. She was just impossible. She'd be elated for a while, and then she'd sit in the living room brooding. Then she'd become almost ferociously hostile. She'd snap at me like a crocodile if I dared to speak to her. I couldn't stand it, finally. There wasn't any point in getting into a fight with her about it; I merely decided that as soon as possible I'd find a place of my own.

The afternoon before the flight we were called to the airport for a conference with Mr. Barker of Sales, and a harassed little man named Casey who was responsible for providing the food and liquor on the flight, and the two senior hostesses with whom we'd be working. They were both brunettes, about twenty-six years old, and they looked at Jurgy and me in an odd amused way, as if we'd just been let out of kindergarten. Their names were Kay Taylor and Janyce Hinds, and I learned later that they'd been flying for nearly five years.

Jurgy and I were just there to listen. The conference was entirely between Mr. Barker and Mr. Casey on the one hand, and Kay and Janyce on the other; and mostly it seemed to be about ice cubes. Kay said, "Mr. Casey, we'll need at least three times the regular supply of ice cubes. I've been on charter flights with guys like these cattlemen before, and they *drink*." "Brother," Janyce said, "and how." The main meal was to be filet mignon with baked potatoes, but this appeared to be unimportant. "Listen Mr. Casey," Kay said, "make it *four* times the regular supply of ice cubes, will you? We can't take a chance of running out of ice in mid-Atlantic. These guys might get awful peeved." Mr. Casey groaned. Janyce said, "And be sure to have a couple of auxiliary gas tanks filled with bourbon, Mr. Casey. You can sling 'em under the wings." Mr. Casey said, "You're going to have enough bourbon and Scotch aboard to sink a battleship." Kay said promptly, "Double up on that, Mr. Casey. We'll need enough to sink two battleships." Jurgy and I listened with awe. They were amazing characters, these girls: good-looking, easygoing, and yet tough as nails and one hundred percent sure of themselves. As the conference broke up Kay said to Jurgy and me, "Kids: make yourselves up real slick tomorrow, eh? We want to impress these cattlemen to death. Maybe when we get to Paris they'll buy each of us a diamond tiara or a glass of milk or something. And, let's see, now: the flight leaves at nine o'clock. Be sure to report in by eight o'clock sharp, not a minute later. We want to check this plane out but good. Okay?" "Okay," we said.

I was alone in the apartment again that evening, which suited me perfectly, because I could get all my ironing done without any mad rush, in preparation for tomorrow's flight, and I could have the hi-fi playing in the background. I couldn't do his when Jurgy was around. Music drove her completely out of her mind. Mozart gave her a headache, Gershwin gave her a headache, even *My Fair Lady* gave her a headache. So I could play the hi-fi only when I was alone, and it gave me the greatest joy. Jurgy was at the Charleroi, this time for a party the cattlemen was throwing in the Empress Room to wind up their three-day convention. I'd been invited, but I hadn't gone, partly because I had so many odd jobs to do at home, partly because I'd be with all seventy of them for the next four days anyway, and one shouldn't overdo these things. Jurgy had assured me rather sourly that she'd be home early; and I had absolutely no cause to worry about her, as far as the party was concerned. She detested liquor in any form. She wouldn't even touch a glass of beer.

At about nine-thirty I was ironing away in a pleasant state of nothingness when the telephone rang. It didn't make my heart go pitter-patter—it rang often enough. Guys I'd had dates with, our friends over at the school, friends we'd made since we started flying—they called constantly. So I lowered the volume of the Mozart I was playing, and picked up the receiver, and said, "Hello," wondering quite vaguely who the caller would turn out to be.

"Hello. Carol?"

And I began to shake like a leaf, just at the sound of that voice speaking my name. I sank onto the arm of a chair and said, "Yes?"

"This is Ray Duer."

I managed to say, "Oh, hello, Dr. Duer."

"How are you?"

"Fine. Just fine. How are you, sir?"

I shouldn't have called him *sir*. I knew that, the moment the word slipped out. I could almost feel him harden. It wasn't politeness, it was just a kind of insolence, a carry-over from those old days when we'd been constantly at loggerheads. But I couldn't help myself.

He answered my question curtly, "I'm fine, thank you."

"How's your hand?"

"My hand? Oh, yes. It's healed, thanks."

"That's good," I said. I was beginning to catch my breath. He said, "Are you doing anything special?"

I said, "I'm still working for Magna International Airlines. I don't know if you'd call that special. It's fun."

"I mean, now. This evening."

I said, "I'm getting ready for an early-morning flight. It's to Europe. I have an awful lot to do."

"Could I see you for a few minutes?"

"I'm sorry," I said. "I'm very sorry."

I guess it had become fixed as a pattern in my brain—Ray Duer only had to say *Can I see you?* and the answer snapped out automatically, *I'm sorry.* I wanted to cry, *Ray, of course, of course, where are you, I'll be there in five seconds, I'll run;* but that pattern in my brain did the answering for me.

He said, "Carol, I want to talk to you."

"I'm sorry."

"You're still mad at me about Donna Stewart?" He didn't wait for a reply. He laughed and went on, "All right, I can tell you what this is about now, it'll only take a moment. Carol, I'll be on your plane tomorrow."

"On my plane?"

"Yes."

I said, "I think you're mistaken. I'm on a charter flight to Paris—"

"I know."

I repeated, "But it's a *charter* flight—"

"I know! I know! That's what I wanted to talk to you about, that's why I wanted to see you. I thought I ought to let you know in advance that I'll be on this flight."

"I still don't understand. Why should you feel you owe it to me to give me this information?"

"Because you might resent it. Because it might do more harm than good."

I said, "Dr. Duer, you happen to be an important officer of Magna International Airlines. I'm nobody. Whether I resent it or not has nothing to do with the facts. If you have authority to fly on that plane, you *fly*, sir."

"I could take another flight."

"Sir, that's up to you."

"By God," he said; and evidently he couldn't trust himself to go on. He hung up.

I didn't move for a long time. I sat, frozen, with the telephone humming in my hand, wondering how all this had happened, how I'd come to reject him again, how I could go on being so stupid and so stubborn, wondering how I could live with myself after this brief and cruel contact with him. I thought, If I'd seen him for a few minutes as he asked, if I'd had enough courage, perhaps everything would have straightened out between us, perhaps—

I put the receiver back and walked up and down the living room, my arms over the lower part of my body as if everything inside me had suddenly become inflamed. But what was Ray Duer doing on this flight in the first place? That plane had been hired from Magna International Airlines by Luke Lucas to transport seventy cattlemen to Paris for a four-day junket. That plane was practically theirs. It had been taken out of regular service. Luke had given a check for the exclusive use of that particular Boeing 707, and nobody could climb aboard it without his permission. The crew, of course. The four little lady hostesses. Ray Duer? Why? He wasn't flying the plane, he wasn't going to sling hash to the passengers. Those cattlemen needed a psychiatrist along with them on this trip as much as they needed a hole in the head.

So, gradually, I realized why Jurgy had been sullen with

me all week, brooding, biting her fingernails. That's how she expressed herself whenever she had something on her mind—like that Saturday morning when she'd brought me here to see the apartment for the first time. So it dawned on me, and I switched Mozart off completely and sat down in silence, in a rage, waiting for her to come back and explain what the hell she thought she was doing.

She walked into the apartment a few minutes after eleven. She didn't speak when she saw me. Her face was cold and blank. She went to her bedroom, and I heard her moving around as she took her clothes off. Then she came clattering into the living room wearing mules and a pale-blue dacron robe, carrying her uniform on a hanger. I hadn't put the ironing board away, although I'd unplugged the electric iron.

She put her hand on the ironing board and said, "Using this?"

"No."

She bent down and plugged in the electric iron, and hung the jacket of her uniform over the ironing board so that she could iron the back first. That's how we'd been instructed to do it: the back, the sleeves, the front, the collar. While the iron heated up she clattered around the room and found herself a cigarette; and, as she lit it, I said, "Ray Duer called."

"Yeah." She clattered back to the ironing board.

I waited until she'd settled again. I said, "He told me he's going to be on the flight tomorrow."

"Yeah."

"You know all about this?"

"Yeah."

"Jurgy, how come you know all about this?"

"He was at the party tonight."

"What was Dr. Duer doing at a cattlemen's party tonight?"

"Luke asked him."

"Why should Luke ask him?"

"Luke took a liking to him."

"Is that so?"

"Yeah."

"What made Luke take a liking to him so suddenly?"

She said icily, "It wasn't so sudden. Luke saw him in a fight with some guy. Luke saw him pick himself off the

287

floor and nearly kill this other guy. That's the kind of thing that goes over big with Luke—he likes a feller with real guts. Duer's staying at the Charleroi with another bunch of student hostesses. We ran into him the other night. So Luke asked him to the party. That answer your question?"

"How come Ray Duer has a seat on the plane tomorrow?"

"Luke asked him."

"Why?"

"I told you once already. Luke took a liking to him."

"You mean to say, you didn't have anything to do with any of this?"

She didn't answer.

"Tell me, Jurgy."

"Yeah. I had something to do with it."

"You suggested it to Luke?"

"Yeah, maybe."

"Did you suggest to Ray Duer that he call me tonight?"

"Yeah, maybe."

"Okay, Jurgy. What's the big idea?"

"You really want to know?"

"Jurgy, I'm just palpitating to know."

"I don't mind telling you, Carol." She bent down and unplugged the electric iron. "Too bad if I burned a hole in my jacket, eh, tonight of all nights." She stubbed out her cigarette carefully, without any hurry, and stood behind the ironing board looking at me. She said, "Honest to God, I really stretched myself to get Duer on that plane tomorrow. Me and Luke, both of us—we had to do some fast talking to get him to come on this junket, just for four days."

"How very interesting," I said.

"You're a bitch, Carol, and no mistake."

"Jurgy—"

"Duer was plain miserable when he came to this party tonight. I never saw anyone so down in the mouth. And you know why? Because he'd got to thinking you might be upset meeting him again. *You* might be upset! Ha!"

"Jurgy—"

She snarled, "You asked me, didn't you? So shut up and let me finish." She began to roll up the left sleeve of her robe. "I had a long talk with the poor guy. I told him to call you. I told you were here all alone, eating your heart out. I told him to invite you over to the hotel. I told

288

him you were still in love with him. I told him all that, and more. I said to him, Pick up the telephone and call her, you'll see. So he called you. And what did you do to him?" She laughed. "You stuck a knife into him, that's all."

"It isn't true—"

"It is true, you know." Her mouth was thin. "When he hung up, he came back to me and said, It's off, I'm not going. He was white in the face, the poor devil. Carol, how many times do you think you can do this to a guy?"

"Jurgy, it's none of your business."

She didn't hear me. "I left him with Luke. God knows if Luke can talk him into flying with us tomorrow. Carol, what the hell would it have cost you to be friendly to him? Just to have given him a friendly word? Eh?"

"I keep telling you—"

"You keep telling me!" she cried. "You keep telling me *what?* You're in love with him, aren't you? You don't have to answer. I know. I live here with you. I've seen you with some of your dates, and, boy! do you keep them at arm's length! You're in love with Duer and no one else, but you can't forgive him for what he did to Donna Stewart—isn't that the story?"

"Oh, for God's sake, be quiet."

"Listen, baby, I'm on a talking jag, and I'm going to talk all I please. You go to your room if you don't want to hear it." She stood scratching her bare arm, staring at me. "Carol. What's the matter with you?"

"This is just getting ridiculous."

"No it isn't getting ridiculous. I'm asking a simple question. What's the matter with you? Who the hell do you think you are?"

I turned to go.

"Wait a minute," she said. "I'll tell you who you are. You're just a broad like any other broad, and it's time you faced it."

"Have you finished?" I asked.

"No," she said. "I've hardly started." She leaned across the ironing board. "Maybe you don't remember, but when we first came here you did me some favors. I told you then, it wasn't a one-way street. I've waited all this time to do you a favor in return; and I figured this was it, getting you and Ray Duer together on this trip to Paris. But you threw it right back in my face." She glared at me. "Now, baby, I'm going to tell you the facts of life. Duer: he isn't a bad

289

guy. He has guts, and that's something these days. He isn't bad-looking. He's holding down a decent job with a big company. He has a future ahead of him. What more does a woman want? Carol, you know the female population of the United States? Around eighty million. Think of that: eighty million broads like you and me, and they'd all jump at a chance of a guy like Duer. And that isn't all, no, sir. We have all these jet planes, don't we? They're opening up the whole goddamn world, aren't they? Boy! Six hours' flying time, and Duer can take his pick of a zillion broads, in all shapes, colors and sizes. You put that in your pipe and smoke it, Carol. If you want that guy you'd better come down off your high horse and do something about him pretty damn quick."

I went to my room.

I couldn't sleep. It wasn't because of anything Jurgy had said, she'd just been shooting off her big mouth. But I loved Ray, God knows why, I still loved him after all these months, I still loved him after what he'd done to Donna, I still loved him in spite of his inhumanity and in spite of everything else my brain could dream up. He'd called me out of affection, and I'd answered him like a bitch (Jurgy was right about that, I had to give her some credit) and I couldn't forgive myself. At about two o'clock in the morning I crept into the living room, switched on a light, and called the Charleroi. I said to the operator, "Dr. Duer, please. I believe he's in apartment 1208."

"Just one moment."

I waited several moments. Then the operator came back on the line and said, "I'm sorry. Dr. Duer doesn't answer."

"Oh. Is that the right apartment number, 1208?"

"1208, that's correct. Do you wish to leave a message?"

"No, thank you."

I crept back to bed.

We reported to Crew Scheduling at five minutes before eight, and met Kay Taylor and Janyce Hinds in the Hostess Room at eight o'clock sharp. Kay said, "Right on the nose, kids. Good for you." She looked us over critically: I suspect Miss Duprez had briefed her to do so. "Carol, do you have a cold?"

"Oh, no. Just early-morning sniffles."

"Sure?"

290

"Absolutely."

"Okay. Now, then. This is how we've decided to work this trip. On the outgoing flight, that's this morning, I'll be the 'A' girl and, Carol, you'll work with me as my 'B.' Aft, Janyce will be 'C,' and, Mary Ruth, you'll be her 'D.' On the return flight we'll juggle the order around so everybody will get a change of scenery. Any questions?"

No questions.

"Okay. Now, then. Meal service. I've checked with the Captain. We're flying one of the special Intercontinentals. He figures our flying time will be approximately seven hours. We aren't serving breakfast—the boys should have had that at the Charleroi. At eleven we'll serve coffee and snacks. We'll start serving lunch at a quarter of one. Three o'clock, snacks again. That breaks up our working day nicely. Questions?"

No questions. God, she was efficient.

She turned to Jurgy and me. "Now, then. You kids haven't flown one of these charter flights before, have you?"

We hadn't.

"Okay." She paused again. "Mary Ruth, you're engaged to one of these guys, aren't you? Just don't take anything I say *personally*, see? I'm only trying to give you a general idea." She went on briskly, "This is going to be a new experience for you two. These guys are cattlemen, which means they're a mighty tough bunch. I'm not saying they aren't gentlemen, or that they won't act like gentlemen. But they've chartered this plane, and they're going to act as if it's theirs, and they're going to do what they damn please throughout the trip. All we have to do is feed 'em, water 'em, and supply 'em with ice cubes. And hand them a bag if they're sick."

She paused and grinned at Janyce. "How am I doing?"

"Great, honey. You're even impressing me."

"I bet." She turned to us again. "I hate to sound like mama, girls, but let me say just this. Mary Ruth, you'll bear me out. These fellows will respect you so long as you respect yourself. You know what I mean, I don't have to tell you. There are seventy of them. That's a lot of guys. They're on a spree. They've worked hard all year, now they're out for some fun. I don't blame them. But no fun on the plane. They can have all the fun they want when they get to Paris. This is one time when you act friendly

291

but you take good care not to act overfriendly. Am I right, Janyce?"

"You sure are. And I know, from hard experience."

"Where was that?"

"Flying down to Rio."

"Oh, boy," Kay said. "Tell me about it sometime." She coughed, clearing her throat. "One last thing. We're going to be mighty formal today. We wear our uniform jackets throughout the trip, buttoned up. Even working in the galley." She laughed at me. "What's the matter, Carol? Have I scared you?"

I must have been completely bugeyed. "Oh, no," I said. "Oh, no. Not at all."

"Leave us not fool ourselves, kids. Seventy big tough guys on a plane for seven hours—that's quite a situation. We're lucky on one respect—we have a real good captain, Frank Hoffer. He won't stand for any nonsense." She looked at us with raised eyebrows. "Any more questions?"

No more questions.

"Okay. Let's go."

We went out to the Ramp Control office with our gear, and signed our names in order of seniority on the Flight Crew list: Kay Taylor, Janyce Hinds, Mary Ruth Jurgens, Carol Thompson. Half of the top-ranking brass of Magna International Airlines seemed to be on hand: the District Passenger Service Manager and, of course, the Transportation Agent, and Mr. Barker from Sales, and Mr. Casey from Commissary, and a large jovial man from Public Relations, and, of all things, a photographer. I guess it was only then, seeing a *photographer*, that I caught on to the fact that this was really, but really, a blue-chip flight. Seventy cattlemen! My God, if they all dug down into their pockets they could probably buy up Fort Knox, and still have enough left over for their carfare home.

And there in the sunshine, right in front of us, was our plane: white, shining, immaculately clean, like something new-born, a huge sleek royal infant outspread on the apron with dozens of attendants waiting on her. The F-6 tankers were pumping fuel into the wing tanks, the commissary trucks were high up on their hoists at the galley doors, the ground air-conditioner truck was humming busily cooling the cabin, the electrical power truck was standing by at the nose, the galley water cart and the toilet-service cart were fussing around, the passenger ramps were in position

orward and aft. Busy, busy, busy, a glorious sight, and as
lways, it made my heart beat faster.

Kay paused to chat to the Transportation Agent and Mr.
Barker, collecting a sheaf of forms from them which she
attached to her clipboard. The passenger list, I knew, was
among these forms. *Duer.* Please, Kay, is there a certain
Dr. Ray Duer officially on the passenger list? Duer—d-u-e-r.
Ray—r-a-y. I didn't have the nerve to ask.

We climbed up the aft ramp. Janyce and Jurgy remained
behind at the aft galley, and Kay and I went forward to
our own station in the far distance. These planes get longer
and longer every day. Now and then Kay stopped to scru-
tinize a seat, or one of the overhead service units—she
couldn't help herself, it was instinctive; but everything was
in order, all the equipment looked new, there didn't even
seem to be a spot of dust anywhere.

My job was to check the galley loading, food, liquor, silver service, and all the commissary supplies, and then I had
to set the lights for boarding and close off the galley. Kay
checked it all with me, and went on to check the emergency
equipment, the lavatory and cabin supplies, and the passenger-service kit. Then she tested the public-address system and the intercom, while Janyce did the same aft. "Everything okay?" Kay asked. Everything was okay, Janyce
answered, everything was hunky-dory. "How's the ice situation your end?" Kay asked. Janyce said, "Boy, we have
enough to sink the *Titanic*." "Liquor?" Kay asked. Janyce
said, "Oodles." "Right." "Right." Click, click.

The cattlemen arrived at eight-thirty. I could see them
from one of the windows, milling around behind the ramp
gates, all of them wearing their Stetson hats; but I couldn't
see Ray Duer. At twenty to nine we were ready to start
loading. Kay went to the forward passenger door, Janyce
went to the aft passenger door; Jurgy and I waited in our
respective cabins; and the men came clomping aboard. I'd
met a few of them when Luke brought them over to the
apartment, but I'd never seen them en masse like this. They
were huge—great powerful men with leathery out-of-doors
faces, shy and soft-voiced, slow-moving. A few of them
were of smaller build than the rest, but they made up for
it in some mysterious way, they managed to look even
huskier and more vigorous. There were men wearing high-
heeled boots and men wearing patent-leather shoes. Some
of them wore tweed jackets and slacks, some of them wore

conservative business suits as if they'd just come from a Wall Street office. Ray wasn't among them.

They were all seated within ten minutes. The crew had come aboard, too; the tow tractor was already attached and we were practically ready to go. Kay took the passenger count all the way from the front to the rear, and I saw her consulting with Janyce, gesturing with a pencil at the passenger list on her clipboard. She was frowning when she returned, and I said, "What's wrong?"

"We're six short."

"Six!"

"They'll probably turn up. We still have time."

I saw Jurgy gesturing to me from her compartment, and I hurried down.

She said in a fierce whisper, "Do you have Luke up there?"

"No. Do you have Duer?"

"No."

We stared at each other.

I said, "We're six passengers short."

"Yeah, I know. The bums, they're probably shacked up with some call girls."

"Jurgy! How can you say that!"

"You don't know what a party they had last night, Carol. It was practically an orgy."

Fine, encouraging words. I went back to my galley with a heavy heart and began to check all the switches—they had to be in the off position before we began to move. Kay wasn't around. I guessed she was consulting with the Captain.

A couple of minutes later she came out of the cockpit and said in a low voice, "I'm going to have a word with the TA about those six no-shows. You'd better go ahead with the oxygen-mask demonstration to keep the boys occupied. Do the whole routine, including the O_2 system. I'll do the life jackets and stuff later."

"Right."

She went out to the passenger ramp to find the Transportation Agent, and I began the oxygen speech. I knew it pretty well after all these months; and, as usual, everybody listened politely without really taking anything in. As my former friend N.B. once said, it's for operations, it's for the birds, it isn't for people. This time, though, I didn't even get to finish. A couple of cattlemen yelled, "Holy gee! Look at that!" and suddenly, without any warning, all those huge men were piling over each other at the port windows, shouting and hollering and roaring with laughter. I thought, My God, what's happening; and ran to the passenger door and looked out.

It was merely that the missing six had arrived. They were all wearing Stetsons, including my beloved, Dr. Ray Duer; they all looked as if they'd spent the night in a ditch, including the man of my dreams, Dr. Ray Duer; and, led by Luke, who was carrying a huge stone jug that was probably full of applejack, they were engaged in a furious war of words with the District Passenger Service Manager and Mr. Casey from Commissary and Mr. Barker from Sales and the TA and the Public Relations man, while the photographer was almost going out of his mind trying to take photographs of the scene for posterity. The cause of the battle stood there mooing piteously, blatting for its mother—a poor, miserable, half-grown calf with a garland of hibiscus around its neck, haltered by a thick red-velvet rope that couldn't have come from anywhere except the Sun King Room at the Charleroi. Apparently the Stetson gang wanted to bring the calf on board so that they could parade it through Paris to show the ignorant natives what a real American calf looked like, while the Magna gang weren't allowing any calf, American or not, to set foot, or hoof, inside their beautiful lily-white Boeing 707. "We paid for the goddam plane, didn't we?" Luke roared; and the District Passenger Service Manager, who'd obviously decided to meet force with force, roared back, "You didn't pay to transport any goddam herd of cattle." "We'll transport anything we goddam please," Luke roared; and the District Passenger Service Manager roared in his face, "Not goddam cattle, you won't. Besides, there's a government regulation against it."

That's the most astonishing thing. I've discovered it, too. There's nothing in this world that will more effectively subdue a great big husky six-foot two-hundred-and-fifty-pound rampaging American male than telling him there's a government regulation against it. We really ought to be awfully proud that our government inspires such respect. Even Luke was stopped in his tracks, particularly when the District Passenger Service Manager went on to quote the regulation in question. "Section 10, Paragraph 3," he said in the voice of authority: "No passenger traveling on any passenger airliner in the United States, or its territories

295

or possessions as proclaimed by Act of Congress, shall transport or cause to be transported or conspire to have transported any poultry, livestock including pigs goats sheep cattle or any other animal whatsoever living or dead, with the exception of such animals as are listed in Sub-section 7 below, under penalty of a fine not exceeding $25,000 or five years imprisonment, or both.—How's that?" Or words to that effect. It wouldn't surprise me if he made it up on the spot—I mean, it sounded just a little too legal to be legal; but it quieted the Stetson gang at once, all the steam was taken out of their sails. Mr. Casey of Commissary added oil to the troubled waters by assuring them that he would take care of the poor little calf as if it were one of his own (I bet), and the Public Relations man said he'd see that next time everything would be different, and the photographer made the entire party, plus the poor little calf, pose for sixteen photographs from all angles; and finally, led by Kay, the six trooped aboard and were reunited with their howling buddies.

We were late now, and in a hurry to get moving. Kay and I seated the six as fast as we could. Luke wouldn't give up that great stone jug, he wouldn't let it out of his hands to fasten his seat belt. I'd guessed right: the liquor in the jug was applejack. "Try it!" he said to Kay. "Made it myself. Best applejack in the whole wide world. Try it, little lady." Kay said, "Not right now, sir. We still have a lot of work to do." The other four cattlemen were fairly easy to handle, but Ray Duer was a mess. God, he was a terrible sight. He was such a sight that I have a theory that the Magna brass just didn't recognize him during the fracas over the calf, otherwise they wouldn't have permitted him to board the plane: they'd have put him under house arrest for conduct unbecoming an officer of the company and a gentleman, or something. He'd lost his horn-rimmed glasses. He hadn't shaved. His face looked as if it had been made up with burnt cork. His hands were black. His clothes were covered with mud. Somewhere along the line he'd acquired a pair of cowboy boots with high heels, which quite obviously were killing him. He was just a picture of masculine beauty and dignity, particularly with the green tinge under his skin and the Stetson hat which merely happened to be a couple of sizes too big and almost came down to his eyes.

He couldn't, or wouldn't, look at me.

I said, "May I take your hat, sir?"

"Hat?" My God, he didn't even know he was wearing it. He reached up and discovered it there on his head, and handed it to me without another word.

"The seat-belt sign is on, sir. Would you mind fastening your seat belt?"

He fumbled around and eventually got it fastened.

"Would you like me to explain how the oxygen equipment works, sir?"

He shook his head.

"How about your luggage, sir? Was that checked in?"

He nodded.

I said, "We'll have some coffee available shortly after take-off, sir. I'll inform you when it's ready."

"Thanks."

We were moving out to the runway. I went around the cabin and checked all the seat belts, while Kay made her announcements over the public address system. Then I set the lights for take-off, and Kay and I went to the forward attendants' seat, where we sat side by side; we put on our shoulder harness and fastened our seat belts and waited for the trip to start.

She said gloomily, "I'm worried about that big bony geezer, the one with the stone jug of applejack. He's liable to make trouble for us."

"Don't worry about him, Kay."

"He has a mean look in his eye: that's what I don't like."

"He's Mary Ruth Jurgens' fiancé. If he gets rowdy, we'll ask her to come and talk to him. He eats out of her hand."

"That's Mary Ruth's fiancé!" Kay sounded astonished. "Well, what do you know!—Sure, I remember now: Molly Duprez mentioned it, but I didn't put two and two together." She wriggled, adjusting her shoulder harness. "Just the same, keep an eye on him, Carol."

"All right."

She added, "And Ray Duer, too. Keep an eye out for any signs of cyanosis throughout the trip. We'll be flying at thirty thousand feet. If they start turning blue, give them a whiff of oxygen."

"Dr. Duer's kind of green already."

"I noticed." She shook her head in wonderment. "I've known Ray ever since he joined the airline, three years ago. We've been to parties together, we've had dates, we've had long talks about this whole flying business, I never knew anyone so dedicated to his job. Honestly, if some-

297

body told me I'd live to see the day when Ray Duer stepped on board looking the way he does, I'd have just laughed at them." She became confidential. "Poor old Ray. He's a great guy. But it's too bad, he's had a rough time lately."

"Oh?" I said.

"Yes. The damned fool—he fell for one of the student hostesses who was staying at the Charleroi. An utter little bitch. You know the type. She led him a hell of a dance, and then walked out on him. According to all reports, he just hasn't gotten over it."

"Gee," I said. "Isn't that awful?"

"It's a shame. He's such a swell guy."

I said, "Who was the girl?"

"Oh, some stupid little cow, I don't know her name. I believe she's from Massachusetts."

The whine of the engines increased, and we began to roll forward.

We served coffee and snacks at eleven. Ray was asleep, dead to the world. His seat belt was still fastened, as it should be on a sleeping passenger, and we decided there was no point in waking him. His color seemed to be improving. Kay inspected him several times and saw no signs of hypoxia. He was getting all the oxygen he needed.

Luke was having a great time in the forward lounge, playing poker with four other men. His color was good; he drank several cups of coffee and wolfed all the sandwiches in sight, which was encouraging, but he wouldn't let go of that stone jug of applejack—he clung to it as if it were filled with rubies.

On the whole, the men were a lot quieter than I'd expected. About half of the group in our compartment were doing some mild social drinking, and the rest were asleep. Janyce reported the same from the aft compartment—no trouble. I saw Jurgy a couple of times and told her that Luke was fine, but she wouldn't come forward to see him. She was rather grim, and she also seemed rather frightened. I said, "Don't worry, Jurgy. We'll take good care of him."

The flight itself was dreamlike. Below us there was nothing but cloud, and an occasional streak of smudgy blue, which was the Atlantic Ocean; and I somehow couldn't get the idea into my head that we were moving closer and closer to Europe and that in a few hours we'd be touching down on French soil. Frank Hoffer, the captain, sauntered through the cabin a couple of times, chatting to anybody who was awake. He was a man of about forty, short and chunky, with tremendously alert dark eyes. Kay had flown with him often: they knew each other well. We had a little conference in the galley, and he said, "Things seem pretty quiet. I guess all the guys are saving their strength for the big time in gay Paree. But if any of them begin to act up, call me at once, will you?"

"You bet," Kay said.

At one o'clock the lunch service began. I set up the trays in the galley; Kay served. Ray was still sleeping, but Kay decided to wake him after she'd served everybody else. "Get some food into his stomach," she said. "That's what he needs." When she returned to the galley she said with satisfaction, "He's fine. He woke up like a baby, and went for the filet mignon as if he hadn't eaten in a week."

We didn't hurry unduly. Kay's idea was to keep the drinking to a minimum. When the entree trays had been collected, Kay served dessert and I served coffee, and we did a good trade, except in the forward lounge where the poker game was going full blast. Luke had his stone jug of applejack, the others had bourbon, and they were all getting a little noisy. Luke was booming and gurgling like an old foghorn.

Kay said, "Hell, I wish I could think of some way to break up that bunch."

"Do you want me to speak to Mary Ruth?"

"Not yet. That's going to be our last resort."

We went on to serve Ray Duer. He'd finished his steak and all the trimmings that came with it, the baked potato and the French-cut string beans and the mushroom caps and the rolls and butter; and my heart rejoiced. He showed little joy, though. He was sitting back staring gloomily out of the window at the clouds twenty thousand feet below.

We were all extremely formal.

Kay said, "I hope you enjoyed your lunch, sir."

"Very much indeed."

"Now, sir: would you care for some dessert?"

"No, thanks."

"Sure? Some fruit and cheese, perhaps?"

"No, thanks."

It was my turn. "Coffee, sir?"

"Please."

He glanced at me for a moment. Then he said to Kay, "This is a fine thing, isn't it?"

"What is, sir?" she said innocently.

"Arriving on board like this."

"Sir: you're going on vacation. Why shouldn't you have a party before you leave?"

He grunted.

I said, "Cream in your coffee, sir?"

"No, black.—Kay, how do I look?"

She laughed. "Not too bad. You know, we have an electric razor you can use."

"Thanks.—Miss Thompson?"

"Yes, sir?"

He scowled. "Nothing. I'm sorry. Skip it."

I knew what he wanted to say to me—not the exact words, but the general theme; and, of course, he couldn't speak with Kay standing there. I don't think he wanted to excuse his condition. He wouldn't stoop to that. I think he wanted to know whether I felt satisfied at last. There he was, almost literally with his pants down, and Iago couldn't have plotted a more subtle revenge. How did I feel about it?

He might have been surprised. All I felt was grief, and love, and the urge to give him more and more black coffee so that he could return to his former estate. I couldn't bear to see him sitting there untidy, unshaven, unhappy. I didn't want revenge, I didn't want to be a witness to his humiliation. I wanted him to be just who he was, not a caricature of himself.

Women are really the key to the universe. I mean, that's where Einstein should have started, not with rays of light bending as they pass a planet, but with this built-in radar that women have, that isn't radar at all. Because, literally, nothing happened between Dr. Duer and me except that I poured him a cup of black coffee, and he then said exactly seven words to me, of which two were my name, Miss Thompson; and Kay Taylor caught it. Her ears flapped, big green blips appeared all over her radar screen; and she was hot on the scent. This is no mixed metaphor: this is precisely what Einstein should have investigated. Because no sooner were we both back in the galley, clearing away the lunch debris, then she began to reminisce about home, how she was longing to see her folks, how she missed her old dad whose hobby was building model ships in bottles, etcetera. Home in her case was Rhode Island, which didn't surprise me: she was a big healthy applecheeked outdoor-type girl. And all this, naturally enough, led on to the most natural question in the world—it couldn't have been more natural if it had grown out of the side of a tree. "Carol, where's your home?"

"Greenwich."

"Greenwich, Connecticut?"

"No," I said: "Greenwich, Massachusetts."

She was stunned. "I didn't know there was a Greenwich in Massachusetts."

There may not have been one there this morning but there sure as hell was one there now. That's who I was and that's where I came from: the stupid little cow from Massachusetts who'd led Ray Duer a hell of a dance and brought him down in ruins. I believe her radar picked this up, too, because she looked at me intently and didn't say another word. When an oral personality like Kay clams up, that's a sure sign that she heard you loud and clear.

The atmosphere in our compartment seemed to change after lunch. I noticed it in the other compartment also, when I walked down to pay Jurgy a brief visit. She still hadn't come forward to visit Luke, and I thought I ought to drop by and give her the latest tidings.

"How is he?" she asked, expecting the worst.

"He ate his lunch."

"H'm. They drinking hard up there?"

"Well, fair to middling."

Her mouth tightened. "Is he getting troublesome?"

"The poker game's a bit noisy, that's all."

"He's hitting that applejack, eh?"

"Some."

"I could kill him. God damn it, why does he have to swill that stuff?"

"I guess he likes the taste. How are things down here?"

"The fellers are getting restless."

"They are our end, too. It's a long trip."

"Yeah." She laughed her old harsh laugh. "Janyce is a real clown. She says we ought to circulate among them slowly, singing hymns. She says the sight of a pure young girl will keep 'em quiet."

I could feel the change in the atmosphere distinctly as I

301

walked back. There were several noisy card games going now. I was stopped half a dozen times and given orders for drinks. I could understand it: these men had been having high jinks at the Charleroi for three days at an alleged convention, and they'd wound up with what must have been a whale of a party last night. Some of them had slept off the effects this morning, some of them had sobered up during lunch; and now they were all set to get going again. One man, a big lumbering fellow with the sexiest brown eyes, said as he gave me his order, "Say, how about joining us and having a little drink yourself?" I said, "I'm awfully sorry, sir, I'm not allowed to. If the Captain saw me I'd be put in irons." The other men laughed, but he didn't. He had his sexy brown eyes fixed on the top button of my uniform—Project A, I suppose. "No kidding," he said: "Sit down for a minute, we'll protect you." I gave him one of my vague idiot smiles, as if he were the wittiest guy in the whole wide world, and walked on. Janyce's idea about singing hymns as we circulated was pretty sound. Maybe it would help, too, if we carried tambourines.

Ray wasn't in his seat. I made a guess that he'd gone to tidy up. There was a tremendous din coming from the forward lounge, and I could hear Luke's voice bellowing out above the rest. I hesitated, and then went to see what was happening. The five men were still playing poker, and several other men had gathered to watch. They weren't breaking up the furniture, although it sounded as if they were. They were just shouting at Luke's antics, and he was shouting back at them and swigging out of the stone jug. The liquor had run down his clothes. He'd pushed his Stetson back on his head, I suppose because he was sweating so hard, and his skin was turning waxy.

He saw me standing there and bawled, "Carol, honey! Come on over here! Come on!" He nudged the man sitting beside him. "Move over, Barney, so Carol can sit down. Hey, fellers, you ever seen a sweeter lil gal than Carol, eh? You ever seen a more innocent pair of eyes? Come on Carol, come sit next to your old Uncle Luke. Move over Barney, don't you hear me?"

But I didn't have to answer him because Kay came through the cockpit door at the end of the aisle, followed by the Captain. They walked over to the card players, and Frank Hoffer edged between the men who were standing there and said to Luke, "Mr. Lucas."

"Hi, Captain! Hi, son! How 'bout a slug, eh?" Luke held up the stone jug.

"Mr. Lucas—"

"Makin' good time, son? We in sight of land yet?"

"Mr. Lucas, I don't want to interfere with your pleasure. I want you and everybody on board to have a good time on this flight. But I'd like to ask you to be kind enough to keep things orderly in here."

"Orderly?" Luke said. He stood up. Barney, the man beside him, pulled him down.

"You know what I mean, Mr. Lucas," Frank said. He turned to the other men. His voice was polite but very hard. "Gentlemen, you'd do me a favor if you'd take your seats. It isn't too safe standing around during a flight. We might run into a little packet of turbulence and then you'd be in trouble."

"Now, Captain," one of the men began.

"May I ask your name, sir?"

"Blythe, Jim Blythe—"

"Mr. Blythe, I've had a plane drop a thousand feet with practically no warning. Had a fellow with a fractured skull once as a result of one of those drops. So, if you don't mind, take your seat, will you? I'd be much obliged."

The men began to drift away.

Luke said furiously, "Hey, Captain!"

"Yes?"

"What's the idea, comin' in here an' orderin' everyone around?"

"That's my job, Mr. Lucas."

"It is? Since when?"

"Since we took off. I'm in command of this aircraft. I'm responsible for the safety of the passengers and the crew. Anything else you'd like to know?"

Luke glowered at him.

"Okay," Frank said. "Just take it easy, will you? And if you don't mind a friendly suggestion, I'd cork up that jug if I were you and hide it away for a while."

"Captain!"

"Yes?"

"Captain, I'll make a deal with you. You take my hand this poker game, I'll fly your ship for you. How's that? Fair enough?"

Frank laughed and walked back to the cockpit. But he'd done exactly what Kay must have asked of him: he'd broken up that rowdy bunch, he'd quelled the noise, he'd restored order in the matter of a few seconds. It was magic, how one man could make himself felt like this.

As we returned to the galley Kay said, "I had to do it. I did my best with that old son of a bitch, but I couldn't even make myself heard, I had to call Frank."

"He certainly fixed them."

"Oh, sure. He's a good guy."

The call chime on the galley panel was sounding constantly. The green call lights were practically sizzling. I said to Kay, "My God, I have half a dozen orders for drinks. The men out there must be furious."

"Let them wait," Kay said.

"But they've waited already—"

"Then go out and pacify them."

"What shall I say?"

"Tell them we're having a little trouble with the electrical connections. That's all."

I might have figured that one out for myself except that I'm not ingenious enough and also I haven't been around long enough. It worked like a charm, of course. I walked up and down saying in a brokenhearted whisper, "Gee, I'm sorry your drink has been delayed, sir, but we're having a little trouble with the electrical connections in the galley," and those big thirsty cattlemen couldn't have been nicer or more sympathetic. They understood. Even the guy with the sexy brown eyes was affected and stopped wondering for a few moments what exotic delicacies reposed under the top button of my jacket. "Did the fuse blow?" he asked, and I said, "No, not exactly the fuse. But we'll have it fixed soon." I felt rather hot inwardly, because I'm not an expert at little white lies. On the other hand I felt morally uplifted —we were really doing these boys a favor, they'd be able to focus much more clearly on the chorines at the Folies Bergère, or wherever they were heading as soon as they hit Paris; they'd get a lot more out of their vacation.

Then, on my way back, I met Ray Duer walking slowly down the aisle. At last, after months and months, we were face to face again. He'd shaved and washed, and he was almost as good as new again except for his cowboy boots— to all intents the same Ray Duer I'd known for a few brief hours, and loved, and wept over, the man to whom I'd offered my bosom as a footstool, only to have it flung back in my face.

He stopped.

I stopped, and everything inside me stopped at the same time.

He said calmly, "Hello, Carol."

"Hello, sir."

His eyes were extraordinarily handsome without his horn-rimmed glasses, but rather cool and inquiring, as if he had a purely scientific curiosity about me, he wanted to know what made me tick. He said, "I'd like to talk to you. Can you sit down for a minute or so?"

"I'm sorry, sir, we're having trouble with the electrical connections in the—"

I caught my breath as I said it, I was aghast at myself. Why was I rejecting him over and over again, like a spoiled brat? Hadn't I grown up in all these thousands of years of loneliness, hadn't I grown a single inch?

He laughed pleasantly, as if on the basis of all the scientific evidence that he'd accumulated this was precisely what he'd expected—another evasion, another cute little remark starting *I'm sorry, sir* as usual. He said, "It's really nothing. I only wanted to tell you, I made up my mind last night not to take this trip." He laughed again. "But Luke Lucas had other ideas. I'm not blaming him, it's my own fault entirely. That's all."

"Ray—"

"Don't worry. I shan't be troubling you any more."

"I'm glad—"

He said curtly, "I thought you'd be glad," and began to edge past me.

I said, trying to keep my voice low, "Why don't you let me finish? I'm glad Luke had other ideas, I'm glad you're here. That's what I meant when I said I'm glad."

He turned with an expression of anger as if I were just mocking him; but he couldn't help seeing the truth. We stared at each other, and the world ceased to revolve. He said, "Carol," but I had to leave him. I'd said what was in my heart at last, there wasn't anything more I could add in public without bursting into tears and making an absolute spectacle of myself; and it ought to hold him for the next hour or so while we pushed on at practically the speed of sound toward the coast of France. We'd be alone there, we'd be able to talk for hours on end without a herd of cattle-men flapping their ears at us; but even with this consoling thought I scarcely made it back to the galley.

Kay was as busy as a one-armed paperhanger, setting up trays of drinks. She didn't look at me, she didn't notice—as Alma would surely have noticed—that I'd been to the fiesta, my voice had changed. And suddenly, as I stood there watching her working so busily, completely out of left field a picture of my other friend, Donna, came into my mind, and somebody—Thompson, and yet not Thompson —said, *My God, I'm glad she isn't here today.* It was nothing but sheer treachery. Not once but many and many a time, flying to New Orleans and Washington and on the Miami–New York run, I'd thought, Oh, gee, I wish Donna were here with me on this flight, we'd have such a ball together—in New Orleans, particularly; in New York, too; even in Washington. Good old Donna. Such a swell gal. So beautiful, so gay, so alive. I missed her like my own right arm.

But not today. Not on this flight. I couldn't even bear to imagine her swishing up and down the aisle with these seventy big husky guys around. It just didn't bear imagining for one moment. I thought, Cut it out, Thompson, you'll be preaching in church next; but it was true—this was the first occasion when I didn't miss her one little bit, when it was almost a pleasure not to have her on the scene, gay and alive and frisky and frolicsome. This was the time to have Kay Taylor around, and Janyce Hinds, who was of the same breed; and Mary Ruth Jurgens, who would hardly give the Queen of England a second look.

"What the hell are you dreaming about, Carol?" Kay said. "Don't just *stand*. Get these drinks circulating."

"Gee, I was miles away."

"Well, snap out of it. How's Dr. Duer?"

"He looks pretty good."

"Ask him if he'd like some coffee—he probably needs it. And don't dally. It's after three, and we have to start the snack service."

I sailed out with a couple of trays. The lounge was noisy again. Luke's voice was if anything boomier than ever, and I wondered whether it wasn't time for Jurgy to pay him a friendly call and tell him in her own sweet gentle way to quiet down. I guess she felt she didn't have the right to interfere when he was having a good time with a crowd of his buddies, it might cause him to lose face. Still, a friendly visit wouldn't do any harm. He was really making a devilish racket.

306

I didn't trust myself to go near Ray until all the drinks were delivered. I couldn't help myself, I was shaking again. He watched me as I approached.

I said, "Would you care for coffee, sir?"

He didn't answer. He stared at me suspiciously. I don't blame him—it's a hell of a question to shoot at the man you love.

I said, "Please try to understand, Miss Duprez ordered us to be absolutely formal on this trip, I'm not even allowed to take my jacket off. Would you care for coffee, sir?"

"*Don't call me sir.*"

"No, sir."

"Just give me a simple answer," he said: "Will you have dinner with me when we get to Paris?"

"I'd love to, I'd really love to, Ray, but I think we'll be too late for dinner. French time is different, remember?"

His eyes were still wary. "Supper, then?"

"Yes," I said. "Nothing would make me happier."

"Maxim's," he said; and before I could even reply to this, the trouble started.

It was Luke. He'd gone berserk, completely berserk. Behind the gold-rimmed glasses his pale blue eyes were almost starting out of his head. Sweat was pouring down his face. He was shouting and cursing incoherently, holding his stone jug in one hand, dragging a man down the aisle with the other hand. The man was Barney, who'd been sitting beside Luke in the lounge playing poker, a big harmless-looking guy whom I'd scarcely noticed. Luke was dragging him by the front of his shirt, just below the collar, so that there wasn't anything the poor devil could do—Luke's great bony knuckles were pressing into the hollow of his throat and choking him. He was gagging wildly as Luke yanked at him and hauled him forward, and it was absolutely impossible for him to break Luke's grip.

Everybody jumped up at the noise—Luke bellowing and Barney gagging and scuffling behind him. I called out, "Please, stay where you are, please sit down," and I said sharply to Ray, "Stay here, just stay here," because I didn't want him involved in this trouble; and then I ran toward Luke.

I said, "Luke! Stop it!"

He was stark staring mad. He didn't seem to see me.

I tried to pull his hand away from Barney's throat.

He said hoarsely, "Keep out of my way, little lady. This lousy stinking son of a bitch, he smirched the name of my Mary Ruth. He's going to make amends to her, he's going to lick her boots, else I'll kill him."

It was nightmarish, because people only spoke like this in old television movies, never in real life. And yet *this* was real life, a jet airliner flying at more than six hundred miles an hour, thirty thousand feet above the earth. God knows who exactly this Barney was, or where he came from; and maybe he had smirched Mary Ruth's name—anything could have happened between those men in the lounge, they were all stupefied with liquor. The only thing was, he might easily die for it.

I began to scream at Luke because the nightmare was too horrible, but he didn't hear me, he didn't see me, he pushed on as if I didn't exist, snarling, shaking his head to get the streaming sweat out of his eyes, swinging the stone jug of applejack like a monstrous club to clear his way. Then I realized that Ray Duer had come up behind me and I cried, "Ray, no! Stay out of this;" but at the same moment I saw Frank Hoffer running toward us, followed by Kay Taylor. She must have rushed directly to the cockpit when she heard this commotion; she hadn't wasted a second, thank God.

Frank shouted, "Lucas! Hey, Lucas!"

Luke stopped. His eyes narrowed. He gave Barney a sudden tug, yanking him around so that he'd be out of Frank's reach. His madness seemed to flare up at this new interruption, his bones seemed to grow bigger.

"What the hell's going on?" Frank said. He closed in, and stared down at Barney for just one moment. "God Almighty, are you trying to kill that man? Let go of him, you fool."

"Captain. Go fly your ship."

Frank said, "Ray," and Ray stepped past me.

Luke turned his head slowly from side to side, peering down at them. He was really like an old dinosaur, huge and crazy and dangerous, towering over them and keeping his eyes on them, aware that these small enemies were hemming him in. He said, "Fellers. Keep clear. Don't do nothing foolish, now."

Frank said, "Let go of that man."

"Hell, no," Luke said, and forced Barney down onto his knees.

Frank called, "Grab his other arm, Ray," and simultaneously they went for Luke. They hung onto him but they couldn't move him; he seemed to be gathering strength to shrug them off. Frank shouted desperately, "Some of you men come and help," and a couple of cattlemen shuffled up tentatively. They said, "Hey, Luke, stop it, willya, cut it out, boy," but he only snarled at them. There was a sort of foam on his lips.

"For God's sake, grab his arms," Frank yelled. "Get that damn jug away from him."

The two cattlemen tried to grab his arms.

"The jug! The jug!" Frank shouted at them. "Get it away from him. He's going to start swinging it."

The four of them were beginning to pull him down. He was fantastically strong. His gold-rimmed glasses had slipped down his nose, the sweat was pouring off him, the white foamy saliva was dribbling from his mouth, he was still clutching Barney's shirt, and he resisted them by the sheer power of his bones. He yielded an inch, and another inch, his knees seemed to be buckling; and then, suddenly, he released his hold on Barney and began to drive the four men off with wild jabs of his elbows.

"Get the jug!" Frank said furiously.

They tried to hang on to him, but he seemed to grow bigger and bonier and madder, and with a last great heave he broke free of them. He said, "Jesus Christ, this is one thing you won't never take from me." He raised the jug over his head with both hands, and hurled it with all his might at the nearest window.

We'd learned a little about those windows during our four days of jet training. Not because we were supposed to wash them once a week, or be able to take them apart, or anything like that; but just as an item in the whole business. Each window, all along the fuselage, consisted of three thick panes of toughened glass: an outer pane, a center pane and an inner pane, sealed for airtightness, and held in position by clips and spring retainers and reveals and heaven only knows what else. Almost nothing on this earth could break through all three panes, but that drunken old dinosaur Luke nearly managed it. The stone jug smashed through the inner pane and the center pane, and shattered the outer pane; and then, maybe because it struck one of the reveals, it bounced back into the plane, onto a seat and onto the floor.

There was a tremendous *whoof!*—an upheaval of noise like the explosion of a bomb tearing the plane to shreds. A great wind rushed past us, carrying the furious rumble of thunder with it. The cabin became dark with swirling dust. Debris was flying around, and loose papers which the wind had caught up. I saw Frank Hoffer running back to the cockpit, his body hunched against the dust and the darkness. My ears clogged, and everything inside my chest seemed to collapse.

I guess in that single moment, Arnie Garrison and Peg Webley and Janet Pierce and Ann Shearer and all the rest of them justified their existence, because after the first split second of disbelief I lost all sense of myself, I almost ceased to exist as a human being, I became a sort of robot, a sort of machine—the cogwheels and the levers inside me began to move automatically. For that tremendous *whoof!* was air exploding out of the plane: our air. That great rushing thunderous wind was air pouring out of the plane: our air, the air that kept our bodies warm and kept our hearts beating and energized our brains and carried the sounds of our voices. It had gone. Our atmosphere was now practically the same as the atmosphere of the black sky outside, thin and icy and incapable of supporting life. Garrison and Company had made damned sure that I knew what to do in this atmosphere. Rapid decompression: God, I knew rapid decompression almost as well as I knew my alphabet.

There were portable oxygen bottles in the racks over Row 7, in the middle of the forward compartment; and over Row 23, at the rear of the aft compartment—but these were for Janyce Hinds and Jurgy, if they were still on their feet. I went to Row 7 and pulled my bottle down, slung the strap over my shoulder, adjusted the mask over my face, turned the yellow knob counterclockwise to release the flow of oxygen—*counterclockwise*, idiot, like opening a faucet. I tested the flow of oxygen by pinching the tube in the bottom of the breather bag, and the bag began to inflate—check. At my side, Kay was doing the same. I wasn't surprised to see her here, she was compelled to be here, just as I was. I knew, too, what was happening in the cockpit. The plane was making a rapid descent—not standing on its nose like a submarine in a crash dive, but going down in a long shallow dive. We could pass from thirty thousand feet to five thousand feet in about a minute, and at five thousand feet we could live, if we remained conscious during the first minute without air and without pressure.

The signs were shining through the murk: *No Smoking. Fasten Seat Belts.* The oxygen-compartment door in the service unit over each row of seats had opened automatically, the four oxygen masks had fallen out of each unit and hung in the air, dangling in front of the stupefied men. Kay made a swift gesture to me to care for the rear portion of our compartment, and then she went forward. That poor devil Barney was trying to crawl off the floor onto a seat; she put her hands under his armpits, dragged him all the way up and slapped an oxygen mask into his hands. Luke was still in a daze: she slapped an oxygen mask into his hands, too. Ray Duer was standing staring at us, a typical idiot of a scientist watching some fascinating experiment; and, thank God, she didn't waste any courtesy on him—she just put her hands on his chest and pushed him down into his seat and planted a mask over his face. Then she went on to the forward lounge.

There was hardly any sound. There was hardly any movement. The cabin was icy, and all the windows had fogged over. Some of the men had already slumped in their seats, and I had to hurry over to each one in turn, raise his head and hold the oxygen mask against his nose and mouth until he stirred and could hold the mask himself. Their eyes followed every move I made: they were practically in a state of shock, they couldn't understand what had happened, they couldn't guess what was going to happen next. It's for operations, I kept thinking, it's for the birds, it isn't for people. I could see Janyce and Jurgy in the aft compartment, utterly fabulous in their uniforms and masks and oxygen bottles, like a couple of raving beauties from Mars; and they were doing just what was I doing, patrolling up and down the aisle, bending down to attend to some man, giving him the precious whiffs that would bring life back to his brain, then passing on to the next man. My God, they were good. They were wonderful. They did it all with complete assurance, as if they'd been dispensing oxygen ever since they were born.

It was a minute as long as a year—longer. The longest and

coldest and darkest minute I ever experienced. But it had to pass. The Captain's voice came over the public address system, grim and tinny: "Gentlemen. I think we've made it." Then the seconds ticked by, and he said, "Both senior hostesses report to me." We could *hear* him—that was the miracle. We had air to carry sound, air to breathe, air to insulate us in a little while from the cold. I pulled off my mask, unhitched the portable oxygen bottle, and returned it to the rack over Row 7 where it belonged. It weighed a ton, I suddenly realized: without it my body felt as light as a feather. Janyce passed me on her way to the cockpit, and gave me a slap on the rump and said, "How you doing, kid?" I said, "Okay. How's with you?" She said, "Not bad, not bad." The men around me were sighing and stretching, some were still holding on to their masks and inhaling oxygen, some were laughing nervously, talking in low voices. A few of them tried to thank me. One pressed a twenty-dollar bill into my hand, and I had to explain politely that we weren't permitted to accept tips. I didn't explain that for some weird reason we were permitted to accept sums *over* twenty dollars because they were considered to be gifts, not tips—there wasn't time to go too deeply into company policy. I made a quick check: everybody seemed to be alive and in reasonably good shape. The man with the sexy brown eyes seemed to have made the fastest recovery on record—I guess the oxygen had stimulated his glands, or something. He grinned madly at my chest and said, "Baby, how 'bout a little drink while we're waiting?" *Waiting for what?* I thought. He looked ready to pounce on me then and there. I said, "I'll have to check with the Captain, sir," and left him.

A couple of men were holding a card table in place over the smashed window. I said, "Thanks for helping," and they grinned at me and one of them said, "Had to do something, miss. It was getting kinda blowy."

And, at last, I saw Ray again.

He sat, and I stood, and we just looked at each other. His face was haggard. He said, very quietly, "Are you all right?"

"Yes. And you?"

"Fine."

He looked away from me. I couldn't speak, I didn't know what to say next; my emotions suddenly overwhelmed me.

312

I knew he was in the same state. We'd come through something together.

He said, "We were interrupted just as we were making certain arrangements. Do I have a date for supper with you later?"

"Yes, Ray."

"At Maxim's?"

"Yes, Ray."

He said, "I think we might have champagne, don't you?"

"That's a wonderful idea."

I stood looking at him for a few moments, not saying anything because there was nothing else to say right now; and then I moved down to the next row, where Luke was sitting. His big bony hands were clasped loosely over his eyes.

I had no chance to speak to him because Jurgy came striding down the aisle. Her face was ashen. I said, "Hi, Jurgy," but she hardly opened her lips in reply.

She gazed at Luke. He knew she was there, but he still kept his hands over his eyes as if he couldn't bear to look at the scene around him. She said, "Luke: I just heard some fellers saying you smashed the window that caused all the trouble."

"That's right, Mary Ruth." He lowered his hands slowly.

"It's true?"

"It's true, Mary Ruth."

She slid the Rock of Gibraltar off the third finger of her left hand, and held it out to him. "Here."

He stared at it blankly.

"Take it," she said.

He began to shake. He couldn't speak.

"I don't need it any more," she said.

He looked at her, pleading. "Mary Ruth, my love—"

"I don't want any argument. Take it."

His voice was piteous. "But, Mary Ruth, my love, every man is entitled to one little mistake."

"One little mistake!" she said furiously. "You drunken bum! You nearly killed everyone on this plane."

Great tears were rolling down his cheeks.

She said, "I hope to God they send you to jail for five years. That's what you deserve—that's the least you deserve."

"You're right, Mary Ruth. I know it."

313

She was crying, too. She said, "Luke Lucas, listen to me. I swear before my Maker, if I ever see you take another drink, I'll skin you alive. I swear it, do you hear me?"

I felt sorry for the poor old guy. If she said she'd skin him alive, she'd *skin* him alive. He'd really picked something for himself in Mary Ruth Jurgens.

I walked on to the galley. Kay was clearing up the debris. She said, "Oh, there you are. Get busy, kid. We're diverting to Shannon."

I said, "We're doing *what*?"

"We're diverting to Shannon for repairs and inspection. We'll be there overnight."

I sighed. That's life. I was only just beginning to get used to its little tricks. You're all set for high romance in Paris in the spring, and you find yourself stranded in Shannon. You have a date for a champagne supper at Maxim's, and you end up eating a ham sandwich in some drafty airline terminal.

But what did it matter, after all? There'd be a hotel, even in Shannon. There'd be privacy. Ray and I could still be alone—

Kay said, "Look: are you going to stand there dreaming all night? We'll be landing in twenty minutes and we have to get the cabin shipshape. Let's buckle down to work."

"Sure thing," I said; and we buckled down to work.